EVERLASTING PROMISES

EVERLASTING | BOOK TWO

DEBRA ST JAMES

Website: www.debrastjamesbooks.com

Email: debrastjamesbooks@gmail.com

Published by: Debra St James Author

Edited by: Cruel Ink Editing

Formatted by: Debra St James Author

ISBN: 978-1-923153-12-7 [Paperback]

ISBN: 978-1-923153-11-0 [Discreet Edition Paperback]

ISBN: 978-1-923153-13-4 [Ebook]

# INSPIRATION

This story was inspired by the lyrics ...

High Hope by Patrick Droney

DEDICATION

To those who have loved and lost too young, this story is for you.
One day, you'll notice colors again.
One day, you won't feel so broken.
One day, you'll be ready to live again.
One day, you'll be ready to love again.

Little by little.

TRIGGER WARNING

One character in this book is a highly trained and fearless K9 officer.
His name is Rex.
Toward the end of this story,
Rex suffers a severe injury in the line of duty.
But I promise he'll be okay.
I'm not that mean! Trust me.

PLAYLIST

High Hope ... *Patrick Droney*
Glitter ... *Patrick Droney*
Sweetest Thing ... *Allman Brown*
Be Slow ... *Harrison Storm*
Stand and Deliver ... *Patrick Droney*
The First Cut is the Deepest ... *Sheryl Crow*
Fall at Your Feet ... *Crowded House*
False Alarms ... *Noah Reid*
I'll Be Around ... *Garrett Kate*
Wild Love ... *James Bay*
If You Ever Want to be In Love ... *James Bay*
Like the Water ... *Patrick Droney*
Sister Golden Hair ... *America*
Ruined ... *Patrick Droney*
Speak Too Soon ... *Wild Rivers*
Magic ... *Colbie Caillat*
Think I'm In Love with You ... *Chris Stapleton*
Yours in the Morning ... *Patrick Droney*
Times Like These ... *Foo Fighters*
Everything has Changed ... *Jasmine Thompson, Gerald Ko*
Don't Stop ... *Fleetwood Mac*

You can check it out here:

https://tinyurl.com/everlastingpromises-spotify

PROLOGUE

HOPE

GRIEF.

The dictionary says it's a noun, but I beg to differ.

How can something that takes over your entire existence be a noun, not a verb?

It grows from nothing at an exponential rate in mere seconds. It's a living entity that molds and changes who you are at your very core, affecting you physically, mentally, spiritually, and emotionally.

The very definition says it's *deep and poignant distress caused by, or as if by, bereavement.* But it's more like an insidious disease that seeps through your mind and body, stealing your hopes ... your dreams. Your future.

It steals the very essence of who you are.

It steals your life.

It steals your soul.

It irrevocably changes the very fabric of your being.

Sitting on the wooden bench, I watch Wyatt push Evan on his favorite swing. Evan's giggles echo through the park, joining the other sounds of children playing, and I grin. *This* is what contentment feels like. Watching the love of my life play with our son.

"Higher, Daddy!" Evan squeals in delight, kicking his little legs.

Wyatt looks over at me with raised brows, asking me if I'm okay with our son wanting to go higher on the swing. We've always been able to read each other's thoughts and communicate silently; I guess it comes from knowing each other for such a long time.

"Not too high," I call out, getting more comfortable on the bench. I know we'll be here a while.

Wyatt pushes him a little harder, and the swing goes higher. Evan cheers, his eyes sparkling beneath the morning sunlight, his hair going every which way as he swings back and forth. He loves flying through the air. I wouldn't be surprised if he becomes a pilot when he grows up.

"I wanna go on the slide," Evan sings, so Wyatt slows the swing to a stop and helps him climb down.

Standing, I hold out my hand to Evan, and he wraps his tiny

fingers around mine. Wyatt's too wide to fit through the tunnel at the top of the slide, so I always end up going with Evan because he's too little to go on his own. When we climb to the top, I glance at Wyatt and see him speaking with a boy wearing a backpack. I smile at my husband as he helps the young boy onto the swing and begins to push him.

Peeling my gaze away from my kind-hearted husband, I situate myself behind Evan at the top of the slide inside the tunnel. A huge explosion bursts through the bird song and children's laughter, shaking the slide and making it unstable. With my heart racing like a wild horse, I quickly scoot us forward, slipping down the slide so we can get to safety before it collapses.

Flames and charred playground equipment become visible as we clear the tunnel, and terror-filled screams pierce the air. I snap my head toward the swings where I last saw Wyatt, but he's not there. As soon as my feet hit the sand at the bottom of the slide, I scoop Evan into my arms and take off at a break-neck sprint toward the swings. Charred limbs send long, ribbon-like fingers of smoke upward, and the stench of burning flesh has me doubling over, crushing Evan against me as I scream until everything turns black.

Jolting upward, my heart pounding like a herd of elephants in my chest, I realize I'm no longer at the playground, but safe in my bed. My throat is raw, my body dripping in sweat, and my sheets twist around me, trapping me in place. My gasp echoes in the silent room as I try to draw a breath that doesn't carry the terror of my dream into my starved lungs. I gulp down air like my life depends on it and tear the sheets from my body with furious hands, then drop back to my pillow, squeezing my eyes closed. When the visual remnants of my dream continue to linger, I snap them open again and stare unseeing at the ceiling.

My chest heaves with a sob, and tears stream down the side of my face, soaking into my hair. Over the years, I've repeatedly had some version of this dream, as if my subconscious is filling in the blanks of my husband's death, even though he was thousands of miles away in Syria when it happened. It's not like I was there. All I know is what the officers told me when they knocked on my door in the middle of the night, almost six years ago.

Not even Shane, Wyatt's best friend, who was also impacted by the blast, could fill in the blanks. Nix, Wyatt's commanding officer, refused to discuss the horrific moment when a young boy carrying a backpack concealing an explosive device asked my husband to play soccer with him.

In the beginning, I had dreams almost every night. Over time, they've lessened, but they still happen occasionally.

This is what living with grief is like.

It's a weird thing. Just when I think I'm beginning to live around *it*, *it* comes up, slaps me in the face, and I land on my ass in proverbial quicksand that sucks me in and won't let go. I can fight *it*, but the more I do, the deeper *it* drags me into *its* depths.

Weeks—sometimes even months—can pass while I live life like everyone else, and then, out of the blue, *it* hits.

Grief.

There's no rhyme or reason. No explanation. No trigger that I can pinpoint. But I've returned to where I was a year after losing Wyatt. The father of my son. My best friend. My future.

We made promises, and he broke his. *I* didn't.

Our promises were meant to be everlasting. Or so I thought.

I was wrong.

I never quite sink back to the depths of despair I experienced during the first year after losing him, but almost six years later, I can't seem to escape *its* clutches completely. *Its* claws latch onto my flesh, tearing at my soul and ripping apart my heart, yet there's nothing I can do to combat it.

I'm helpless. At *its* mercy.

For the last two weeks, I've cried myself to sleep every night and woken every morning with tears soaking my cheeks. This morning is no different as I swipe angrily at the moisture on my face. I know I'll always carry pain in my heart and a heavy ache in my soul, but feeling this way all the time is exhausting. I'm tired down to my very marrow.

Curling into a ball around Wyatt's pillow, I make myself as small as possible beneath the burden that's become too much to carry.

In my heart, I know Wyatt would be disappointed. He'd be pissed that I'm not moving forward at a pace he'd deem appropriate. He was never one to surrender to negativity, but he's not here. He can't comfort me, and he certainly can't tell me that everything will be okay.

Because it will *never* be okay.

"Mom, are you awake?" Evan calls softly through my door.

"Yeah, big guy." I swipe my cheeks again, trying to remove the evidence of my pain.

"Can I come in?"

I smile wistfully. Ever since he walked in on me dressing, he's started knocking to check if it's "safe" to enter, instead of walking in unannounced like he used to. I appreciate it. I do. I'm just sad he's already at that age.

I place Wyatt's pillow back on his side of the bed, wipe beneath my eyes, and then sit up. "Sure." When the door opens, I pat Wyatt's side of the bed and encourage Evan to step beyond the doorway. "Come and sit with me for a minute." He climbs onto the bed, and I wrap my arm around him, sliding my fingers through his soft hair. "How are you feeling about starting middle school tomorrow?"

He shrugs. "Okay, I guess."

"Did you and Elliott work out a place to meet?" I hate the thought of him being all alone, but what I hate more is that Wyatt isn't here to see his son moving onto the next stage of his education. He missed Evan's first day of kindergarten—and first grade—because he was deployed, but we video chatted so he didn't miss out completely. Now, though, we can't even do that.

"Yeah, sorta." He looks up at me with his big brown eyes, just like his dad's. It doesn't get any easier to look at Evan and not see Wyatt. The older Evan gets, the more he looks like his father. Even some of his mannerisms are like Wyatt's, and I would've thought that, with the limited time they had together and Evan's young age, he wouldn't be so much like his dad.

I was wrong.

About so many things.

I muss his hair a little, noting the length. "I think I'll trim your hair after breakfast." I meant to do it last week, but it totally slipped my mind.

He dips away from me, swatting my hand with a frown marring his young face. "I don't need a trim."

My eyebrows shoot up. "You do. All the kids have fresh cuts for the beginning of the year. I'll only tidy up the ends a little, but I'm cutting your hair."

He pouts and climbs from the bed, and I follow suit on the other side, grabbing my robe. "Dammit. Having a hairstylist for a mom is the worst," he snaps over his shoulder.

I chuckle to myself as I pull my hair free from my robe. "Watch your mouth." I raise a brow at him. "Meet me downstairs. I'm making pancakes."

He pops his head back around the doorjamb with a hopeful expression. "Chocolate?"

"I guess I could be persuaded." We head downstairs, and when Evan sees me place the chocolate chips on the counter, he whoops loudly. He sets the table for two while I mix the batter, and then he stands beside me while I cook the pancakes. "So, what would you like to do on your last day of freedom?" I flip the pancake over, waiting for his answer.

He shrugs. "I was just gonna play Fortnite with my friends."

I glance out the window. "It's a nice day. We should do something outside."

He huffs, folding his skinny arms across his chest. "You always make me go outside just because the weather's nice. I don't wanna."

I press my lips together, hiding my grin at his adorable pout. "I'll tell you what. After breakfast, I'll cut your hair." His frown deepens, but I ignore him. "Then, humor me and join me on a bike ride, and I'll leave you to do your thing with your friends for the rest of the day."

His eyes narrow as he contemplates my offer. "Hmmm, you drive a tough bargain, but okay. That sounds reasonable."

"Fantastic," I say as I carry the pancakes to the table. Evan wastes no time dropping a couple onto his plate and diving in, as if I haven't fed him in a week. "Hey, slow down."

"I can't! They're too good," he mumbles around a mouthful of food.

I can't argue there, this batch tastes exceptionally delicious for some reason.

We clear the table, and Evan wipes the dishes as I wash. Then, I set up a chair on the back porch and trim his hair.

As the brown strands slide through my fingers, I flash back to a time when Wyatt would let me cut his hair while I was training to be a hairstylist. I chuckle under my breath. Some haircuts I gave him were hideous, and he'd have to wear a hat to cover the disaster, but he never once denied me when I asked to practice on him. My heart flips in my chest as I remember his steadfast support, which never wavered during the time we were together.

2

HOPE

I JUMP ON ONE LEG TO PUT ON MY SECOND SHOE. "C'mon, Evan, you're gonna be late for your first day!" I call out as I fasten the last buttons of my work shirt.

Mom's better at keeping Evan on time, but I wanted to take him on his first day of middle school. She's such a godsend, looking after him, so I can open the salon each morning. I don't know how I'd manage without her.

"I'm coming!" he shouts down the stairs.

By the time I've grabbed my purse, he's puffing and panting at my side. "Let's go."

We climb into the car, and I load up Evan's favorite playlist to hopefully make him smile. His nerves fill the interior of our car like a suffocating cloud, and I want him to start his day in a better headspace. We pull up to the kiss-and-drive section, and he releases his seatbelt, ready to climb out as soon as we stop.

"Hey, have an awesome day. I love you, big guy, and I can't wait to hear all about your first day when I pick you up." When I stop, I lean back as far as I can to plant a kiss on his cheek, but he climbs out of the car, leaving me hanging.

"Thanks, Mom. See you later." He slams the back door and races toward the gate.

I exhale a long breath and shake my head. *Where's my baby gone? Why does he have to grow up so fast?* I blink away the sting at the back of my eyes and suck in a shaky breath, then put my foot on the gas and drive out of the drop-off section, heading to work, all the while wishing Wyatt were here for this milestone.

Blinking, I swallow the lump in my throat and press my lips together to stem my emotions. I'm so tired of being an emotional wreck. I turn up the music as a distraction and direct my focus outward instead of inward; it's something I learned at the *coping with grief* group I attend when I'm really feeling low.

With a few minutes to spare before I need to be at work, I drive through Starbucks to grab coffee for myself and the girls. I'm sure Sophie will need one too, since James started second grade today. I take a deep breath and push my shoulders back to hide my emotions and breeze through the back door. After dropping my purse in the cupboard, I head out front, where Sophie and Lucy are already working with clients.

"Morning, ladies."—I hold up the coffee—"I brought you guys a treat."

Sophie shimmies and blows me a kiss as she wets my client's hair, ready to shampoo. "Thanks, lovely!"

Lucy makes grabby hands. "Gimme, gimme, gimme!"

I chuckle at her theatrics as I deliver the drinks to the girls, setting Sophie's at the reception desk and placing Lucy's on the small gold table closest to her chair.

"How nervous was our boy for his first day?" Lucy asks.

She stops mid-cut, waiting for my answer, and I shrug. "He jumped out of the car before I could kiss him goodbye." My lip trembles as I share my disappointment, but I take a deep breath to regain my composure. After years of practice, I'm a pro at pushing my tears away in public.

"James was the same. What's wrong with these boys? Don't they know we need momma hugs?" Sophie chuckles and I force myself to do the same.

Mrs. Davies pipes up, "I was always so grateful to send my boys off to school after summer vacation. My sanity was barely hanging on by a thread, and I was desperate for peace and quiet." Sophie rolls her eyes as she massages her scalp, and I know exactly what she's thinking. Mrs. Davies' boys were probably just as happy to be at school—and away from her.

Sophie finishes up and grabs her coffee from the reception area. She's our receptionist, and I'm not sure how we managed before she started working here a few months ago because she steps in wherever she's needed. It feels like she's always been part of the team. I know she won't be here forever; she has different dreams from working in a hair salon.

The phone rings, and Sophie answers it as I lead Mrs. Davies to my chair. I run the wide-tooth comb through her shoulder-length bob and catch her eye in the large, gold-framed mirror. "What would you like done today?"

A twinkle appears in her eye, making the hairs on the back of my neck stand on end. "I thought you could surprise me. I'm ready for a change." She smiles broadly and sits up straighter in her chair.

Ugh. I hate it when clients do this, and Mrs. Davies has done it before. She ended up hating what I did to her hair, even though it looked amazing. I raise my eyebrows with a fake grin—another thing I've mastered—as I run my fingers through the fine, wet strands. "So, you won't mind if I dye it hot pink and give you a mohawk?"

Her whole body shakes as she chuckles. "Well, no ... I mean yes, obviously, I don't want anything like that. Be sensible, dear."

I somehow suppress an eye roll. "How about bangs? Are you ready for that much of a change? I could layer the hair here"—I slide my fingers through a portion of hair on each side of her face —"so it frames your face. It would give you more movement and a fresh look."

She draws her mouth into a thin line. "Hmm, that would

mean I have to come back to see you more often to keep my bangs out of my eyes. I'm not sure I like that idea."

"If I make them long enough for you to still pull back into a high ponytail, you wouldn't need such regular maintenance. I know how busy you are," I suggest.

She nods as her cheeks rise slowly. "Yes, I think that sounds perfect."

"Great."

I separate portions of her hair and twist them, holding them in place with sectioning clips, then start cutting an inch off the length. As I cut her hair, we chat about the latest episode of *The Bachelor*.

"That brunette girl ... what's her name?"

I rummage through my memory and the girls that are left. "Bianca?"

"Yeah, that's her. I want her to win. She's a real sweetheart."

I grin. "She is, but I think he's more interested in Candy's boobs. He's always talking to them."

Mrs. Davies chuckles. "I think you might be right."

Once I'm happy with the cut, I blow dry and straighten her silver-streaked hair, using my fingers to comb it into position. "There, what do you think?" She turns her head side to side, and I hold a mirror up behind her so she can see the layers I've added. "It's still long enough to tie up for everyday convenience, but you now have some volume and movement for when you want to leave it down."

"I love it, Hope. As usual, you've done an amazing job."

I spend the rest of my day cutting, coloring, and styling, and as soon as the clock hits three p.m., Sophie and I walk out the door to collect our boys from school. I'm grateful Marina allows me to work around Evan's schedule. It means I get to spend essential time with him. I've been with her ever since I started out as a stylist and have always considered myself extremely lucky to have her as my boss. She's always been amazing and flexible with my work hours to accommodate my being a single parent. Let's face it, even when Wyatt was alive, I might as well have been a single mom.

I spot Evan the moment I pull into the pickup line. He's talking with a group of boys I don't recognize, and I grin. I'm so glad he made some new friends today. He hasn't noticed I'm here, so I quickly shoot him a text, then check my rearview mirror. Cars are lined up behind me, and I watch kids climb into them. *C'mon, Evan. I can't wait here all afternoon.*

Sure enough, the woman behind me beeps her horn, and I wave to acknowledge her. Evan glances at his phone, leaves my message unread, and slides it back into his pocket. Damn it. I'm going to have to loop around the block.

Pulling onto the road, I drive around the corner and wait for ten minutes to give him time with his new friends. Then, I continue around the block and pull into the pickup line again. There are only a dozen or so kids left waiting, and the line is empty. Evan's standing on his own, and when I come to a stop, he stomps toward my car, climbs in the back, and slams the door, startling me.

The vibe coming from my son is not what I was expecting, especially after watching him laugh with the group of boys I saw him with earlier. "How was your first day?"

He shrugs, looking out of the window. "You're late!" he snaps.

I narrow my eyes, keeping my gaze on the road. "I wasn't late. I was here on time. I even texted you, but you were busy with your new friends."

He grumbles and slumps in his seat, dragging the seatbelt across his body and clicking it into place.

"What's with the attitude?" I ask, turning on my blinker and glancing at him in the mirror.

We drive in silence, but the air in the car is stifling. I'm not sure what's happened to put him in such a foul mood, but I don't appreciate it. I know the first day of middle school can be overwhelming, so I'll give him a pass. He's probably had a big day, and his emotions are all over the place.

"I thought we could grab a milkshake before we go home. How does that sound?" I push as much enthusiasm into my voice as I can, but I'm really not feeling it.

"Whatever." The single word drips with his surly attitude.

Oh-kay then. "Or ... we can go straight home. Your choice."

I watch him roll his eyes in the mirror. "If you want a shake, we can get a shake."

"I'm asking what *you* want, Ev. You usually love *Declan's Diner*, so I thought we could celebrate your first day. But if you'd prefer to go home, we can do that."

"I just wanna go home."

"Okay. Let's do that." I take the cue from him and shut my mouth. He's obviously in a mood—which has been happening more often than not lately—and I find it best to give him some space when he gets like this. He usually snaps out of it pretty fast—well, he used to.

The second I turn off the engine, Evan climbs out of the car, slamming his door. He stomps up to the house and waits impatiently for me on the porch. As soon as I open the front door, he storms inside and upstairs, banging his bedroom door behind him.

I stand frozen and blow out a long breath. Some days I don't recognize this kid, and I don't know how to deal with him when he's like this. There have been occasions over the last few weeks when he's been moody—which I've assumed was due to being nervous about middle school, and I guess today's been a big day— but this is beyond anything I've experienced with him so far.

Give him grace. Give him grace. Give him grace. I repeat the mantra to remind myself to stay calm and give him space when I really want to follow him upstairs and reprimand him for his behavior.

Pushing away from the front door, I hang my purse on the hook, head into the kitchen, and pull out the ingredients to make brownies. Maybe some chocolate will cheer him up. I know it'll make *me* feel better.

As I'm pulling the brownies from the oven, footsteps sound on the stairs and I grin. *Worked like a charm.* He drags a stool out from the counter, and I keep my back to him, pretending he's not there as I place the tray on the cooling rack and take out two plates. I toss some frozen berries, coconut milk, and ice cream in the blender to make a smoothie and pour it into two milkshake glasses.

Being a single parent is tough, though I should be used to it by now; I've been one for more than half of Evan's life. It's tiresome having to be both parents, and it's not what I signed up for. I have nobody to bounce ideas off of or to get a second opinion about what I should do in different situations. I flounder with confrontation, and it would be great to have someone else here to be the tough guy sometimes. If Wyatt were here, he could be the one to speak with Evan about his behavior. But it has to be me. It's always me.

My gut tenses and guilt grows. I hate how my thoughts narrow to blaming Wyatt for leaving me in this position. This isn't his fault. He wouldn't have left us willingly.

I draw in a deep breath and blow it out slowly, trying to cleanse my thoughts as I plate up two generous slices of warm brownie. I silently slide a plate and glass across to Evan, and then bring mine to the counter and sit beside my son—the one piece of Wyatt I have left. We don't speak for the longest time, and I wonder if this is how it's going to be from this point forward.

Evan swallows the last bite of his brownie, then uses his fingers to collect the crumbs. "Thanks, Mom. That was yum," he says with a wide smile. "Can I have another piece?"

"You're welcome, and sure, but make it a small one. I don't want you to ruin your dinner." *Should I say something about his behavior? Do I risk asking him about his day now that he seems to have calmed down, or will my questions set him off again?*

I feel like I never know the right thing to do.

He grabs a piece and returns to his seat. "I'm sorry I was in a bad mood," he mumbles around a mouthful of chocolate, and I do my best not to grin. *There's my boy.*

"Thanks for apologizing." I glance at him, then return my gaze to my food. "I'm not the enemy, you know."

"I know." He stuffs another forkful into his mouth and chews.

I sip my smoothie to give us some time to breathe. "Anything you wanna talk about?"

"Nah."

My heart sinks, and I struggle to think of what to say next. Lord knows I haven't had the emotional strength to deal with much since losing Wyatt, but I need him to know I'm here whenever he needs me.

"Well, I'm always here if you change your mind."

He grabs his empty dishes and carries them to the sink. "I know." Without looking back at me, he leaves the kitchen and heads back upstairs.

I can't be left alone with my thoughts, so I turn on the television for background noise and collect a load of laundry to do while I prepare our lunches for tomorrow. We'll be back to our usual routine in the morning, so I need to be organized.

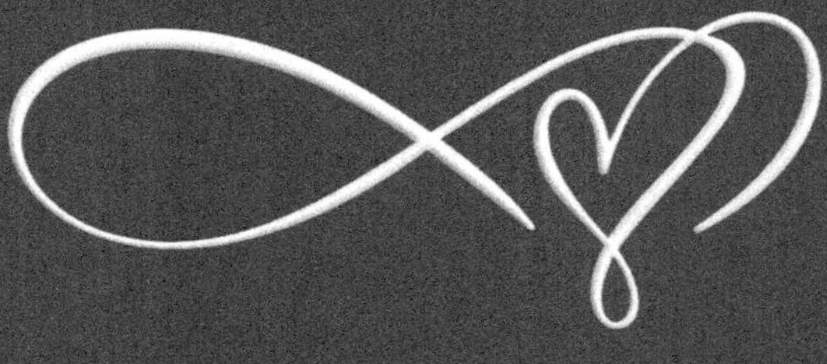

3

BEN

"C'mon, Rex, time to work out!" I say, skimming my fingers over his dark fur as we head out to the backyard, which overlooks the ocean. He's the best workout partner a guy could ask for. Selecting my favorite playlist, I turn up the volume, ready to work up a sweat and burn off enough calories to allow me to enjoy my favorite cookies later.

I do some warm-up stretches, then lie on the grass to do sit-ups as Rex's paws hold my feet in place. "Woof!" he barks, then licks his chops when I reach one hundred. He's pretty smart, but I don't think he can actually count. His response is more about him recognizing my body language when I'm about to stop. After all, we're trained to be highly in tune with each other.

I rub the top of his head, then flip over to do push-ups. Rex climbs onto my back and gets comfortable, licking the back of my neck every now and then.

"Thanks for the encouragement, buddy," I grunt out.

He's not a light dog, but having him on my back while I do these provides the added resistance I need. Next, I grip the pull-up bar beneath the back porch, and Rex stands on his hind legs so I can wrap my legs around him. I lift him as I do my curls, admiring the ocean view.

"All right, buddy. You ready to run?" He leaps up, his front paws landing on my shoulders, and licks the side of my face, making me chuckle as I rub the dark fur at his flanks.

After I lock the house, we head through the front gate to the sidewalk and jog slowly for two blocks to warm up. The briny air fills my lungs with each breath, and my smile spreads. I look out across the horizon at the waves crashing and breaking as my feet pound the pavement. This never gets old. I'm so grateful my job gave me the opportunity to move here from Piney Lakes—it's the fresh start I needed, and I haven't looked back. Leaving everything behind, except for my best friend Sebastian, was the best decision I've ever made.

"I'm on Fire"—the ringtone Seb added when he officially became a firefighter—sounds from my pocket, and I slow to answer my phone with a grin; speak of the devil. I press the green button and hold it to my ear.

"I need a wingman next Saturday night. Tell me you're not working," he says before I can get a word out.

I chuckle warmly. "Depends," I hedge. Not that I mind being his wingman. It's always entertaining.

"We responded to a fire alarm in an apartment building last night, and this hot-as-fuck chick told me she's going to be at *Brady's Pub* next Saturday night with her girlfriends. You gotta come, man. If Lucy's friends look anything like her, you'll be in luck."

I enjoy *Brady's*, and they often have a band playing on Saturday nights. "Sure. But I have an early shift on Sunday, so I can't be out late." I'm not looking for anything right now, and I'm not interested in one-night stands like he is.

"Yeah, yeah. No problem. Meet you there at eight."

"Sounds good."

"Thanks, man. Gotta go." He disconnects the call before I can say goodbye.

Rex and I continue our run, enjoying the early morning sun

and fresh air, then head home to get ready for our visit to the shelter. He leaps into my restored truck, and I climb in, roll the windows down, and pull onto the street.

When I park in front of *The Paw Palace*, Rex props his paws on the passenger door and almost hangs his whole body out of the window as his tail thumps wildly against the seat.

I chuckle at his excitement. "Yeah, boy, we're here." I attach his leash and lead him inside.

When Tori looks up, her smile is instant. "Ahhh, Rexy!" She steps out from behind the counter and drops her knees to the polished concrete to fuss over Rex.

"Hi, Tori. Nice to see you, too," I joke, my voice thick with sarcasm.

"Oh, you big baby. I was getting to you." She climbs to her feet, still fussing over Rex. Once he's satisfied he's said hello properly, he sits, his thick tail sweeping back and forth across the smooth floor. He loves coming here on our Saturdays off. "C'mon, I'll show you who we have available for the kids today."

Tori, Rex, and I make our way through to the back room to check who's here. My black Converse squeak on the polished concrete, and the smell of disinfectant hangs heavy in the air as the dogs bark excitedly. Most of the dogs aren't here long, but occasionally, there are one or two who take longer to find their forever homes. We stop at each door to meet the occupants, and Rex excitedly bounces on his paws as he says his hellos.

I usually let the kids and dogs figure out who wants to hang out with whom, then we head out back so the kids can play with the dogs. Some choose to stay inside if Tori has kittens. Sometimes, she even lets the kids bathe and groom the animals.

"Most of these dogs will be fine, but I'd steer the kids clear of those two." She points to two of the dogs. "They've been a little aggressive since coming in. I think they've been abused."

Fuckers! My hands form fists at my sides, and Rex stills beside me. I abhor people who abuse animals. I push my shoulders back and stand tall. "Have the owners been charged?"

She curls her shoulders inward and shakes her head slowly as she watches the two dogs. "I don't think so. There's not enough evidence." Damn. That pisses me off. "It'll make it tough to find them new homes, but we'll try to work with them and see if we can rehabilitate them."

I nod, and we turn the corner to head through another door to see the cats and kittens. My eyebrows shoot up as I look around the space. "Not a single adult cat. That's gotta be a first."

Tori grins. "I know. How amazing is that? But we do have some six-week-old kittens. I think the kids will love them. They came in yesterday, and we've checked them all. We'll need to keep them here for another two weeks before we can find them new homes."

Two of my regular kids, Eva and Michael, are introverted and prefer to sit inside quietly with the kittens or smaller dogs, so they'll probably hang out in here today.

The children who join me here are kids I've apprehended. They mostly come from broken homes, or they've lost a parent and are having trouble adjusting—hence acting out. They're not bad kids, just misunderstood and struggling. Bringing them together with the cats and dogs waiting for their forever homes kills two birds with one stone. It gives the kids someone else to think and care about, while also giving the dogs and cats the one-on-one attention they need. It's something they don't get enough of. Tori and the team do their best, but they're swamped with the day-to-day running of the place, and while they ensure the animals get regular time outside and snuggles, the kids provide something a little extra. Both animal and child are always much happier by the end of our time here.

We head back toward the front, and Rex bounds away from me with a happy woof. When I look up, Donnelly's walking toward us with a giant grin. He drops to his knees when Rex reaches him, and they greet each other like the old friends they are. Donnelly's been with this program for the longest—two years. He was the first kid to join me when I had the idea to start this program and approached *The Paw Palace*. I chuckle as I watch them together. Rex is a fucking intimidating dog when he's on the job, but here, with the kids, he's a playful puppy.

"Hey, Ben," he calls as he rests his cheek on Rex's head.

I step closer. "Hey, Don. How are things with you?"

He looks up at me and swallows. "Not so great. I got suspended for a day last week for back talking and swearing at one of my teachers."

I study him closely, noting the disappointment suffusing the surrounding air. Donnelly has trouble regulating his responses. "What brought that on?"

He shrugs and turns away from me. "Dunno. Just having a bad day, I guess."

I crouch next to him so I'm on his level. "Any ideas how you could have responded instead of lashing out?" I ask gently.

"Yeah." He sighs. "Shoulda taken a breath and kept my mouth shut, like you've taught me. It wasn't worth it, and now, because I've had a suspension, I can't go to school camp. Sucks."

I squeeze his shoulder. "Definitely sucks, man. But we've talked about consequences. The school has to follow through, or everyone will do whatever they want."

He blows out a hot breath and his shoulders drop when he looks up at me with remorse swimming in his gaze. "Yeah, I know."

Carrying a book beneath her arm, Eva wanders in next, and the entire welcome process begins again until each of the nine kids have arrived. My chest puffs out with pride; we have a full house today. The kids choose their companion for the next couple of hours, and we head out into the yard so they can play and run. As anticipated, Eva and Michael choose to stay inside with the kittens, and I know Tori will hang out and chat with them when she can.

"All right, gather 'round with your pups." I collect the slicker brushes Tori left out for us. "Tori needs us to help her by giving these guys a brush. Remember to be gentle." I demonstrate with Rex, though the kids don't really need it; they've done it enough times before.

The kids watch closely, then turn to their companion and practice what I've shown them while I move around the group. "Brett, your friend seems to like the attention you're giving his tummy."

He glances up at me with wide eyes and a broad grin. "I know, right? He's so friendly. I wish we didn't live in an apartment. I'd love to take him home with me."

"I bet he'd love to come home with you. Maybe when you have a home of your own one day, you can have a dog."

He nods enthusiastically. "I'm definitely planning on that. I'm gonna get a good job and a house with a yard, so I can have a dog of my own."

I grin. Brett used to have trouble thinking about what his life might look like in the future. He didn't care that the path he was on was so destructive. It makes me happy to hear him talking about his future in a positive light. "That's a brilliant plan. Let me know if there's anything I can do to help make that happen."

At the end of our two-hour session, we put the dogs back into their kennels. The kids and I thank Tori, and I walk out to the front of the shelter and wait with them until they're collected by their parents. When it's just Rex and me, he looks up at me, tilting his head as his tongue lolls out the side of his mouth. I squat down and kiss his snout as I rub him behind his ears. "You did good, buddy. Let's go home and eat some lunch."

He kisses me, and we climb into my truck to head home. Happiness for a job well done fills me, and I grin. I've watched these kids grow over the last couple of years, and if the worst they get is a suspension now and then, I'm happy with the results of our time together, and consider it time well spent.

4

HOPE

"C'mon, Hope," Lucy whines. "Come out with us. You might actually have fun. And if Sebastian's friend is half as hot as he is, you'll thank me later," she says, glancing over her shoulder and wiggling her eyebrows up and down. "Maybe you'll even get lucky."

Tension builds across my shoulders, and my smile grows more and more forced the longer she nags me to go out with them. "I don't want to get lucky. I'm happy where I am right now." I slide the key out of the lock and double-check that the door's secure.

She sighs and rolls her eyes. "You're not happy. You're scraping by through life. Mr. Right's not just gonna turn up on your doorstep, you know."

My stomach twists and folds in on itself. She says the words so flippantly, but I already had my Mr. Right. If I can't have him, I don't want anyone else.

I had my one true love with my soulmate—my one and only chance at happiness.

As hard as it's been to accept that, at thirty-four, I've had my great love and lost it, I know I need to make peace with it some-how. I need to find happiness within myself, not depend on someone else. And some days I do. Even for weeks at a time, *if* I'm doing well.

Savannah wraps her arm around my shoulder. "At least come out. Evan's with the in-laws for the weekend, and you should hang out with your girls. No pressure to talk to anyone of the opposite sex. I promise." She squeezes me close. "I'll personally keep all men away from you." She releases me and flings her arms and legs out in some type of wacky karate move, causing laughter to bubble up and escape, and her purse drops to the pavement. The contents scatter everywhere—typical Savannah style.

The three of us rush to collect everything and stash it back inside. I guess it wouldn't hurt to go out with the girls. They're always asking me, and I always say no. Maybe it would help lift my spirits and get me out of this funk I can't seem to shake. I look at my colleagues and friends as they watch me with hopeful expressions.

I need to start living again. Maybe I should try to have some fun.

"Okay. I'll come." They jump up and down, squealing in delight, and I hold up my hands, freezing them on the spot. "On one condition." I hold up one finger and they nod. "I'm honestly not looking to date. I'm not ready, and at this point, I don't think I'll ever be ready, so please promise me you won't pressure me to do something I don't want to do."

Their eyes go all soft and some of their excitement drains away. They reach forward, each taking one of my hands. "Promise."

I nod sharply, as if convincing myself I've made the right decision. "Okay. But the second either of you breaks your promise, I'm out. I mean it." I'll drive myself there so I can escape if I need to.

"We've got you, Hope." Lucy squeezes my hand. "I'm just happy you've finally agreed to come out with us."

Savannah tugs me into her. "We'll take care of you. Promise."

I CHECK myself in the mirror while a mixture of dread and a touch of excitement roll around in my stomach. I press my hand against it and try to push away the urge to text Lucy and cancel. I study my reflection. My eyes lost their sparkle the day the military police showed up at my door to tell me that my husband wasn't ever coming home, and the light that used to gleam there has never returned. My eyes glisten as I trace over the rest of my face, noting the fine lines between my brows.

I see myself in the mirror every day at work, but I never take the time to look properly, and as I study myself now, sadness creeps over me. I look older than I should. Weighed down. Burdened. Sad. I wonder if strangers can see it, or maybe it's not obvious to people who have never met me before.

Bringing my fingers up to my mouth, I lightly trace my quivering lips. Lips that haven't been kissed in such a long time. The tears become too much to hold back, and they spill out over my bottom lashes. They track down my face slowly, then gather intensity while I fight to remember how Wyatt's lips felt against mine as he kissed me; but the memory is just out of reach.

Oh, god.

My stomach clenches as I search and search for how his mouth felt on mine, but the feeling is nowhere to be found. A sob bursts out of me, and I bend at the waist in acute pain. C'mon! A memory can't just disappear completely. I *know* we kissed, and I can see us together, but the feeling of his mouth on mine ... *it's gone.*

How can it just disappear? It must be there somewhere; I'm just trying too hard right now. Maybe if I relax and think about something else, it will come to me.

Dropping to the edge of my bed, I grip the mattress with white-knuckled force to stop myself from falling. My heart twists as horror fills me.

Is this what happens? Will my memories of Wyatt slowly disap-

pear? Vanish into the ether? Fade, one by one until there's nothing left to remember?

This night's already a disaster. I should stay home. There's no point ruining the girls' night out with my melancholy mood. It's not fair to them. A sob shakes my body, and I roughly wipe beneath my eyes.

Decision made, I lean over to grab my phone to text Lucy. It lights up before I touch it, and I snatch my hand back. Lucy's name glares at me with accusation, like she knows I'm about to cancel. With a shaky hand, I wipe my tears again—*I'm so sick of crying*—and grab it to answer her call.

"We're outside." Music blares in the background, and excitement radiates through her voice. I was going to drive myself. I guess they figured if they picked me up, I wouldn't be able to bail on them.

I twist my fingers in my curls. "Uhm ... I-I—"

The music disappears, and there's a knock at my front door, making my shoulders curl forward. Damn.

"I'm at your front door. C'mon, Hope. Let's go," she urges.

Staying where I am, I press the phone against my ear. "Uh, I don't think I can do this," I murmur with a sob. My heart pounds like a bass drum, the vibrations reverberating through my body and thrashing in my ears, and I sniffle.

"Can you let us in, please?"

I turn toward the door but remain where I am. I can't face the girls. I'm so embarrassed. It's been almost six years, and the idea of going out is terrifying. "I-I can't. I'm so sorry. I just can't do it."

"Oh, sweetie. Let us in." Her voice softens, the excitement from a moment ago vanishing. "We don't have to go anywhere, but we can't leave you alone like this," she says gently.

I swipe my cheeks and drop my head. "I don't want to ruin your night," I murmur. "You guys have fun."

"Do you really think we can have fun knowing how much pain you're in? Please let us in. We can watch a movie and hang out with you." The rustle of fabric and lowered voices fill the phone. "Savannah's gonna go get some wine and goodies so we can have a girls' night in."

They're clearly not going to give up. I swipe my cheeks and use my fingers to wipe beneath my eyes and nose as I head for the front door, drowning in guilt for ruining their plans. The second I open it, Lucy wraps her arms around me. "Oh, sweetie. You don't have to push us away when you're having a tough time. We're not just good-time friends, you know."

I nod against her shoulder. It's not that I mean to push them away. It's that I feel so damn broken and uncomfortable sharing my misery with them, and after almost six years, I really feel I should be able to go out with friends.

Everybody keeps telling me that Wyatt died, not me, but a huge part of me died with him. I don't know how to be here without him. I know it's something Wyatt's best friend Shane also struggles with, and I've said those very words to him. I don't understand why I can't take my own advice.

Lucy drags me inside, closing the door behind us and leading me through my living room. "Oh, I love those new bookshelves," she gushes as she runs her fingers over the smooth wood.

"Shane stopped by last weekend and built them for me. I was running out of room." I keep buying new books even though I have no desire to read—haven't picked up a book since Wyatt died. It's the worst book slump I've ever had.

Her cheeks turn pink at the mention of Shane, then she turns her attention back to my books, running her fingers across the spines. "So ... how is Shane?"

I wrap my arms around my middle. "Still the same." I think she has a crush on the stoic man. However, I get the feeling he may be off the market soon, if he can move past his guilt.

She nods slowly. "Oh, what's this book like? I've seen it all over social media."

I move closer to see which book she's talking about. "I have no idea. Haven't read it yet. You can borrow it, if you want." It's not like I'm going to read it anytime soon; I've completely lost my reading mojo, but I like to keep up with my favorite authors' new releases.

"Thanks, I'll grab it before I leave." She heads into the kitchen and collects three wine glasses, three bowls, and three spoons.

While she's doing that, I go to the bathroom to wash my face. Mascara is smudged beneath my eyes, making me look like I've had a hard night out. My eyes are red and puffy, and my nose is pink and shiny—a familiar look. I wash my face and dry it, then head out to the living room to tidy up a little. There's another knock on the door, and I let Savannah in, taking the shopping bag from her hand as she leans in to embrace me.

"I grabbed all the good stuff." She grins as she holds two bottles of wine above her head. "We're in for a great night, ladies."

She struts—yes, struts—to my kitchen and immediately pours three drinks. I place the shopping bag on the counter and pop the second bottle into the fridge for later. She passes Lucy and me a glass each and holds hers up for a toast. "To a fabulous girls' night in." We clink our glasses together and simultaneously take a drink of the sweet Moscato.

I watch my two friends, dressed similarly to me in hip-hugging jeans and cute tops, and my heart swells with appreciation for them. I don't know how they're still my friends after years of neglect on my part. All of my energy has gone into barely surviving, which has left nothing to invest in my friendships. How they're still here supporting me is beyond my comprehension.

"Thanks, ladies. I don't deserve you." My nose tingles, and I press my lips together to stop them from quivering. I should just put on my big girl panties and go out with them. "You shouldn't have to spend your Saturday night stuck here with me instead of meeting your hot firefighter and his friend."

They move to either side of me, wrapping themselves around me. "We wouldn't be anywhere else," Lucy announces.

"Yeah, we don't leave a girlfriend in need behind," Savannah adds.

I force a smile. "Thanks, girls. I appreciate you so much."

"We know. All right, let's get started." Savannah places her glass on the counter, then starts dragging items out of the shopping bag. Chocolate ice cream, a six-pack of Hershey's chocolate bars, Hershey's chocolate sauce, brownies, and a giant bag of Reese's. "Welcome to death by chocolate, ladies."

We all chuckle. "What a way to go," Lucy moans as she opens the bag of peanut butter cups and inhales.

We load up our bowls with ice cream and chocolate sauce, then carry the remaining treats into the living room and turn on my favorite trashy TV—*The Bachelor*. I try to stay on top of as many trashy shows as I can, because I find it provides the best conversation starters with most clients. Most people want to either talk about their kids and grandkids, complain about their partner or work, or talk about what they've read or watched. Sometimes, I feel like I know my clients better than their therapists do.

As we get caught up watching the dates while Lucy and Savannah give a humorous running commentary, I do my best to stay in the moment, laughing at the right times so as not to get lost in my head. Hours pass as we watch episode after episode, only pausing for bathroom breaks and wine refills. They've done an incredible job of dragging me out of my misery for a few hours, but the night has ended, and that crushing feeling from earlier returns.

We walk to the front door, and they both come in for hugs. "We love you, Hope," Lucy says as she pulls away, gripping my arms and trapping me in her gaze. "When you're ready to go out, we'll go out. Until then, we're happy to spend nights in with you."

My heart squeezes with gratitude. They could have easily gone out and kept their plans without me, but they chose to stay and support me. It felt kinda nice.

"You guys are the best. Thank you for tonight. For everything." I push my mouth up into what I hope looks like a genuine smile, because it is.

"Anytime, lovely," Savannah says as she gives me one last squeeze. "See ya at work on Monday."

"Yeah, see you guys on Monday." I walk them out to Savannah's car, wrapping my arms around my middle as I watch their taillights shrink.

Turning to walk inside, I lock the front door and head into the living room to clean up. The house feels so empty. So silent. I wash the dishes and leave them to dry, throw out the trash, and as I turn out the kitchen light, my laptop catches my attention.

I rarely use it. I have it to pay bills and store our photos and videos ... *our memories*. Flipping the lid, I pull out a chair to sit at the table. I navigate to the photos, click on the video I'm looking for, and press play. Dragging the progress bar until I get to the part I want, I sit forward and study every inch of Wyatt's handsome face, then hit play. He dips me low and my startled chuckle fills the silence, then his lips are on mine and he devours me. Applause and cheers echo in my silent kitchen as I grip the back of his neck and kiss him with abandon.

When the kiss finally ends, we stand with our eyes locked together. My lips are swollen from his attention and the smile stretching them is as wide as the Mississippi.

Salty tears touch my lips and I spread them across the pillows with my finger. It's almost like I can feel the ghost of Wyatt's thumb as he rubs my smeared lipstick, a proud grin decorating his face.

Will this ache ever go away?

Swiping at my cheeks, I shut down my laptop, then switch off the lights, leaving the room lit only by the moonlight streaming in through the kitchen window.

I move through my nightly routine with an emptiness that won't ebb, and when I finally climb into my lonely bed, the tears I'd pushed away earlier come tumbling out.

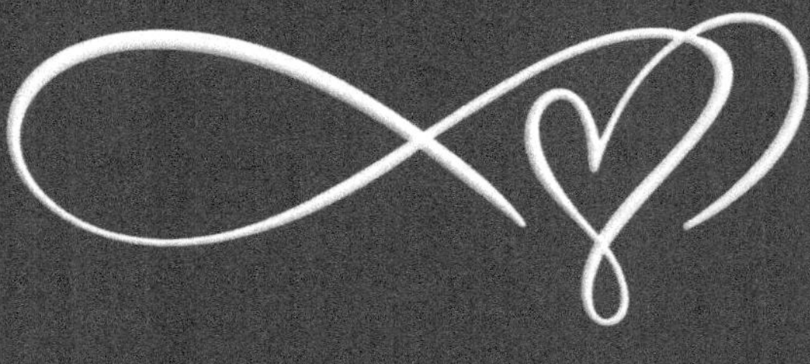

5

BEN

I moan as I take a bite of my sugar cookie and turn to the next page of the old album. I can't help but grin at the goofy photo of Sebastian, Tahlia, and me. We did some stupid shit when we were young.

A chuckle bursts over my lips, spraying cookie crumbs down my T-shirt, when I look at the next photo Seb took. I have my arm wrapped around Tahlia's shoulders, and I'm poking my tongue in her ear. She's wearing a disgusted face as she tries to push me away, but I remember how I held on tight, so she couldn't escape my torture.

I can't believe it's been nine years since I saw her smile or heard her laugh. My heart stutters, and I pause to draw in a deep breath as I squeeze my eyes shut.

Growing up, the three of us were inseparable. People often called us The Three Musketeers, and we loved it. Tahlia was such a tomboy and fit in with me and Seb effortlessly. We were the best of friends until the unthinkable happened and we lost her.

At eighteen, we were too young to experience such a tragedy. But cancer doesn't discriminate. It doesn't care about age, hopes, or dreams for the future.

I brush away the scattered cookie crumbs, then trace my finger over the curve of her face, swallowing the lump that always forms in my throat. She had a beautiful soul and such a fun spirit. She taught me to let go and have fun, to break out of the mold my parents had created. She helped me understand that things didn't need to be so serious all the time. I had a lot of love for her—I still do. We were as close as two friends could be. Tahlia and I had something special. A connection that transcended explanation.

People often speculated if we were a couple. They couldn't understand how we could be so close and remain platonic. She had boyfriends, and I had girlfriends, and through it all, our friendship stayed true and strong—it never deviated. I loved her ... dearly, but not in *that* way. Never like *that*.

I would do anything for her, as she would for me. Anything to make her happy. And in the end, I did my best to fulfill her dream. My mind skips back to the look on her pretty face when I—

My phone lights up with my boss's number, interrupting the memory, and I place the album on the coffee table so I can answer the call immediately. Something must be wrong if he's calling on our day off. I press the green button. "Taylor."

"We need you and Rex out at the Bosworth Trails. A four-year-old girl has wandered off. Her mom can't find her. We've told the officers at the scene to block off the area for you guys."

"On it." I end the call, head to my bedroom, and shove my feet into my sneakers. Rex follows me, sensing my urgency. "We have work to do, buddy." I rub the top of his head and down his flank. His tail swishes eagerly, and I quickly grab my tac vest from the hook beside the front door. "C'mon. Let's go, boy." He follows me out of the house, jumps into the back of our cruiser, and within a few minutes, I pull onto the street.

I park the cruiser amid several police vehicles and civilian cars and head straight to the officer who looks to be in charge. Holding out my hand, I introduce myself. "Sergeant Taylor, Sir. I have Officer Rex in the cruiser, ready to search."

He nods once as he shakes my hand. "Thanks for coming out

so quickly. We need to find her before it gets dark. She went missing at thirteen hundred hours. Mom searched for her and didn't call us until fourteen-thirty, when she realized she wouldn't find her on her own." He points toward a distraught woman. "She has some of her daughter's clothes waiting for Rex."

"Thanks." I glance at my watch. Fifteen-thirty-five stares up at me. That's two and a half hours. I glance around. She could be anywhere. Not an impossible task to find her, so long as a stranger hasn't taken her, but it won't be quick.

I grab Rex, then attach his vest and lead. As soon as his vest is secured, his demeanor changes and he's ready to work. With his intensive training and years of experience, he knows exactly why we're here.

"Ma'am. I'm Sergeant Taylor, and this is Officer Rex." I point my chin downward. "We're here to help locate your daughter."

Her tear-filled eyes drop to Rex. "Oh, thank goodness. We were at the playground. I've been working so much and wanted to treat Mia to an afternoon off prekindergarten so we could spend the afternoon together. I should have just left her in school where she belongs," she tells me on a shaky breath. "I turned my back for only a minute to grab her water bottle from my purse, and when I turned around, she was gone," she says through violent sobs.

I give her a reassuring smile. "We'll start looking for her immediately. I believe you have some of her clothing for Rex."

She nods quickly and races to her car, returning with a dress. "It got sticky with ice cream, so I changed her into shorts and a T-shirt." She passes it to me, then rubs her hands up and down her arms.

"Can you show me the last place you saw your daughter, please?"

"Sure." She leads us to a small climbing frame. "She climbs everything at home, so I like to bring her here," she says shakily, wrapping her arms around her body.

"I bet she loves it." I smile softly. "Okay, I'm going to let Rex familiarize himself with Mia's scent, and then we'll start our search. Stay strong."

She nods and I crouch down to Rex, holding out Mia's dress. He takes a good sniff. "Find Mia, Rex."

I stand, and Rex drops his nose to the ground. He leads me around the playground, circles back to the climbing frame, then seems to catch a scent and he's off. With his nose to the ground and his tail swinging side to side, he leads me away from the playground and to the area where several park trails begin. He doesn't pause, obviously locating Mia's scent. Additional officers follow us at a distance, keeping out of Rex's path, but ready to step in when needed.

Rex quickly weaves through the long grass as he follows Mia's trail. He pauses for a moment and looks around with his tongue hanging out, then drops his nose again. My heart and feet pick up speed to keep up with him as he works.

He lives for this stuff, and he's incredible at what he does. Together, we've found dozens of missing people of all ages.

We leg it over the terrain for forty minutes, Rex still going strong and my adrenaline running high. The temperature has been mild, but as the sun drops closer to the horizon, the warmth of the day is waning. Children are small, and they have less tolerance for temperature fluctuations. We need to find her—soon. Rex pauses every now and then, but moves on quickly.

As we clear the crest of a low hill, my heart sinks when I spot a craggy outcrop. *Shit, I hope she didn't climb those.* The jagged rocks would have been an enormous temptation to Mia with her penchant for climbing.

Rex doesn't slow, and my heart pounds a heavy staccato against my ribs as he heads straight for the boulders. He sniffs around the base of the outcrop, then walks around the area for a bit, his ears twitching. This isn't promising.

Picking up her scent again, he climbs over the rocks, then sits and barks, indicating he's found her. I peek inside the crevice between two large boulders and, sure enough, little Mia is curled into a tight ball, asleep—oblivious to the worry she's caused.

Relief fills me, and a gush of air escapes my tight lungs as I drop to my haunches to praise Rex. "Good boy. You found Mia. Great job, Rex."

I rub each side of his neck vigorously, and he soaks up my attention. His tail thumps against the rocks, and his tongue swipes up the side of my face. I stand and he leaps up, resting his paws on my pecs as I scratch down his sides. He loses his footing on the uneven terrain and slips, dropping to all four paws heavily and scratching my pecs on the way down. *Ouch!* I rub my chest with the heel of my hand, certain he's left scratch marks.

I keep Rex close as the officers who were following move forward to collect the sleeping child. They bring her to Rex so he can sniff her, concluding his search. His rump tips side to side, and he licks her arm. He looks up at me expectantly, because he knows his job is now complete and he's ready for his reward.

"Great job, Officer Rex!" the other officers praise him, and he rejoices, spinning around, his butt moving so fast with his wagging tail that I'm surprised he doesn't knock himself over. Finding what he was searching for is the best game to him.

I drag his toy out of my pocket and hold it alongside his nose, and like the good boy he is, he sits on his rump and waits for my command. As the officers head back toward the playground, I give him the command to play, and he immediately snaps his jaws, grabbing the rope roughly so we can play a game of tug-of-war as an additional reward. He shakes his head back and forth with a playful growl, pulling on the rope with all his might.

Laughing, I tug on the toy, digging my heels into the dirt and leaning backward for leverage. Rex's hind foot slips out from beneath him again, and he lands heavily on his back flank, whimpering as he falls. *Shit!* That's twice in the last few minutes, and he seems to have hurt himself this time.

I quickly tuck his toy in my pocket and squat down, but Rex

leaps back onto his feet, nudging the side of my jeans. He wobbles a little and whimpers again, so I carefully rub his back flank.

"What happened, boy?" When he tries to free his leg from my grip, I know he must be hurt. Shit. "You'll be okay. Let's get back to the cruiser, buddy."

I collect his lead and walk a few steps, then realize he's unable to bear any weight on his hind leg, so I bend down and carefully scoop him into my arms, ensuring I don't aggravate his injury. I'll have to take him to the police-sanctioned vet to get checked out. I kiss the top of his head as I carry him back to the playground. Sweat coats my back, and my muscles scream the longer I carry Rex—all eighty-seven pounds of him—back to the parking lot to find the mother and her daughter happily reunited.

With her daughter tucked safely in her arms, the mother makes a beeline for Rex and me. "Thank you so much for finding Mia. I don't know how I'll ever repay you. Words just don't seem enough."

"Seeing you together and safe is all we need." My arms tremble. I need to put Rex down before I drop him.

Her eyebrows dip, causing creases to form between them. "Is he okay?" She points her chin down at Rex.

I glance down at my partner. "He slipped and hurt his back leg, so I need to take him to the vet." The sooner I get him into the back of the cruiser, the sooner he'll get the help he needs.

"Oh, no." She holds her daughter with one arm and reaches out with her other to stroke Rex's fur. "Thank you for finding my baby girl, Rex. I hope you feel better soon."

Mia lifts her head from her mother's shoulder and reaches over to stroke Rex, too. "Mommy, can we get a doggy?"

Rex's tail wags as his tongue lolls out of his mouth. Even though he's injured, he still laps up the attention they're giving him.

Typical.

I settle Rex on his bed with a treat and set the timer for his next ice session. My phone rings, and I grab it with a wince as Seb's name lights up the screen. Accepting the call, I hold it to my ear. "Sorry, Seb. I have to bail."

"What, why?" he whines.

I sigh and run my hand over the top of my head, then grasp the back of my neck. "Rex and I had a search and rescue this afternoon, and he's injured his hind leg."

"Oh, shit. Is it bad?" Seb's shock and concern translates clearly through the phone.

"It's not too bad, but he'll be out of action for a few days. I need to make sure he rests, and I need to ice it on and off through the night, so I can't leave him."

I hear him moving around and the rattle of keys. "I'm on my way. I'll pick up beer and pizza. I haven't had pizza since that night at Brady's, so I'm overdue."

A laugh bursts across my lips; the guy is a fiend for pizza. "Thanks, man." I end the call and grab a bag of peas from the freezer, then drop my ass to the floor to hold them on Rex's hind leg. "You really did a number on yourself, buddy."

He raises his head and looks at me, then drops it on top of his front paws with a sigh. I lean my head against the wall while I hold the makeshift ice pack in place.

Closing my eyes, my cheeks rise at the memory of the little girl curled up in a ball in between the rocks. After her solo adventure, she must have been exhausted. Thankfully, Rex is amazing at what he does, and we were able to reunite mother and daughter. Warmth fills my body with pride for a job well done today. A successful rescue is what Rex and I live for. It's one of the reasons we do this job.

Rex barks a second before the front door bangs open. "Stay," I command, standing to greet my friend.

"Honey, I'm home," Seb calls.

I chuckle as his footsteps sound down the hallway, and he arrives at the kitchen door. Grabbing the pizza from him, I drop it to the counter and put the peas back in the freezer. Seb places the beer next to the box and heads straight to Rex. He squats next to him and rubs from the top of his head down his side to his rear. Rex's tail wags like crazy, and I'm proud of him for remaining on his bed and off his leg. Seb nuzzles his head. "You okay, boy?"

Rex licks the side of his face and Seb chuckles. He turns to me, then climbs to his feet. "How did the search go?"

I pop the top off two beers, open the pizza box, and hand Seb his drink. "A four-year-old wandered away from her mom at Bosworth Trails. Found her curled up asleep between two boulders. If she'd walked another twenty feet, she would have fallen over the ridge."

He scrapes his fingers through his short beard. "Shit."

I nod as I take another drink and swallow. "She wandered about a mile and a half on her own. I was relieved when we found her safe."

Seb grabs a slice of pizza and takes a bite, shaking his head in disbelief. "I bet her mom was beside herself. People don't realize how fast and far their kids can get in a short amount of time."

I grab the pizza and lead Seb through to the living room, then grab Rex's bed with Rex on it and carry it over so he can hang out with us.

When I return, Seb's studying the photo album I was looking through earlier. Happiness shines from his eyes as he studies the photographs.

"She was such a great chick," he comments as he turns the page, then chuckles. She really was. The world definitely lost a little of its sparkle when she left this earth. "Remember that time her mom's car broke down, and we had to get out and push it? She drove it into the ditch, and the damn thing tipped onto its side." He chuckles as he shakes his head.

A laugh bursts from deep within. "I forgot about that. She was so pissed."

"So was her mom, if I remember correctly." He nods as he flips to the next page, and I take another bite of my pizza. "So many good times." He grows quiet, and his expression turns somber. "I still miss her."

My heart squeezes while my stomach tightens. "Yeah, me too. Me too."

6

BEN

"Car three-Adam-twenty-five, theft in progress at 576 South Street, at the gas station. Offenders are three youths. No other description at this time. Manager called it in." Katie's voice comes across my radio.

I'm about five minutes from the location, so I flick my blinker and turn left.

"Ten-four, car three-Adam-twenty-five en route," I respond.

It's not an emergency, so I don't bother with lights or sirens. Stopped at a set of traffic lights, I glance out my window and watch a guy about my age walking his German shepherd while pushing a stroller. My thoughts immediately go to Rex. I hope he's been staying off his feet. I'm sure everyone at the station will make sure he's resting, but he tends to get excited when he's around our colleagues.

Pulling into a parking spot near the entrance of the gas station, I climb out of my vehicle. Inside, I see an older gentleman holding a youth by the collar of his shirt, causing my hackles to rise. He shouldn't have his hands on a kid; he wouldn't do that to an adult.

The doors slide open as I approach, and I get my first decent look at the boy. He looks to be about ten or eleven, and I don't sense the usual teenage attitude coming from him. He appears more ashamed than anything else. I glance around, noting he's the only youth present.

Where are the others? Katie said there were three.

The rotund man, who I assume is the manager, drags the boy forward as he storms toward me, all bluster. "About time you got here. Two of the scoundrels escaped." He flings his arm out toward the door, highlighting their escape route. "I want to press charges."

I hold up my hand and glance down at the boy. "I'm Sergeant Taylor. Please release the boy."

"He'll run if I let him go," he snaps.

I step closer and speak to the boy. "You'll stay where you are if he releases you, right?"

He drops his gaze to the floor, and his freckled cheeks turn pink. "Yes, sir."

I lift my eyes to the manager and raise my eyebrows. "Release him, please." He's just a kid, for fuck's sake, and I've seen enough troublemakers to know he's a good kid who's made an error in judgment.

The manager finally releases him, and the kid steps closer to me. "I want him arrested."

Calm down, old man. "What's your name, sir?"

"Mr. MacDonnell. Are you going to arrest him now?" he asks with raised brows.

I pride myself on being a patient man, but this guy and his demands are already pissing me off. "Can you please tell me what happened?" I make a production of dragging out my notepad and pen while my blood simmers.

"That one"—the manager points at the boy with a stubby, shaky finger—"and two other troublemakers were walking around my store and stuffing their pockets with candy. They stole sodas and drank them right in front of me, like they were taunting me!" He narrows his eyes at the kid as I write a few notes.

I look down at the boy. "What's your name?"

"Evan Sullivan, sir."

"Evan, can you please empty your pockets?" I tighten my fingers around the smooth plastic of the pen and my notebook, and drop my hands to my hips.

"I already emptied his pockets. The other boys got away with their pockets full," the manager says angrily, slapping his hands against his thighs.

Raising my chin, I ask. "So, he doesn't have any stolen goods on his person?"

"No ... but he did!" he snaps.

I hold my hands out in a placating move. "Without evidence, I'm afraid I can't charge him with theft." *Did he forcefully remove the items from Evan's pockets?* "Did you remove the items from his pockets, or did Evan remove them?"

The manager's face turns scarlet. "I have CCTV footage. I have all the evidence I need." Jesus. Evan looks up at me with big brown eyes, resigned to his fate.

I shift on my feet, getting more comfortable. "Sir, I understand you're angry and upset, but did you or the boy remove the items from his pockets?"

His body trembles with anger. "I removed them."

I turn to Evan. "Did you give Mr. MacDonnell permission to remove the items from your pockets?"

Evan shakes his head. "No, sir."

"The items in his pockets belonged to me. I don't need permission to get my stock back!" he shouts, spit flying from his mouth.

Evan looks up at me and shrugs. "I didn't mind. I did the wrong thing. The stuff belonged to him."

The old man points at Evan again, his hand shaking in anger, and I'm worried the guy's going to collapse at any moment. "I'm sick of these young kids coming in here and causing trouble. Something needs to be done."

"I agree, sir. This behavior is unacceptable, and you've done the right thing by calling it in to the station. However, in this instance, I don't think a charge is necessary. I'll have a chat with

Evan, take him home to his parents, and discuss the events of the afternoon with them. Often a ride in the police cruiser and a stern chat are enough of a deterrent. I'll also ensure he undertakes community service at the local shelter. Would that be satisfactory for you?"

The manager grunts and drops his hands to his hips as he studies Evan for a few moments. "Of the three boys, he was causing the least trouble, and I guess he didn't drink a soda." His posture softens as his shoulders drop. "To be honest, he looked reluctant and seemed like he was following the other two."

Evan raises his head and looks at the manager. "I'm sorry, sir. I was just doing what my friends wanted me to do. I was trying to fit in. I promise it won't happen again." His bottom lip trembles as he delivers a genuine apology without being prompted. That says a lot about his character, supporting my initial assessment of him.

"You need to get yourself some new friends, young man," the manager suggests.

Evan nods and shrugs. "Not sure if they're really my friends," he mumbles.

"Evan." He looks up at me. "Do you want to press charges against Mr. MacDonnell for putting his hands on you?"

Evan's eyes widen comically and he shakes his head with vigor, looking between me and the old man. "N-n-no. I-I-I did the wrong thing, and he was just getting his stuff back."

MacDonnell's shoulders stiffen and he aims a murderous glare my way, but before he can open his mouth, I nod. "All right. I'm going to take Evan home, and I'll have a chat with his parents. Enjoy the rest of your afternoon, Mr. MacDonnell."

"You, too, Officer. And I don't want to see you back in my gas station, Evan. Do you understand me?"

He nods. "Uh, yes, sir."

The glass doors open, and I lead Evan out to my cruiser, opening the passenger door for him. "Get in and put your seatbelt on." I climb in and start the car. "What's your address?" He tells me, and I punch it into my GPS, then call the station to let them know I'm taking one of the kids home and that the other two offenders were not at the scene. I could use this time to question the boy about his friends and find out more information, but sometimes it's best to let the kids stew a little.

I'm about five minutes out when I notice him adjusting his position. Glancing his way, I find him peering out the window as he bites his bottom lip. "Will your mom and dad be home?"

"Mom will. My dad died in Syria," he mumbles.

My heart cleaves open for this kid. "Sorry about your dad, Evan. That's gotta be tough." I watch him shrug and drop his eyes to his lap.

I think he's a good kid who's lost his way a little. Dad's gone, so there's possibly no father figure at home, and Mom's probably busy working and holding down the fort. He's the perfect candidate for my project at *The Paw Palace*. Hopefully, his mom will agree with my suggestion for him to take part in the program.

I pull up in front of a neat, dove-gray, two-story weatherboard home with white trim around the windows and doors. They don't live all that far from my place. Climbing out of the car, I open Evan's door, and he leads the way along the concrete path to the porch. I take the three steps as he flings the screen door open and storms inside.

"Mom!"

The hair on the back of my neck rises. The door was simply left unlocked. Some people underestimate their own safety. Evan's silhouette, followed by that of a petite woman not much taller than he is, comes into view as he leads her to the front door. She pushes open the screen door, and her eyes widen when they land on me. The air in my lungs leaves on a gush, and I straighten my spine.

Jesus. She's beautiful.

All soft, delicate features, wild curly hair, and clear eyes. My heart gallops in my chest, and I have to consciously take a breath.

Her head snaps to her son, who bears the same freckles across his nose and cheeks as she does. "What on earth is going on?" she asks Evan, but he drops his gaze to his feet and shuffles in place without answering her. His shoulders hunch, and the scent of shame fills the air as he fidgets with the hem of his T-shirt.

Her eyes rise to meet mine, the stunning aquamarine overflowing with questions, so I step forward and hold out my hand. "Sergeant Taylor."

She slides her small palm along mine, and the warmth from her touch scalds me, sending flames licking up my arm as I wrap my fingers around hers. "Hope Sullivan. What's this about, Sergeant?" When I release her hand—much too soon for my liking—she raises it to stroke Evan's hair. "S-sorry, where are my manners? Would you like to come inside?"

"Sure. That'd be great." She steps inside and holds the screen door open for me. I wipe my boots on the mat, then step closer to her and Evan. I'm immediately enveloped by her soft vanilla scent that's reminiscent of my favorite cookie. Everything about this woman is femininity personified—from her delicate bone structure and petite frame to her curly, honey-colored hair and the fragrance she wears. My protective instincts kick into overdrive.

"Do you realize you left your front door unlocked?" I ask as we wander down the hallway, passing photo after photo of a young, loved-up couple, gradually aging into a family of three. The man wears a military uniform in several of the images, and one shows Hope wearing a pink tutu and pointe shoes. It's like a timeline, showing their life over the years. Hope looks different in the images. Happier. Lighter somehow.

"Was it? I guess I forgot to latch it," she says, unbothered, as voices filter from the living room where I assume the television is on.

"May I suggest you ensure it's always locked, ma'am?" I tell her as I follow her into an open kitchen/dining room that leads back into the living room I passed on the way in. It's light and airy, with mixing bowls and cooking trays spread across the countertops.

She reaches up into a cupboard, exposing an inch of pale smooth skin above her fitted jeans. "Yeah, sure. I usually have it locked. Do you want a cup of coffee?"

Since I'm on patrol, I shouldn't stop for long. I should explain what happened and invite Evan to join my program, but I'll be damned if I can tear my eyes from this beauty. "Sure, coffee would be great, thanks."

"How do you take it?"

"Black, thank you." I drag a stool out, adjust my pants that are growing tighter by the second, and sit at the counter next to Evan.

"So is anyone gonna tell me what's going on?" Hope asks as she makes our drinks.

I nudge Evan. "Are you gonna tell your mom, or should I?" I lean in close to his ear and lower my voice. "It usually works out better if you come clean yourself."

He looks up at me with a miserable expression and drops his shoulders in defeat, then tells her what happened.

She passes my coffee to me across the counter, and then slams her fists into her slim hips. "Evan Wyatt Sullivan," she snaps. "We did not bring you up to be so disrespectful. How dare you steal property and disrupt someone's business? I thought you were at Elliott's house!" Her eyes narrow. "So now you're lying to me?" Hurt reverberates in her voice, and I sense their relationship is a little fractured.

He drops his head, shifting on the stool. "I'm sorry, Mom."

"Why would you lie to me?" she asks softly, her worried gaze locked on her son as she leans on the counter across from us.

One small shoulder rises and falls as Evan traces an imaginary pattern on the counter. "I'm just trying to fit in and make new friends."

Hope's eyes rise to mine, her face full of disbelief and pain.

"What happens now? Will he be charged? We can go back so Evan can apologize, and I'll pay for anything he stole."

I shake my head. "Evan didn't actually steal anything. According to the gas station manager, his friends were responsible for most of the trouble. Evan has already apologized for his part, and even though the manager was upset and angry, he conceded that a warning would be enough this time." I look down at Evan. "Because it's not gonna happen again, right?" I raise a brow and wait for him to respond.

"No, sir. It won't happen again."

"It better not, Ev. I'm gonna have to take your computer games away from you, and you're grounded for a month." I wince. I'm glad she's taking this seriously, but that's probably a little harsh.

Evan's shoulders curl inward. "Yes, Mom." He looks up at his mom, his eyes beseeching. "Can I still play soccer?"

Hope blows out a long breath and runs her fingers through her curls. "I guess. It wouldn't be fair to let your team down, but that's it, Evan. And we'll be going back to that gas station so you can apologize again."

He nods, still focusing on the countertop. "Can I go to my room?"

With an exasperated sigh, Hope nods.

Evan hops down from his stool and looks up at me. "Thanks for talking to the manager about not pressing charges and for bringing me home. I'm sorry." He leaves the room with slumped shoulders before I can say anything further, and Hope sags against the counter as she watches him leave.

"I'm so sorry and embarrassed. You must think I'm a terrible parent, because I didn't know where my son was or what he was up to." Pink tints her porcelain cheeks, making her freckles stand out. Her bottom lip trembles, but she presses her mouth into a tight line, and I watch as her posture stiffens.

"Not at all. Kids can be pretty creative when they want to be, and I get the impression he's learned his lesson. I don't think he'll repeat the behavior. I believe he's trying to fit in with his friends." I shrug. "Sometimes kids make a bad judgment call."

"He started middle school, and it's changed him. He's been more moody and angry, but I never expected this from him." She slides her fingers into her hair, holding them there for a moment, keeping the curls away from her face and exposing that smooth swathe of perfect skin at her waist again. "I don't know what's going on with him. I guess it's hormones—or whatever." She seems lost. They both do.

I adjust my position, preparing to ask a tough question. "Can I ask about his father? Evan said he died in Syria." Maybe it only happened recently.

Her eyes instantly darken with sadness as she drops her gaze, and I watch her slender throat move when she swallows. "Yeah. Almost six years ago. He was ... uh ... he ... uh ... he ... died in an explosion." Her fingers flutter up to her delicate collarbones. "Evan was only five when we lost his father." She swallows again, glancing at me, then quickly averts her gaze, but not before I see the tears forming.

I watch her curl in on herself, wrapping her arms tight around her body as if she's trying to hold herself together. Every instinct in my body is fighting to peel her arms away and replace them with mine, but I lock those thoughts down. That would be highly inappropriate.

"I'm sorry for your loss. I can only imagine your devastation." I don't want to tell her I appreciate her husband's sacrifice for our country; it doesn't seem right to say the words, because I bet she doesn't want to hear them. His sacrifice has cost her and Evan dearly. This is the other side of the cost of war, and it's devastatingly painful.

Hope nods once. "It's been ... uh ... difficult."

I bet. Shifting on the stool, I grasp the back of my neck. "I promised the manager that Evan would participate in community service."

Hope nods, her eyebrows drawn tight. "Fair enough. What do we need to do?"

"I run a program for kids around Evan's age down at *The Paw Palace* every other Saturday morning. The kids spend a couple of hours with the dogs and cats, grooming them, exercising, and playing with them. They hang out with the animals and give them some much-needed attention. I started the program to help kids who were making poor decisions and finding themselves in trouble. It helps the team at the shelter give the animals some one-on-one time, too. It's a win-win for everyone involved. I'd like Evan to join us, if you're okay with it. I think it'll be good for him."

Her fingers slide into her hair again, clearly a nervous habit. "I feel like that would be more a reward than a punishment for Evan. He's always wanted a dog."

I smile softly. "I don't have a problem with it being a reward, and you shouldn't either." Her eyebrows slant down, and she opens her mouth, but I hold up my hand. "Sometimes redirecting behavior works better than punishment does. Several kids in the program have lost a parent, and it'll give Evan the opportunity to see he's not alone. These animals are homeless. Some of them have experienced abuse. Working with the animals gives the kids a sense of purpose outside of themselves, and I find it helps the kids get out of their own heads. The kids in the group are supportive of each other, and they'll welcome Evan into the fold. It'll provide him with community—people his own age with similar experiences." She nods thoughtfully, and I stand. I've lingered too long, and if I stay any longer, I may never leave. "Think about it. We'll be there at ten a.m. next Saturday." I rap my knuckles on the counter. "I hope I'll see Evan there. You're welcome to stay the first time so you can see what we do, but after that, I prefer the kids to be on their own. He's more likely to engage with the other kids if you're not there."

She nods again. "Thank you. I'll bring him down. It may be exactly what he needs."

My stomach flips at the thought of seeing her again. Hope follows me to the front door, past the shrine of a family that once was, but no longer is.

I don't think Evan is the only one in this house struggling with the loss of his father. It's clear Hope is lost, too. I step over the threshold of the front door, reluctant to leave, but I'm on patrol and can't linger here for the rest of my shift. I have paperwork to do.

"Thanks for bringing him home and for speaking with the manager on his behalf. I appreciate your compassion and understanding."

One side of my mouth rises. "You're welcome. If possible, I prefer not to take a hard line with kids. They make mistakes. We all do. It's how we learn who we are and what we're made of. It's how we make sense of our place in the world." I trace my eyes over her pretty face, cataloging her delicate features and storing them in my memory. "Enjoy your evening, Hope."

"You, too. Bye, Sergeant."

"You can call me Ben."

She bites her bottom lip and nods. "Okay. Thanks, Ben."

I head down the porch steps, and once I'm on the pavement, I turn around. "Make sure you lock your doors." My tone is firm, brooking no argument.

She uses two fingers to salute me. "Yes, sir."

My cock twitches in my pants, and I smirk at her sassy comeback. Oblivious to my reaction, she spins on her heel and walks back inside. I hear the click of the lock and, knowing they're safely secured inside, I walk the short distance to my cruiser.

Once inside, I drop my head back against the headrest and blow out a long breath. I can't remember the last time I felt that level of attraction. I glance up at the house one last time, then start the car, pulling onto the road. I can't wait for next Saturday.

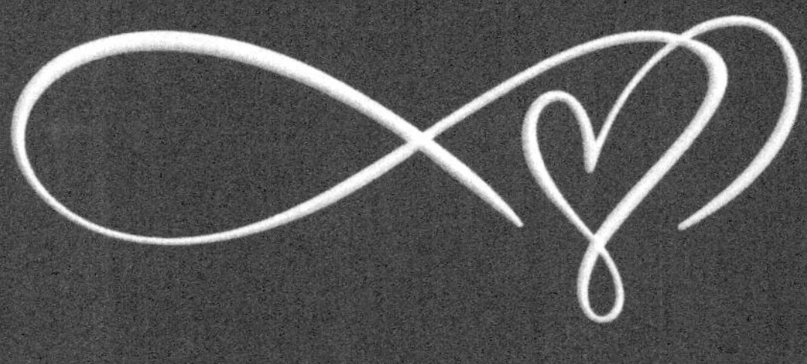

7

HOPE

I SLOWLY WAKE, THEN FOLD INTO A TIGHT BALL beneath my covers as awareness rolls through me—it's the anniversary of the worst day of my life. Anxiousness has been my constant companion leading up to today. I've barely eaten, and it's been a struggle to function.

I was determined to face this day differently than I have before.

I wanted to be stronger this time. I want to be over *it*, for fuck's sake.

My stomach twists, and my heart stutters.

I'm so fucking weak.

I wrap myself tighter in the sheets and curl inward as if I can somehow protect myself from this pain. *But how do I protect myself when the pain is inside me?* It's relentless. The devastation of my loss—*our* loss—steals my breath and breaks my heart daily. It twists my mind into dark and treacherous places, and I don't know how I'm supposed to move forward and break out of the clutches of this tragedy.

Dragging Wyatt's pillow into me, I trap it against my body, burying my face in the softness. Wyatt's scent is long gone, but I feel closer to him, knowing he rested his head here. I ache for one more of his hugs, one more kiss, one more touch. To see his smile and share a laugh one more time. I would give up everything to have one more single moment. To make one more memory.

Maybe not *everything*. I'd never give up Evan. Not for all the new memories in the world.

I don't want to face today.

It's supposed to get easier.

Scrunching my eyes closed, I let my tears fall freely as the ache in my chest expands; my body's weighed down like an anchor is holding me out at sea in rough waters, and I'm too exhausted to fight against it. I'm battered—body and soul.

I'm so tired.

Exhausted to the very center of every cell in my body. I can't remember the last time I felt anything but this soul-crushing pain.

I desperately need it to stop.

THE BED DIPS BEHIND ME, and an arm slides around my waist. The corners of my mouth press upward, and I snuggle back. "Mmm, Wyatt," I murmur.

I grip his hand and tangle our fingers which feel all wrong, then my eyes snap open, and my reality slaps me in the face.

"Sorry, babe. It's just me," Clara whispers, then kisses the back of my head.

I close my eyes, and a sob explodes past my lips. My body shudders, and my sorrow comes out in full force. Tears that should have dried up long ago stream down my face and my nose runs like a damn faucet. I release my grip on my best friend's hand and wipe away the snot. Her hold tightens, providing me sanctuary as I fall apart. Her mouth presses against my hair, and her fingers gently slide over my tangled curls. Just when my cheeks become dry, a fresh wave of tears fall.

PEELING MY GRITTY EYES OPEN, I notice the brightness filtering around the edge of my curtains, stretch out my aching body, then flop to my back. Staring up at the ceiling, I try to pull my thoughts together. I can't keep doing this. It's not fair to Evan to see me like this all the time. For the past six years, he's never seen me truly happy.

What does that do to a kid? It can't be good. Just look at what happened yesterday.

Disappointment washes through me like a tsunami; I've let our son down in the worst possible way and now he's acting out. He lost his father, and I've been emotionally broken for so many of his formative years. I can't even say I've done my best to get us through the loss of Wyatt, because I haven't. Far from it. I've been so selfish in my grief.

I throw back the covers and climb out of bed with renewed determination to do better, then head straight to the shower. The warm water runs over me, and I dip my head back to wet my face and hair, letting it wash away my dried tears and pain. Taking my time, I wash my hair and body. I shave and scrub. I methodically cleanse myself from head to toe, like I can somehow wash away my mistakes and start fresh.

Today's a new day. Why can't I—*we*—start fresh?

I flip my hair over and condition it, working through my hair routine. When I step out of the shower, I feel better, and my determination to face the day is at the forefront of my mind. Laying one of Wyatt's T-shirts on my bed, I plop my curly hair into it and wrap it, then get dressed and head out of my bedroom.

Low voices drift upstairs, so I follow them to the kitchen. As I get closer, I recognize Wyatt's parents' voices and Clara's chuckle. *I didn't imagine her earlier.*

Clara and I met in middle school and became inseparable. Then, I met her older brother and fell in love. She was over the moon when we got married; everything was perfect … *until it wasn't.*

Stopping just out of sight, I watch Wyatt's dad talk and laugh with Evan while my mother-in-law stirs something on the stove. Guilt wraps itself around me. Evan can laugh with him, but not with me, and I'm ashamed we never laugh like that.

I'm not surprised they're here today. They probably knew I'd be a mess. I know they mean well, and they find comfort in spending time with their grandson—their last link to their son—but I think I would have preferred to be alone with Evan today.

My boy notices me first, and his posture stiffens as the smile drops from his face. He lowers his eyes to the counter as if he's been caught doing something he shouldn't, and my heart stops beating. We're in worse shape than I thought. I paste on a smile and step into the kitchen, heading straight for Evan. "Morning, everyone." I wrap my arms around his shoulders and kiss the top of his head. "Morning, big guy." I squeeze him extra tight and drop my mouth next to his ear. "I'm sorry."

He turns his head and forces a smile my way. "It's okay."

"It's not, but things are going to get better for us," I whisper, then muss his hair and greet Wyatt's parents with a hug and kiss. "Thanks for coming over. I'm sorry I slept in, but I'm sorta glad I did because this smells delicious."

"I hope you don't mind," Wyatt's mom says as she mixes the scrambled eggs in the pan.

I kiss her cheek. "Not at all, Mom."

Walking over to Clara, I wrap my arms around her, and we sway from side to side as I kiss her cheek. "Thanks, Clara."

She winks at me. "You're welcome. Come and sit while I make us all coffee."

"Breakfast is almost ready. Evan, can you set the table, please?" Mom asks.

I jump in. "I can do that. You and Grandad looked like you were having a great time." I wink at my boy and grab the silverware. Once everything's on the table, I collect enough plates and place them on the counter.

Tracey dishes everyone's breakfast—no, brunch, since it's almost eleven—and we carry our plates to the table. Everyone is quiet for a few minutes as we eat, and I feel I should break the silence, but I'm embarrassed. After six years, I should be coping better. Doing better. Being a better mom. I wonder what they really think of me. *Do they worry if I'm taking proper care of their grandson?* They've never come out and said anything directly to me, but I see their side glances, I hear their sighs, and I watch relief slide over their faces once a month when I drop Evan at their house for the weekend.

"Thanks again for coming over today." I swallow roughly, fighting the tingle in my nose and sting behind my eyes. "I'm sorry I've let you down." I look around the table at Wyatt's family. "I realize I need to do better from now on. I promise ..." I drop my eyes to my half-eaten food as my heart hammers. "I promise this is the last time you'll have to step in to pick up the pieces." I blow out a long breath and smile shakily at the people who were so very important to Wyatt. The people who still are very important to Evan and me.

Mom slips her hand over mine and squeezes. "You haven't let us down, honey. Far from it. We know how much you loved Wyatt, and none of us can imagine how heartbroken you are. Yes, we lost our son and Clara lost her brother, and by god, we're devastated. But Wyatt was your future ... Evan's too, and that future was stolen from both of you in the most violent way. None of us begrudge you your tears and sadness, Hope." When I look up at her face, all I see is empathy and love. "But we truly hope you can somehow find happiness again for your own sake." Clara and Wyatt's father, Graeme, nod in agreement.

"We love you so much, and we need you to come out the other side of this. Wyatt wouldn't want you to still be so sad," Graeme says gently.

I know losing their son has taken a toll on them—they aged almost overnight—so for them to say this to me must mean they're desperate for me to climb out of my grief. I shrug. "I'm doing my best, but I'm going to try harder."

Clara smiles softly. "You'll get there, and we'll be here for you every step of the way."

8

HOPE

WE PULL UP TO THE CEMETERY IN THREE SEPARATE CARS, so we can each go our own way after this visit. I grab the bottle of beer from the passenger seat and turn back to Evan. "You ready?"

"Do I get a choice?" he snaps.

I frown. "What do you mean?"

"I don't wanna be here. *He's* not here. It's just a creepy, empty place." He pats his heart. "He's in here." Then he touches the side of his head. "And here ... mostly," he murmurs the last word as he turns his gaze out of the window. "I hate coming here."

God, I don't know my son anymore. He used to always want to come here to talk to his dad. He'd tell him all about school and soccer, about his friends and what he was watching on TV. He'd make Lego cars and bring them along, showing them to the headstone with pride. I swallow around the lump that's lodged in my throat. "I-I-I'm sorry. I had no idea."

"You wouldn't. I can't talk to you about this stuff," he snaps with venom, and my eyebrows shoot up my forehead.

"I'm sorry I've let you down the most, Ev." I pause to look out the windshield. "If you wanna go, we can leave."

He opens his door and climbs out, then ducks back inside. "We're here now, and everyone's waiting." He slams the door and heads toward his aunt and grandparents, leaving me to feel like a steamy pile of shit.

With shaky hands, I open my door and climb out of the car. I'm not a fan of coming here myself. I hate the finality of the place. I hate seeing Wyatt's name carved in the cold, unforgiving stone. I hate the permanence of it. But I come here out of respect for the love of my life. For the father of my son. For my best friend. Most of all, I come because I hate the idea of him always being here all alone.

I push away the hurt and the tears that threaten and follow everyone toward Wyatt's final resting place. Clara drops back and weaves her arm through mine. "You okay?"

I smile tightly. "Not really." No point lying. "But I'm going to work hard to do better."

"You're doing better than you give yourself credit for." She tugs me in close. "I think you're so brave," she whispers. "I don't know how I'd cope if I lost Ryan, and we've only been married for three years. I'd be completely devastated."

Nobody understands my grief. How can they, unless they've experienced it for themselves? "I just miss him so much."

"I know. I do too. He was the best big brother a girl could ever ask for. Sometimes I talk to him when I'm alone just to feel closer to him, but as each year comes and goes, I feel like my link to him has lessened. Ryan's been amazing and has really helped me honor Wyatt's memory in positive ways. I don't think I'd be in the place I am today without him in my corner."

I squeeze her tight. "I'm happy for you. Ryan is an amazing man." I drop my voice as we stop in front of Wyatt's grave. "Wyatt would have really liked him."

She laughs. "Only after he'd kicked his ass."

I chuckle too. "True."

Tracey and Graeme fuss about, pulling out weeds and wiping down the headstone as I wrap my arms around my middle to hold myself together. I promised myself no more tears today, and I'm determined to keep that promise. Once they're satisfied with everything, they sit on the grass and the rest of us join them. I open the bottle of beer and slowly pour it onto the grass for Wyatt.

"I'd really like it if we could all share a happy memory of Wyatt today," Tracey says.

Graeme nods and a low chuckle escapes. "I'll never forget my son's face when he first laid eyes on you, Hope. He was only fourteen, but I could tell how much he liked you." My heart skips at the memory and my somber smile widens.

"I thought he was so cute, even though I was only twelve and boys weren't really on my radar." I glance across at Evan and he screws up his face.

"That's just gross," he grumbles.

We all chuckle.

Tracey smiles wistfully. "Yeah, then he would find any excuse to hang around whenever you came to visit. Clarissa would get so annoyed, telling him you were *her* friend, not his." Clara chuckles and Tracey drops her gaze to the headstone. "We knew as soon as you were both old enough, he would ask you out. We couldn't have been happier."

We were each other's firsts for everything. So many good times and fantastic memories. My eyes flick to Evan. He's studying me closely, as if he's seeing me in a different light. I should make more of an effort to think about our good memories—our *happy* memories—instead of being swallowed by the most tragic memory of all. We were so lucky to have Wyatt in our lives, and I'm beyond grateful he gave me Evan, but I've done a terrible job of keeping his memory alive for our son.

I draw oxygen deep into my lungs and glide my hand over Evan's hair and down his back slowly. My heart warms as I think about the memory I want to share today. "I'll never forget the look on his face when I told him I was pregnant. I swear a light breeze could have knocked him over. It was such a surprise. He immediately went into protective daddy mode and catered to my every whim while he was home. He kept track of your development during my pregnancy, even while he was deployed," I tell Evan as I wrap my arm around him, pulling him in close. "He was so excited to be your daddy, and he loved you so much."

Evan pulls out of my embrace and shoots to his feet, then storms away from us. I'm frozen with confusion, my thoughts in a muddy swirl.

Graeme jumps to his feet. "I'll check on him." He jogs to catch up with his grandson, and I watch helplessly from my place on the grass.

Maybe I should be the one to go after him, but he doesn't talk to me, which is completely my fault. I get too upset, and I've been in a constant state of sadness. *How would he possibly think he can talk about his father with me?*

I bury my face in my hands. I've failed him. He didn't just lose his father; he lost me, too. Tears flood my cheeks, and I gasp to take in a breath at my sudden realization. I have to fix this before it's too late. *Damn it!* I promised no more tears today.

Arms wrap around my shoulders and waist on either side of me. "Shhh, Hope. Things will get better," Wyatt's mom murmurs against my hair.

My body shudders, and I take a hiccupping breath. "I need to do so much better for him."

Clara's arm squeezes my waist tighter. "You're doing okay, and I think things have changed for you today. I can see the determination in your eyes." She kisses my hair. "Small steps starting today, Hope. That's all you can do. It's all you can ask of yourself."

Thank goodness for these two amazing women.

When I glance in the direction Evan went, he and Graeme are walking back toward us. I climb to my feet and tentatively make my way to them. The smile I give Graeme is shaky at best. He squeezes Evan's shoulder, then my hand, and leaves the two of us alone with a sad smile.

In the middle of the cemetery, we stand a foot apart, but it may as well be a mile. Evan's face is tilted toward the grass, his chest rising and falling with exaggerated breaths. I take the step needed to close the distance between us so I can wrap my arms around him, and instead of pulling away like I was scared he would, he falls against me, burrowing his face in my chest and wrapping his arms tightly around me. A sob breaks free, and his body trembles against mine.

I slip my fingers through his hair as my heart breaks for the not-so-little boy in my arms. Tears escape and track down my cheeks as we hold each other, and I kiss the top of his head, holding still, drawing in his boyish scent, as we stand quietly in each other's arms. It's the closest we've been in too long, and I make a promise to myself to hold him more. To be more present for him. To be more emotionally available and less broken.

"I'm so sorry, Ev. I've let you down in the worst possible way." I kiss his hair again, then look up at the sky. *God, how many times have I apologized? How many more times will I need to?*

He pulls away from me slightly, and his wet eyes shatter me. "I-I-I can't remember stuff. I'm scared I'm gonna forget him."

I cup his freckle-covered cheeks—something he got from me. "I won't let you forget. Things are gonna change, Ev. I promise. We'll talk more, and I'll share more stories about your dad."

His body loses some of its stiffness, and he smiles sadly. "I'm sorry I've been a jerk. I've just been scared."

"You haven't been a jerk, Ev." I pull him back in close. "I love you so much, baby."

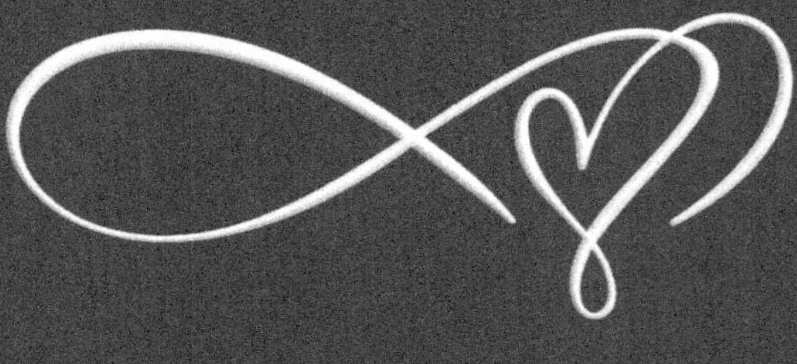

9

BEN

I'M NERVOUS. I'M MAN ENOUGH TO ADMIT IT.

I don't get nervous.

And especially not for a woman.

But. Hope's not just any woman.

As the clock ticks down to ten, the butterflies in my stomach feel more like hummingbirds. Even Rex is picking up on my nervous energy and is pacing around me like the fantastic guard dog he is.

"Are you okay?" Tori asks from behind the counter. We've already gone through to see the dogs and cats so she could show me which ones were suitable for the kids today.

I twist the leather band on my wrist. "Yeah, why?" I roll my eyes at myself. After two years of coming here, it's probably obvious to her that I'm not my usual self.

She waves her arm around. "Not sure. You seem … agitated."

I wander over to the counter. "I have a new boy starting with the program today. I'm hopeful he'll show up. His father died in Syria, and he got into some trouble last week."

Her smile drops, and her shoulders sag. "Oh, no. Poor kid."

The front door opens, and Francine and Donnelly walk in.

"Morning, Ben," they call as they walk toward us, dropping to their knees to say hello to Rex. "Morning, Tori."

"Morning, guys. Glad you could make it. We have some puppies today!" I tell them, and their eyes light up.

The other kids arrive soon after. Once we're all gathered and the clock strikes ten, my stomach drops.

They're not coming.

I really thought Hope would bring Evan today. She seemed genuine about following through. Maybe something came up.

As we're filing through the doorway to the back area where the dogs and cats are housed, the front door opens in a rush and in steps Evan. Before I can actively think to go to him, my feet change direction on instinct, and I head back the way I came. My cheeks are stretched as far as they can go when Hope bustles through the door behind her son.

"You made it." My lungs finally fill with a full breath, and Rex heads straight for Evan, his tail moving so fast, his rump shakes from side to side. He loves to make new friends. Evan's hands immediately slide into Rex's fur, making his tail go ballistic.

"I'm so sorry we're late. I had to wait for the load of laundry to finish, and then we caught every red light on the way," Hope apologizes in a rush, her pale cheeks flushed pink. Rex immediately transfers his welcome from Evan to her, and she chuckles. "Who do we have here?" she asks as she rubs the top of his head.

"I'd like you to meet Officer Rex. He's my partner."

Her brows shoot up, and her eyes shine when she looks back up at me. "Oh, I didn't realize." Her eyes narrow slightly, and I can tell she's thinking about something. "Was he in the back of your cruiser when you brought Evan home? He could have come inside with you." I appreciate her concern for Rex, not that leaving him in the cruiser is a problem since his space is climate-controlled for his comfort.

"I didn't have him with me. He was recovering from a sprain at the station while I was out on patrol. He was out of action for a couple of days, but he's fully recovered now."

"He's a beautiful dog," Hope says as she rubs between Rex's ears.

"Rex is a boy, Mom. You should probably call him handsome," Evan suggests with a grin.

We all chuckle. "He'd probably prefer deadly, intelligent, or powerful. Wouldn't you, Rex?" He looks up at me and barks. I hitch my thumb over my shoulder. "You ready to head through and meet the others?"

"Will I get to hang out with a dog?"

"You sure will. I'll introduce you to the others, and then you can choose who you'd like to spend your time with. We even have some puppies here today," I say as I open the door. The noisy barks ring out, and Evan beams when he sees the stalls full of dogs. "We also have cats if you'd prefer to sit and play with them."

"No way. I love dogs. I want a dog, but Mom won't let me have one." He slides his brown eyes to Hope.

My eyes drift over to her. "A dog will get lonely with me at work and you at school all day, Ev."

"You're always welcome to come hang out with Rex on his days off." My mouth runs away before my brain catches up, but it's a terrific idea, so I'm not mad about the offer.

Evan's eyes are almost glowing with excitement. "That'd be awesome."

Hope looks shell-shocked, opening and closing her mouth several times. "Oh, we wouldn't want to impose."

I wave off her concern. "Rex loves company. No imposition at all. In fact, you'd be doing me a favor."

The other kids stop what they're doing when they spot Evan and Hope. "Everyone, I'd like you to meet our newest member, Evan, and his mom, Mrs. Sullivan."

Hope titters and slides her curly hair behind her ear. "You can call me Hope. Mrs. Sullivan is my mother-in-law."

Tori and the kids call out their hellos, and I introduce them one by one. "Okay, so we usually spend a few minutes saying hello to each of the dogs. Evan, you can choose any dog to spend time with while you're here. Just let me or Tori know, and we'll bring them out of the kennel for you and take them outside."

Tori and I get the kids settled with their cats and dogs, and while the kids are busy loving on their chosen pet for the day, I make my usual rounds to talk with each of the kids.

Normally, I have no issue being in the moment and focused solely on the child I'm speaking with, but today, my gaze keeps being drawn back to Hope. She chose a puppy, and I've been watching her play and laugh. Her blue-green eyes sparkle in the morning sunlight, along with the natural golden highlights in her hair.

I thought she was beautiful last week, but when she smiles ... man ... her beauty dials up to a whole new level.

"Are you even listening to me, man?" Donnelly snaps.

I drag my mind and gaze back to him. "Sorry, come again."

He rolls his eyes with annoyance. "I told you. I asked my teacher if we could start a running club at school, and he said yes. He's even going to help me set it up."

I rest my hand on his shoulder and squeeze. "I'm proud of you, Don. That's an awesome initiative, and I'm glad your teacher is supporting you with the project."

"Yeah, it feels pretty good to get positive attention at school instead of always being in trouble."

"I bet. When does the running club start?"

"Next week. Only on Friday mornings to start, but I'm hoping to do it most mornings if the teachers will let me." He lifts his chin toward Evan and Hope. "How'd he get on your radar?"

"He was causing trouble in a gas station with some of his friends. I think he was just trying to fit in. He lost his dad in Syria." I glance back at the woman who has me fixated. "He could do with some new friends." Don is a couple of years older than Evan, but they may go to the same school since they live in the same school district. Evan could do with someone to have his back in case the boys from the gas station give him any trouble.

He acknowledges me with an arrogant chin lift. "His mom's hot as fuck."

I snap my head around to Donnelly, narrowing my eyes and straightening up. "Watch your mouth and don't be disrespectful."

He holds his hands up in surrender. "I didn't mean anything by it. She's too old for me, but you're single." He looks me up and down. "You're probably good-looking enough to bag a chick like that."

I shake my head in exasperation. "Do I need to teach you how to be respectful toward women?"

"Nah, man. The chicks at school love me." He rubs his knuckles on his chest. "I don't need lessons from an old guy like you."

"Hey, I'm only twenty-seven. I'm not *that* old," I say, standing up, slightly affronted. Rex immediately comes to my side, ready to move on. I've been saving Evan for last because I wanted to let him relax, but I also want to check in with him. "I'm gonna keep moving. I haven't checked on Evan yet."

Don winks at me with a tip of his chin in a cavalier move only a teenage boy can pull off. "Sure thing, Ben. Whatever you say."

I don't bother responding. No point defending myself. Hope's puppy is lying on his back as she rubs his tummy, his hind legs doing an odd kick every now and then while Evan's puppy is chewing on the bottom of his jeans, making Evan chuckle. They both look so different from the last time I saw them. Something's definitely changed.

I lower myself to my butt between the two. "How're things going over here?"

"These puppies are crazy." Hope chuckles as she continues to scratch the pup's stomach, and he twists his body around to nip at her slender fingers.

Evan looks up at me with a wide grin. "I've had so much fun."

Rex moves closer to Evan, using his paw to engage with his pup, enticing him to play. The two dogs run a short distance together, and Evan climbs to his feet to follow them, leaving me alone with Hope. We watch him play with both dogs for a moment in silence.

Then, just as my eyes have done all morning, they find their way back to Hope. She's watching her son with a soft smile. "How's he been this week?"

She swallows and turns her attention to me. Having her eyes on me has me shoving my shoulders back and pushing down my nerves. "We had a tough day last Saturday. It was … uh … the sixth anniversary of my late husband's death." My stomach sinks and rolls as she glances back at Evan. "But I think we've turned a corner. He hasn't been as moody, and he's really been looking forward to today."

"Anniversaries are tough. I'm glad to hear he's doing better, and that he was looking forward to today. Sometimes we need something positive to look forward to." I tear my gaze away from her. "And how have you been?"

Out of the corner of my eye, I watch as she subtly shifts. "As good as can be expected, I guess. I … uh … haven't coped the best with losing my husband. I've let Evan down, and I promised him, and myself, that I'll do better. I think the gas station thing woke me up a little. He deserves a mom who's more emotionally stable and engaged. Not someone who's just going through the motions."

I rub my hand over the top of my hair. "Grief is tough and unpredictable. I'm sure you've been doing your best." Dropping my hand to the back of my neck, I squeeze, tearing my eyes away from her. "Does Evan have a male in his life he can go to?" *Yeah, I know. I'm fishing for information. Sue me.*

Her pup climbs to its feet and runs off to join the others. "He has a few … my dad, Wyatt's dad, and Shane, Wyatt's best friend.

Although, Shane doesn't come around so much because I asked him to give us some space. I felt like we were relying on him too much and holding him back from his own life. He carries a lot of guilt about Wyatt, and I didn't want him watching over us out of obligation."

Interesting. Maybe he wasn't watching over them out of obligation, but attraction. I can certainly relate to that; Hope is a beautiful woman. Part of me settles at the idea that she has people she can rely on, while another, more selfish part wants her to grow to rely on me. I want to be that person for her and Evan.

I shake my head and snap my thoughts away from that archaic nonsense. Tahlia's mom would slap me up the back of my head as she preached to me about how strong women are in the face of adversity. "Why does he feel guilty?"

Silence ensues and worry worms its way through my gut that I've pushed her too far, too soon. She doesn't know me. "He survived the blast that killed Wyatt. He didn't come out unscathed, but he felt he should have been the one to die so Wyatt could come back to us." Keeping her eyes downcast, she plucks at the grass. "He felt his life wasn't as important as Wyatt's because he didn't have a family." The desire to drag her into my lap and wrap my arms around her is strong, so I pluck at the grass in front of me, too.

Fuck. That's heavy. "I can't imagine"—I look off into the distance—"can't fathom the pain he experienced to feel that way."

She sighs heavily. "Yeah. He's a really great guy and has been so good to me and Evan. I just want him to be happy. I want Evan to be happy too, you know."

"What about *you*?" The words escape my mouth before my brain can engage to stop them.

Her eyes dart up to me, brows dipping low. "What do you mean?"

I stop tugging the grass and lock eyes with hers—my gray to her aquamarine. "What about *your* happiness?"

"I'm happy when Evan's happy." Her cheeks rise a little. "He's happy today. Happier than I've seen him in ages, and that makes me happy." She steals her eyes away and murmurs, "I had my turn at happiness." She shrugs carelessly, like she didn't just shatter my heart into fragments that I'm not sure I'll be able to piece back together. "It's their turn now."

"Why does it have to be your turn *or* their turn? Why can't you all be happy?" *I need to understand.*

Her shoulders push back, and I watch her as she steels her spine. Her eyes find mine and lock me in place. "Have you ever promised someone forever, Ben?" She doesn't stop so I can respond; she pushes on. "Because *I* did. And even though Wyatt's not here to hold up his end of our promise, *I* am. Every day for the rest of my life, I will keep my promise to love him. It's not easy when I miss him with every fiber of my being, but a promise is a promise." I swallow, absorbing her pain and loss as it hits me like a wave. "Happiness is scarce when your hopes and dreams are stolen abruptly with no time to prepare or come up with contingency plans. My life is no longer how I want it to be. My plans ... destroyed. Devastation resides in its place. Happiness can't survive in that environment." She swipes angrily at her freckle-covered cheeks.

The urge to reach across and take her hand in mine to offer her comfort is overwhelming.

She's still buried so deep in her grief; I'm surprised she's functioning at all. I look at her with new eyes and admiration for the steel in her spine and the strength it's taken for her to still turn up every day for her son.

"You're amazing. You know that, right?" Questioning eyes look my way. "To be able to raise your son on your own when you've lost so much. I bet the temptation to hide from the world was immense, yet you keep showing up, day in and day out."

She swallows harshly and flicks her eyes away from me with a shrug, then pulls her knees up beneath her chin and wraps her arms around them. She curls in on herself, as if trying to shield herself from our conversation, and I realize it was too much too soon, and way too heavy for a setting like this.

"I wouldn't say I've shown up every day," she says. "I've let Evan down more than I should have. It's probably why he got tangled up with those boys from school."

I wave her comment off. "Kids do stupid shit all the time. Doesn't make them bad kids. Certainly doesn't make their parents terrible."

Tori walks over. "Hey, Ben. Some of the parents have arrived. Should we wrap up today's session?"

I glance at my watch. "Shit, sorry, I lost track of time." I leap to my feet and call out to the kids. "Okay, time to get the dogs back inside. Let's go."

Tori giggles. "It's okay. The dogs love being out here with them. I just didn't want a bunch of parents complaining they've got better things to do on a Saturday than wait for their kids." She rolls her eyes. We've had that happen before. If Hope met some of the other parents, she wouldn't be so hard on herself.

We wrangle the dogs back into their kennels, and the kids leave with their parents—except for Donnelly. His mom is often late. Sometimes, she even forgets to pick him up.

Fussing over Rex, Evan and Donnelly talk until Don's mom comes speeding into the parking lot. I grit my teeth, reminding myself I'm off duty. If I talk to her about her driving and the safety of other road users or pedestrians who may be using the sidewalk, she'll probably stop bringing him, and I don't want that to happen. Hope looks at me with raised brows, and I roll my eyes, blowing out a frustrated breath.

"See ya, Donnelly. Good luck with the running club," I call as he climbs into the car.

"Thanks, Ben. See ya, Ev."

"Bye." Evan waves to the retreating car.

Hope drags her keys out of her purse. "Well, Ev. We should get going. Thank Ben, please."

I'm not ready to say goodbye.

Evan looks up at me. His entire face lit with happiness. "Thanks, Ben. I had the best day. Can I come back next time?"

I chuckle and muss his hair. "Sure. We're here every other Saturday at the same time. You're always welcome, and if you have any trouble getting here for one reason or another, call me. I'll pick you up." I hand him a slip of paper with my number on it.

"Oh, you don't need to go to any trouble. There may be some Saturdays when his grandparents will have to bring him because he stays with them once a month. Other than that, I'll be able to bring him." I hook my thumbs through the loops of my jeans and rock back on my heels as I tuck that little piece of information away.

Evan drops to his knees and buries his face in the scruff of Rex's neck. "Bye, Rex." Rex's tail swishes wildly, tipping his rump from side to side.

"Rex and I were going to enjoy some burgers on the back deck for lunch. Would you guys like to join us?" We really weren't, but I'm not retracting the invitation. *I don't want to say goodbye.* "I'm sure Rex would appreciate the company."

Evan leaps to his feet with wide eyes. "Can we, Mom? Please say yes."

She chuckles and tucks her honey hair behind her ear as her eyes rise to mine, then dart back to her son.

10

HOPE

HE'S SO HAPPY. *HOW CAN I SAY NO?*

Especially if it means keeping that smile on his face.

It's such a rare occurrence. I'd do anything.

I should feel uncomfortable accepting Ben's invitation. He's a virtual stranger, and he's inviting us to his home. Under normal circumstances, I would say no, but accepting his invitation doesn't feel like the wrong thing to do. He seems safe, and I feel at ease in his company.

I also can't ignore the fact that I've shared more with him in fifteen minutes than I have with anyone else in a long time. He's familiar somehow, and he seems to understand my grief. Ben's given Evan an amazing opportunity, and while he spends time with Rex, his smile is permanently etched on his cute little face.

What could it hurt?

Maybe if Evan plays with Rex, his desire for a pet will be satisfied and he won't ask me to get a dog of our own ... *again*. It's getting harder and harder to say no, especially when I know how desperately he wants one. With both of us gone most of the day, I can't, in good conscience, agree; it wouldn't be fair to a puppy. But I still feel bad. I want to give Evan everything.

I grin at my son as he patiently peers up at me, waiting for my answer, a hopeful expression painting his face. "Okay," I tell him as I look up at Ben. "Only if you're sure we're not imposing." His shoulders seem to drop, and he releases a breath like he was as desperate for my answer as Evan was.

"No imposition." Ben claps his hands together as his cheeks rise, making deep crinkles at the corners of his eyes appear, telling me this man smiles a lot. "Great. You can follow me."

Suddenly unsure, I glance down at Evan. His grin is so broad, his eyes so hopeful. I'm many things, but I'm not a monster. With resignation, I gesture toward my car. "Uhm, is there anything we can bring? If you give me your address, I can stop at the store and we can meet at your place." I fidget with my keys. "It's bad manners to turn up empty-handed."

He shoves his hands into his pockets and rocks back on his heels. The muscles beneath his tattooed forearms tense with the action and the denim of his jeans pulls tighter around his firm thighs. He's in great shape, but I guess that's to be expected since he has to be in top condition for his job.

With muddled thoughts, I snatch my eyes away.

Why am I noticing his arms and thighs?

My cheeks burn with shame, and I shuffle on my feet. I fix my gaze just beyond his shoulder while I wait for his response—with a racing heart and suddenly clammy hands. I let the high of playing with the puppies and Evan's desire to play with Rex cloud my judgment, and I could kick myself for agreeing to spend the afternoon with Ben and Rex. From the corner of my eye, I watch him studying me, his smile diminishing the slightest touch.

"I need to pick up a couple of things at the store. You can follow me." He pats his thigh, and Rex sits beside him obediently. He's such a good dog.

I force a nod. "All right. Come on, Ev."

We make our way to my car and climb inside. "Thanks, Mom," Evan says from the back seat. "You're the best."

My eyebrows shoot up as I start the car to follow Ben out of the parking lot. "I don't know about that," I mumble underneath my breath. *Who goes to a stranger's home for a meal after knowing him for what ... a couple of hours tops?*

And just because he's an officer of the law, that doesn't make him completely safe.

My breaths grow choppy as we pull into the store's parking lot. I tighten my hands on the steering wheel until my knuckles turn white as I park the car. After I turn off the engine, I twist in my seat to face Evan. "I don't know if this is such a good idea, Ev. We don't really know Ben, and we're going to his home."

He scoots forward and rests his hand on my shoulder. "We don't have to go, Mom. It's just ... I-I-I really like him. He's never once spoken to me like I'm a problem. Not like some of the teachers do. He didn't give me that sad look when he found out about Dad. You know the one ... like I'm broken because he's gone. Not like Shane and everyone else does," he murmurs the last part, and fissures spread across my already shattered heart. "I feel like a normal kid with him."

He feels like a normal kid.

I can't take that away from him. He's had so many years of grief in his young life, and I promised things would be different. That I'd try harder. He needs this ... and maybe I do too, because Ben doesn't look at me like I'm broken either.

He makes *me* feel normal, too.

He didn't give me platitudes when I told him how I felt. He looked at me as though I'm strong—not like I'll shatter at any moment.

I glance out the windshield and spot Ben waiting patiently with Rex on a leash by his car. Drawing in a deep breath, I decide to do this—for Evan ... and maybe for me, too. "C'mon, then. Ben's waiting." We climb out of the car, and Ben leads us inside. "Are you allowed to bring Rex into the store?" I know some stores allow pets, and I guess Rex isn't technically a *pet* since he's a working dog, but he's not working now.

"Oh, yeah. They love Rex here. They get upset when I come without him. He's a local celebrity." Ben chuckles and leans down to rub the scruff of Rex's neck. "Hey, Rex. They love you, don't they?"

Rex looks up at Ben with pure adoration for his ... *owner* ... *boss* ... *dad*? I don't know. They seem more like friends and equals than dog and master.

When we step inside, the staff call out their hellos to Rex like he is an actual celebrity. Ben tells Evan to grab a cart, and we make our way through the store. He adds more to the cart than I would have expected for a simple lunch of burgers. Suspicion grows when he asks Evan what some of his favorite snacks are and adds them to the cart as we go. "Were you really having burgers?" I wave my hand out toward the cart.

He looks down and shrugs. "Yeah. I need to get groceries for a few days because I'm back on days this week and won't have time to shop. Hope you don't mind." That still doesn't explain why he's grabbing some of Evan's favorite foods.

"Of course not. Do what you need to do. If we're in the way, let us know."

"You're not in the way. I'm almost finished," he says smoothly.

"What should I grab for dessert?"

Evan's eyes light up. "Can we get apple pie, Mom?"

I glance up at Ben, about to ask him if he likes apple pie, when he freezes on the spot. "You like apple pie?" he asks Evan with wide eyes.

"Uh, duh. Who doesn't?" Evan responds.

"Exactly. Let's go get apple pie."

"It won't be as good as Mom's homemade apple pie, but it'll have to do this time." I hear Evan gush over my apple pie to Ben as they walk away, and I smirk to myself. My kid is a fiend for sweets. Completely my fault since I love to bake.

"Really? Do you think your mom will make me an apple pie?" Ben asks.

"I don't see why she wouldn't, if you ask nicely." He looks up at Ben. "Mom bakes all kinds of things. She's really good at it." I should feel annoyed that Evan's volunteering my baking services. Instead, I feel warmth filling my chest that he loves my baking.

We grab the apple pie and ice cream, and Ben pays for everything, even though I try my best to keep the dessert items separate. So now we're still turning up at his house empty-handed.

11

HOPE

WHEN WE PULL INTO THE DRIVEWAY BEHIND BEN, I barely hold in a gasp when my eyes land on his gorgeous home. A sweet bungalow with stonework at the base, pale blue weatherboard with white trim, and black shingles covering the roof—and it's only one street away from the beach.

Climbing out of the car, Evan makes his way straight to Ben's car, releasing Rex from the passenger seat, but I can't tear my eyes from the home in front of me. The guys carry the groceries into the house, and I finally get myself into gear and grab the last bag from the trunk.

"You have a beautiful ho—" The words fade into the ether when I see the view spread out in front of me. The entire back of his home is glass. Vast windows overlook the ocean that seems to go on forever. Dazzling blue water dances beneath the sun.

Huh? That's weird.

The water hasn't looked that blue in such a long time. He must have some type of film on the glass that enhances the colors.

Ben looks back at me with a grin after opening the glass folding patio doors to let the ocean breeze in. "Nice, huh?"

Nope. No film on the glass. The water really is that blue. *Wow!*

"It's gorgeous. I love the ocean, but with my fair skin and freckles, I don't get to enjoy it as much as I'd like."

"Rex and I run along the beach every day, and he loves to play in the waves," he tells me as he unpacks the groceries. I push my way in and unload the bags to make myself feel useful. I can't just stand around gawking at the beautiful view while he does all the work. "Ev, you wanna take Rex out back and play with him while I sort this out and get the burgers started?"

"Sure." He pats his thigh. "C'mon, boy."

They disappear through the door, leaving me alone with Ben. I put the cold food in the fridge and freezer, noting his preference for healthy foods, while Ben puts everything else away. Then he gathers what he needs to make the burger patties.

"How can I help?"

"You wanna put the fries in the air fryer and slice the buns?"

"Sure."

We easily work together to prepare our lunch. My eyes keep dropping to the play of his muscles beneath the smooth, decorated skin of his forearms. His long, capable fingers mix the mince until all the ingredients are combined, and heat rises to my cheeks. I blow out a long breath and focus on cutting and buttering the buns. "How long have you lived here?"

He stops for a moment, narrowing his eyes in thought. "I moved here about four years ago now. I used to live in Piney Lakes."

"Oh, wow. That's quite a change of pace." He nods, murmuring his agreement. "What made you move to the city?"

He swallows harshly and returns his focus to the patties he's shaping. "There were more opportunities in the police force here. I didn't want to be a small-town cop." He waves his hands around, gesturing to the house. "And I figured I may as well make the move since this house was left to me when my best friend's mom passed away." He places the patties on a tray. "It used to be their family's vacation home that hadn't been used in a long time, and it needed a fair amount of work, but I'm happy with the results."

I swallow the lump in my throat at the change in his tone when he shares the loss of his best friend's mom. *I wonder why the house was left to him and not his best friend?* "I'm sorry for your loss." He simply nods and returns his attention to the burgers. Opening the fridge, I peer inside. "Well, you've done a fantastic job." I move a few items aside, but still can't find what I'm looking for. "Do you have ketchup?"

"Yeah, it's in the pantry." He gestures toward a door with a tip of his chin.

The fridge door bangs closed with a heavy thud, as disbelief washes through me, swift and strong. "In the pantry?"

"Yeah?" he responds slowly, his eyes narrowing slightly.

I can't believe he keeps the ketchup in the pantry. *Heathen.* Opening the pantry door, my eyes widen when the unexpectedly large space greets me. He has a full butler's pantry hidden behind the simple door. "Oh wow, this is amazing," I say, already imagining what I could do with all of my baking supplies in a space like this. I grab the ketchup from the mostly empty shelf and wave it around as I exit the meticulously kept space. "Everyone knows you keep the ketchup in the fridge."

He turns and leans his ass against the granite counter, folding his arms across his chest, and I can't help but notice how his muscles shift and change. The way his T-shirt stretches around his biceps and pulls across his pecs. "I don't like my ketchup cold. Room temperature works best for me. Even Heinz says it's shelf-stable. I checked."

My eyebrows shoot up. I'm impressed. "Fair enough. I was always taught it goes in the fridge. I never thought to question whether I could safely store it in the pantry." You learn something new every day.

Evan barges in through the back door with Rex by his side.

They've certainly become fast friends. "Are we eating soon? I'm starving." My eyebrows shoot up at his familiarity with Ben.

Ben chuckles. "Sure. I'll cook the patties. You think you can survive another fifteen minutes?"

Rex heads over to his bowl and greedily slurps the water, then drops to the floor, resting his head on his front paws. His golden eyebrows shift as he watches us move around the kitchen with intelligent brown eyes.

"I guess so. I'm thirsty, though. Can I get a drink?" He heads to the fridge and yanks it open.

"Manners, Evan." I frown at him. *What the hell?* "You don't just help yourself. You wait for your host to offer you a drink. And where's the *please*? You know better than that."

He closes the fridge and drops his eyes to the oak floor. "Sorry." Then looks up at Ben. "Sorry, Ben."

"That's okay, I'm a terrible host. I should have offered you and your mom a drink when we got home. My mom would be very disappointed in me. Manners are really important to her," Ben says in a tone that suggests his mom would be *more* than disappointed in him as he grabs some glasses from the cupboard above the sink. Pointing with his elbow toward the fridge, he tells Evan to choose a drink for all of us and then pours them as the burgers sizzle in the grill pan.

Once they're cooked and we assemble the burgers, we load up our plates with fries and carry them out to the back deck. Rex follows us and lies quietly at Evan's feet. Completely enamored, my son can't tear his eyes away from his furry friend as he eats. I don't think I've ever seen a more well-behaved dog, but I guess it makes sense, given he's a police dog. I bet his training is intense.

The briny breeze blows my curls around my face, so I twist them around until they form a temporary knot to keep my hair out of the way. I only half listen to Ben and Evan's conversation about soccer and running as I stare at the view in front of me. The glistening sparkles of the sun on the bluest water and the white crests of the waves as they crash onto the shore have me mesmerized. I wonder if Ben's lived here so long that he takes this spectacular view for granted, or does he appreciate how lucky he is to have it to enjoy?

"Donnelly goes to the same school as me. He told me he's starting a running club next week. I think I'll join because it'll help my fitness for soccer," he tells Ben, then turns to me. "Do you think Nanna would mind taking me to school earlier on Friday?"

I shrug. "I don't see why she'd mind, especially if it's so you can exercise. You know how much she loves to run." At sixty, Mom still runs every day. "She'll probably start bugging you to join her when she runs her half marathon," I say, nudging his side.

"I've done a couple of half marathons. They're great fun." Ugh, another weirdo who likes to run. Ben raises his eyebrows at me. "What? You don't like to run?"

"Nope. I couldn't think of anything worse than running." Much to Mom's disappointment. I readjust the twist at my nape. "I get winded too quickly and feel like I'm going into cardiac arrest." It's not pretty—or fun. I don't understand how people find it therapeutic.

Ben glances at me, then looks at Evan. "Maybe we should train your mom."

I hold my hands up in a defensive move. "Nope. Don't even think about it. My mom's been trying to get me to run since I was a teenager. It's not gonna happen now. I'm too old to start. Ballet was enough to keep me fit."

Ben chuckles. "We'll see."

He can chuckle all he wants, but we *won't* see. The guys continue to chat over apple pie and ice cream, and warmth—not just from the afternoon sun—unfurls through my chest at their easy camaraderie. It's like they've known each other a lot longer than they actually have. It all feels very comfortable.

Too comfortable.

The sun is sinking in the sky, reminding me we've been here for a while and should get home. I have things to do, and Evan has a homework assignment to complete.

Standing, I collect the dishes. "Ev, we should head home. I'm sure Ben has stuff to do, and so do we."

Evan's smile disappears, but I pretend I don't notice. We can't hang out here all afternoon.

Ben drops his large hand to my forearm, and I freeze in place, lowering my eyes and noticing the differences between us. Where my complexion is fair, he has a gorgeous tan. Where my fingers are long and slender, his are thick. Once he has my attention, he removes his hand, and the seized air in my lungs escapes.

"Leave all of this. I can do it. I don't have plans other than laundry. Rex and I usually take it easy on the weekends when I don't work."

I raise my chin. "I insist. It won't take five minutes, and then we'll be out of your hair."

He must recognize my determination in the stubborn way I'm holding my chin, because he nods and then helps me carry everything inside. I search for rubber gloves, but come up empty. "What are you looking for?"

"Uh, dishwashing gloves?"

"Sorry, I don't have any. I can wash the dishes."

Dishwashing detergent is terrible for my hands and nails, but I can suck it up this once. "That's okay. I can do it." I quickly wash the dishes and set the kitchen right to the best of my ability without knowing where everything goes. When I spin to face the kitchen, Ben is bent over, returning the grill pan to the cupboard, and my eyes automatically drop to his firm backside.

What the hell is wrong with me today?

It's like my eyes have a mind of their own. I snap my gaze away and swallow guiltily.

"Thanks so much for this morning and for lunch. Evan had a wonderful time, and it's been fantastic to see him so happy." I wipe my suddenly clammy hands on the cotton covering my thighs.

"It was my pleasure." He pauses a moment, his intelligent gray eyes studying me. "How about you?" He tilts his head to the side a little, as though my answer is the most important thing in the world.

My lips tip up in a way I've perfected to show the outside world I'm fine. Inside, I'm anything but. I've found myself appreciating another man like I didn't make a commitment to be faithful to my husband. I'm appalled and ashamed.

"It's been great. And when Evan's happy, I'm happy." Evan moves beside me, and I slide my arm around his shoulder to pull him in close and steady myself under Ben's watchful gaze. Something tells me he doesn't buy my act. It really has been a great day, a nice change of pace. Ben's easy to talk to, and Evan seems to have a lot of respect for him—something he's been lacking with Shane and me in recent months. But now guilt is settling like a lead ball in my stomach, and it's easier to fall back into the patterns I'm more used to. I squeeze Evan's shoulder. "It's time to go. Say thank you to Ben, please."

Evan thanks Ben, and we make our way out of his home and to the driveway. The heaviness that had been absent this afternoon returns with each step as I get closer to my car—and regular life. For a few hours, I lived in the moment. I allowed myself to feel joy and just *be*. Something I've been struggling to do.

When I release the locks on my car, Ben opens the doors for me and Ev, then stands back with his hands relaxed at his sides, drawing my attention to his thick thighs. Rex sits beside him without instruction, his tongue hanging out of his mouth.

"Is it okay if I come to the shelter again?" Evan asks.

"Absolutely. I was hoping you would." He looks down at Rex and then back at Evan. "And you can stop by anytime to play with

Rex. He loved having you here today. I think he gets sick of always being stuck with me."

"That would be so cool. Thanks, Ben." He drops his butt onto the back seat. "See ya, Rex." Rex almost dances on the spot, his tail wagging happily as Evan closes his door.

I shuffle my feet and look down at the grass. "Thank you for being so welcoming, but it's probably not a good idea to give Ev an open invitation. He'll be around here all the time. Especially since we don't live that far away." I chuckle, looking back up at Ben.

"I don't mind, really. I'd love his company." He glances at Evan in the back seat, and I figure that's the end of the conversation, so I twist my body to climb into my car. "The invitation is open to you, too, Hope. Anytime you feel like company, you're welcome to stop by."

My heart stalls, and my lungs feel like they're burning. I freeze mid-sit and my eyes must be as wide as saucers. "Th-thank you," I stutter like a fool. "That's very kind, but I don't want to be a both-er." Not only that, it would be weird to seek another man's company. "Thanks for today. Bye, Ben." I quickly close myself inside my car where I'm safe and start the engine before he can respond.

Pulling onto the road, I wave politely through the window and blow out a long breath. My heart beats an irregular rhythm, and I tightly grip the steering wheel with clammy hands.

Evan sighs in the back, and I glance at him in my mirror. "Can we get a dog, Mom? I promise I'll feed and walk him every day."

So much for my theory of him getting his fix and being satis-fied. "And what will the dog do all day at home by himself, Ev? Do you think that's really fair?"

He's quiet for a long time. "What about two dogs? They'd keep each other company," he says, his voice filled to the brim with excitement, because in his mind, he's solved the problem.

"We can't have two dogs, Ev." Guilt moves through me like a landslide. I hate saying no to him. I wish I could say yes. I wish we could go back to *The Paw Palace* and get one of those cute puppies we played with today, but I have to be the realistic one in this situation.

It's lonely being the only adult in the house. Every decision lands on my shoulders. I don't have anyone to share the load or to take turns being the mean parent. I'm *always* the mean parent. It's exhausting, and it's not how things were supposed to be.

12

I STAND IN FRONT OF *THE PAW PALACE* WITH MY ARMS firmly crossed in front of my chest in an attempt to keep from fidgeting. Rex circles my legs, picking up on my anxiousness. I drop my hand to slide my fingers through his fur to settle him and ground myself, and he drops to his butt beside me. "You're okay, boy."

For the past two weeks, I haven't stopped thinking about the slip of a woman with long curly hair and aquamarine eyes. She's filled every waking moment, and I've had to wrestle my thoughts away from her to concentrate on important stuff, like my job.

I loved having Hope and Evan at my house, and I hated it when they left. The house suddenly felt too quiet, too big, too empty. Something changed in Hope, and she seemed in a hurry to get away. I'm not sure if I did or said something to upset her, but I didn't like the sudden shift in her demeanor—I felt responsible somehow. I thought we'd spend the entire afternoon together. I was even about to suggest a walk along the beach when she suddenly stood to clear the table.

The last two weeks have felt like a decade has passed, and I've counted down every minute until I get to lay my eyes on Hope again. It certainly doesn't hurt that Evan already feels like a friend.

I hear the door open and close behind me, and Tori comes to stand by my side. "Hi, Ben." She crouches to greet Rex with a scratch behind his ear. "How come you guys are waiting out here?"

"Hey, Tori." I look down at her. "No reason." *Just waiting for the woman I can't get off my mind as if I'm a kid waiting for the fair to open when it comes to town.*

"We only have a handful of puppies, but we got some kittens early in the week. They've had all their checks, so they're ready for the kids."

"Okay, sounds good."

"Are you okay?"

I glance down at Tori. "Yeah. Why?"

She swipes her tongue over her bottom lip, making it shimmer, and shrugs. "You don't seem yourself."

Wrapping my arm around her shoulder, I tug her into my side and squeeze. "I'm fine. Promise."

She smiles up at me, then pulls away. "Okay. I'll head inside and get everything ready."

As each child arrives, my nerves kick up another notch. What if Evan doesn't show? I don't have Hope's number to check on them. I guess I can always go around—

Hope's car pulls into the parking lot, and when she stops at the front door, the air trapped in my lungs wooshes out. Evan leans forward and kisses her, then climbs out of the car. She watches him run toward me and waves politely, then drives out of the parking lot. My body deflates and my shoulders drop. Disappointment takes the place of my anxiousness to see her, and I don't know how to feel about her not staying. I've been waiting for two weeks to see her again, and that thirty seconds wasn't nearly enough.

"Hey, Ben."

"Hey, Ev," I reply as I watch her car disappear down the street.

He crouches low, resting his head on Rex's back as he rubs his fingers through his dark fur. Rex is equally happy to see his new friend, trying to spin around so he can lick Evan's face, making him laugh loudly. As I watch them, I realize I need to pull my head out of my ass and get with the program. I'm here for the kids. No other reason.

"You ready to head inside?" I ask Evan as I open the glass door.

He stands with a beaming smile and a sparkle in his eyes. Hope would be thrilled to see him so happy. "Yep. Come on, boy." He pats his thigh, and Rex trots inside beside him, leaving me behind like I'm chopped liver.

We walk through to the back part of the shelter where the cats and dogs are. Tori's already there with the others, explaining which animals they can spend time with today. Once the kids are settled out in the yard with their dogs, or inside with their kittens, I make my rounds as usual, checking in with the kids about how they've been since we last caught up.

Donnelly tells me all about the running club, and I don't think I've ever seen him so animated. He and Evan seem to have developed a friendship, which is exactly what I'd hoped for. It'll give Evan a support person at school and Donnelly someone to watch over.

As the session winds down, my stomach twists. I need to think of something to do so I can spend time with Evan and Hope. I probably should have thought of a plan before this, but I'd hoped she'd come to the session like she did last time. She seemed to enjoy spending time with the pups, and I figured she'd want to do it again. I didn't count on her not attending, which is my fault; I guess. I only invited her to the first session and told her it was best if she didn't stay, so Evan would bond with the other kids.

I watch out the front windows as the parents pull in to collect their kids and finally, an idea hits. "Hey, Tori. Do you need any dogs bathed today?"

She grins brightly at me. "You betcha. Are you offering?"

A sense of lightness flows through me because, if I do this right, I might get to spend some time with the woman I can't stop thinking about. "Of course." I move next to Evan and keep my voice low. *I know I'm evil using Evan's love for the dogs, but a man's gotta do what a man's gotta do.* "Hey, Ev. Do you have time to help me bathe some dogs this afternoon?"

His eyes grow as wide as full moons. "That'd be awesome. I'll ask Mom."

Bingo!

My grin is instant and broad. Now, let's hope his mom agrees. Some of the kids organize to catch up with each other next weekend, making my heart expand. I started this program to give the kids an outlet and something positive to look forward to. I never dreamed it would also give them the opportunity to build strong friendship connections.

Donnelly leaves with his mom, leaving me and Evan alone. "Do you have any plans for the weekend?"

"Nah. Mom'll probably want to go for a bike ride"—he rolls his eyes—"because she's always trying to get me outside in the fresh air." He does air quotes around *fresh air,* and I smirk. "Not that there's much to do inside now that I'm not allowed to go on my computer."

Hope pulls into the parking lot, and I walk with Evan toward her car. "Let's see if your mom's happy for you to help me bathe the dogs." *And hopefully offer to stay and help, too.*

He flings her door open, startling her. "Mom, can we please stay and help Ben wash the dogs?"

She holds her hands up with a grin. "Woah, slow down. What's happening?"

He sucks in a long breath. "Ben has to bathe some of the dogs today and asked me if I'd like to help. Please say I can stay and help." She glances up at me, giving me one of those fake smiles she so easily shares, then turns her attention back to her son. "Please, Mom."

"Okay, sure. How long will it take?" She flicks her clear eyes that look more blue than green today back to me.

"About an hour. You could stay if it makes it easier for you?" *Please stay. Please stay.*

She nods, then drops her eyes back to Evan. "We don't have plans, so I guess it'll be okay. Let me park the car, and I'll come inside."

Yes! I mentally jab my fist into the air. I hate to admit it, but I'm giddy to spend more time with Hope.

Rex dances around Hope when she steps inside the shelter. *I know how you feel, buddy.* She ducks down, cupping each side of his face in greeting. "Hello, Rex."

She chuckles when he swipes his tongue up the side of her face, and jealousy burns through me thick and fast. Her genuine smile is still in place when she looks up at me, and I have to suck in a sharp breath. It's fucking beautiful.

She's fucking beautiful.

I scrape my fingers along my short beard to stop myself from sliding a loose curl behind her ear and running the back of my hand down the side of her face. I bet her skin's as soft as a rose petal. "He's happy to see you," I tell her. *So am I.*

She chuckles. "Seems that way. So where are these dirty pooches?" My eyes dance over her face, unsure which feature I want to stop on. She's stunning. I'd forgotten exactly how beautiful. "Ben?"

"Oh, right. Uh ... through the back. Follow me." When we make it through to the back, Tori's already set up the bathing area and is bringing out the first dog. She explains the process to Hope and Evan and then leaves us to it. When it's just the three of us, I take the lead. "Evan, do you want to rinse him?"

"Can I?"

"Sure." I position the dog in the tub, and Evan uses the sprayer to rinse him with warm water. "We need to keep the water and soap away from his eyes, okay?"

He nods, keeping his attention on what he's doing. "Okay. Mom, you'll be good at this."

Hope chuckles. "Yeah, I guess so, but my clients don't wriggle around as much as these guys."

"Mom's a hairstylist. She washes people's hair all the time," Evan explains.

I raise my eyes to Hope. "Oh, yeah? Where do you work?"

"Oh, over at *Beyond the Fringe*?" The tone of her voice rises at the end, as if she's unsure. The name's familiar, and I search my memory for its location. She points to the north-east. "About fifteen minutes in the other direction from our houses."

I nod, picturing the location. "I know where it is. I'll have to stop in for a haircut." She glances up at my hair, which I'm sure is a mess from me running my fingers through it all morning—a nervous habit that's only worsened at the thought of seeing her again.

I watch her slender throat move as she swallows and the flutter of her pulse at the base. What I wouldn't do to have the privilege of kissing that spot. "Or I can cut it for you at home. Your style is pretty straightforward." Her eyes widen slightly and fill with panic, like she didn't mean to offer to cut my hair.

I should be a gentleman and give her a way to opt out, but I'm not gonna. "That'd be great. Lemme know when you're free, and I'll come over."

She tucks a long, curly lock behind her ear, revealing a pink flush up the side of her neck. *Beautiful.* "Okay."

Evan guffaws, bringing our attention back to him. The dog is shaking his entire body, showering him from head to toe.

"I'm afraid that comes with the job, Ev." I chuckle and grab a clean towel to wipe him down.

Hope steps in, grabs the shampoo, and lathers up the mutt's fur. Her long, slender fingers massage the dog, and I've never been the jealous type, but I'm envious of the attention she's giving him. He lifts his snout up to the ceiling in obvious enjoyment, and I can only imagine how good it would feel to have her hands on me.

Once she's finished, Evan rinses him and gets treated to

another shower, then Hope towel dries him. I clip his nails, brush his fur, and return him to his kennel. We repeat the process twice more, then go in search of Tori.

"Are you guys finished already?" she asks from behind the counter.

"Yep. All done. Many hands make light work and all that. We'll see you in two weeks."

"Thanks, guys. I really appreciate the help. I've got two sick cats and a dog in recovery after surgery in the hospital today, so you've saved me a job and given me more time to sit with them." Her gratitude glows from her eyes. I know she appreciates as much help as she can get.

We say goodbye and stroll to the parking lot.

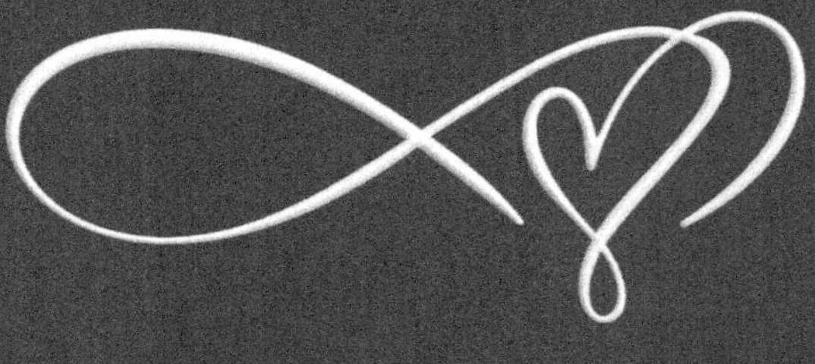

"Mom, I'm hungry. Can we get something to eat?" Evan moans, and I could cup his cheeks and kiss him right now.

"Me too." I rub my stomach for theatrics. "Rex and I were going to grab some fish and chips from the *Blue Goose* down at the beach."

Evan's head snaps up to his mom. "Can we get fish and chips, too?"

I should feel ashamed, but I don't. Using a kid to spend more time with his mom is underhanded ... not very upstanding ... but I am a man beneath the uniform and badge I wear. The badge to which I swore to serve and protect ... to uphold laws and keep the community safe. Technically, I'm not breaking any laws.

She messes up his hair and leans in close, taking a whiff. "You smell like wet dog. We can grab lunch at home after you shower and change." Evan's face drops, and so does mine. Both of our shoulders roll inward with disappointment. Rex barks up at Hope, and she chuckles as she looks at the three of us. Rolling her eyes, a hint of a smile touches her lips—a genuine one this time. "All right, then. I guess the shower can wait."

Evan cheers loudly, but I keep my celebration close to my chest, only sharing a simple smile with Hope. "Fantastic. Let's go."

Rex and I climb into my truck, while Evan and Hope climb into her car, then we make our way down to the beach and the *Blue Goose*. We grab a table on the terrace overlooking the water, so we can sit with Rex, then I head inside to order lunch after arguing with Hope because I refused to take her money. She's clearly used to being independent.

I guess even when her husband was alive, he would have been frequently absent and she would have been the primary caregiver and responsible for their welfare. That builds a toughness and strength not all women have. It's admirable ... not to mention sexy.

On my way back to the table, I pause a moment, watching Hope and Evan laugh about something. Without knowing them all that well, I imagine there hasn't been a lot of laughter in their home over the last six years.

There's been an obvious change in Hope since I first met her. She seemed heavily weighed down in her grief. She was closed and guarded. Then she opened up a little last time at the shelter and shared a little of her pain with me. Today, I watched her laugh and smile with Evan. They weren't fake like her previous smiles, and I wonder if I can help Hope, so all her smiles are genuine.

The breeze blows a honey-colored curl across her cheek, and she raises a slender finger to pull it away, tucking it behind her ear without breaking her attention from her son. They seem close. I can't imagine the strength of their bond forged through devastation.

I know after Seb and I lost Tahlia, our bond strengthened because we experienced shared pain, even though I was closer to her. He still felt the devastation of losing our best friend deeply.

Hope glances up, and her eyes catch on me; the aquamarine is so light, almost sparkling out here in the afternoon sunlight. She smiles gently, but it isn't fake, so I'll take it.

My feet move of their own accord, carrying me back to the table. I plop the number and our sodas in the middle and take a seat. "Thanks for helping me bathe the dogs today. We got through them much quicker than I would have on my own."

"I had fun, even if I stink like a wet dog now." Evan gives his mom the side eye, then leans forward and takes a whiff of her. "Ha! You smell like a wet dog, too, Mom." He points at her as he leans away like she smells offensive.

I lift my T-shirt to my nose, then pull it away quickly. "Pretty sure we all smell like wet dog at this point."

Evan leans in for a smell. "Yep, you stink too!"

"Evan!" Hope snaps, creases forming between her brows as she looks at her son with disapproval. "Where are your manners?" She looks at me. "I'm sorry. Wyatt and I instilled manners in Evan, even if he seems to forget them whenever he's around you."

I wave off her concern. "We're just having some fun." A server drops off a large basket of chips, fish, and calamari rings, along with salt, vinegar, and ketchup. Evan's eyes widen comically. I grab the steamed fish for Rex and then wave my hand across the table. "Dig in."

Hope tucks her loose hair behind her ear. "Thank you for lunch again," she says as Evan reaches into the basket and grabs a handful of chips, stuffing them into his mouth unceremoniously. "Evan! Oh, my gosh, Ben's going to think you have absolutely no manners at all. What is wrong with you?" Her neck and cheeks flush that gorgeous pink I love so much.

He drops his eyes and curls his shoulders inward. "Sorry. I'm just so hungry, and Ben doesn't mind."

As much as it doesn't bother me, I need to support Hope. "As much as I love that you're comfortable with me, you need to listen to and respect your mom. She's trying to teach you how to be a good person, and how to behave in different situations."

He nods slowly. "Sorry, Ben."

Hope's posture visibly softens, and her features relax. She mouths the words, "thank you" and I feel her appreciation fill the space between us. Supporting her in that moment felt right, and I know I'll strive to always do so. I'm drawn to this woman like I haven't been to anyone before her. The connection I feel to her and Evan is too strong to ignore, and I'm going to make it my mission to become an integral part of their lives.

It sounds weird, but I believe I was destined to meet Evan and Hope—to make them mine and keep them forever. I glance up to the clear sky; maybe Tahlia had something to do with it.

I pop a chip into my mouth and chew. "So, Evan, what's your favorite subject at school?"

He pauses and looks at his mom, a frown marring his features. "I don't like school."

"I wasn't a fan of school either, but I always loved PE and social studies." I shrug. "There must be something you like."

He drops his chin to his chest. "I like writing stories," he mumbles, and my eyebrows shoot up. He brings his warm brown eyes to mine. "Don't tell the other kids. Mom's the only person who knows."

"I won't." I glance at Hope. "Your secret's safe with me. What types of stories do you like to write?"

His eyes brighten as he sits up straight. "I like to write crime stories with twists and turns that you don't see coming." He looks at Hope. "They're like the books Mom likes to read."

"They're really good too," Hope says, pride warming her voice.

"I bet they are. Well, if you need any help with the law enforcement side of things, I'm always happy to give advice," I offer.

He pushes his shoulders back. "Really? That'd be awesome."

I turn to Hope. "So, who are your favorite authors?"

She rolls her eyes to the roof above us. "I haven't read for several years now, but I loved John Grisham, James Patterson, and Patricia Cornwell. I still buy their new releases, even though I've lost my reading mojo." She forces a chuckle, like it's no big deal that she's lost her reading mojo, but as she tucks her curls behind her ear, I sense she misses the hobby more than she lets on.

"I have to admit, I'm not a huge reader. I find it difficult to sit for long enough to enjoy a book. I'm more inclined to watch a show on TV."

"Mom always has the TV on, even when she's not watching it," Evan declares.

I look at Hope, wanting her to open up and tell me something else about herself, but I don't want this to be an interrogation, even though I want to know everything about her, so I keep my mouth shut.

She raises and drops one smooth shoulder carelessly. "I like to have it on for background noise. When Evan's upstairs doing his schoolwork or playing his games, it's too quiet downstairs." *And lonely, I suspect.* I hear exactly what she's not saying.

14

HOPE

I press my hand to my stomach, feeling fuller than full. The salty breeze coming straight from the ocean is cool, sending goosebumps scattering across my flesh, and I shiver.

Ben notices and stacks our dishes in the middle of the table, then stands. "We should head out. You're cold." Like the obedient dog he is, Rex immediately makes his way to Ben's side.

I watch as disappointment washes over Evan and wave off Ben's concern. "I'm okay." I stand and position the strap of my purse across my body. I'm sure he wants to be on his way. "Evan, do you want to walk along the beach before we go home?" It's such a gorgeous afternoon, and if I can keep Ev busy here for a little while longer, it leaves less time for him to spend cooped up in his room.

He looks out at the waves and along the shoreline, taking notice of younger kids making sandcastles under the watchful gaze of their parents, while bigger kids toss a ball with their dads. His brows furrow, and he shrugs. "If you want to." His voice lacks enthusiasm, and I know he's only doing it for me.

Great, it seems he's only enthusiastic about things when it involves Rex and Ben. "Evan, what do you say to Ben?"

He raises his head to Ben. "Thanks for today. And for lunch. I'm sorry I forgot my manners."

Ben chuckles and raises his hand to Ev's head, messing up his hair. "You're welcome."

My heart skips as I watch their easy companionship. Shane's been awesome with Evan, stepping in as much as he could when Wyatt died. He's been determined to keep his promise, but we couldn't keep relying on him. We were holding him back, and I couldn't live with the guilt. Thankfully, since I asked him to give us space, he has, but Evan's missed him terribly. Guilt has been my constant companion, but I needed to release Shane from his obligation to us. He needs to get on with his own life, not be weighed down by a promise he made more than a decade ago.

Watching Evan with Ben, as he soaks up his attention like a sponge, is heart-wrenching. At the same time, it makes me happy that he's made a new friend. Maybe I should be wary that Ben's so much older than him, but I think he'll be a wonderful role model, and I know he'll encourage Evan to make good choices.

"Thanks for lunch. Are you sure I can't pay for some of it, at least?"

He waves off my offer. "Nah. It's cool. But do you mind if Rex and I join you for a walk?"

I swallow my surprise. I thought he was in a hurry to get home, using my goosebumps as an excuse. "Sure. If you'd like."

Evan cheers and then pats his thigh, running toward the beach. "C'mon, Rex. Let's go, boy." Rex follows him like he would follow my son anywhere. At least he's excited to spend time outside now. That's something, I guess.

I chuckle. "He loves Rex so much." I glance up at Ben and then return my gaze to Evan and Rex. "He asked for a dog after we left the shelter last time. I wouldn't be surprised if he doesn't try to steal yours."

Ben pushes his hair back from his strong forehead. "He's welcome to spend as much time with Rex as he'd like."

I remove my sandals, then head toward the water so I can wet my feet as we walk. Ben removes his shoes and socks as well, and we walk side by side in comfortable silence for a while. I don't feel the need to fill the quietness that's fallen between us, enjoying the gulls overhead, the laughter of the children, and the swooshing of the waves on the shore. Why I feel so at ease in Ben's company so quickly is beyond me.

Now that we're out in the sunshine, it's considerably warmer. The breeze feels incredible as it kisses my skin, and the sun is warm without being scorching. It's the perfect afternoon. I grin in appreciation.

"What's that smile for?" Ben asks, and my smile drops.

A curly lock blows across my lips, and I use the moment to pause as I grip it between my fingers and tuck it behind my ear. I look up into his gray eyes surrounded by thick, dark lashes. "I was just appreciating the perfect afternoon. The sun's shining and the breeze feels phenomenal." My eyes sting, and my nose tingles when I realize I've enjoyed this outing—and not once have I thought about missing Wyatt. I tear my gaze from Ben's, not wanting him to see my pain, and return them to the horizon, swallowing my grief the best I can. "We bought our house as close to the beach as we could afford because Wyatt loved to surf. When he was home, he'd wake early and hit the waves, then he'd come home to collect me and Evan and bring us down here for a couple of hours. We've sort of avoided it more than we should have. It's been nice to be back here."

I'm not sure what made me blurt all of that out, but I think I needed to bring Wyatt into the conversation—as a reminder. There's something about Ben that has me opening up to him, and I'm not sure what that is, but I need to remember where my loyalty lies. Our hands brush occasionally as we walk, so I put more space between us. If he notices, he doesn't say anything.

"Growing up in the country, I didn't live close to the ocean, so I'm not an experienced swimmer, and I can't imagine how hard it is to learn to surf. But I enjoy living as close as I do to the ocean now, so I can run or walk along the shore. I love watching the waves and tide roll in. I enjoy watching others enjoy the beauty of the water. The sunsets from my back porch are stunning, and I wouldn't give them up for anything now that I've experienced them."

Appreciation warms me to my center. I'm so grateful that he shared his experience with me instead of trying to soothe me with unnecessary platitudes.

Ben pauses and his eyes narrow as his body stiffens. When I follow his gaze, there's a young man running away from the shore, carrying a pink backpack. The woman shouting after him is obviously torn between leaving her children and running after him. Ben drops his shoes and takes off, pointing toward the guy. "Rex! Go! Guard!" His voice is firm and unyielding.

Rex's ears perk up, and in an instant, his fun-loving personality flips. He turns in the direction Ben points toward and takes off in a sprint—I don't think I've ever seen a dog run so fast. Ben's hot on his heels, and even though he's fast, he can't keep up with Rex.

Evan comes over to me. "What's going on?"

I point toward the young guy who's running away and then back toward the lady. "I think that man stole her backpack. Ben and Rex are chasing him down."

His eyes widen. "Woah. That's so cool!"

I nod in agreement. I guess when you're a cop, you're never off duty. I collect Ben's shoes, and we wander closer to the lady as we watch everything unfold.

Rex catches up to the guy and leaps onto his back, knocking him down. The backpack goes flying out of his hand, and then Rex seems to be growling at the man, his fur spiking up and ears erect. His stance looks incredibly threatening, but he's not attacking the guy—more like keeping him in place.

Quite a crowd has gathered to watch the spectacle as Ben

catches up to them, holding his phone to his ear. He doesn't seem to be in a rush to call Rex off the thief.

Rex maintains his stance, growling at the young guy while Ben talks on his phone. Then, he pockets the device and stands with his hands on his hips, assessing the situation. My heart pounds in a heavy rhythm against my ribs.

He didn't hesitate to act. Not for a single second.

The woman who had her backpack stolen, brings her hands up to her chest. "Oh, my god. That man and his dog stopped the thief."

I step a little closer. "He's a police officer. Actually, they both are."

She turns toward me, her wide eyes falling on me. "Seriously?"

I nod. "Yeah. That was incredible to watch. I've only ever seen the fun, playful side of Rex. He's amazing." *If not a little terrifying.*

When I look down at Evan, his mouth is gaping, and his eyes are wide like moons. "Rex was amazing, Mom. Did you see him?"

"I did." It was a little frightening to watch. *He's so gentle and playful with Evan, but what if he turned on him suddenly? Should I be so trusting of him with my son?*

A few minutes pass, and when a police car pulls up, Ben drags the young man to his feet. They talk for a few minutes, then an officer heads toward us with Ben and Rex, while the other stays with the thief.

Ben hands the backpack to the woman with a smile, his straight white teeth surrounded by his short, dark beard almost sparkling beneath the sun. "Your backpack, ma'am."

"Oh, thank you so much," she gushes, her cheeks flushing pink. "You're my hero." Her appreciation seems excessive, and the way she leans forward, showing her cleavage, is making *me* feel uncomfortable.

I narrow my eyes, unsure if I like the way she's looking at Ben.

Not that I have any right to feel any kind of way about anything to do with him. He's not mine.

Objectively, I know he's a handsome man. He has an impressive body, beautiful eyes, and amazing hair—among other great qualities you only learn about as you get to know him. His easy smile is definitely swoonworthy. I can see why she's looking at him like a piece of meat, and I wonder if that happens to him a lot.

Even though he's off duty, he remains professional. I don't understand this feeling that's erupted through my body. All I know is it makes me uneasy and I feel out of my element.

A hand touches my arm, and I jump, my heart leaping into my throat. "Are you all right?" Ben asks.

I was so lost in my thoughts that I hadn't noticed he'd finished with the woman. I look up into his worried gaze. "Yeah, it took me a moment to work out what was going on when you took off." I hand him his discarded shoes.

"Rex was incredible!" Evan shouts as he drops to his knees, wrapping his arms around Rex's neck and burying his face in his fur.

Now that I've seen Rex in action, I'm not as comfortable with Evan being so familiar with the dog. "Evan, I don't think it's a good idea for you to play with Rex like that. He's a working dog." My heart pounds, and the rush of blood through my body is almost louder than the waves. I'm not sure why I didn't think about it before. I guess seeing him in action made the reality of what Rex does hit home. Evan doesn't release his hold and my breathing picks up speed. "Evan. Let Rex go, please, and step away."

Creases form between Ben's eyebrows as he watches me. "Are you okay?"

I wave my arm toward his dog. "I'm just concerned. What if he attacks Evan?"

Ben shakes his head and places his hands on his hips. "He would never. He didn't attack that guy because I never gave him the instruction to do that. Hope, his training is impeccable. You have nothing to fear. Evan is completely safe. I give you my word."

Instead of being offended, he offers me a genuine promise that my son is safe. My shoulders relax, the worry releasing from my body, and exhaustion takes hold. I trust his word. I trust *him*.

"Rex only went after that guy because *I* gave him the command to. He would never take chase, attack, or guard without a command from me and me alone. Evan and you are both one hundred percent safe in his company. As is everyone who comes into contact with him, unless they're a criminal," he tells me with his stormy eyes locked on mine, putting me further at ease.

"Thank you. I hope I didn't offend you. It's just ... Evan's all I have left and—"

He holds up his hand, shaking his head slightly. "You don't need to say any more, Hope. I get it. It can be confronting when you see Rex in action for the first time, and I completely understand where you're coming from." He digs a rope out of his pocket and holds it out to Rex, who obediently sits at his feet, looking at the toy with longing. "Play."

Without pause, Rex latches onto the rope and begins a game of tug-of-war with Ben. Playful Rex is back. The muscles beneath Ben's tattoos tense and shift with the game, and as I watch them play, a small smile tugs at my lips. I can't believe he's the same dog who just went after a thief.

Rex shakes his head side to side and digs his back feet into the sand, but Ben's not giving him an inch.

"Good boy, Rex," he encourages, and Rex responds with a playful growl.

"Can I do that too?" Evan asks.

My pulse leaps, and Ben looks to me for guidance. I know I should nod or say something to give him the okay, but I can't find it in myself right now to agree to the game. I trust Ben, but what if Rex is still hyped up from the chase and he bites Evan by mistake?

Ben must read the indecision in my eyes. "Maybe another time, Ev. Give your mom some time to get used to the idea. Okay?"

Evan's bottom lip drops into a pout. "I guess." I know he's not happy, but Ben's right. I need some time to get my head around it.

"We should probably head home, Ev." His shoulders drop, but he doesn't argue. Thank goodness for small mercies.

Ben pushes his hair away from his forehead again. "I'll walk with you to your car."

We make it to the parking lot, and I put my sandals back on while Ben puts on his shoes and socks, pushing his hair back again as he stands.

"Would you like to follow us home? I can cut your hair. I have everything I need, and it would save you from coming into the salon," I offer. Shock has my mouth slamming shut and my eyes widening.

His eyes widen slightly, along with his lips, like he's as surprised as I am by my offer. "Only if it's no trouble. I don't want to put you out."

"It's no trouble at all, and it's the least I can do since you've bought us lunch twice now."

"You don't owe me anything for that. I was happy to have company." He's mentioned company a few times now. He hooks his thumbs through the loops of his jeans while I shift on my feet and wonder if he's a little lonely like I am. "Are you happy for me to bring Rex, or should I drop him home first?"

"Mom, say Rex can come too. Please."

Now I feel terrible because Ben thinks I don't trust Rex. "Please bring Rex with you. I can't bear the thought of him being left at home alone."

"If you're sure." I nod. "All right, I'll follow you home then."

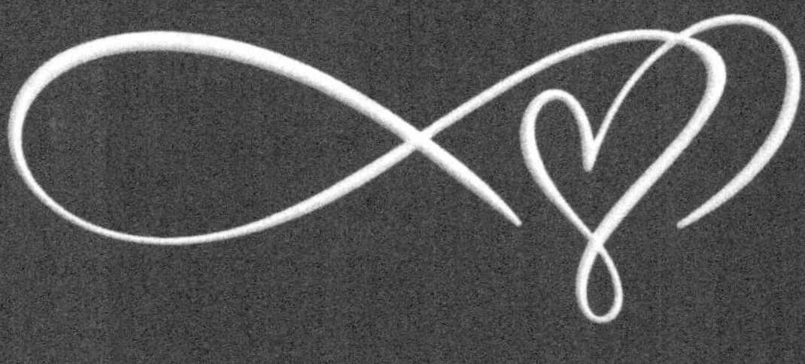

15

HOPE

We each climb into our vehicles and drive home. It's unnerving knowing a police officer is driving behind me. Keeping an eye on my speedometer, I stay a couple of miles under the speed limit and make sure I flick on my blinker well in advance. And where I would normally drive through a yellow light, I stop. When I pull into my driveway, my shoulders slump and I blow out a long breath, then stretch my neck from side to side to release the tension from my shoulders and neck—*that was so stressful*.

Ben pulls in behind me and climbs out of his car with a knowing grin. "You always that careful on the road?"

Heat flushes up through my cheeks—he knew what I was doing. "Of course."

He nods slowly with a chuckle and a raised brow. "Sure." *He totally doesn't believe me*. Rex leaps out of the car and Ben engages the locks, and after Rex sniffs around our front yard, they both meet me and Evan at the front steps.

I unlock the front door and step inside with Evan, Ben, and Rex close behind. "Evan, can you please take a dining chair out to the back porch while I get my gear?" I still haven't gotten around to buying chairs to match the outdoor table.

He heads to the kitchen and grabs a chair while Ben locks the front door behind us. Once I have everything set up on the back porch, I gesture for Ben to take a seat. "Evan, can you please fill one of the ice cream containers we have in the bottom of the pantry with water for Rex."

"Okay, Mom." He strolls back inside to look after Rex.

Once Ben's seated, I run my fingers through his hair. It's so soft. I love hair. I've loved it since I was a little girl and used my dolls as clients. There's something soothing about the strands sliding through my fingers. "Do you want me to follow what you already have here, but make it shorter?"

He runs his fingers through the strands, colliding with mine, sending tingles fizzing along my skin. "Yeah, that'd be great."

"Do you know how low you have the clippers on the sides? That'll give me an idea of how much to take off," I ask as I continue to run my fingers through the soft, dark brown strands. I can't seem to stop myself.

Gosh, he smells great this close.

I shake my thoughts away. I should not be noticing how great he smells.

"Usually a two."

I nod. "That looks about right."

Evan brings Rex back outside and they play in the backyard, with Rex following Evan around like they've grown up together. Their bond blossomed fast, and I love seeing my boy so happy and carefree.

I fasten the cape around his neck, ensuring it covers his clothes, then grab my clippers, attach the number two guard, and collect my comb. "You have gorgeous, thick hair." A lot of women would love to have this sort of thickness.

"Uh, thanks." His strong, tanned hands rest over the top of the cape on his thighs, and I watch him curl his thick fingers to make fists, turning his knuckles white.

Starting at the bottom, I comb the hair into the clippers and work my way around the base of his hairline and upward until I reach his ears. Once I'm happy with that, I wet the longer strands left on top and exchange the clippers for scissors to blend the longer length with the shorter sides. I work my way around his head, ensuring I keep the length consistent, but getting longer as I get closer to the top.

Moving around to the front of his body, he opens his legs wider so I can slip in between them, my outer thighs touching his. When I glance down at his face, the muscles in his jaw clench, and I watch him swallow harshly. My pulse pounds in my veins as my blood rushes through my body, and his eyes seem to be locked at the base of my throat.

Can he see how fast my heart's beating?

My response to him is a little embarrassing, and I know I'm blushing because of the heat in my cheeks. I've never experienced this type of reaction to a man other than Wyatt. I cut men's hair all the time, and I've *never*, not once, felt the flutter in my stomach like I do right now.

What the hell is happening to me?

Shame swiftly floods through me, drowning me in guilt and making my stomach sink like the Titanic.

I'm a married woman. I'm a married woman. I'm a married woman.

I chant the words over and over again to remind myself I shouldn't be looking at Ben or reacting to his proximity. I made a promise to Wyatt, and I intend to keep it. Ben's here because he's Evan's friend. I'm just doing him a favor to thank him for being so good to my son.

The son I had with Wyatt.

Wyatt, my husband.

Taking a step back, I swallow past the guilt lodged in my throat. I lift my eyes back to his hair and work through the strands, using the comb and my fingers to gather and measure the length before I cut each section, keeping things professional and squashing the attraction I feel to him.

I'm utterly mortified.

If Ben could read my thoughts, I'm certain he'd run a mile—and then Evan would miss out on having such a great role model in his life. Without Wyatt in the picture, my priority is ensuring Evan has good men in his life he can turn to. Wyatt's friends—Shane and Nix—have been fantastic. My brother Cole lives too far away to offer any support, but Dad and Wyatt's dad are regular fixtures in his life, which is a blessing. Another stable man to provide guidance would be amazing, especially since I've asked Shane to step back.

Pressure lands on my hips, and I jump a little. Looking down, I find Ben's warm hands causing the pressure where they rest gently on my slight curves, as he looks up at me with furrows across his forehead.

"Are you okay?"

When I raise my eyes to his, I notice small patches of amber near the pupils in his concerned gray gaze. So pretty.

What is going on with me?

His hands are so big. So warm. So *terrifying*.

I swallow, then lick my dry lips, and put on an air of nonchalance. "Yeah," I say, but the single word comes out raspy and on a shaky breath, which is not convincing at all.

He doesn't remove his hands, and neither of us looks away. For a few long moments, we're caught in each other's gaze. My heart beats like a drum—thick and heavy. A pulsing rhythm that sends my blood gushing through my system and into my ears. My eyes drop to his lips and his eyes drop to mine. The heat up the side of my neck intensifies.

I'm the first to look away. Returning my focus to his hair, and the task, I desperately try to gain control of my hormones and thoughts—thoughts wholly inappropriate for a married woman.

Finally, he removes his hands, placing them back on his thighs.

I *should* feel relief at the reprieve, instead I feel cold and left adrift. Everything's so confusing. Maybe it would have been better if he'd come into the salon. It wouldn't feel so intimate. It would be safer.

Evan's feet pound on the steps, followed by the click of Rex's nails, as they make their way toward us. "Mom, can you cut my hair like Ben's?"

I turn toward my son with eyebrows halfway up my forehead. "You hate getting your hair cut. I always have to bribe you."

He drops his head, looking at his feet. "Yeah, well. Ben's hair is cool." He looks back up at me. "If you cut mine like that, I wouldn't mind so much."

I'm not sure I'm ready to change his boyish hairstyle, but ultimately, it's his hair, and his decision. "Okay, I'm almost finished here, and you guys can swap places."

"Thanks, Mom."

"Can you please bring out the lemon tea and three glasses? I'm sure Ben would like a drink."

"Okay." Evan heads inside, and the screen door bangs shut behind him.

I shake my head with a chuckle and look down at Ben. "Please only ever use your influence over him for good and not evil."

He draws his finger across his heart and then repeats the process in the opposite direction. "Promise." He winks at me, sending a flutter through my stomach, and shows his perfect teeth when he grins. All he needs is a pair of dimples, and he'd be completely irresistible.

I fidget with his hair, getting it just right, then clip around his ears and along his hairline to tidy everything up. I dust the chopped hair away from the back of his neck, ensuring I get every last strand. "Okay. I'm done. There's a mirror in the bathroom if you'd like to take a look."

He waves me off. "I trust you."

I wince when I feel a hair splinter stuck beneath my fingernail, an unfortunate hazard of the job. Pinching my finger, I search for the offending hair.

Ben moves closer, taking my finger between his and studying it closely, sending tingles racing like fire up my arm. "What's wrong?"

"Nothing. Just a hair splinter." I pull my hand back and direct all my focus on removing the tiny hair to block my unwanted reaction to the man standing too close to me. Suddenly, the porch feels too small as he towers over me, and I take a step back to keep space between us. In an attempt to regain my equilibrium, I close my eyes as I suck my finger into my mouth to soothe the sting.

My eyes snap open and my lungs deflate when Evan steps out with a jug and three glasses, breaking the tension. Filled with relief, I take them from him to place on the outdoor table so I can pour us each a drink. We each grab a glass, and Evan sits in the chair Ben vacated.

"All right. Are you ready?"

He nods eagerly. "Sure am."

"Are you sure? Your hair will be a lot shorter than it is now." I study his face, looking for any sign he's having second thoughts, but come up blank.

"Yep."

I tip my head to the side. "Okay, then."

Picking up my clippers, I repeat the process with his hair and as his locks fall at my feet, sadness washes over me because I know he's going to look less like a little boy and more like a teenager. Something I'm not ready for. *At all*. I feel like I've missed a lot of the last six years because I was too busy drowning in my grief and barely surviving. And now it's too late to get those years back.

He sits still as I shape and cut his hair, and the second I'm finished, he bolts inside to look at himself in the mirror. He races back out a few minutes later with an enormous grin and throws his arms around me. He's behaving more like the old Evan used to, not the moody boy he's become since he started middle school.

"Thanks, Mom. It looks awesome." His excitement diminishes a little as he turns to Ben, looking unsure. "Do you wanna read my stories?"

Ben's eyebrows rise, and I can read the surprise in his expression.

16

THE RHYTHM OF MY HEART SKIPS, AND MY BROWS RISE at the privilege he's bestowing on me. My chest fills with warmth at his willingness to share his stories with me—stories only his mom knows about.

"Evan, I'm sure Ben has things he needs to do at home," Hope says softly, running her hand over the top of his fresh cut. The heartbreak of cutting his hair was plain to see on her face, but she fulfilled her son's wishes over her own because she's a fantastic mom.

There's no way I'd turn Evan down when he's sharing a part of himself he doesn't share with anyone else. "I'd love to."

"Thanks, Ben. You wanna come up to my room?"

"How about you bring your books down here?" Hope suggests.

"Okay." He rushes inside, and Hope brings a broom and another chair outside. I take the broom from her and help sweep up the hair while she cleans and puts away her equipment. By the time we're finished, Evan returns with several notebooks. "Which one do you want to start with?"

"How about you select one or two for Ben to read for now?"

Hope tells him. What she doesn't realize is that I'll read every single story if it means I can stay longer.

When she was standing between my legs—so close that I could see the blue-green striations of her irises and watch her pulse flutter rapidly at the base of her sexy throat—it made me never want to leave.

As much as I think it pains her, I sense she's equally attracted to me. The way she flushed pink and the breathiness of her voice were a dead giveaway. It's been six years for her, and I wonder if she's ever considered dating. Our conversation from a couple of weeks ago suggests she probably hasn't, which means I need to take things slow.

He shuffles through the books and sets one aside, then shuffles through them some more, pulling out a second one. He picks them up and hands them to me. "I think these two are my best."

Hope smiles, then heads toward the back door. "I'll leave you two to it." She disappears inside, and I miss her instantly, but return my attention to Evan and the gift he's offering me.

"All right, give me a quick overview of each story, and I'll choose which one to read first." His eyes brighten as he explains each story to me. I hold up the blue notebook. "Okay, I'll start with this one."

Evan can't contain his excitement as I flip the cover open, get comfortable, and start to read. Rex rests obediently at our feet, and Evan leans his chin on his fist, watching me. His brown eyes bore into the side of my head, and self-consciousness makes my neck itch, but I push through the discomfort and continue to read.

It's a terrific story. I can tell it's written by a kid, but it's fantastic—better than I expected. I lift my eyes to Evan and smile at him.

"What did you think?"

I raise my eyebrows. "I have to be completely honest. I wasn't expecting much, but I really enjoyed it. You have great characters, and the tension kept me turning the pages. I wanted to find out if the killer was who I thought—and if they'd catch her. It was the perfect length to keep my attention."

His eyes widen. "Really?" He can't hide his surprise.

I nod. "Yeah, really." I place it on the table and grab the second book. "Is it okay if I read this one too?"

"Yeah."

As the sun sinks closer to the horizon, I open Evan's second story and lose myself in the world he's created. The lead detective is the same; he's just solving a different murder this time. The story is equally engrossing as the last one, and I'm eager to see how it ends.

Delicious smells waft from inside, and my stomach rumbles in response. Rex raises his head and sniffs the air where he rests between me and Evan. Tangerine and rose colors paint the sky, and the air is considerably cooler when I finally close the second story.

"Evan, I dunno what to say, man. You write fantastic stories. Do you think you'll write for a living?"

He scoots closer to me. "Do you think my stories are good enough? I mean, Mom says they are, but she's my mom; she has to say they're good."

I shrug. "As I said before, I'm not much of a reader, so I'm not really an expert. But I didn't want to stop reading and if they can make me"—I jab my chest with my thumb—"keep reading, they must be pretty great. Don't you think? And I don't think your mom says stuff she doesn't mean."

"Well, yeah, I guess so." He grins at me. "Thanks for reading my stories and liking them, Ben." He collects his books and heads inside to put them away.

I guess that means my time is up. My chest pinches at the idea.

Reluctantly, I stand and tap the side of my leg. "C'mon, Rex. Time to go."

He looks up at me, tilting his head to the side as his ears twitch. Even he can tell I don't want to leave. I carry the dining chair inside and place it at the table.

Hope's cutting cabbage at the counter, and whatever she has

cooking smells incredible. I watch her slender fingers wrapped around the knife as she slices into the vegetable, noting her wedding rings on her left hand as she listens intently to Evan. "Ben thought my stories were good. He thinks I'm good enough to be a writer!"

She gives him a proud, genuine smile. "I've told you that, but you never believed me."

He shrugs. "Well, yeah. You have to say my stuff is good ... you're my mom."

Hope drops the knife and jabs her hands into her hips. "Are you calling me a liar?"

It takes a second for Evan to realize what she said. I can tell the moment her words sink in, when his eyebrows shoot high above his wide eyes. "What? No! I never said that."

Hope giggles. It's such a beautiful sound. "I was kidding, Ev."

The relief on his face is instant as his shoulders drop from around his ears. He runs his hand over the top of his head, then pulls it away. "My hair's super short now."

Hope bites her bottom lip, and I can tell she's trying to hold back a laugh. Her eyes sparkle like the sun glinting off the ocean, and in this moment, she looks so damn beautiful my chest aches.

The last thing I want to do is leave, but Hope's preparing dinner, so I should get out of their hair. Knowing I'm going home to an empty house fills me with a sense of loneliness I've pushed aside for too long.

"Uh, thanks for the haircut and for sharing your afternoon with me and Rex. We should get going so you can get on with your evening."

"No! Stay for dinner," Evan almost shouts, then looks at his mom. "They can stay for dinner, right, Mom?"

Hope's eyes snap up to me, and a blush spreads up her neck. "Uh, sure. If he'd like to, but he might have things to do or a date or something, Ev."

My eyebrows rise and my neck heats. *Was she fishing for information?*

My chest expands with a relieved breath that I don't have to leave just yet. "No date tonight or any other night." Hope's mouth drops open a little and she lowers her eyes back to the chopping board. "I'd love to stay for dinner."

Without looking at me, she says, "Great. Evan, can you please set the table on the back porch for three?"

He does as asked and sets the table for dinner without an argument.

"Can I help?" I move around the counter until I'm standing beside Hope. I can't stay away from her. It's as if I'm the ocean and she's the shore.

She lifts her gaze to me, uncertainty written across her face, so I step back a little to give her some space. I watch her swallow, then lift my eyes to study her. Her features are so fine, like a ballerina's, with pale skin, a sprinkling of freckles across her nose and cheeks that remind me of cookie crumbs, and a sun-kissed pink tinge from this afternoon's walk along the beach across the same area. I pause on her pale pink lips with the perfect bow, wishing I could lean forward and press a kiss to them. I bet they're softer than silk. They look even more perfect when she smiles.

She tears her gaze from mine and points toward the sweet potatoes on the counter. "Would you mind peeling those and cutting them into wedges?"

"Sure." I wash my hands at the sink, noticing the rubber gloves she must use when she washes the dishes. She digs into a drawer, grabbing a peeler, and I get to work. "What smells so good?"

Using her elbow to point to the pressure cooker on the other counter, she says, "I'm cooking pork in barbecue sauce, so we can have pulled pork sliders, coleslaw, and a side of sweet potato wedges."

My stomach grumbles. "Oh, man. That sounds so good!" I widen my eyes in delight.

"It's one of my favorite dinners," Evan adds.

Rex raises his head, tilting it to the side. "Yeah, buddy. You're gonna miss out, but I'll give you a treat later."

Hope bites her plump lower lip and looks down at Rex. "I have some leftover roast chicken and potatoes in the fridge. Will he eat that? I don't want him to go without."

Her concern for Rex warms my heart. "That would be appreciated. I can always replace it tomorrow."

She waves off my offer. "Don't worry about it. He deserves it for his bravery today."

I was worried after she expressed her concern about Rex this afternoon. It would've been terrible if she couldn't move past it and feel safe with him, but it seems she's okay with him. Her acceptance feels as though she trusts me—at least a little—and that's all I need for now. A woman like Hope, who's been hurt so deeply, won't trust easily, so each time I earn a little of it, I'll celebrate the win.

"Evan, can you please take a shower, wash your hair, and get changed so we don't have that wet dog smell at the dinner table."

He leaves the room without an argument—something I would have done when I was his age—leaving Hope and me alone in the kitchen. "He's a really great kid."

"Thanks. We had a rough patch there for a little while. His attitude stunk, and he didn't seem to care about anything. I think it was a turning point for both of us when you brought him home from the gas station. I hate to say it, because I can't believe he did what he did, but it's like I have my son back." She opens the fridge and brings out a bottle of wine, holding it up to me. "Would you like a drink?"

"Sure."

She pours two glasses and slides one across the counter. "He was only five when we lost Wyatt, and I recently discovered he's been worried that he's going to forget his dad." Hope takes a delicate sip of her wine, and I mirror her, tasting the crisp sweetness.

I'm not much of a wine drinker, but I'll never say no to sharing anything with her.

"Do you talk about Wyatt with him very often?"

Her eyes slide away as she swallows another mouthful of wine. "I haven't been the best parent. I've been too overwhelmed by my grief over what we've lost. He didn't feel he could talk to me about his dad for fear of upsetting me. But I made a promise to him that things would change, and we've both been doing better. I've made a concerted effort to talk about Wyatt, and I think it's helped ... both of us." She twists the stem of her glass between her slender fingers. "It hasn't been as hard to talk about him as I thought it would be." She raises and drops a smooth shoulder. "It's been kinda nice."

"I bet. I know this is nowhere the same as your loss, but I lost one of my best friends nine years ago, and it really helped to have Sebastian, my other best friend, to talk with about her. It helped keep our memories of her alive."

Hope's gaze fills with compassion as she moves closer and reaches across the counter to rest her hand on mine. I flip my hand over and link our fingers together, dropping my eyes to where we're connected as my blood fizzles beneath her touch. The connection between us is so strong that I lose my breath for a moment. When I glance back at her face, she has creases between her brows, and her eyes are fixated on our joined hands, like she can feel the same connection I do.

Slowly, her gaze rises to mine, and I watch her throat move as she swallows. I expect her to pull her hand away, but she doesn't. She says nothing, but she doesn't need to. I can feel her compassion and empathy filling the space between us. It's like she's absorbing my pain and giving me back a warm hug without wrapping her arms around me. She understands. Just as I understand her pain, even though they're not on the same level. I'm not sure how long we stay like that, but I don't feel the need to add to our conversation right now.

"What was her name?" Hope murmurs as she squeezes my hand, and I pray she doesn't let go because I'm not ready to give this moment up.

My lips tip up a little. "Tahlia." My smile falls away. "We were eighteen and had just finished our senior year when everything went to shit. We'd been best friends since elementary school. Everyone called us The Three Musketeers." I chuckle dryly. "We saw each other every day and never fought or tired of each other's company. We were there for her when she lost her dad—and for Sebastian when he lost his mom in a factory fire."

She presses her lips together, her eyes soft and warm with a glassy sheen to them. They've never looked more beautiful. "Can I ask what happened?"

I lift my glass to my mouth and take a sip of the cool wine. "Sure." It's not as hard to talk about since so much time has passed. "It started out small. Little things that she'd brush off with a laugh and we thought nothing of it. But looking back, they were warning signs that shouldn't have been ignored. Maybe ... maybe if we'd paid attention, things would have been different for her. I don't know." My free hand grows clammy, so I wipe it on the denim covering my thigh and draw in a deep breath. As much as I've come to terms with Tahlia's death, losing her still hurts. "She was incredible with science and math. Her brain was quick and accurate, like a calculator. She was planning to go to college to study structural engineering." Hope's eyes widen. "Tahlia was the smartest girl in our year in both subjects, but at the end of our senior year, she struggled with calculations. Things she'd normally solve in a few seconds took much longer. She'd laugh it off and put it down to the stress of finals, and we didn't think to question it. Then she started to bump into doors and desks and lose her balance going up and down stairs. She even sideswiped a car in the parking lot one day, and even though she laughed it off, we knew it shook her up."

Hope squeezes my hand again in quiet support and moves a

little closer, her thigh brushing against mine. "If you wanna stop, you don't have to tell me anymore. I don't want to push."

I drop my eyes to the counter for a moment to gather my composure, because this next part is brutal. My heart pounds double time, sending my blood rushing through my veins. The whoosh of my life force pulses loudly in my ears. "I haven't shared this story with anyone else, but I'd like to share it with you, if that's okay?"

She nods. "Of course."

"Anyway, one night she was watching TV with her mom, and she lost the feeling in her left leg—like a terrible case of pins and needles. She couldn't put any weight on it, but eventually, the feeling disappeared, and she thought nothing of it. Then, about a week later, we were hanging out at my place and her speech became slurred like she was drunk, and then she convulsed and passed out. It scared the shit out of Sebastian and me." Hope's gasp rings out like a gunshot in the quiet kitchen. "We called an ambulance and her mom, and they transported her to the hospital. At first, the doctors thought she'd had a stroke, so they ordered special scans, but instead of a blood clot, they found three huge tumors in her brain."

"Oh, god." Hope's slender fingers tighten around mine, and pain radiates from her, hitting me like a tsunami. I silently absorb it as the waves crash over me, tracing her features slowly with my eyes.

"There wasn't much they could do for her. She was having treatment to shrink the tumors and steroids to reduce the symptoms, hoping it would extend her life. A month later, she had a catastrophic stroke and passed away a few days later." I shake my head as I think back to that time. We were shattered. "The loss devastated us. She was so young, so smart. Funny and loyal. It felt like a part of me died with her. If her mom and Sebastian hadn't been there for me, I think I'd still be lost." I couldn't rely on my parents to be there for me. They were always too caught up in themselves and each other.

Hope's shoulders slump. "Life's so unfair sometimes."

"Yep. They say only the good die young, and I think I believe that. She was the best out of the three of us."

The air fryer beeps as Evan's footsteps sound on the stairs, dragging me from my memories. Hope quickly untangles her fingers from mine and wipes beneath her eyes, turning away from me, leaving me feeling cold, lost, and disoriented. I didn't plan to share my loss with her; she's already drowning in grief for her husband and the father of her son. She didn't need to know about mine, but it felt cathartic to share it with someone who understands the devastation of loss.

"Is dinner ready yet?" Evan asks as he steps into the kitchen, looking between me and his mom, a frown marring his forehead.

Hope shares one of her fake smiles when she looks at him. "It sure is. I'll just make the sliders."

I slip off the stool. "Can I help with anything?"

She glances at me over her shoulder. "You can grab the chicken and potatoes out of the fridge for Rex. Evan, grab an empty ice cream container for Ben, please."

We each set about our tasks and, in a short amount of time, we're slipping into our seats at the table outside, ready to dig into the delicious meal Hope prepared. "Thanks for the invitation to dinner. This looks fantastic."

"Mom's the best cook," Evan declares proudly, his eyes bright.

Hope chuckles quietly. "I don't know about that."

I swallow a seasoned sweet potato wedge. "I dunno. This tastes pretty great."

She tucks a long, curly lock behind her ear, exposing pink splotches along her sexy throat. Her lips tip up at the corners and her eyes crinkle slightly. "Thanks."

We eat quietly for a while, enjoying the meal too much to talk.

Hope tops off our wine, and as our initial hunger is somewhat abated, the conversation begins again.

Hope takes a sip of her wine and places the glass back on the table. "Does stuff like today happen often?" I tilt my head to the side and narrow my eyes, trying to figure out what she's asking. "You know ... chasing after people when you're not working?"

I finish chewing the food in my mouth and lean back in my chair, hooking my arm behind the wooden back. "I wouldn't say it happens often. It's happened maybe a dozen times during my career, but when it does, I can't turn my back on the crime I witness. Technically, I'm always on duty. I swore to serve and protect, and I take that vow seriously. It's why I became a cop. I like to help people and keep them safe. It's what gets me out of bed in the morning and gives me purpose."

"Do you think I should be a cop, Mom?"

I turn to Evan. "What happened to writing?"

"I can do that too. You don't work every day. I can write on my days off," he shoots back like he's had all the time in the world to think about it.

Hope's already pale complexion lightens further beneath the porch light. "Uh." Her eyes flick up to mine. "Why would you want to do that?"

"So I can help people like Ben does," he answers casually, like he didn't just flip my heart around in my chest. "It was really cool what he did today." Warmth flows through my body, starting from my chest and making its way to my extremities. Hope turns toward me, her eyes soft and glistening.

17

HOPE

I MOAN AT THE SWIPE OF WYATT'S TONGUE THROUGH MY throbbing pussy. With my thighs resting over his strong shoulders, I push my hips up to press harder against his mouth, seeking the friction I know he can give to me. The unexpected rasp of his short beard creates more sensation than I'm used to and I frown at the foreign feeling.

Perspiration coats my skin and my hair sticks to the side of my face as my temperature builds to the level of an inferno. My heart races and my muscles tighten as I grow closer to my release. He's so good at this. His fingers pump in and out of me, feathering against the spot he knows so well. Another soft moan escapes and my eyes roll back in my head as sparks fly through my blood and I explode in a supernova of white light.

When I slide my fingers back into Wyatt's short hair, something feels off. The texture's wrong. It's too soft, slightly too thick. The shoulders beneath my thighs are somehow broader, opening me wider and stretching my hips. I narrow my eyes in concentration as awareness slides over me that the fingers inside my body feel thicker than what I'm used to. I drop my eyes down my body to work out what's going on when instead of warm brown eyes, I'm greeted with playful gray ones.

My eyes snap open, and I jolt. Fast, uneven breaths escape as my already fragile heart pounds loudly in my ears, and I furiously kick away the tangled sheets wrapped around my sweaty body. My pussy throbs while tears of despair flood my eyes.

The deep ache in my chest cleaves open with each gut-wrenching sob that leaves my body, and I don't know whether to hold my chest to keep it intact or cover my face to hide my shame.

I turn my head and drop my eyes to the empty side of the bed. Wyatt's side. I still don't sleep there. I don't know why. It's not like he's ever coming back.

Guilt wraps around me like a python, crushing me from the inside out, and I drop back to the bed, fold over, and make myself as small as I can. The muscles in my back and across my stomach tense with each sob that shudders through me, and I wrap my arms around my knees, pressing them tighter to my chest. Like I can hide from what just happened.

I'm a dirty cheater.

A fresh flood of tears track down my cheeks at the revelation.

Devastation at losing him all over again builds from my core, spiraling outward until I feel it in every cell of my body.

How could I dream of another man?

How could I break my promise?

Overloaded with too many destructive thoughts, my mind shuts down as I stare into the blackness of my bedroom, curled into a ball with salty tears painting my cheeks. The darkness hiding my shame from the light, but not from me.

"Why did you have to leave us?" I whisper into his pillow.

Desolation fills my heart, spilling across my bed, and oozing across my bedroom.

I OPEN the door to Mom, just like I do every other weekday

morning, except today I can't look her in the eye for fear she'll see my shame.

"Morning, sweetheart," she sings, then kisses my cheek as she passes.

"Morning, Mom." I push the door closed behind her, then pull it back open when I spot Dad climbing the porch steps. "Morning, Dad."

He wraps his arms around me, tugging me in tight to his body, and I wonder if he can tell that I cheated on my husband. "Morning, sweetie."

"What are you doing here?"

He tilts his head to the side as he slips off his boots. "Can't a guy stop by to say hello to his daughter and grandson once in a while?"

"Well, yeah, but it's odd to see you when you're normally at work."

He shrugs as he steps past me. "Felt like saying hello. Felt like a day off."

I smile. "Well ... hello."

He chuckles as we head toward the kitchen where Mom's chatting with Evan. Her wide eyes lift to me, and a devious grin stretches across her face. "Really? He stayed and watched *Guardians of the Galaxy* with you guys on Saturday night?"

"Yeah, and Rex fell asleep with his head on my feet. It was so cool."

Mom giggles and plucks at the longer strands on top of his head. "I love this new style."

Oh, god.

"Yeah, it's exactly the same as Ben's," he says excitedly, not realizing the fuel he's adding to Mom's imagination. Her eyes snap up to me, sparkling with delight, and her mouth forms a small *O*. "You should have seen Rex and Ben chase down a thief at the beach after we had lunch at the *Blue Goose*."

Geez, Ev. Shut up already. He never talks this much when it's just the two of us. Now he's decided to share every moment of his Saturday with Mom and Dad. Seriously?

"Ev, have you packed your backpack for school?" I widen my eyes, waiting for his response.

His eyebrows scrunch together, and he looks at me like I've lost my ever-loving mind. "Well, no. I just woke up."

"Well, get ready for school. I've gotta go." *Before Mom starts her inquisition.* I can't deal with it this morning. I had to put on extra concealer this morning to hide the dark circles beneath my eyes.

I grab my coffee and kiss Ev on top of his head. "Be good for Nanna and Grandad, and have an awesome day at school." I widen my eyes. "Behave."

He rolls his eyes. "I've been good, Mom. Promise."

"Keep it up! I'll see you at our usual pick up spot after school. And don't be late; you have soccer practice this afternoon." I lean into Mom. "Thanks, Mom. Have a great day."

"Oh, I will." She grins, and I can tell by the excitement in her eyes—and the tone of her voice—that she's made assumptions she has no business making.

Dad wraps his arm around my shoulder and whispers in my ear. "Your mother is going to be unbearable today. I can tell." He kisses my temple. "Have a good day, sweetie."

I smile at him. "Thanks, Dad. You too." I step away and grab my purse. "Don't work too hard on your day off." I'm sure Mom has a list of things to do waiting for him at home.

He jabs his thumb to his chest and widens his eyes. "Me? Never!"

I make my escape out the front door and exhale a long breath. My hand curls around the door handle of my car, and the tightness across my shoulders releases.

"Sweetheart?"

My muscles lock tight again as I open my door. Mom steps up

close and leans her arm on top of my door, ensuring I can't close her out. "It sounds as though Evan really enjoys Ben's company."

I nod. "Yeah, he does. They've become fast friends." I toss my purse across to the passenger seat and drop into the driver's seat, situating my coffee in the cup holder.

"That's nice." She pauses and I slide my key into the ignition and start the engine. "And … uh … have you made a new friend, too?"

I shrug. I don't know what Ben and I are building, but I'm uncomfortable with the way he infiltrated my dream. We connected in a way I haven't connected with anyone before. Our common experience with devastating loss and grief created a bond I wasn't expecting. My already mangled heart broke for him and the loss he experienced at a young age. "I've gotta go, Mom. I'm gonna be late."

She draws her mouth into a tight line. "Okay, sweetheart. Have a great day. See you tomorrow."

"Thanks. You too." I reverse out of my driveway and pull onto the street, keeping my face averted. She knows me too well, and I'm sure my face reveals the guilt I feel over last night's dream.

Rationally, I know that after six years, nobody would think badly of me if I moved on with my life, but my heart won't let go. I promised my heart, body, and soul to Wyatt to keep forever. It was a promise I took seriously, and until recently, thought I'd have no problem keeping. However, a certain gray-eyed man with a kind heart has caught my attention—and he's starting to get under my skin.

I have no problem with him spending time with Ev, but I clearly need to put some boundaries in place.

18

HOPE

I UNLOCK THE BACK DOOR, TURN OFF THE ALARM, AND turn on the recessed ceiling lights, creating pretty reflections on the gold trim decorating the mirrors and walls. Then I turn on the matching gold pendant lights, stow my purse in my locker in the lunchroom, and head to the front of the salon.

Taking a long drink of my coffee, I log into the computer and check the bookings for the day. We're all booked back-to-back, which is not unusual for us, and it's exactly what I need today, so I'm thankful. I need to stay busy so I can keep my mind from the dream I had last night … and Ben.

Frowning, I walk down the short hallway to the laundry room to swap out the towels in the washer and dryer, loading another pile of dark teal towels that match the paint on the salon walls. Picking up the first dry towel, I fold it in half twice, then stack it on the shelf. I continue the mindless work, trying to sort through my muddled thoughts.

His understanding of my loss made so much more sense after he told me about his best friend, Tahlia. At any age, it would have been horrific to witness a friend convulsing and then to find out they had terminal brain cancer, but at eighteen? I shake my head in disbelief. I can't fathom what it was like to watch her deteriorate and pass away. An experience like that isn't something you quickly forget, especially since they seemed as close as two friends could be.

I wonder if they were ever tempted to take their friendship to another level? Stop it! You're not supposed to be thinking about him. I sigh and run my hands through the front of my hair and grasp a handful at the roots. His playful gaze flashes in my mind, sending heat pooling between my thighs and flooding up my neck. Shit!

Shaking the thoughts from my head, I turn on the sound system and choose a playlist for the day. Scanning the selections, I settle on the Patrick Droney mix. His raspy voice sounds over the speakers as I ensure we have enough cash in the drawer.

"Morning!" Sophie calls as she heads toward the lunchroom.

"Morning," I call back.

She comes back out, carrying a pile of freshly folded towels, and places them on each cart, ready to be used. She then adds the dark teal capes we use to protect our clients' clothes. Once she's stocked the carts, she restocks the towels at the basins, and then she comes over to me.

"How was your weekend?"

I drop my head and lick my lips while my stomach free falls. "It was okay. How was yours?"

She tilts her head to the side, then focuses on the computer, clicking the mouse to wake it up. "You okay?"

"Yeah. Why?"

She lifts her eyes to my face and studies me. "You look tired."

"Oh." An awkward chuckle escapes my lips. "Had trouble sleeping last night."

The back door slams shut, and Lucy and Savannah chat as they walk through to the lunchroom.

"Any reason?" She asks the question like it's no big deal if I answer or not, but I know the girls here worry about me. I glance away from her and swallow past my confession. I'd really like to get someone's take on my dream and if they consider it cheating, but it's so personal. She lays her hand on my forearm, concern filling her eyes. "You can talk to me."

Lucy and Savannah join us and immediately pick up on the mood. "What's going on?" Lucy asks.

Sophie shifts her gaze to her. "I was just asking Hope why she had trouble sleeping."

Lucy and Savannah move closer. "Are you okay, hon?" Savannah asks.

It's such a private thing ... but perhaps they can give me some perspective. I feel like such a dirty cheater, but maybe it's natural for something like that to happen. It's not like they've experienced loss like I have, but I desperately need to talk to someone ... to get this burden of guilt off my chest.

"You know this is a safe space, right?" Lucy reminds me.

I nod, then lick my lips. "I sorta don't know where to start, but last night I had a sexy dream about Wyatt and me." The girls grin and wiggle their eyebrows up and down.

"Oh, I like the sound of this," Sophie adds as she leans her hip against the counter, getting more comfortable.

"It's not like I haven't had them before, you know ... but this time it was different."

"Good different or bad different?" Lucy asks.

"Bad different." I scrubbed my body so hard in the shower this morning because I felt so dirty. I'm surprised I didn't take off a layer of skin.

They move in a little closer, worry shrouding their features. "What happened, hon?"

"Well, Wyatt made me ... you know ... with his mouth and fingers"—my neck heats like it's sunburned—"but when I looked down, it was *Ben* looking up at me."

Lucy's mouth drops open, but it's Savannah that speaks. "Ben? The cop who brought Evan home?"

I nod.

Their eyebrows shoot up, and it would almost be comical if I weren't so distressed by the events of last night. "I ... I think it's because we spent a lot of time together on Saturday. After he bought us lunch, I offered to cut his hair at my place, and then one thing led to another and he ended up staying for dinner. Then, we watched a movie with Evan, and I couldn't help but notice how fantastic he smelled and how soft his hair is. Oh, and he has really nice arms and a tight butt. He smiles really nice, and his gray eyes have this amber color close to the pupils." I point to my eye, unable to stop the word vomit, and while the girls appear shocked, I'm drowning in embarrassment. "Now I feel like I cheated on Wyatt because I had a sex dream about another man," I rush to add.

"You cut his hair?" Lucy clarifies with wide eyes. "At your house?"

I nod. "Well, he'd bought us lunch after Evan and I stayed behind at the shelter to help him bathe the dogs. He kept brushing his hair away from his face, and I ... well, I thought it was the least I could do. He's been amazing with Evan. Ben's so kind and he's been so compassionate and understanding. And then Evan wanted me to cut his hair in the same style as Ben's." Their eyes soften. "And he read a couple of Evan's stories and made a big fuss about how well-written they are, and it was close to dinnertime by the time he finished." I shake my head as I remember how eager Evan was to continue spending time with Ben. "Evan didn't want to let him go, so he asked if he could stay for dinner. It's like he's so desperate for a man's attention ... and Ben's more than happy to give it to him. I couldn't say no." I draw in a long breath. That was a lot to get off my chest.

"And then you dreamed about him last night?" Savannah asks softly.

I nod slowly, my tongue too tangled to let any more words come out.

"Well, I think it's completely normal," Sophie says with confidence. "He's spending time with your son, who you love to pieces, and it's making him happy, which makes you happy. I think it's to be expected that he'll morph into other areas of your thoughts and psyche." She rubs her hand across my shoulder. "He's the first guy that you've spent any time with since you lost Wyatt."

"Shane used to come around a lot. Did you ever have dreams about him?" Lucy asks, then takes a sip of her coffee like the question she asked wasn't a bombshell.

I shake my head. "Nope. I know he's handsome, but he's been nothing more than Wyatt's friend helping us out. I've never ... uh ... never felt that way about him." I swallow the boulder in my throat, cursing my suddenly dry mouth. "I ... uh ... find Ben incredibly attractive. And the way he treats Evan is so appealing." My eyes burn, and my nose tingles. My stomach free falls with my confession, and I cover my face with my hands.

"Awww, hon. This was bound to happen at some point," Savannah sympathizes as she tugs me in for a hug.

"But I promised Wyatt forever. I shouldn't find anyone attractive. I shouldn't have sexy dreams about a man who isn't my husband. It's not right." I wrap my arms around my middle.

Savannah studies me closely with deep creases between her brows. "Do you honestly believe Wyatt would want you and Evan to be alone for the rest of your life?"

"I promised him."

"*Until death*, Hope," Lucy murmurs.

"Yeah, well, I'm not dead," I snap.

The girls roll their eyes, and I feel their patience slipping away. "You're being ridiculous now. We know how much you love Wyatt, but there's no way he would hold you to that promise now that he's no longer here," Lucy tells me. "He would want you to find someone to love you and Evan. Someone to look after you both and make you happy."

Logically, I know they're right. But my heart doesn't work on logic.

"Let me put it to you this way. If you passed away and Wyatt was left behind, would you want him to stay true to his promises to you?" Savannah asks.

I open my mouth but immediately slam it closed as my mind wars between wanting him to stay true to me but also wanting him to be happy.

Wyatt was always emotionally stunted, and he wouldn't be able to give Evan the softer love and support he needs to thrive. Evan would need a woman around to give him that softness. He missed a lot of Evan's early years because of his deployments and they would have almost been strangers if Wyatt had to leave the army to care for our son—*if* he chose to leave. The army was his life.

As much as I hate the idea of another woman sharing Wyatt's bed, I would rather he be happy and Evan looked after. Tears well behind my eyes and the ache in my heart becomes unbearable at the realization. Sharp claws dig at my battered soul, and I cover my face with shaky hands as the tears fall, my shoulders shuddering with each agonizing sob that breaks free.

The girls surround me, wrapping me in their embrace and holding me tight. My knees weaken and my body shakes, but I stay standing as my friends offer me their love and support.

"Oh, Hope," Sophie murmurs.

"I'm not ready," I sob.

"You take all the time you need, hon. Nobody's saying you have to do anything about anything right now," Lucy reminds me.

Savannah pulls away slightly. "And while you're waiting to be ready, don't feel guilty if you dream about another man. It's only a dream. No harm done."

A knock against the glass door breaks our moment, and we separate. I dip my face to the floor and head to the bathroom to wash my face and reapply my makeup, doing the best I can with red, puffy eyes.

I PARK THE CAR, and Evan climbs out. "Have a good practice session and make sure you listen to Coach Mathers."

"I will." He slams the door and heads toward the field where the rest of his team is gathered.

I climb out of the car and sit on the hood so I can watch, and while my eyes are on Evan, my mind is still stuck on Ben. All day, it's been a struggle to keep my thoughts away from the man. It's been such a long time since I've felt any sort of attraction to anyone that the all-consuming thoughts are foreign and unsettling.

The girls helped me realize something Shane's been trying to tell me for a while now—that it's okay to move on. Wyatt's not coming back. I twist my wedding ring around my finger as my heart wrenches, and my stomach twists with the thought, but it's true, and it's time I accept that. I don't think I'll be ready anytime soon, but at least I'm not dismissing the idea completely—like I've done in the past.

That's progress, right? At this point, I'll take anything.

Out of the corner of my eye, I notice a car pull into the parking lot, and when I turn to get a better look, my breath catches. I snap my head back around toward Evan and lick my parched lips. It doesn't mean it's him just because a patrol car pulled into the parking lot, but it's not a regular patrol car. It's like the one I saw parked in Ben's driveway.

My heart explodes into an erratic rhythm, and my stomach flip-flops. The crunch of tires over gravel in the space next to my car makes the hair on the back of my neck stand on end, and when I hear the door open and close, I do everything in my power to maintain a steady breath. Footsteps crunch closer, and my heart pounds a wonky rhythm in time with each step.

Oh, god. It's him. I recognize his aftershave as it wafts around me and fortify myself, hoping he can't tell I had a dirty dream about him last night when he looks at me.

"Hey, Hope. I was driving by and noticed the kids playing

soccer. Thought I'd stop on the off-chance one of them was Evan."
He beams like he's won the lottery.

I can't help but smile too. "Hey." I point to the field directly in
front of us. "You found him."

He rests his hands on his duty belt, making the muscles in his
forearms tense beneath his intricate tattoos, and I grip the edge of
the hood with white-knuckle force to keep my balance.

The first time we met, he was wearing his uniform, but I was so
stunned by the entire episode that I didn't appreciate how fine he
looks in his dark blue shirt and pants. When my eyes finally make it
back to his face, I'm greeted with a slight smirk. Heat rushes up my
neck and into my cheeks as embarrassment washes over me.

"Yeah, it seems I did." He moves closer and leans his ass against
the hood of my car, folding his arms across his broad chest. Slowly,
he peels his eyes away from me and turns to watch Evan. "He's
quick on his feet."

I tear my gaze away from his profile to see Evan sprinting down
the sideline with the ball close to his feet, and a genuine grin
spreads across my face. "We practiced a lot to increase his speed. He
went from being one of the slowest kids on his team to being the
fastest."

I see Ben nod in my periphery. "You're a great mom."

My shoulders tense. He keeps saying those words, and I
wonder what I've done to give him that idea. Most of the time I
feel as though I'm failing Evan. I haven't given him the emotional
support he's needed since losing Wyatt, so my instinct is to deny
his compliment, but I don't want Ben to think poorly of me.

"It can't be easy raising him alone." *How does he always seem to
understand?*

I close my eyes briefly to stem the sting of tears. I've already
had an emotional day, and I don't want to have another breakdown in front of Ben. His gaze sears the side of my face, and when
I'm certain I have my emotions under control, I open my eyes and
turn toward him. "Thanks."

Studying my face, he simply nods, as though he knows how difficult it is for me to accept his compliment. We both turn back to watch Evan, and I do my best to ignore my reaction to having Ben this close. It's like my body remembers exactly what he did to me, even though it was only a dream.

It takes a mammoth effort to concentrate on the kids on the field and ignore the ache that's growing stronger by the second. A gentle breeze blows across the field, and I push my curls away from my face with a trembling hand.

I glance at Ben's cruiser, wondering where Rex is. "Have you finished for the day?"

He shakes his head and turns to me. "Nah, just on a break." He glances down at his watch. "Actually, I should get going." He raps his knuckles on the hood as he glances back at the field. "Will I see you next Saturday?"

I chuckle as I grip the edge of the hood and lean forward. "I don't think anything would keep Evan away. He loves spending time with the dogs so much."

He grins. "That's good to hear, but will I see *you* there?"

His gaze is intense as he observes me closely, like he's trying to solve a puzzle, and my mind freezes for a moment, then I nod. "Well, I'll need to drop him off and pick him up."

Rocking back on his heels, a slow smile spreads. "You can come in, too. I know how much you enjoyed playing with the puppies."

"Oh, I thought it was a kid-only type thing."

"Well, it's supposed to be"—he lifts and drops a shoulder carelessly—"but I can make an exception for you."

My pulse skyrockets, pounding in my ears at an almost deafening level. "You're too kind, but I don't want to intrude on your program. I see how much it's helped Evan, and I'd hate to get in the way."

"You'd never be in the way, Hope." He winks at me, sending a kaleidoscope of butterflies fluttering in my stomach. "Anyway, say hi to Ev for me."

"I will. Bye, Ben." I raise my hand and wiggle my fingers in goodbye.

"Bye." He climbs into his cruiser and pulls out of the parking lot.

My shoulders roll inward, and feeling light-headed, I draw in a much-needed breath. Thank goodness he's gone.

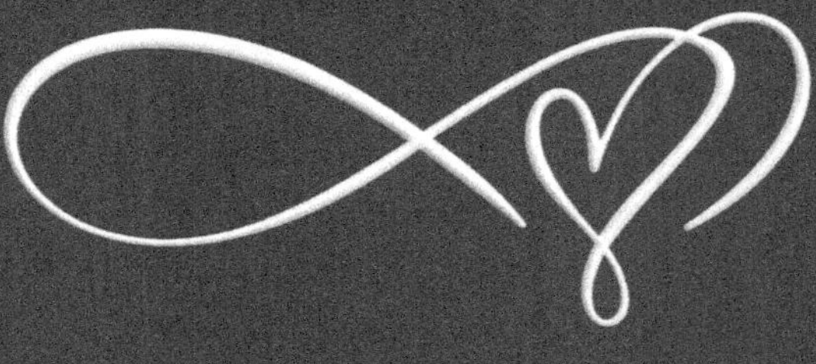

19
BEN

I trace the condensation on the outside of my almost empty glass and watch the way the droplets change shape. Hope always looks beautiful, but she looked stunning with the afternoon sun highlighting the natural golden hues in her hair. Her lashes looked dark and thick, and when she looked down, they fanned across the apples of her cheeks. I don't think she has any idea how breathtakingly beautiful she is.

A full glass of beer slides across the table in front of me, and I glance up at Sebastian. "Thanks."

He tips his head and drops into the seat opposite me. "You okay? You seem distracted."

His concern is apparent, and I realize I've been flaky tonight. I've only been half-listening and not fully participating in the conversation. My mind is so full of Hope and Evan that I've had a hard time concentrating on anything else. The only time I've been completely switched on is when I'm working, and even that's been a struggle. The rest of the time, I move through my day on autopilot, my mind a million miles away. "Sorry."

Creases appear between his eyebrows. "Why are you sorry?"

I shrug. "I've been shitty company tonight, and it's not like we get to spend a ton of time together with our rosters." I straighten in my seat, vowing to push Hope and Evan from my thoughts so I can give Seb the attention he deserves. "How's work been?"

"Had to use the jaws of life to cut a young guy out of his wreck last weekend. He was a mess. I'm not sure if he survived. His vehicle certainly didn't." He takes a long drink of his ice-cold beer. "I wish these young guys would take speed limits more seriously." Placing his glass back on the table between us, he adds, "I'm pretty sure I heard the paramedics talking about a blood alcohol level of 0.15."

I'd like to say I'm surprised, but I'm not. I shake my head with disappointment. "Alcohol and speed are a tragedy waiting to happen."

"Yep. They think they're fucking indestructible." We're both quiet for a few moments. We've seen too many serious accidents resulting in permanent injury or death because of stupid, risky behavior. Stuff that could have been avoided if the kids had taken a moment to consider their actions and possible consequences. Seb takes another drink, never taking his eyes from me. "So, what's up?"

I take a moment to gather my thoughts, but it's like wrangling a litter of rambunctious puppies. I take another drink and swallow it down. I open my mouth, but nothing comes out, so I try again. "A few weeks ago, I picked up a kid after being called out to a gas station. There was a group of kids shoplifting. By the time I arrived at the scene, there was only one kid, so I took him home." Seb nods to let me know he's listening. "We spoke a little in the car, and I discovered his dad was killed while serving in Syria."

"Ah, man. That's gotta be tough to lose your dad like that." Seb leans forward and places his elbows on the table, bringing him closer to me. If anyone knows what it's like to lose a parent on the job, he does.

I nod. "Yeah." I sigh, remembering the pain in his voice when he told me. "I really felt for the boy. When I took him home, I met his mom." Just thinking about Hope makes my blood heat. "She was clearly upset when she saw me on her doorstep with her son." I flick my eyes up to my best friend's face. "She was so fucking beautiful; she stole my breath."

A slow smile tips up his lips. "Like, how beautiful on a scale of one to ten?"

"She's not even on the scale, man." I inhale a deep breath as his eyebrows rise halfway up his forehead. I never talk about women like this. I've never been so affected before.

"Tell me you asked her out."

I shake my head. "She invited me inside so I could tell her what happened, and I literally watched her heart break. It's obvious she's still grieving the loss of her husband and hasn't moved on at all. She's so emotionally devastated, but she's still doing her best to raise her son. Her strength makes her even more attractive to me, but I can't do a thing about it."

He narrows his eyes and tilts his head to the side a little. "Why not?"

"I invited Evan to join my program at the shelter, so we've spent a little time together. She's a great mom, a strong woman, and sexy in all the ways that turn me on, but she's still completely in love with her late husband." I look out into the crowd.

"Damn. That's tough. You can't compete with a ghost."

"I know and I don't wanna compete with a ghost. To me, there's no competition. If I were ever lucky enough to gain her attention, I wouldn't ever expect her to stop loving him," I tell him, my voice gruff as I struggle with my emotions.

Seb's eyes widen, and he reclines against the seat. "You're a better man than me. I wouldn't want her thinking of anyone else but me."

I shrug and lean forward. "That's the thing. Normally, I'd feel the same way, but I'd be satisfied with even a fraction of her affection." I smile a little when I remember how she was checking me out at the soccer field. "I think she's attracted to me. I've caught her checking me out, but I don't think she'll ever act on it. She still wears her wedding rings after six years and is fully committed to the promises she made her late husband."

Seb leans forward, engrossed in my situation. "What are you gonna do?"

"I'm not proud to say I've been creating situations with Evan so I can spend time with her." I drop my eyes to the table, ashamed that I've stooped so low, but desperate times call for desperate measures. "Don't get me wrong. I love hanging out with Evan. He's an amazing kid, smart, and easy to be around."

Laughter erupts from Seb, and he takes a good minute to get himself under control. "I've heard everything now." He slaps his palm against the table. "Just ask her out, man."

"Did you not hear me? She's still in love with her husband."

"I heard you, but I also heard you when you said you caught her checking you out." He takes a drink of his beer and swallows. "Ask her out. She may surprise you and say yes."

I shake my head. "I doubt it. I just need to keep spending time with them. Hopefully, if I give her enough time, when she's ready to move on, I'll be right in front of her."

"Yeah, but by then, you'll probably be in the friend zone, and she'll be asking you to babysit her kid so she can go out with some other dude."

My pulse pounds in my ears and my hand forms a fist at the idea of her going on a date with someone else. "Fuck that."

His eyebrows shoot up, and he gives me that look that says, *you know I'm right.* "Unless you want to let her slip through your fingers, you need to step up your game." I nod thoughtfully, trying to formulate a plan for when I see her tomorrow. *If* I see her tomorrow. "So, what are you gonna do?"

"I'm spending the morning at the shelter and had planned to ask Hope and Evan out for lunch afterward. Other than that, I have no idea."

"I'm sure you'll figure it out."

I hope so. I don't like the idea of being in the friend zone.

20

BEN

I ROCK BACK ON MY HEELS, TWISTING THE LEATHER band around my wrist. Rex looks up at me, tilting his head to the side as his eyebrows shift and move. "I'm okay, boy."

He gives a short, shrill bark, then licks his lips, turning his attention back to the driveway where the kids will arrive any minute now. I do the same, but my mind won't stop working through my options with Hope. I don't think she's ready for me to ask her on a date. I'm certain if I take that step too soon, I'll ruin any chance I may have. My best course of action is to spend time with Evan *and* her, giving more of my focus to Evan until she grows more comfortable and relaxes a little. If I take the time to get to know her and give her time to get to know me, I think I'll have a better chance of her agreeing to a date when the time is right. I nod to myself, happy with my plan.

Michael and Peter arrive first and, after our usual greeting, wander inside. The rest follow soon after, leaving Donnelly and Evan still to come. I should go inside since most of the kids are here, but I don't want to miss seeing Hope. Even if it's from a distance, I need to get my fix. She pulls into the parking lot and makes a wide circle to drop Evan right at the front door. He waves from the back seat and jumps out as soon as the car comes to a stop.

"Hi, Ben!" He slams the door and Hope winds down the front window.

"Remember, we can't stay today, and please come out on time. I'm in charge of the cookie booth at 12:30."

Cookies? My eyebrows shoot up in interest and my stomach growls.

"Yeah, Mom. I know." He rolls his eyes as he heads inside, waving at her over his shoulder.

I lean on the roof of her car. "Hey." I can't stop myself from tracing every freckle and curl with my eyes.

"Oh, hey." Pink makes its way up her neck, and her slender throat bobs. "I'm sorry we were late, but I had to wait for the cookies for the bake sale to finish baking." Her eyes scan my face, then dart toward the windshield.

"Cookies, you say?" I ask lightheartedly.

"Uh, yeah." Her eyes flick back to me. "Evan's school is fundraising for some new gym equipment, so they're holding a giant bake sale today. I need to get home and make a few more batches, then come back to collect Evan before heading to school for my turn to manage the cookie booth." She looks a little over-whelmed with everything she needs to get done.

"I can bring Evan to school after the session today to save you a trip."

"Oh, I couldn't ask you to do that. I'm sure you're busy."

What is it with her always assuming I'm busy?

She couldn't be more wrong. I work, exercise, and spend time with Rex, occasionally hanging out with Seb or the boys from the precinct. "You didn't ask. I offered, and it's no problem. I wouldn't mind stocking up on some home-baked goods, particu-larly cookies, and if the money goes to a good cause"—I shrug—"all the better."

Her expression turns to disbelief. "You eat cookies?"

I pat my trim stomach. "Of course! Who doesn't eat cookies? They're my favorite. I'm not a weirdo, you know."

My playful response garners a genuine chuckle, and I feel like a king. "Good to know."

"Anyway, I can bring Evan after we finish here."

Does she trust me enough?

She looks out the windshield for what feels like an eternity, and I don't like that her eyes are no longer on me. "It would certainly help, if you don't mind."

Yes! I clear my throat. "I don't mind at all. As I said, I wouldn't mind stocking up. I miss Tahlia's mom's baking, so it'll be a treat."

Her shoulders relax. "Okay, thank you so much." Her clear eyes land on me again, and I stand a little taller. "I guess I'll see you at school."

I tap the top of the roof. "I guess you will." I give her my best smile. "I look forward to it." Hope nods, and I take a step away from the car, then call out as she pulls away. "Oh, and Hope."

She stops. "Yeah?"

"Save me a cookie or two, yeah?"

Blotches instantly cover the entirety of her neck, her eyes widen, and she chuckles awkwardly.

I grimace when I realize how that sounded. "Sorry, that may have come out wrong."

She waves off my concern with a flick of her wrist. "What's your favorite cookie?"

You.

I do have a favorite, but I find I want to drag out our conversation for as long as I can. "Hmm, tough to choose just one."

She raises her eyebrows. "Top three?"

My lips tip up. "Chocolate chip cookies come in at number three. Number two would have to be white chocolate macadamia nut, and my number one favorite cookie is the humble sugar cookie." My mouth salivates at the thought of eating half a dozen warm sugar cookies straight out of the oven. "Crispy around the edge and thick in the center." I make a chef's kiss. "Perfection." My eyes almost roll into the back of my head at the thought.

Hope chuckles warmly. "I'll see what I can do. I need to get going or I'll be late." She grips the steering wheel. "I need to bake three more batches, have a shower, and put some makeup on. I don't wanna scare away prospective customers."

"You needn't worry, you look beautiful as you are." I tap the top of her roof again. "See you there." I walk away before she can respond. The compliment flew out of my mouth before I could stop it, and I wince slightly as I walk inside while the engine of her car revs and she pulls out of the parking lot.

21

BEN

"I wish we could have brought Rex with us," Evan pouts as we pull into a parking spot on the street. The school parking lot was overflowing, and it took some time and patience to locate a place we could park.

I turn off the engine and angle my body toward him. "Me too, but it isn't always appropriate to bring him with me. There will be a lot of kids and excited energy here, not to mention loads of sweet treats, which are Rex's favorite. He's a big dog, and even though he's well-behaved, not everyone is comfortable around dogs like him. I need to consider the comfort of others and the situation."

His shoulders sag. "Yeah, I guess. I just love him so much." He looks up at me, his eyes overflowing with love for Rex.

"I know you do. He loves you too." And he does. He took to Evan like a duck to water. "C'mon, let's go find your mom." We climb out of my truck and head across the street to the school. Even though I've never been here, it's easy to find our way to the gym with the number of people heading in that direction, as well as those walking toward us with bags of baked treats. "It looks like the school has a good turnout."

"Evan!"

Evan and I turn toward the voice, and I see a young kid, probably the same age as him, jogging toward us. "Oh, hey, Elliott," Evan greets the boy. "I just got here."

Elliott's gaze slides to me, his eyes full of questions. "You're lucky. I've been here for three hours already, and it doesn't look like I'll be outta here anytime soon."

Evan laughs. "How bad can it be with all the cakes and cookies and stuff to eat?"

My thoughts exactly.

We walk toward the gym, and Elliott waves his hands in the air theatrically. "Pretty bad when Mom won't let me have anything."

"Damn."

"Yeah."

The gym is a hive of activity when we step inside. Tables line the far back and side wall, while a pop-up café, juice bar, and an ice-cream parlor are spaced equally along the opposite side wall— each with a line of at least twenty people waiting.

Music blares over speakers while cheerleaders perform a polished routine. Most of the tables and chairs in the center of the room are occupied by people enjoying sweet treats with coffee or juice as they watch the show. It's obvious the organizers have put a lot of thought into the event.

I move my gaze to the tables along the side and back walls looking for Hope, and they land on her immediately, like they knew exactly where she was. My breath catches in my lungs as it does every time I see her. She's gorgeous. It's almost like I forget how pretty she is. Evan's telling Elliott about the shelter and what he does there with me, but I don't hear a word. My sole focus is on the woman across the room—the one who's invaded every thought since I met her.

A man steps in front of her table and says something I can't hear from this far away, but I watch her tuck her loose curls behind her ear and give him one of her fake smiles. She shifts on her feet, leaning back, and her posture screams, *I'm uncomfortable.*

Without thinking, I head over to her, the hackles on the back of my neck rising. When I get closer, I hear the man's voice over the music. "I'll buy everything on this table if you'll go on a single date with me," he says, standing like the cocky asshole he is.

Red clouds my vision, and every muscle in my body tenses.

Hope's discomfort rolls like a wave from her, and I can't stand here and do nothing, so I step around the table with a grin, slip my hand around her waist with a familiarity we don't have, and kiss her temple. Her vanilla scent floats around us, blending with the smell of freshly baked cookies. "Sorry I'm late,"—in a millisecond, I scan her table and trace her face with my eyes, noting how, in this light, her freckles resemble cookie crumbs scattered across her nose and cheeks—"Cookie." Her eyes widen slightly. "Evan and I had trouble finding a parking spot."

She tenses as she looks up at me, but when I shoot her a wink, her body melts against mine. I can't ignore how well she fits against me, with her softness against my hard planes and her lithe shape burrowed against my straight edges. Drawing in a sharp breath, my chest expands as I watch her hand resting on my pecs rise. Her warmth burns me through the cotton of my T-shirt, and when I lift my eyes to hers, gratitude shines back at me.

I cover her hand with mine, and we stand in our own bubble as the cocky asshole becomes a vague memory. Her stunning, clear eyes soften measurably, and we could easily be the only two people in the gym right now.

"Mom!"

Like a bullet through glass, the moment shatters in a split second, and she takes a hasty step away from me as her eyes flick around the gymnasium. My hand drops to my side, and my heart stutters from the loss. I run my hand through my short hair to cover my disappointment and paste on a smile.

Hope grins at her son as she steps around the table to greet him with a hug, but he moves away swiftly, avoiding her embrace. Her smile drops momentarily, but she recovers quickly. "Hey, big guy. How were the dogs today?"

"What's going on?" he asks with eyebrows drawn tight together, creating deep creases between them, his suspicious gaze flicking between me and his mom.

Hope swallows. "Nothing, Ev. Ben just rescued me from an uncomfortable situation." She combs her fingers through his short hair, making the strands stand up.

"What kind of situation?" he asks, disbelief dripping from every word.

I clear my throat and rub the back of my neck. "I saw a guy standing at your mom's table, and she looked uncomfortable, so I came over and pretended to be her boyfriend so he'd leave her alone."

His shoulders drop half an inch and he returns his focus to Hope. "Are you okay?"

"Yeah, Ev. The guy left once Ben stepped in." She turns to me. "Thanks for your help."

"Any time." I shrug. *Maybe one day it won't be pretend.*

"Thanks for helping Mom."

"No problem." I glance across the table, noting the different varieties of homemade cookies. "Did you bake all these?" There seems to be a lot here.

Hope scoffs. "Ah, that'd be a no. The school coordinated groups of parents to bake various types of treats. Cookies, cakes, muffins, cupcakes, pies, slices, meringues, puddings, candy. You get my drift."

I nod, impressed. "I've never seen a bake sale on such a huge scale."

She looks around, pride lighting her eyes. "It's pretty spectacular. Since we're new to the school, this is our first year, but I think they do it every other year."

Potential customers step up to the table, and Hope goes to work. Evan and I wander around the gym, and I purchase more than what I really need. Everything looks so damn good. How am I supposed to resist? Evan's quiet, which is unusual for him.

"Would you like a juice or something?" I ask.

He looks across at where the pop-up stores are set up, then back to me. "Yeah, sure," he answers, but his voice lacks his usual enthusiasm.

We wander over and line up at the juice bar. The cheerleaders are still performing to the music playing over the speakers. Once we have our drinks, we find an empty table and take a seat. I pull out the caramel slice I bought and offer one to Evan. He takes a piece but remains quiet, wearing an expression of concentration.

"Everything okay?" I ask gently.

He looks up at me and takes his time to finish chewing the food in his mouth. "I thought you were *my* friend."

His words catch me off guard, and I'm momentarily stunned. "Yeah, I am," I say, slowly and clearly.

"But you like my mom," he states bluntly.

"Well, yeah." I swallow. *Why do I feel like I'm walking into a trap?*

"Do you like *her* more than *me*?" he asks, narrowing his eyes.

I shift in my seat and lean against the back of the plastic chair, stretching my legs beneath the table to hide my discomfort. "I like you both for different reasons." I won't lie to him. I respect him too much for that.

He turns away, directing his focus to the cheerleaders, and I drink my juice, giving him time to gather his thoughts. He's an intelligent kid, and I'm sure he has more to say.

"Would you still like me and spend time with me if my dad were here?"

My heart pounds, and my eyebrows rise at his question, but I lean forward and look him in the eye without delay. "Yes, I would. Though, to be honest, I think if your dad were still here, you wouldn't have gotten mixed up with those kids and found yourself in trouble at the gas station. We might've never met."

"Maybe," he mumbles.

We both fall quiet, and I can see the questions and doubts

forming behind his eyes. I could try to soothe him, but I think I'd do more harm than good. I need to be patient and let him work through his thoughts.

He straightens in his chair and takes a drink, then swallows. "Do you wanna date my mom?" he whispers softly, not looking at me.

I trace my eyes over him, noting the freckles scattered across his nose, just like his mom's. His soulful brown eyes that must be his dad's and the boyish shape of his face that will begin to change soon as he grows into a man. "Would it be a problem if I did?"

"She still loves my dad."

I nod slowly. "I know."

His eyes widen slightly. "You don't mind?"

"Why would I?" He shrugs. "We can love lots of people at the same time. You love your mom *and* your dad. I assume you also love your grandparents, aunts, and uncles. You probably love Shane too, right?" He nods. "Each time you love someone new, do you have to stop loving someone else to make room for them?"

He shakes his head. "No."

I lick my lips. "Because our heart is elastic. It stretches to accommodate the new people that come into our lives." I grin slowly. "I don't expect your mom to stop loving your dad. I would never expect that. He will always have her love, and that's okay with me because I know that if I were lucky enough to have your mom's love, she'd have enough for me, too."

His eyes widen. "So you love her?"

I chuckle. "Not yet. I like her a lot and would really like to spend some time getting to know her better. Love comes in time."

"So you wanna date my mom?"

Man, this is worse than meeting the girlfriend's parents for the first time, but Evan's approval is far more important. I wipe my sweaty palms on my jeans beneath the table. "I would, but I need to work out the right time and the right way to ask her." I pause for a moment. "Would you be okay with it if we dated? Not saying your mom's even interested, but if she were and I asked her, would that be okay with you?" I clench my fists on my thighs to keep them from shaking as I wait for his answer.

He watches me for a moment as he considers his answer. He's only eleven, but he's the most important person to Hope, and his opinion means a lot to me. "Yeah, I think that'd be okay."

My grin is instant as relief whooshes through my body. He smiles too, and the heaviness that fell between us disappears.

"Should we grab a coffee for your mom and head back?"

He grins. "Good idea."

As we're lining up, I think about our talk. I don't want him to keep secrets from Hope, but I don't want him to share what we've spoken about. I have no idea what the protocol is in this situation. "Uh, Ev?"

"Yeah."

I wave my hand between the two of us. "Would you mind keeping this between us? I don't—"

He holds up his hand. "You don't need to say anything. This is between us. Man to man." He winks at me, and I chuckle.

"Man to man."

22

HOPE

I'm certain I'm not imagining it.

When he pretended to be my boyfriend, and I sunk into his warmth and felt the steady beat of his heart beneath my hand, I got lost for a moment. If Evan hadn't come over when he did, I'm not sure what would have happened next.

Thank goodness he showed up.

Ben called me *Cookie*.

I wonder if it's because he thinks I crumble like a cookie. I shake my head at the ridiculousness of the thought. He's never once looked at me like I'm weak or broken. I guess he was caught on the spot, and since we were surrounded by cookies, it kinda makes sense. Wyatt never gave me a nickname, so I'm not sure how I feel about it.

I smile, take money, and hand over tray after tray of cookies. In between customers, I lift to my toes to see where Ben and Evan are. I expected Ben to drop Evan and leave, not stick around for as long as he has. I scan the gym until my eyes land on them, sitting at a table, sharing a treat, and drinking juice. Evan's smiling and nodding, and I admire the way Ben's T-shirt stretches across his taut, muscular back. More customers stop at my table, and I lose sight of the pair as I focus on serving.

Out of the corner of my eye, I see a woman step around my table. When I glance up, my eyes land on Mom and I smile. "Hey, Mom. I'll just be a sec."

"Hi, sweetie. You do what you need to, and I'll help where I can." She shuffles closer, checks over the table, then grabs extra stock from the crates behind us to restock.

"Thanks. Where's Dad?"

She chuckles. "He's buying up a storm at the table selling candies." That makes sense. He has such a sweet tooth. "Where's Evan? I thought he'd be here." She presses up on her toes to look around the gym. I know the instant her eyes land on her grandson, because a wide smile pushes up her cheeks. "Oh, there he is." Her grin drops. "He's talking to a man," she adds, a hint of worry in her tone.

I don't have time to put her mind at ease before another customer approaches the table and asks about the various flavors of cookies for sale.

"Nanna!" my son's voice rings out, and the next thing I know, a streak of red flings himself into her waiting arms.

Hmpf. He wouldn't hug me. I was lucky he let me play with his hair. I brush off my hurt feelings and watch them embrace. I guess he hasn't seen her since yesterday. Well, that's what I tell myself to lessen the sting of his earlier rejection.

He pulls away and tugs on her hand. "Nanna, come meet my friend, Ben."

Mom's eyes widen comically, then she snaps her gaze to me and raises her eyebrows. "Oh, I'd love to meet *your* new friend." She pats her hair down and readjusts her blouse as she follows my boy a few feet away to Ben.

Poor Ben. I didn't have time to warn him. She'll have us married with babies within the blink of an eye, and he won't even see it coming. I'm just thankful Wyatt's parents are out of town this weekend—*that* would be awkward.

Another wave of customers approach my table, and I get busy dealing with them and restocking. Once they're gone and the table's full again, I reorganize the crates of cookies, stacking the empty ones off to the side for collection.

Mom slips next to me, and her smile reminds me of the Cheshire Cat from *Alice in Wonderland.* "Ben's a lovely young man. It seems he and Evan have formed a strong friendship."

I ignore the excitement in her tone. "Yeah, they have. Evan really enjoys his company, along with Rex, his dog."

"Mmhm," she responds.

"Evan's been a lot calmer and happier since he started volunteering at the shelter with Ben and the other kids every other week. That's where he was this morning and why Ben's here. He gave Evan a ride, so I had more time to bake and get ready." *Shut up already, Hope.* The more I speak, the bigger Mom's grin grows.

"Such a helpful young man," she remarks, her eyes practically sparkling with delight.

"Yeah, he is."

"Mmhm."

"What's that supposed to mean?" I ask defensively, widening my eyes. "Mmhm?"

She presses her lips together, like she's trying to hold back her smile, but it's a lost cause at this point. She can't hide her delight. "I was just agreeing with you. I've noticed the difference in Evan, and he loves to talk about Ben. It was lovely to meet him. That's all." She raises her eyebrows, her eyes gleaming beneath the gym's overhead lights.

I narrow my eyes. "That's all?" I grouse. "Why don't I believe you? I know your mind is working a million miles a minute."

She leans in close. "Would it be so bad if I were thinking how nice it would be if *you* also happened to develop a friendship with Ben? Maybe something a little more?"

A fresh wave of customers interrupts our conversation, and I send up a thank you to whatever higher power rescued me. We sell more trays of cookies, and I bend to the crates to collect more to restock the table again. When I stand, Mom sidles up close.

"I bet he looks fantastic in his uniform," she says.

I flick my eyes to Ben, hoping he didn't hear, only to find him shaking hands with Dad. I guess there was no avoiding it since he's with Evan. Dad'll talk to anyone, and the fact that he's with his grandson makes him a prime target.

"Oh, look. Stan likes him, too."

I roll my eyes skyward. "Dad likes everyone, Mom."

She nods sagely. "True. But I can tell he *really* likes Ben."

I slowly turn my head toward her, my expression dripping with disbelief. "They've spent less than a minute together, Mom. Settle down."

She flicks her wrist toward me. "After forty years of marriage, I know your father better than I know myself most days."

That's probably true, seeing as it was the same for me and Wyatt. We were together since I was sixteen, married when I was twenty. Then, I lost him when I was twenty-eight. A weight falls on my chest, threatening to force me to my knees, but I take a deep breath and bring my focus back to the present—just like my grief counselor taught me in group.

After another hour, the gym finally empties, and we pack down our tables. I have two trays of cookies left. Not bad. Ben, Dad, and Evan help where they can, Mom stacks chairs, and I collect the empty crates to store behind the gym. When we're finally finished, we walk out to our cars together. I pull my sweater tighter around my body to ward off the chill in the late afternoon air.

Mom wraps her arm around Evan's shoulder and tugs him to her side, leaving me to walk alongside Ben and Dad. He goes willingly, wrapping his arm around her waist. "Would you like to come for a sleepover? We can watch a movie, and I can make waffles and bacon for breakfast."

He turns to me, his eyes wide and excited. You'd think he'd get sick of seeing Mom every day, but he loves her so much. "Yeah, can I, Mom?"

"Good idea, June. He can help me harvest the veggies for dinner," Dad adds, mussing up Evan's hair.

I almost pout. That means I'll be home alone tonight. I hate being in the house on my own. Even with the television on, it feels too quiet. Too empty. But I paste on a smile. "If you want to." I look up at Mom. "What time would you like me to pick him up tomorrow?"

"Why don't you come for lunch?"

I nod. "All right. That sounds like a plan."

I say my goodbyes to Mom and Dad and then pull Evan into me to hug him, which he allows. "Have fun and be good. I'll see you tomorrow."

"I will."

I kiss the top of his head. "Remember, I love you all the way to *Knowhere* and back again."

"I love you too, Mom." He squeezes me quickly, then pulls away. "See ya tomorrow." He turns to Ben. "See ya later, Ben."

"See ya, Ev." Ben waves.

"It was so lovely to meet you, Ben. Hopefully, we'll see you again soon." Oh, god! *Seriously, Mom, could you be any more transparent?* "Evan's birthday is coming up next month. Perhaps we'll see you then?"

Ben chuckles, showing his perfectly straight teeth. "Nice to meet you, too. If I'm lucky enough to score an invite, I'll definitely be there. Enjoy your evening."

"Bye, Ben," Dad calls as they head off. I watch them pile into Dad's car and pull out of the parking lot, leaving me alone with Ben.

"Thanks for all of your help today." I take a step toward my car. "I'll see you later?" I tug my purse straps higher up my shoulder, preparing to make my escape.

"Happy to help whenever you need it." He doesn't seem to be in a hurry to leave, and I sense he wants to linger for a little while, even though it's getting colder. "I guess you have the evening to yourself, huh?"

My shoulders sag. "Yeah. I always get the first weekend of the month to myself because Evan stays with Wyatt's parents for the weekend." I look down at the cracked sidewalk between us. "I hate it."

"It's great that they still get to keep that connection with their grandson."

I wrap my arms around my body. "Of course. I would never deny them," I say a little defensively.

Ben holds his hands up. "I-I didn't mean it that way."

"A lot of people are surprised when I tell them, and I can never understand why." I soften my tone. "They're as much Evan's family as mine are. It would seem unfair for them to lose their son and then never see their grandchild because of that."

He nods. "Agreed. They've already lost so much." He pauses. "You all have," he adds, leaning a little toward me. His hands twitch at his sides, like he wants to reach out for me. To comfort me somehow.

My stomach falls and rolls, twists and tangles on itself. "Yeah." He's always so caring and understanding whenever Wyatt pops up in the discussion.

We stand awkwardly at the edge of the almost empty parking lot. Since I dreamed about Ben going down on me, I can barely look the guy in the eye. I feel like I somehow took advantage of him against his will when he's been nothing but respectful—a true gentleman. I drop my eyes to his hands, and my neck heats at the reminder of what his fingers felt like when they were inside me.

Not that I know what they feel like, but the dream was so real.

Oh, god. And now I'm thinking about it while I'm standing right next to him. *What the hell is wrong with me?*

He tilts his head to the side. "Are you okay?"

I twist a curl around my finger, buying time to get my head out of the gutter. "Uh, yeah?" He studies me closely. He's not buying my answer. "I guess I'm a little thrown. I wasn't expecting to be on my own tonight." I chuckle awkwardly.

Thankfully, he tucks those thick fingers in his jean pockets and out of sight, but I can't tear my eyes away from the way his tattoos move as his muscles shift. Wyatt only had his army ranger tattoo over his heart. I never realized how much I like tattoos. Or maybe I just like Ben's tattoos. "I guess you could call your girlfriends and go out, or something."

My stomach sinks remembering the last time I tried to go out with the girls and failed epically. "Ha. They'd probably love that, but I'm not much for going out these days." I shrug and drop my eyes to my feet. I sound like a loser.

"I don't go out that much either." *How can that be?* I raise my eyes to his, and he reads my unspoken question. "My best friend is a firefighter, so our schedules rarely align. The most we do is occasionally enjoy a quiet beer at *Brady's*." He drops his chin with a boyish smile. "I guess we're not that different."

My eyes widen in disbelief. "Uh, yeah we are. I'm a miserable single mom. You're a young, good-looking guy." I wave my hand around the vicinity of his body. "You should be out there, meeting women and having fun." Even though I say the words, they taste like cardboard on my tongue.

His eyes twinkle as he raises his eyebrows, and a cheeky grin lifts his lips. "Maybe I don't need to go out to meet a woman. Maybe I've already met a woman I'd prefer to spend time with." His eyes bore into mine, and I get the distinct impression he's referring to me, but I can't be certain—and I don't want to assume anything. It's better ... *safer* if I assume he's talking about someone else. I'm certainly not ready to go down that road. I'm not sure I ever will be.

"Oh. Well ... that's great." I hook my purse straps up higher just for something to do. A sick feeling forms in my stomach. It feels a lot like jealousy, and I have no idea why. I have no relationship with Ben. He's not mine.

Nor will he ever be.

Not thirty seconds ago, I decided to ignore the prospect that he was referring to me. *I* decided I'm not ready. It's like my mind is a seesaw. "Anyway, I'd better be going. Thanks again for today. Enjoy your evening." I spin on the heel of my boots to head toward my car.

I don't like the way he makes me feel.

It feels wrong.

His footsteps sound behind me, crunching over the gravel. "Uh ... would you like to maybe eat together rather than both of us eating alone?" My feet falter, and I come to an abrupt stop. Blood rushes through my system like a hurricane, tearing through my veins with such speed that dizziness assaults me. Ben reaches out to steady me, his hand burning through my sweater as he grips my arm firmly. "You okay?"

I swallow thickly, trying to steady myself as I nod slowly. "Yeah. I think so." I chuckle awkwardly. I must be fifty shades of red right now.

"Was it because I suggested we have dinner together?" he asks softly. I nod once and try to push past my embarrassment. "Sorry. I didn't mean to put you on the spot or make things awkward." He shrugs and almost makes himself smaller, as if it's his size that makes him intimidating.

"No. It's totally my fault. You ... uh ... caught me off guard and I'm just an awkward mess." I flap my hands around myself to drive my point home.

"I just thought we could share a meal ... as friends. I always eat alone, and it'd be nice to have company for a change." He offers a kind smile.

Well, that explains why he's always keen to eat with me and Evan. He must get lonely. It's not like he's asking me on a date. We'd just be sharing a meal because we're both alone and have to eat. It makes sense. I can make dinner for both of us.

I force a smile. "Sounds good. I can cook something for both of us if you'd like to come over around seven," I say before I can change my mind.

His mouth tips down. "I wasn't angling for a home-cooked meal. I can grab something on the way to your place so you can have a night off. I imagine you have to cook every night."

I wave him off. "Nah, it's okay. I enjoy cooking, and maybe I can make something suitable for adults for once." It might be nice to have adult company for a change.

"If you're sure?" I nod and he grins. "Sounds like a plan. I'll bring something for dessert, and I'll see you at seven."

Flutters make themselves known in my stomach, and I swallow past the feeling that this is wrong. "Sure. See you then."

ACID BURNS IN MY STOMACH, and sweat coats my forehead and down the curve of my spine. *What was I thinking?* I never should have agreed to dinner. And I definitely shouldn't have invited him here and offered to cook for him.

I must have lost my freaking mind to think I could do this.

I pace around the island in my kitchen, berating myself for my stupidity. I can't have Ben here. *Alone.*

It's okay when he's here to spend time with Evan, but this is different. I'm attracted to him, and I shouldn't be. The backs of my eyes sting, and that telltale tingle fizzes in my nose. Hot tears well until they become too heavy and slide down my cheeks. I swipe at them angrily.

I can't do this.

I don't know why I thought I could.

Snatching up my phone, I navigate to my contacts and find Ben's number. As I'm about to press his number to call, my phone rings, startling me, and I fumble to keep hold of the device.

It's *him*.

I answer with a shaky finger and hold the phone up to my ear. "Hello?" My blood races through my body too fast and I grip onto the counter for support.

A long sigh sounds on the other end of the phone. "Hey, Hope. I'm so sorry to have to do this, but Rex and I have been called into work. An elderly woman with dementia has gone missing, and we need to help find her," he says. Each word drips with regret, and I can imagine him running his thick fingers through the short strands of his hair. "This happens sometimes and I can't say no. It's part of the job. I'm so sorry to cancel. I was really looking forward to dinner."

I look out my kitchen window to the darkness beyond and shiver—it's only sixty degrees outside. That poor woman is wandering, probably lost and disoriented, out there somewhere.

"Oh no, Ben. Please don't apologize to me. I completely understand." Guilt washes over me at the relief I feel from him canceling. But then I think about *why* he canceled, and I feel terrible for the missing lady and her worried family. "Your job is important, and it's cold out there. Finding her and making sure she's safe is far more important than dinner. Please don't give it a second thought."

He blows out a breath. "Thanks for being so understanding. Maybe we can have dinner another time?"

"Yeah, sure. Good luck with your search."

"Thanks. Bye, Hope." Regret is thick in his voice, but all I feel is relief.

Sweet, *sweet* relief.

"Bye, Ben." I sag against the counter as the phone goes dead.

23

BEN

I'VE NEVER FELT PISSED ABOUT BEING CALLED INTO work before. Even when it's happened in the middle of a date. It's part of the job. The job I love. But tonight, I'm pissed. What's worse is that I got the impression Hope was relieved I had to cancel. I shouldn't have suggested that we have dinner tonight. It was too soon. But it was impossible not to jump on the opportunity to spend some time alone with her, and now I've probably spooked her.

I pull into the parking lot of the nursing home and push my hectic thoughts away to focus on the task at hand. "Are you ready, Rex?"

He barks loudly in response, and my lips widen. *This* is what we live for. We climb out of the cruiser and head straight to the lead officer, who takes long strides straight toward us with his hand outstretched. "Taylor." We shake hands. "Rex." He rubs Rex's scruff. "Thanks for coming out so quickly."

"No problem."

"We have an eighty-five-year-old female with dementia. Anne Sinclair. The home didn't know what time she left the building, but we've looked over security footage and discovered she left around fifteen-thirty hours. They only discovered her missing when she wasn't in her room when they went to collect her for dinner." My eyebrows shoot up and he nods sagely. "Footage shows her wearing a cotton dress and no shoes. In the past when she's had lucid moments, she's attempted to escape from the facility. It seems she succeeded today."

"Jesus. She'll be freezing."

He nods, a grim expression tightening the area around his eyes and mouth. "Yeah. Time is of the essence. If you head to the reception desk, they have an item belonging to Anne for Rex. We need to hurry."

"Got it." I tug on Rex's lead. "C'mon, Rex. Let's get started."

We head inside, where it's significantly warmer, and I wonder how on earth someone known to have dementia can walk out the front door without being stopped or, at the very least, noticed.

The receptionist hands me a plastic bag with what looks to be a pillow case inside. "Once the police requested an item of Anne's, we thought it best to seal it in a bag to prevent our scent from being added to it."

I tip my head and give her a grateful smile. "Thank you. Appreciate it."

The woman fidgets. "I feel so bad. I left the desk to go to the bathroom. I was only gone a few minutes. That must have been when she wandered out with a group of visitors. I'm so sorry."

It's not me who she needs to apologize to, so I just tip my head in acknowledgement, then crouch down to Rex and pull the bag open. "Okay, Rex. Take a deep, long sniff. Let's find Anne and bring her home safely."

He buries his nose into the bag and sniffs the fabric, then drops his snout to the carpet, sniffing the surrounding area. I climb to my feet, holding the bag in case he needs a refresher along the way. I never know how long a search will take, because it's impossible to predict how far someone's traveled in the time they've been missing. He moves toward the large glass doors and they slide open, exposing us to the chill of the night.

Rex obviously has a potent scent, and I follow his lead.

One hour passes—and another. White clouds form in front of my face with each breath I take, and there's still no sign of Anne. Her lack of appropriate clothing for the cool of the night increases my concern by the minute. She's not even wearing shoes on her damn feet.

Rex heads into a playground and sniffs around the swings. "What is it, boy?" He looks up at me, his tail wagging. "Where's Anne?"

He barks in response.

He takes off again toward the opposite side of the playground, stopping at the slide and the climbing frame. We head down the sidewalk and keep moving through the darkened streets, lit every ninety feet by the soft yellow glow of the street lamps.

We've traveled a good eight miles so far, and still no sign of her. My stomach drops as my worry for her well-being grows. Rex has an exceptional search-and-find success rate, one of the best on the force, so I'm confident we'll find her. My concern is for what state she'll be in when we do.

Yet another hour passes, and we're closing in on 10:30. The temperature's dropped since we started our search, and she's been missing for seven hours now.

Rex veers off the sidewalk, passes through a rusted metal gate, and steps onto a stone walkway that's overgrown with weeds, leading up to a porch with more rotten planks than I would trust to support my weight. The smashed windows of the home are dirty with years of grime, and it looks as though it's been abandoned for decades.

Rex bolts to the darkest corner, and a lump comes into view. My heart sinks as I drop to my knees beside the elderly woman. She's unnaturally still, and I rest my hand on her back, noting the lack of body heat and movement. I shift my hand up and over her shoulder, placing two fingers on the side of her throat, and dip down so my cheek is next to her mouth and nose.

Nothing.

Devastation washes over me, and I drop my head out of respect. "I'm sorry, Anne." I shake my head and remove my jacket, gently placing it over her body, covering as much of her as I can. I know it won't make any difference, but it feels wrong to leave her exposed to the cold.

I make the call that I've found her and give our location, then drop to my butt to sit beside her, taking her frozen hand in mine.

Rex whines and drops to his stomach on her other side, lying close and sharing his body heat with her.

My thoughts go to her family and the pain they're about to experience with the loss of their loved one. She was possibly someone's wife, mother, aunt, sister. She was definitely someone's daughter. She lived a long life, and this is how it ends for her—frozen and alone. It's so damn tragic. And so unfair.

While I wait for support to arrive, I can't help but think about the relief in Hope's voice when I told her I had to work. I'm man enough to admit it stung a little. I had hoped we were at least beginning to build on the initial stages of friendship—and maybe we are, but she's scared.

I've caught her checking me out, so I think she's attracted to me on some level. Maybe she feels guilty when she promised herself to Wyatt, but I doubt he'd want her to be alone for the rest of her life. If she were my wife, I know I wouldn't want that for her.

There are no blue and red flashing lights when the team arrives, and we efficiently and respectfully work together to do what needs to be done for Anne.

It's almost midnight when I finish with the necessary paperwork and head out of the station. I'm beat. And starving—I didn't have time to eat dinner. The thought of going home to an empty house is unappealing after seeing Anne curled into a ball, alone on the porch of an abandoned house.

My phone buzzes, so I drag it out of my pocket.

COOKIE

I hate to bother you, but I wanted to check if you found the lady you were looking for

I can't turn my mind off … I just keep wondering

If you can't share that information with me, I understand

She's still awake. A grin explodes across my face, and suddenly I don't feel so tired. I'm not surprised she was concerned; she has such a empathetic heart.

I'd love to see her, so instead of answering, I head toward her house. "Do you think she'll let us in, Rex?" I hope so.

When I pull up in Hope's driveway, the soft glow of the television shines around the edge of the curtains. I grab Rex, lock the cruiser, and head straight for her front door with my heart racing. I have to physically pause and take a deep, calming breath to stop myself from banging down her door.

Slow. Slow. Slow.

I knock softly, in case she's asleep. As time ticks on and there's no answer, my shoulders curl inward, and fatigue begins to overwhelm me.

"Who's there?" her soft, lyrical voice comes through the door. The porch light turns on, bathing me and Rex in a soft glow.

She's still awake!

I clear my throat. "It's just me." I drop my head to study my sneakers. *What was I thinking, turning up on her doorstep at midnight?* "Sorry. I know it's late. I shouldn—"

The click of the lock rings out and sends my pulse spiking. The door swings open, revealing her gorgeous face, free from makeup, and her curls piled haphazardly on top of her head. I can't see her body because she's hiding behind the door.

"Everything okay?" she asks, worry pinching around her eyes. I swallow, unable to speak, as she steps out from behind the door in an oversized army sweatshirt and long knitted socks that reach above her knees, leaving a couple of inches of her toned thighs exposed. She looks fucking adorable. "Ben? Are you all right?" she asks as she unlocks and pushes open the screen door.

"We didn't have a positive outcome tonight and the thought of goi—" Before I can finish, she has her tiny body pressed against mine, her face buried in my chest, and her slim arms wrapped around my waist.

"I'm so sorry," she mumbles against my jacket.

My breath stutters in my lungs at the feel of her against my body. I close my eyes and cup the back of her head as I hook my other arm around her waist to hold her close. We fit together perfectly. Like she was always meant to be in my arms.

Rex whines at our feet, and when I look down at him, he's looking up at us, his ears pricked and eyes questioning. Hope pulls away from me to crouch so she can say hello to Rex, and now I'm wishing I'd dropped him home first.

"Would you like to come inside where it's warm?" She rubs Rex's scruff. "You do, don't you, boy?" She looks up at me from her crouched position and a sudden vision of her on her knees, taking my cock deep down her throat, assaults me.

My dick wakes up. *Down, boy.* This isn't the time to show off.

"Have you eaten?"

I shake my head, trying desperately to shove the illicit image from my mind. "No."

"I can reheat the dinner I made," she offers.

Now I feel like an asshole. I never apologized for wasting her time in the kitchen preparing dinner for us. "I'm sorry about tonight."

She shrugs, her marine-colored eyes sparkling beneath the porch light. "Don't worry about it. Come inside."

She steps to the side, allowing us to enter her home. It's considerably warmer, and I instantly feel better after the discovery Rex and I made tonight. Just being in Hope's presence is enough to wipe away the image of Anne curled up on what we discovered was the porch of her childhood home. We found out, from her niece, that she had never married or had children—that she was pretty much alone.

The knowledge added to the devastation of our discovery and only highlighted the aloneness and isolation of the life I've created for myself. I see Sebastian every few weeks—at best. I have friendly banter with the crew at work, but I haven't developed any solid friendships. City life is quite different from country life—where everyone knows everyone—making it difficult to create bonds.

I'll never regret moving to the city, because I needed to escape the memories and toxicity of my hometown, but I find living here lonely ... until Hope and Evan. They've been a bright spot in my otherwise routine life, and being in her company makes me feel ... better.

Hope steps into the kitchen and flicks on the light, then heads straight to the fridge. "Take a seat and I'll heat this up. It'll only take a couple of minutes."

I watch her move around the kitchen with ease. She said she loves to cook and her fridge and pantry certainly look well-stocked. Leaning my elbows on the counter, I angle forward as she bends over to reach something at the bottom of the cupboard. The oversized sweatshirt she's wearing—that I suspect belonged to Wyatt—still covers her ass, but I'm treated to a little more thigh. When she stands with two empty metal dog bowls for Rex, my brain goes haywire.

Pointing to the dishes, I ask the obvious question, "Are those for Rex?"

She looks down at them, as if to clarify what I'm talking about.

"Well, yeah. I bought them on my way home today, so he'd have something to use whenever he comes over." Her eyes widen, and she slams her mouth closed as if she's shared a secret that's not hers to share, but her words give me hope that something can grow between us. Especially if she's thinking about Rex coming over regularly, because we both know Rex won't be coming here alone. Pink races up her neck, and I can't tear my gaze away from her and the startled expression she's wearing.

I climb to my feet and, without taking my eyes from her, make my way around the counter until I'm in her space. The bowls press against my abs, and I look down into her uncertain gaze. She tilts her head back and swallows roughly.

"You didn't have to do that, but I'm not gonna lie, I appreciate it." I flick my eyes between hers. "I know you were uncertain about Rex, so it means a lot to me you trust him in your home. It means even more to me you think enough of him to have bought these." I take them from her hands, dropping my gaze to her lips. I'd do anything right now to lean down and press my mouth to hers to show my appreciation.

Slow. Slow. Slow.

I break the moment and spin toward the sink to fill one bowl with water and place it on the floor beside the counter.

Still frozen in the same spot, she watches me. "You're welcome," she murmurs as she finally moves toward the fridge. "I cooked him some chicken and vegetables for dinner. I'll just ... uh ... grab it from the fridge."

It's my turn to freeze as she grabs the container and empties it into the second bowl, then places it on the floor beside his water. "You made him dinner?" Rex wastes no time and digs in. He didn't get to eat either, so he's starving.

"Yeah. I assumed he'd come with you. I didn't want him to go hungry." Her thoughtfulness touches a place deep inside. Her assumption that I'd bring him with me and planned accordingly warms my heart.

"I hadn't planned to bring him with me, but thank you for thinking of him." I could keep going with my gratitude, but the microwave beeps, letting us know my midnight dinner is ready.

Hope points to the opposite side of the counter and tells me to sit, then grabs my plate out of the microwave and slides it in front of me. I draw in a deep breath of the delicious smelling dish.

"Beef stroganoff," she tells me, then tips some milk and chocolate into a saucepan on the stove. "I hope you like it." She grabs a bottle of water from the fridge and passes it to me.

"It smells delicious, and I'm starving." I collect my fork. "Thanks for this."

"You're welcome," she says easily as she stirs the milk and chocolate on the stove. I take my first bite without taking my eyes from her exposed thighs.

When the first creamy bite lands on my tongue, I moan. I chew the tender beef and swallow, quickly scooping up another bite. "This is really good."

"Glad you like it. I can't make it for Evan because he doesn't like mushrooms." She pours the chocolate milk into a mug, then pulls out the stool beside me and sits, wrapping her hands around the warm ceramic. We're both quiet for a few moments. "Do you want to talk about what happened tonight?"

I swallow the food in my mouth. I guess that's partly why I came here. I didn't want to be alone. I needed to know there was someone around. Someone who would listen if I needed to talk. Anne isn't the first person we've searched for who didn't make it, but her passing is fresh. Normally, I'd go home, have a couple of beers and push everything away. But I don't have to do that tonight.

"The person we were searching for walked out of a nursing home. She was there because she had dementia, and I'm struggling to comprehend how she could walk out of there with no one noticing. They said she often tries to escape when she's lucid, but still ..." I swallow past my anger at the poor management of the facility. "She was wearing a cotton dress. Didn't even have shoes on. Security footage showed she walked out at 3:30 p.m. with a group of visitors who were leaving, but nobody noticed her missing until dinnertime."

Hope gasps. "That's awful."

I nod. "I know. Rex and I searched for more than three hours and eight and a half miles before we found her curled up in the darkened corner of the porch of an abandoned house. She was so still and so cold. I covered her with my jacket and held her hand while Rex and I sat with her until my team arrived."

Hope's hand slides across the counter between us and covers mine. Her warm fingers wrap around mine, and she squeezes. I flip my hand over and link our fingers together, much the same way I did last time. Dropping my gaze to where we're connected, I note how pale her skin looks against mine, how small her hand is, and how right it feels to be accepting her quiet support.

"We found out she used to live there as a child." That was probably the most heartbreaking knowledge of the night.

I raise my gaze to Hope's face. Tears fill her eyes and topple over her lashes to trail slowly down her porcelain cheeks. "Oh, god. That's just so tragic."

I spin on my stool, bringing me closer to her, and raise my hands to cup her face. Using my thumbs, I gently wipe away the tears on her cheeks. Cheeks that should never glisten with tears, only rise with happiness. Her eyes flick between mine and my lips, and the temptation to lean forward and press a kiss to hers is almost too much to fight.

It wouldn't take much.

A slight pitch forward.

But then I glance back up at her eyes, and all I see is confusion. It's like someone's opened the back door and let the chilly night air in. It's a reality check. One I needed.

Leaning back, I put more space between us and slide my hands down her cheeks to her neck, across her slim shoulders, and reluctantly pull them away. Turning forward again, I sever the connection, and in my periphery, I see her shoulders sag and hear a soft breath leave her mouth. I'm such an ass. Touching her like I have the right to.

Grabbing my fork, I scoop up more food and nod. "Yeah. Rex and I have had a few searches over the years that haven't ended well, but this one felt ... different somehow."

"I can't even imagine," Hope murmurs.

I focus on eating my dinner while Hope drinks her hot chocolate. No more words are spoken, but the silence isn't uncomfortable. Rex has finished eating, so he's lying on the floor with his head resting on his front paws, his stomach full and satisfied.

When I'm finished eating, I collect Hope's empty cup and my plate and carry them to the sink to wash the dishes.

"You don't have to do that," she says as she rises.

I look at her over my shoulder. "Yes, I do. You made a delicious meal for Rex and me. I've intruded on your sleep. It's the least I can do."

She flicks her wrist, waving off my words, then bends down to grab Rex's empty bowl. We work together to clean up, and I no longer have any reason to stay. She needs to sleep, and I should get home. I wipe my hands on my jeans.

"Thanks for letting me come in, for feeding me, and for listening. I couldn't face going home to an empty house."

She smiles sadly as we walk to the front door. "I'm glad I could be here for you. I completely understand about the empty house part." She waves her hand around, gesturing toward the emptiness of her house. "It's not much fun."

I scratch my short nails through my trimmed beard, so I don't reach for her. I've already crossed the line tonight, and I don't want to do it again. "No. It's not."

She opens the door and pushes the screen door open, wrapping her arms across her middle as she holds it open with her body.

Rex steps onto the porch first and looks up at her as if to thank her for dinner, and she rubs the scruff of his neck. "See ya, Rex. You did good tonight, even if it didn't have a happy ending." He licks her while his tail wags, making her chuckle. She stands to her full height, bringing the top of her head in line with my chin. "See ya, Ben. Get some sleep."

"You, too. Thanks again." I lean in and kiss her cheek lightly, and then head down the porch steps before I wrap my arms around her lithe body and pull her tight against me so I can taste her properly.

24

HOPE

"Mom! Look, I can make a rainbow!" Evan shouts across the yard as he holds the spray up to the sky.

I chuckle as I push the mower forward. "It looks pretty, Ev."

Satisfied that I've seen his rainbow, he returns to washing the suds off the car, and I turn the mower around and head back in the opposite direction.

The upkeep of the house feels like a never-ending job, and even though Dad, Graeme, and Shane have offered numerous times to help, I refuse. They all helped us so much over the last few years, and I'm determined to become independent this year. I know it's been hard for them to step back and give us the space to learn to do things for ourselves, but I'm happier knowing I can do things on my own. And Evan's older now, so he can help and is happy to do so ... mostly.

I finish mowing and put the mower away, then grab a bucket so I can dig the weeds out of the garden beds. Evan meets me on the front porch with two glasses of lemonade. "You have a missed call from Uncle Nix," he tells me as he hands my phone over.

I put it on the step between us. "I'll call him later." I take a long drink, the cool liquid soothing my throat. "Thanks for the drink. I was thirsty."

The phone rings, and when I look at the screen, Nix's name glows brightly. I grab it and answer with a smile. "Hey, Nix. Long time, no speak." Conversations between the two of us used to be awkward. As Wyatt's commanding officer, he held a lot of guilt for Wyatt's death. He felt responsible for allowing Wyatt and Shane to play soccer with the boy who was carrying the explosive device that ultimately stole Wyatt from us.

"Hey, Hope. Yeah, it's been a while. Sorry about that, I've been busy and time seems to disappear," he says, but there's a note of stress in his voice.

"That's all right. Is everything okay?" I ask as my eyes scan the garden beds for weeds that need to be removed.

There's a long pause on the other end of the line, and I check the screen to see if our call has been disconnected. "Uh, I don't know how to tell you this, so I'll just say it."

My heart races, and my hands shake. Blood rushes through my ears, and my mouth fills with cotton. It all happens in an instant as panic hits me like a freight train. "What's wrong?" I stand, no longer able to be seated.

Evan twists his head in my direction, his face pinched tight.

"A rattlesnake bit Shane this afternoon, and Violet rushed him to the emergency room," he says, his voice full of tension, and I can tell it must be serious by his tone.

My hand flies up to cover my mouth. Panic threatens to drag me under, but I concentrate on my breathing. "Oh, my god!" I pace the walkway, twisting a curl around my finger. "Is he gonna be all right?"

Evan jumps to his feet. "What's happened?"

"A rattlesnake bit Shane. He's in the hospital," I rush to tell him.

Nix's voice steals my attention back to the call. "They took him straight in for treatment when they arrived, and he's still there. Violet hasn't heard anything more. I'm on my way. I'll keep you updated."

"No, we'll head over." I look at Evan with wide eyes. "Which hospital is he at?"

"Mercy Vale. Go to Emergency. I'll meet you there."

I climb the steps and hurry inside. "Okay." I disconnect the call. "Evan. Get changed, we have to go."

He rushes behind me. "Is he gonna be okay?"

I stop in my tracks, sensing that my son needs reassurance. Shane means a lot to him—to both of us. I grip his shoulders firmly and lock my gaze with his. His eyes, so much like his father's, almost knock me on my ass, but I take a deep breath. "He's in the best place to get the help he needs. He's going to be okay, but I'd like us to be there to support Violet and Jasmine. Okay?"

He nods quickly. "Okay."

"Go get changed, and wear something comfortable. Layers are a good idea. I'm not sure how long we'll be," I call after him.

"Okay."

I quickly change, shove some snacks and bottles of water in my purse, and we head out, locking the house behind us. We're both quiet in the car as I drive us across town toward the hospital. I wonder what happened? My hands tremble against the steering wheel, so I grip it tighter.

He has to be okay. He can't survive an explosion overseas only to come home and not survive a rattlesnake bite—not now, when he's met the woman of his dreams and is finally living the life he deserves.

Life can't be that cruel. But that nagging voice in the back of my head reminds me it can.

I glance in the rearview mirror at Evan. He stares out of his window, lost in thought. "He'll be okay, Ev. He's strong and healthy." I take a deep breath, hoping I haven't just lied to my son.

His only response is to nod.

We pull into the parking lot, and I find the only empty spot. Of course, it's the farthest away from the emergency entrance. We couldn't possibly find somewhere closer when I'm in a damn hurry. We quickly climb out of the car and head through the giant glass sliding doors. We make our way to the emergency area waiting room, finding it packed with people. And the way they're gathered together, I can only assume they're all here for Shane.

Nix walks toward us, says hello to Evan with a handshake, and wraps me in a hug. With his arms around me, my bravery leaves me and a sob breaks free. He pulls me in close, and I bury my face in his hard chest. "I'm sorry I had to call you. Violet thought you'd like to know."

I look up at his stern face. "Thank you. Of course I'd want to know. He's important to us." Pulling away, I swipe away my tears in embarrassment. Guilt—my constant companion—washes through me because I've pushed Shane away over these last months, and we haven't seen him all that much. "Any news?"

He shakes his head solemnly. "Not yet."

My mouth turns down, and worry makes my stomach twist. "I should talk to Violet."

He nods stiffly, and I walk over to Violet, who's holding her sweet daughter, Jasmine. We smile sadly at one another and embrace the best we can with her gorgeous little girl between us. I don't know what to say to her. I don't want to give her platitudes; I'm certain I wouldn't want to hear them if I were in her shoes. Instead, we seem to have a silent conversation, offering each other support just by being close.

"Anything I can do for you?"

Violet shrugs, her eyes red and swollen. I can only guess how many tears have fallen. "Pray he's okay," she murmurs, her voice dripping with despair.

I nod and shift so I can get a better view of Jas's cute little face. "How are you, Jas?"

She pulls her tear-stained face out of the crook of her mother's neck. "I'm sad. My daddy's sick!"

Daddy.

Oh, my. I figured things were pretty serious, but I had no idea they were *this* serious. My heart feels like it's floating with happiness for them. That they found each other and have become a family. He'll definitely pull through this—there's no way he'd ever leave these two behind.

"I know. But the nurses and doctors are looking after him, and he'll be all better soon." She nods, acknowledging my words, and I return my attention to Violet. "What happened?"

"We decided to go on a picnic. We'd been there a while, and I was taking photos, so Shane and Jas went for a walk."

"There was a rattlesnake under the bush, and Daddy picked me up so it wouldn't bite me, but it bit Daddy and made him sick," Jas adds quickly.

I reach out to rub her tiny arm and look back at Violet, continuing our unspoken conversation. *Lucky he was there.*

I know. Thank god he saved Jas. She holds her daughter a little tighter.

Imagine if the snake had bitten Jas. There's no way she would have survived something like that. He saved her life with his quick thinking. But that doesn't surprise me. Shane's all about caring for the people around him.

We all stand, sit, or pace the floor of the waiting room as we wait for news. Violet's mom and her partner gather Violet's nieces and Jas to take them home—I'm surprised when Jas leaves willingly. Violet breaks down, and we all gather around her to give her the support she needs as we remind her how strong Shane is. We all know he'll be fighting hard to stay for her and for Jas.

It feels like an eternity passes before a nurse comes out through the doors. "The family of Shane Sutton," she calls.

We all leap to our feet, Violet's sister, Cassia, supporting her. "That's us," she tells the nurse.

The nurse scans the group. "I can only take two people through."

Violet seems to shrink a little, but finds her voice. "Can you give the rest of us an update at least? Is he ... is he okay?" she asks shakily.

The nurse's gaze wanders over each of us. "He was in pretty bad shape. The amount of walking he did before he received assistance meant the venom made its way through his system. However, he was brought in within two hours of the bite, and we immediately started antivenom treatment. While he didn't have an allergic reaction to the treatment, his condition worsened, and we had to give him another dose and move him to the ICU"—my breath wooshes out of me—"where he'll be monitored closely and continue to receive further treatments every six hours."

I can't believe this is happening. It feels unreal that such a giant of a man is so unwell. He always seems so invincible. So strong. So vital.

Violet loses her fight to stand on her own, and as she collapses, Toby—her brother-in-law and world-famous musician—catches her and holds her up. I watch her find her strength and face the nurse. "Will he be okay?"

The nurse's eyes scan our group and land back on Violet. "He's improving, which is a positive sign. I can't tell you any more than that. You'll need to speak with his doctor. But I'm happy to take two people through to see him."

Evan and I move away from the main group while they have a discussion about who's going to go through with the nurse. We wrap our arms around each other in support. Nix and Toby hug Violet, and she disappears through the doors with Shane's mom.

"Mom, do you think he's gonna be okay?" Evan's been so quiet throughout everything, internalizing his worry, so I'm glad he's finally speaking.

"You heard the nurse. He's improving, which is a positive sign. Rattlesnake bites can be deadly, but if he's improving, I think he'll be okay." His shoulders drop from around his ears and I massage the back of his neck and across his shoulders.

"Do you think we'll get to see him?"

I shake my head. "I don't think so. Not tonight anyway, because it's so late. We can come back and visit with him when he can have visitors."

"I'm not ready to leave yet."

"Me neither." I'd rather be here with the people who love him the most, than be at home. At least here, if there are any updates, we'll hear them along with everyone else.

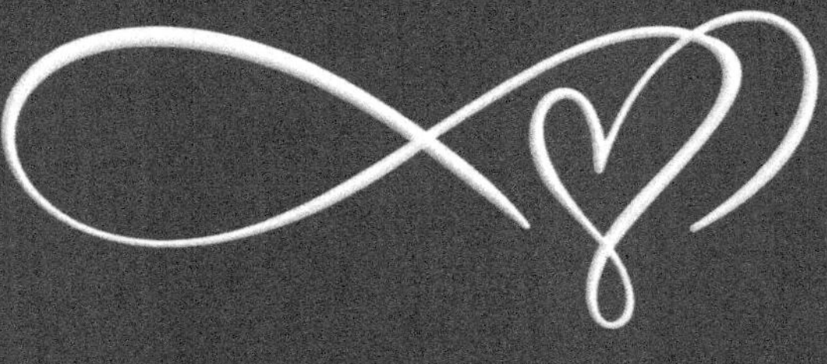

25

HOPE

Wrapped in Wyatt's hoodie and a blanket, I hold my morning coffee in two hands while I watch the sunrise from my front porch.

We sat with everyone, until eventually, Shane's mom returned to the waiting room, leaving Violet to stay with Shane alone. Evan was curled up across two seats, asleep, and I figured it was time to head home. I left my number with Cassia and asked her to pass it on so I could be kept up to date. Evan and I stumbled through the door, said goodnight to each other, and disappeared into our respective bedrooms, exhausted.

I can't stop thinking about how Shane saved Jasmine's life. Even though I was exhausted last night, I couldn't sleep because my brain wouldn't shut down.

He was so angry that he survived the bomb blast when Wyatt didn't. He felt that his life was somehow worth less than Wyatt's because he didn't have a wife and child waiting at home for him. I know there were dark times for Shane—times when he didn't want to survive. Times I completely understood, because if it hadn't been for Evan, I think I would have given up on this life to be with Wyatt.

But now I'm wondering if he was meant to survive for a reason. And maybe that reason was to be here to save Jas.

Shaking my head, I lift my coffee to my lips and drink, savoring the warmth as it slides down my throat. If I consider there was a reason Shane survived, then I also have to consider there was a reason Wyatt didn't, and that's too difficult to contemplate. I refuse to accept any reason would be good enough to take him away from us. But I can't deny the idea that Shane was meant to be here.

A shiver works its way up my spine, and I shudder as I look out across the street, noting the glint of the rising sun off the windows of the houses opposite us. Glancing upward, I suck in a sharp breath at the beautiful purplish-pink shades stretching across the sky. I didn't notice colors after Wyatt first died. I didn't notice the color of the flowers—or how green the grass was. I didn't see the changing colors of the seasons, and I completely missed changes in Evan because I was too entrenched in my grief.

Now, I realize it's important to appreciate the little things— the changes and shifts caused by the passing of time and the beauty in the world around me. I promise myself to pay more attention to Evan and to never miss another milestone.

As I PULL into the hospital parking lot, I glance at Evan in the rearview mirror. "Remember, we can't stay too long or you'll be late for soccer practice, and you need to be there to show Ben what to do."

He nods. "Yeah, I know."

Imagine my surprise when Evan called Ben to ask him if he could coach the team at practice tonight because Shane's in the hospital. He did it without consulting me while I was busy finishing the gardening I didn't get to on Saturday.

We climb out of the car and walk inside, searching for the room number Violet sent me yesterday.

"It's here, Mom." Evan steps through the door, and I follow close behind. "Shane!" he calls as he closes the distance to the bed.

I glance around quickly, hoping Evan hasn't disturbed anyone, then my eyes land on Shane. It's weird seeing him lying prone and being still. He's always active, needing to do something to keep busy.

Shane smiles at Evan. "Hey, big guy."

Evan studies the giant of a man, tracing his eyes over every part of him with concern, even though he's covered with a sheet and cotton blanket. "Hey."

Shane tips his chin toward me. "Hey, how are you doing?"

"Better than you," I say as I step closer to his bed. Now that I've finally seen him with my own eyes, my heart finally slows to a normal rhythm.

He shrugs. "Yeah, well ... better me than Jas."

"While we were waiting to hear if you were going to be okay, Jasmine told us all about how you saved her from a rattlesnake." I lean down to kiss his bristly cheek. "You did good," I tell him.

He shrugs again like it's no big deal he saved Jasmine's life. "Better me than her," he repeats.

I agree with a nod. "I haven't stopped thinking about it all." I bite my bottom lip because I'm not sure how to say what I want to say. I can't even believe I'm going to say the words. "And I was thinking ... maybe ..." I glance at Evan, then study Shane's face closely. "Maybe you were meant to survive the blast so you were here to save Jasmine's life," I say on a shaky breath.

His face pales to an unhealthy shade and, after a moment, he nods sharply, then turns toward Evan with his usual stoic expression in place. "Sorry I can't make it to practice this afternoon."

Evan's been worried about how Shane would feel when he found out that Ben was going to take his place as coach while he's unable. He looks down at the floor. "That's okay. Ben said he'd help, even though he doesn't know anything about soccer. He said I could tell him what you usually do, and I could be his assistant coach." I know he doesn't want to hurt Shane's feelings, but he's so excited Ben's coming to practice.

"Who's Ben?" Shane asks as he glances between me and Evan. I shuffle on my feet and adjust the strap of my purse on my shoulder. I've been pushing Shane away, determined to be independent, and now here we are telling him that someone else is going to take his place. I swallow, suddenly uncomfortable with the discussion.

"He's the police officer that ... you know," Evan says, dropping his eyes to the floor as pink stains his cheeks.

Shane's eyes flick between me and Evan for a few moments, then his lips slowly spread, forming a wide grin. Crinkles form around the corners of his eyes, and he genuinely seems happy. He musses Evan's short hair. "That's great. Please thank him for me, and if he gets stuck, he can give me a call."

Evan's head snaps up and his wide eyes land on Shane. "You're not mad?"

Shane chuckles. It's a foreign sound coming from him. He's normally such a stoic man, but I love the sound of his happiness. It's exactly what I've wanted for him. It's what he deserves. "Why would I be mad? I'm grateful he can step in to help."

Evan blows out a relieved breath, and his shoulders relax. Then he grins as he looks up at Shane. "He said he can help out as long as you need, provided he's not working." He moves in closer and whispers, "I was worried it would hurt your feelings. I'm glad you're not mad. Ben's really cool."

I smile to myself and chuckle. "Ben and Evan have become fast friends, but I think Evan loves Ben's police dog, Rex, more than he loves Ben."

"Well ... Rex is pretty cool."

Violet walks in with a tray of drinks and snacks, closely followed by Shane's best friend and boss, Toby Summer. I can't believe how down to earth the guy is considering he's a world-famous rock star. When we met him the other night, he was so warm and friendly to Evan and me.

We all say hello, and it's plain to see how happy Shane is to see Violet. However, I can't miss the tension that seems to snap between him and Toby, and I wonder what's happened between them to cause such disharmony.

"All right, Ev. We need to get moving if we want to be on time for practice." I lean down and kiss Shane's cheek. "I'm so glad you're okay."

"Me too," he whispers, and I know he really means it. A part of me settles knowing he's going to be okay—and not just from the snakebite, but in general. He's found his place, and he's finally happy. Wyatt would be thrilled for his friend.

I say goodbye to Violet and Toby, offering my help if they need it, then hook my arm around Evan's shoulders and lead him out of the room.

26

It's chaos.

Organized chaos, but it's still chaotic. There are kids everywhere with moms, dads, and even a few grandparents in tow. Hope's car isn't in the parking lot, but I head to the same area I saw Evan playing a few weeks ago and cross my fingers I'm in the right place.

Looking around, I spot other coaches placing out cones in some type of formation in their designated area. I have forty minutes to coach the kids, then we pair up with another team for a game that lasts an hour. Apparently, that's a shorter time than a regular game.

After Evan asked me to coach his team because their friend, Shane, was hospitalized with a snakebite, I checked out some YouTube videos so I wouldn't be at a complete loss as to what to do. I've never played soccer, never even watched a game, but in the last twenty-four hours, I've binged enough material to help me feel like I know a little about it.

Since nobody's setting up in this area, I'm going to assume I'm in the right spot, so I grab some cones and place them in a grid. The parents and kids watch me with uncertainty until one boy grows brave enough to approach me.

"Who are you?"

"I'm Ben. I'm taking Coach Shane's place for the day," I tell him, offering a friendly smile. "What's your name?"

He folds his arms across his chest with a huff. "Ronald. Where's Coach Shane?"

I stop what I'm doing and give Ronald my full attention. "I'll explain where he is and why I'm here once everyone arrives. That way, I only have to say it once. Okay?"

He dips his chin. "Who's your kid on the team?"

I rub the back of my neck. "I don't have a kid on the team, but I'm Evan's friend."

Ronald huffs again like it's an Olympic sport and rolls his eyes. "He's a bully."

My eyebrows shoot up. "I find that hard to believe."

"He pushed me over for no good reason. He's a bully. I don't care if you don't believe me," he snaps.

Well, this isn't a good start. I didn't anticipate dealing with team politics this afternoon, but I guess it's inevitable with any sports team. Satisfied that I'm aware of Evan's flaw, he spins on his heel and returns to his mom.

When I glance up, a flash of red catches my eye in the parking lot. I look more closely, and some of the tension I was holding across my shoulders dissipates. I'm used to being in unfamiliar territory with work, but this is different. This is important, and I want to make a good impression.

I watch them park and climb out of the car. Evan runs toward me, while Hope follows behind at a steady pace after grabbing a camping chair out of her trunk. She's so damn beautiful with the afternoon sun behind her, making her hair look like golden honey. Her tight denim jeans hug her slender thighs, and her baby blue sweater perfectly complements the color of her eyes.

"Hey, Ben. Sorry we're late," Evan says, stopping in front of me. "We stopped at the hospital to check on Shane."

I grip his shoulder and squeeze it gently. "That's okay. How's he doing?"

Hope joins us after setting up her chair on the sideline. "He's gonna be okay. Thankfully." The relief on her face is unmistakable.

They both care about Shane, which is completely understandable with their connection. Once again, it makes me wonder if there was ever anything more than friendship between Hope and Shane. I dismiss the idea in the same breath. There's no way Hope would have gone there. Six years later, and she's still not ready to consider a relationship with anyone other than her husband.

"I'm not sure how long he'll be out of action, though."

"That's okay. We'll play it week by week. I'm happy to help if I'm not working." The other kids gather around us, and I nod my head to the team. "Do you guys want to explain what's going on? It's probably better coming from you."

Hope nods. "Sure."

I clap my hands loudly. "Can everyone gather around, please? We'd like to have a quick chat before we start today."

The kids and parents move in close, and Hope explains what happened to Shane. Immediately, one mom decides to organize a collection so the team can buy him a card and a gift. They all seem to have a lot of respect for the guy, and I hope I get to meet him at some point.

PRACTICE WENT OFF WITHOUT A HITCH—MOSTLY. That is, until Ronald took the opportunity to prove his earlier point about Evan being a bully. Ronald provoked Evan until he pushed him over. And while I don't condone Evan's behavior, he was clearly defending himself. Ronald didn't appreciate it when Evan pointed out that I'm a cop and told him I'd *investigate* the incident and file a police report. The kid soon fessed up and apologized for his errant behavior.

Other than that, I think the session went well, and if I have to help again, I'm pretty sure I'll do even better next time. I would imagine it'll take some time for Shane to be back on his feet. Though, I know army guys are pretty tough, particularly those in the Rangers. The guy didn't let a bomb blast keep him down; I doubt a rattler's gonna stop him.

The boys collect all of our equipment, and store it in the shed, which is busy as adults—wearing soccer gear—collect larger posts and nets to set up for their games.

"One day, I'll play on the grown up team," Evan tells me as he puffs out his chest.

"Yeah?" I confirm as we make our way over to Hope, who's waiting at the edge of the parking lot.

"Yeah. They play when it's dark. I wanna play for the *Monday Knights*. Those guys are really cool." We stop at Hope and my stomach sinks, knowing they'll go home to their place and I'll go home to mine. I hadn't realized how lonely I was until I started spending time with them. Rex is great company, but I miss regular human contact that's not part of my job. "Mom, can Ben come over for dinner?"

I try to keep the relief filling my veins from showing on my face when I steal a look at Hope to wait for her answer.

Her gaze lifts to mine, and a slow smile teases at her lips. "I was going to invite him over," she says to Evan, keeping her eyes locked with mine—the aquamarine looking darker beneath the twilight. "Would you like to join us for dinner? I made Shepherd's pie."

I don't care what we eat. The fact she's invited me into her home ... *again*, is more than enough for me. Even if they sat and ate dinner in front of me without offering me a single bite, I would never refuse. "Thanks. That'd be great. I'll quickly go home and feed Rex, then I'll come over. Can I bring anything?"

"Can you please bring Rex with you?" Evan asks, linking his hands together and holding them beneath his chin.

I chuckle and look up at Hope to confirm if it'll be okay with her.

She nods, smiling gently. "Please bring him. I have enough left over from last night's dinner for him."

"All right. I'll pick him up and then come over." I walk them to their car, hold the door open for Hope, and watch them drive away. Then, I head to the store, refusing to turn up empty-handed.

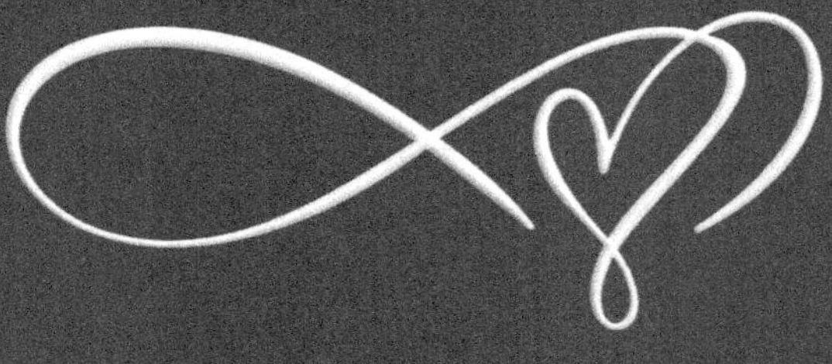

27

BEN

Rex races for the front door, landing on the porch in one leap, and I chuckle. "Are you excited to see them, too?" I rub the top of his head when I get to the porch, and he looks up at me. Once he realized where we were headed, he couldn't sit still in the truck.

I knock on the door, and within seconds, the sound of footsteps come toward us. The door bursts open, revealing Evan wearing an excited grin. "Rex!"

Rex half stands on his back feet and barks, matching Evan's excitement as he unlocks the screen door. My heart pounds because I know I'm about to see Hope again. Rex leaps up and rests his paws on Evan's shoulders, excitedly licking his face, eliciting bright laughter from the boy who's wormed his way into our hearts.

I hold the store-bought brownie and bottle of wine I grabbed on the way over above my head, and edge past the two. "Remember to lock the door, Ev."

"Okay."

As I walk down the hallway toward the kitchen at the back of the house, where I assume Hope will be, I pause for a moment and study the family photographs on the wall. Evan is like a mini version of his dad, but I see some aspects of Hope in him, too.

I skim my eyes over the various photos of Evan and Wyatt, Wyatt and Hope, Hope and Evan, and all three of them together.

Even though Hope hasn't changed all that much, she looks different now. There's an inherent sadness about her that isn't present in any of these photos. Her eyes were brighter, and I could swear she was glowing. And as gorgeous as she is, there's something to be said for the slightly more pronounced curves she had back then.

She was so happy. Content.

I've only ever seen brief glimpses of the Hope I see in these photos, and it's only when she seems to forget for a moment and allows herself to be in the here and now, which doesn't happen often. Soft music drifts out from the living room, making a change from the television I've grown accustomed to hearing.

Out of the corner of my eye, I see her step from the kitchen. She pauses a moment, then comes closer, looking at the photographs as she stands beside me.

She sighs, then points to a photo where Evan is tiny. "That was the day we brought Evan home from the hospital. Wyatt had been deployed, and we weren't sure if he was going to make it home in time. He missed the birth, but he was here to bring us home." She points to another one. "This was Evan's fifth birthday. It was the last birthday he got to share with his dad."

I wedge the bottle of wine beneath my arm, hook my free arm around her shoulders, and she sinks into me. "I'm sorry, Hope. Life's unfair sometimes."

"Yeah," she murmurs, then looks up at me. We're so close that it would be easy to dip down and press a kiss to her soft lips. "I've been thinking ..."

My pulse stutters at her expression, and I'm balancing on a knife's edge as I wait for her to share. "Yeah. What have you been thinking?"

I trace her gorgeous face with my eyes, wishing I could run my fingers down her cheek until I reach her chin, then tip her face back and take her mouth in a kiss I hope would make her weak in the knees.

She licks her lips, making them shine. She has no idea what she does to me. How sexy she is.

"With everything that happened to Shane, I feel like he survived the blast so he could be here to save Jasmine from the rattler." She shrugs and I study her closely, waiting for her to finish. "But then I would also have to accept there was a reason Wyatt didn't survive."

My heart tumbles out of my chest and sinks through my body until it's in a mushy mess at my feet. I tug Hope's body around until she's pressed against me, and her hands drop to my waist, holding onto my sweater. I kiss her forehead, then rest my chin on top of her head and breathe her sweet scent deep into my lungs, holding her to me with one arm.

"Not necessarily. Sometimes shitty things happen to good people without rhyme or reason."

She pulls her face away from my chest and tips her head back to look up at me. "I guess. Because I can't think of a good enough reason for him to be taken from us so soon."

I release her and slide my fingers through her hair, slipping it gently behind her ear. "There is no good reason. And I'm sorry you and Evan have had to experience his devastating loss. You will always love him and hold him in your memories. He will never diminish in your heart."

Her eyes flick between mine, and I hope she knows I'm being sincere. A shaky smile forms, and she drags her hands up my flanks until they're resting on my pecs. She'll definitely feel how hard my heart is beating for her, but I don't want to hide it. I'm so far gone for her, and we haven't even kissed.

If this is all she'll ever give me, I've decided it'll be enough. My rational mind says: *what the fuck, man?* But my affection for her doesn't come from a rational place. Our gazes lock for a moment, and this close, her warm breath coats my chin.

She licks her lips again, and my eyes drop to watch. "Dinner's almost ready," she murmurs.

Evan hustles past us with Rex, but doesn't bat an eye at our closeness, as if he's seen us standing together in an embrace before.

"Smells delicious."

She drops her gaze from mine, curls her hands into fists, and pushes away from me. When she spins toward the kitchen, my body deflates and I follow behind, my eyes dropping to her cute ass that's wrapped in denim. She's ditched the boots and replaced them with over-the-knee socks—like the ones she was wearing the night I turned up on her doorstep at midnight.

One day, I wouldn't mind having her legs resting over my shoulders while she *only* wears those socks. Never in my life would I have thought I'd find long socks sexy, but on her ... *damn*.

When I breach the kitchen door, I come to a stop. Rex's bowls are in the same place they were the other weekend, already filled with food and water for him, like he's part of the family. The table is set for three, and a salad is already sitting in the middle of the table. The Shepherd's pie is resting on the stove, and the counter-tops are free of mess.

She's worked hard since coming home from soccer practice, and it hits me ... she probably always works too hard. She's holding down a full-time job, running a household, and raising her son alone.

She doesn't *need* a man or anyone else in her life because she already has everything covered. But I'd bet there are times when she'd love to take a break. To kick back and just breathe. To take some time for herself. To be cared for instead of being the one to always do the caring.

She'll never *need* me. But I'd love for her to *want* me one day. To allow me the privilege of being the one to care for her and Evan.

I place the store-bought brownie on the counter, along with

the bottle of wine. "How about you take a seat, and Evan and I will serve dinner?" I lead her to the dining room and pull out the chair at the head of the table.

"Oh, this is your seat," she tells me, that distinctive flush I love so much rising up her slender throat.

Words escape me.

She sat me at the head of the table. Growing up, that spot was designated to the man of the house. It would have been where Wyatt sat when he was home, and warmth fills my body that she would even consider giving me the honor.

I shake my head. "*You're* the head of this household. You should sit there, Hope."

She swallows and shakes her head a little. "I-I-I can't sit there."

I nod. "Which seat is yours then, Cookie?"

She points to the seat on the left, so I pull the chair out, and she sits. I guess that means Evan's on the opposite side. I move the table setting from the head of the table to the seat beside Hope. She studies me closely, but I ignore the questions in her eyes. I want to show her I want to be here alongside her and Evan. That I'm not here to *replace* her husband.

"Evan, can you pour yourself a drink, please?" I walk around the counter to serve the pie, placing a portion on each plate. I hold a plate out for Evan to take. "Here ya go."

"Thanks, Ben." He takes a sip of his drink, then carries his glass and plate to the table. I follow him with our plates, then grab two wine glasses and the bottle I brought with me.

Holding it up to Hope, I ask, "Wine?"

She holds up her glass with a small smile. "Please."

While I pour, I ask Evan, "So how do you think practice went this afternoon?"

He swallows the food in his mouth. "Pretty good, I think. Maybe next time, bring a whistle."

I nod, then pour wine into my glass. "Good idea. It'll save my voice." I hold my glass up to Hope, and she taps hers against mine. Dipping my head, I say, "Cheers."

"Cheers."

The first mouthful of the meal Hope prepared is divine as the flavors of meat and potato burst across my tongue. She certainly knows how to cook. Every meal I've had here has been delicious. "This tastes fantastic. Thanks for inviting me to dinner."

Hope adjusts her position. "Thanks, and you're welcome," she says without looking at me.

Her mood's changed since she first said hello and we shared our moment in the hallway. She's grown somber and distant. She's rebuilt her walls, denying the friendship we're building. I'm not gonna lie to myself and say I'm not disappointed, because I am, but this is to be expected. If I want a chance with her, I need to bide my time and show her there's a life beyond the grief she's been drowning in.

Even though I'm aware of every single movement she makes, every breath she takes, each bite of food she swallows, I turn my attention to Evan. "How was school today?"

He shrugs. "Okay, I guess. It was school. Same as every other school day."

I nod. "Fair enough. Tell me one thing you liked best today, then."

He chews while he thinks. "We're starting a new topic in English. Creative writing." A slow grin grows. "I think I'll enjoy it."

My eyebrows shoot up. "I think you'll more than enjoy it. This is the perfect opportunity for you to share your talent. I look forward to reading what you write."

28

BEN

Hope stands abruptly, using the backs of her legs to shove her chair back noisily on the wooden floor, and hurries from the room. We both watch her until we can't see her any longer. I catch Evan's gaze across the table, and his only response is a shrug.

"Is she okay?" I thought I was doing the right thing, focusing on Evan instead of her, but maybe not.

"She does that sometimes," he says with another shrug and returns to eating.

"Should I check on her?"

He shrugs again. Typical boy. "Dunno. She usually comes back after a while and pretends nothing's wrong."

She does this sometimes? But then why does my gut tell me it's because of something I've done? Do I stay here, eat dinner, and wait for her to return? Pretend nothing happened? Or do I check on her and try to talk about it? The easier option would be to sit here and pretend nothing happened, but I'm not one for taking the easy route.

I stand, pushing my chair out with the backs of my legs. "I'm just gonna check on your mom."

He gives me a thumbs up and a smile. "Good luck!"

I grin at him. "Thanks."

I wander through the part of the house that leads to a guest room and bathroom. Listening carefully, I step down the hallway. A quiet sob breaks the silence, and I head toward the door at the end of the hallway. It happens again, and I lean my head against the door, pain ripping through my chest, threatening to take me under. I tap lightly. "Hope?"

"I'll be out in a minute," she answers, but I can hear the pain in her voice.

"Can I please come in?"

"No," she snaps. I haven't heard her speak like that before. "I just need a minute, okay?" she says, softening her tone.

"I just thought we could talk about whatever I did to upset you." I throw it out there, hoping she takes me up on my invitation.

Her sigh sounds through the door, and I can almost taste her defeat. The knob turns, so I step back a little to give her space, and the door opens an inch. It's enough to see her tears and make my stomach twist.

She drops her chin to her chest. "It wasn't you. Please don't think it was you." She's quiet for a long time, and I think that's all she's going to say.

I wish she'd open the door and literally let me in so I can wrap her up. Soothe her. Wipe away her tears.

She blows out a long breath, her shoulders rising and falling dramatically. "It ... it just felt so normal." I tilt my head to the side, and she shakes her head a little, still keeping her face averted. "It's normally just the two of us, but you were there and asking Evan about school ... it ... it reminded me what it was like when Wyatt was home. He'd talk to Evan about school and his favorite parts because Evan's never liked school."

And now I get it. I scratch my short beard so I don't reach for her the way I want to. "I'm sorry, Hope. I didn't mean to open a wound that's still raw."

She glances up at me, her eyes shiny from her tears, then drops her gaze back to her feet. "You couldn't have known. It was sweet and exactly what Evan needs." She releases the door, and it edges open a little more.

I take half a step, bringing me closer, and use my fingers to tilt her chin up so I can look at her pretty eyes. The sadness there is like a knife to my chest, but I push through my discomfort. "It's okay to tell me if I overstep. I'm not here to take the place of anyone. It's important to me you know that."

Her throat moves as she swallows.

"I see how much you still grieve for Wyatt. I'm not trying to replace him, Hope. Really, I'm not. But I'm going to be completely honest here, and it may get me kicked out." I drop my hands and hold them out. "I want to be transparent with you."

She nods slightly.

"I'm interested in being more than your friend. More than Evan's friend." I draw in a deep breath, hoping this doesn't bite me in the ass. "When you're ready, I'd like to take you on a date sometime."

She opens her mouth, and I know she's going to tell me she's not ready, so I hold up my hand.

"No time limit. I'll wait as long as it takes. When you're ready, I'll be here. In the meantime, nothing needs to change, and you can tell me if I overstep and I'll back off. To be clear ... I'm not going anywhere unless you tell me to leave."

Her eyes widen. I don't think she was expecting any of that, but I'd prefer to be up front with my intentions, so we both know where we stand.

I nod once and turn back toward the kitchen. "I'll leave you to compose yourself."

When I return to the table, Evan's almost finished his meal and mine is a little cold, so I heat it for a minute in the microwave, then grab Hope's dinner and do the same.

"Is Mom okay?"

"Yeah, bud. She'll be okay."

He drops his gaze to his plate, moving his salad around with his fork. "She gets upset a lot."

"She's sad."

He heaves out a sigh. "I know." He flicks his eyes up to me. "Do you think you can help?"

"I'm not sure, but I'd like to try." Hope strolls back into the kitchen as the microwave beeps, and I point to it with my fork. "I reheated your dinner."

She smiles softly. "Thanks." Once she has her dinner, she returns to the table. "Sorry about that." She takes a sip of her wine and focuses on eating. Even though she's composed herself, her sadness fills the room, permeating every nook and cranny.

My phone lights up, blaring "*I'm on Fire*," and breaking the tense silence. Hope's eyebrows shoot up, and Evan laughs. "Sorry, that's my friend, Sebastian. I'll call him back later."

"You can talk to him now. We don't mind."

The song continues to blare. "I don't wanna be rude."

Hope shrugs. "Take the call."

I rise from the table and grab my phone, accepting the call before wandering away from the dining area, ending up in the living room. "Hey, Seb."

"Hey. You wanna catch up? I have the night off."

My eyes skim over the photos on the mantel, freezing on one of Hope and Wyatt on their wedding day. Happiness radiates from her, and she looks completely different. I remember Tahlia had a very similar look on our wedding day. It's the look of a woman fulfilling her most treasured dream.

"Can't tonight. I'm having dinner with Evan and Hope."

"Bring them along. I want to kick your ass at mini golf." He chuckles. "And it would be awesome having witnesses."

"Who kicks who's ass?" I grumble playfully. "I distinctly remember handing yours to you last time."

"Ha! Whatever, pretty boy." I hear the fridge open. "Go ask them to come along. I'll wait."

I rub the back of my neck. "It's a school night. I doubt they'll come."

"It's only 6:30. Finish dinner, and it'll be seven. We'll meet at 7:30, play for an hour, and the kid'll be in bed before nine."

True. I guess. "All right. I'll ask them." They could do with a little fun, and this may just be what they need.

"Great."

I hold the phone to my chest and step back into the kitchen. "Seb wants to catch up tonight."

Disappointment clouds Hope's features, setting off a buzz of excitement through my body, which I know makes me an ass. "Oh."

"When I told him I was having dinner with you guys, he invited you both along."

"Cool. What are we gonna do? Are we going to a bar for a drink?" Evan asks, as he moves to the edge of his seat, his eyes wide with excitement.

I chuckle. "Would you be disappointed if I said we sometimes play mini golf?"

His eyes widen further, and he leaps from his seat. "Mom, say we can go. Please!" He holds up his hands like he's begging.

She chuckles at his excitement. "It's a school night, Ev. And you haven't done your homework yet."

"I'll get up early and do it before school." He shakes his hands to emphasize his request. "Please say yes."

"You'd be home and in bed by nine, if that helps," I offer.

Her shoulders drop, and she blows out a long breath. Pointing her fork at Evan, she looks at him sternly. "You'd better do your homework in the morn—"

"Yeah!" He throws his hands up. "I'm gonna kick your ass, Ben!"

"Evan Wyatt Sullivan. Watch your mouth!"

Woah, triple named!

He drops his head with apology. "Sorry, Mom."

"It's not me you need to apologize to."

He lifts his brown eyes to me. "Sorry, Ben."

I dip my chin. "So, should I tell Seb to meet us there?"

Hope nods. "Sure. We'll just finish dinner and we can go."

"We'll have to drop Rex at my place."

Hope drops her eyes to Rex, who's stretched out on the floor beside Evan. "He can stay here, if you think he'll be okay on his own."

"He should be. He's used to being in different environments and he's grown quite comfortable here."

She nods and I walk back into the living room. "You there?"

"Yeah. Evan sounds excited."

I chuckle. "He is. Thinks he'll kick my ass."

Seb laughs. "Get in line, kid. That's my job." He pauses for a moment. "I'm looking forward to meeting the duo that has you tied in knots."

We make the arrangements to meet, and I step back into the kitchen to finish my now cold dinner. But I don't care, because I'll be spending the next couple of hours with all of my favorite people.

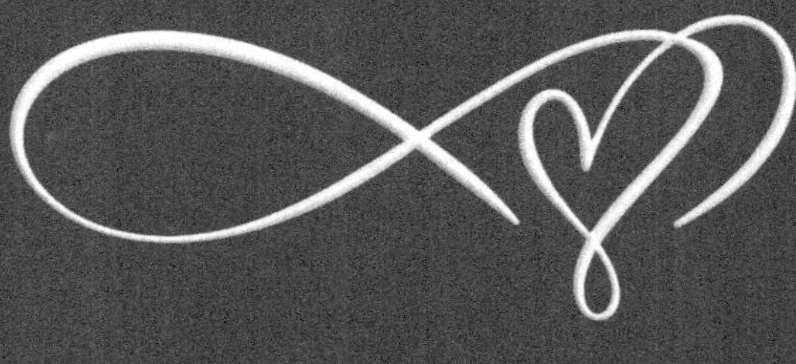

29
HOPE

I stand with my hands on my hips as I survey the mini golf course.

It's literally an entire golf course shrunk down to miniature, complete with greens and bunkers. None of this crappy fake turf BS on a flat concrete surface with metal bars surrounding the edge. This is a state-of-the art quality golf course right here.

I didn't even know this place existed. Huge overhead lights make it feel like daytime, and the guys are enjoying a beer while Evan and I each drink a soda as we make our way around the course.

"All right, Ev. I need you to get a hole in one this round to knock Ben out of first place," Sebastian urges.

I watch Evan's chest puff up, and his eyes twinkle with mischief. He's loving the attention he's getting from Ben and his best friend, Sebastian. I'm guessing Piney Lakes only produces hot, sexy men if these two are anything to go by.

"I'm gonna do my best." He swings his club, and Sebastian moves in behind him.

"Hang on. You need to adjust"—he twists Evan slightly—"yourself a little this way. Right. Go ahead," he tells Evan with a sharp chin lift in the direction of the hole.

"I just want to point out that you two are ganging up on me, and it's throwing me off my game," Ben says, tongue in cheek, as he holds his beer off to the side.

Sebastian whispers something in Evan's ear, and they both chuckle. Then Evan lines up the ball.

For the first time in forever, I'm relaxed and enjoying the moment. The guys' playful banter continues as Ben tries to distract Evan, and one of my favorite songs comes over the speakers. I move my hips in time with the beat, singing the lyrics under my breath, *"Will you meet me in the middle? Will you meet me in the end?"* as I tap my feet.

Evan hits the ball, and we all hold our breath, watching as it lands on the green and rolls toward the hole. It rolls about three inches past the hole and comes to a stop. "Damn it!" Evan cries.

I open my mouth to remind Evan about his cursing, but Ben beats me to it. "Hey, Ev. None of that."

Sebastian claps Ev on the back. "Yeah, Ev. A gentleman never curses in front of a lady." He tips his chin toward me with a wink, and I feel heat rise up my neck.

Evan dips his chin to his chest. "Sorry, Mom."

I smile at my son. "I know." I tip my head toward his wayward ball. "Pretty sure you'll get it in this time."

He shoves his shoulders back. "I know I will." He struts to his ball and hits it, but it rolls about two inches on the opposite side of the hole. I watch his hands tighten around the club and his mouth form a straight line. He tries again, and the same thing happens. Again and again. With each pass of the ball missing the hole, I watch his temper burn hot, but he holds it in. Finally, his ball rolls into the hole, and we all cheer. "About time!" He dips down to grab his ball out of the hole. "Stupid ball. It should have been an easy shot."

Seb shakes his head and pats his shoulder in consolation. "Bad luck, Ev. Happens to the best of us."

"Yeah, well, that sucked."

Ben wraps his arm around Evan's shoulder. "I notice you kept your cool under pressure," he tells Evan, his voice dripping with sincerity. "Even though that hole totally sucked for you." He pushes away playfully. "But it was awesome for me!" He laughs as he dances away from my son like a big kid.

"Hey!" Evan shouts playfully as he chases after Ben. "I'll get you next time," he declares with a grin.

I giggle under my breath, so happy to see him having a good time. We need to do more activities like this, though I think we're having so much fun because of the guys and their youthful playfulness. I love how they've taken Evan into their circle.

Ben chuckles, places his beer on the high-top table, and steps up to the tee to drop his ball. As he positions his feet and lines up the shot, I sigh at the way his back muscles move beneath his sweater and his ass fills out his jeans.

Sebastian sidles up next to me with a raised brow and a smirk. *Busted!* My neck heats with embarrassment, and I feel it flaming all the way up my throat. He watches me with amusement filling his eyes, and I die a little on the inside. Thank goodness he keeps any comments to himself, although his thoughts are written all over his face.

The *thwack* of the club against the ball draws Sebastian and me back to the game, and, much to Sebastian and Evan's dismay, Ben lands a hole in one. He's not humble about it either, streaking across the green, cheering like he's won an Olympic gold medal. With his arms high above his head, he reveals a sliver of toned abs, and I can't miss the trail of dark hair that disappears under the waistband of his jeans.

A sensation that I thought I'd never feel again takes me by surprise, and I squeeze my thighs together. Tingles erupt in that area I thought I'd buried along with my husband, and I glance around to ensure nobody can tell how turned on I am.

Since it's a Monday night, we're the only people here—a blessing, considering how obnoxious we've been. To be fair, I don't think we'd be as noisy as we have if there were other groups on the course.

"Your turn, Cookie," Ben says as he saunters back toward us, blowing his knuckles and rubbing them on his sweater, looking proud as punch.

My heart does a little skip at the nickname he's given me. I figured he used it to make us seem like a couple when the guy at the bake sale wouldn't take no for an answer, but this is the second time he's used it since then. My stomach flips and my body warms at the intimacy of Ben calling me Cookie.

I shove those feelings aside quickly because I shouldn't feel all gooey inside—I'm not even sure how I feel about him giving me a nickname when my husband never did.

I step up to the tee and drop my ball. Feeling three pairs of eyes burning into me is a little intimidating, but I try my best to focus.

"Should I tell her she needs to twist a little to the right?" Evan whispers conspiratorially to the guys, like I can't hear him, so I shuffle a little to the right.

"Is that better, Ev?" I ask, glancing over my shoulder.

He gives me two thumbs up, and I grin, turning back to the hole, but not before I notice Ben's eyes on my ass. I'm tempted to give it a little wiggle, but I don't want to lead him on after what he said to me earlier in the bathroom.

Why a man like him would be interested in a mess like me is beyond my comprehension. He's a cop, though, so his instinct is to help people, but I don't need anyone feeling sorry for me.

I hit the ball, and it goes flying through the air, landing way beyond our hole in the shrubs on the next green. The guys practically fall over laughing, and I roll my eyes but can't stop the giggle that bubbles its way up my throat. It really was a terrible shot.

"Cookie ... that's the best hit of the night!" Ben calls out and I think maybe I like having a nickname after all.

"The best. Mom should get a trophy for that one," Evan splutters between bouts of laughter.

"Ha, ha, boys. Laugh it up at my expense. I don't care." And I don't mind because I haven't seen my son smile and laugh so much in years. I trudge across the course in search of my ball as I chuckle, feeling so much lighter than earlier.

We play the next hole with the guys behaving in much the same way, continuing their smack talk and jokes as we each take our shot. Of course, I take the most number of shots to get the damn ball in the hole. To be expected, I guess, since I have the coordination of a baby panda.

This next hole's a little trickier. I have to hit the ball beneath a waterfall and around a bend, which then goes up a slight slope. There's no way I'm going to get this ball in the hole. The guys couldn't do it, so I'm not holding my breath. I line up the ball and whack it hard. It has a long way to go, and I want to make sure I have a slim chance of getting it close to the hole. It rolls beneath the waterfall with speed, then ricochet's off the rocks, sending it around the bend and disappears from view. I make my way to the green and can't see my ball anywhere. "Great. It's disappeared again, only this time I have no idea where it could be."

Evan races up to me. "It's okay, Mom. We'll help you find it."

I ruffle his hair. "Thanks, Ev." The four of us search, pushing back shrubbery, but turn up nothing. "Darn it, I've lost my ball this time."

"Uh, Hope," Ben calls. When I turn in his direction, he's crouched near the flag. With a surprised expression, he points to the hole. "Found it."

My heart picks up speed with excitement and disbelief. "No way!" I race over and peer into the hole and sure enough, there's my ball. I leap around the guys like I've won the million-dollar lottery. "Oh, yeah!" I shimmy my ass with my hands raised in the air, enjoying my fluke shot. "Take that, boys!"

Even while I'm celebrating, I know with all my heart there's no way in hell I could replicate it. It was a totally lucky shot. It'll never happen again, so I make the most of it.

Ben scoops me up with his thick arms wrapped around my thighs and runs around the course like a maniac! "Oh, yeah! She did it! That's my girl!" He jostles me as he runs, and I'm laughing so hard that I fall over his shoulder. My hands land on his tight butt, and in the heat of the moment, I give it a firm squeeze and a slap.

My hair flies all over the place, and I bet my face is as red as a tomato with my hysterical laughter, but it feels so good to laugh this hard. It's been such a long time since I've had anything to laugh about.

Finally, we settle down and finish the last hole of the night. I'm actually sad the evening is over. "Thanks for inviting us along tonight. We had so much fun," I tell Sebastian. "Right, Ev?"

"It was all right, I guess." He toes the ground with his shoe.

I press my mouth into a straight line to hide my grin. Such a sore loser. "I know you had fun, too, Ev."

Sebastian leans in to hug me goodbye. "We'll have to do it again some time."

I return his friendly embrace. "Definitely. Just maybe not on a school night next time."

He nods in agreement, tucking his hands deep into his jean pockets and making the fabric stretch across his thighs. When these two go out together, they must get a ton of attention from the ladies. A strange pinching feeling occurs in my chest at the thought of Ben being the center of female attention that isn't mine. I don't like the thought of women looking at him, and I certainly don't like the feeling the image evokes in my body.

"We'll work out when our schedules align next." Seb says. He and Ben exchange a bro-hug, and Seb climbs into his truck while we climb into Ben's.

I can't wipe the smile from my face as we drive home. I'd forgotten what it was like to have fun. To laugh. To be playful. To be in the moment.

"Seb's really cool," Evan blurts.

The glow of the dashboard highlights Ben's grin. "He is. He's been my best friend since kindergarten."

"Woah! You're really old, so that's a long time," Evan says.

I nudge him with my elbow. "Evan, don't be rude."

Ben chuckles. "I'm only twenty-seven. I'm not *that* old."

Twenty-seven? Yikes.

He's so much more mature than his twenty-seven years. I sort of calculated his age when he told me about Tahlia, but hearing him say it out loud makes me feel old at thirty-four. I shouldn't be noticing his tight butt and firm abs. If I only consider his age, he's too young for me, but I can't deny the pull I feel toward him.

30

HOPE

WE SLOW OUT FRONT OF MY HOUSE AND BEN PARKS behind my car, then we all climb out. When I reach the door, I pull out my key, and as I slide it into the lock, the sound of claws tapping on my hardwood floors makes me smile.

A sharp bark comes from inside, and Evan grins. "He's excited we're home."

"Sounds like it." I unlock the door, and when it swings open, Rex leaps around with his tail wagging so much that his rump tips from side to side like he hasn't seen us for an entire week, rather than a couple of hours. "Is he always this happy to see you when you leave him home?" I ask Ben.

"Yeah. We don't spend a lot of time apart, but he's always happy to see me," he tells me as he rubs Rex's neck. He jumps and licks his dad's face, making Ben laugh. "Good to see you too, buddy."

"Mom, can we *please* get a dog?"

I heave a huge sigh in my head. Here we go again. "We can't, Ev. Our dog would be left home alone too much and would get lonely. It wouldn't be fair."

His shoulders slump in defeat, and I feel like a terrible parent.

"Your mom's right. Dogs need a lot of attention. Especially

when they're puppies," Ben says, and I could kiss him right now for having my back.

Evan folds his arms across his chest and rolls his eyes. "Not you too. I'll never get a dog at this rate."

"Probably not, big guy," I say. "Now say goodnight to Ben and off to bed."

"But I'm not tired," he whines.

I shoot him my best *don't mess with me* look. "No arguments. Off to bed. I'll be there to say goodnight in a minute."

He faces Ben. "Thanks for taking us to mini golf. I had a lot of fun. Even though I lost," he mumbles the last part under his breath.

"You didn't lose. I did," I remind him.

He turns to me. "You don't count. You were never gonna win anyway," he says matter-of-factly.

Ouch!

"Hey, don't be mean to your mom."

Evan sighs. "Sorry, Mom. I didn't mean it in a *mean* way. I was joking." He widens his eyes.

Ben reaches out and squeezes his shoulder. "Thanks for coming. Seb and I usually have fun, but having you guys there made it even better."

Evan says goodbye to Rex and then heads to his bedroom, leaving me alone with Ben. I look up at him with a heart full of gratitude. "Thank you for tonight. I can't remember the last time I saw Evan have so much fun."

"I'm guessing that applies to you, too." He steps closer, making me nervous, so I lean back a little until my shoulder blades are pressed against the front door.

I swallow, trying my best to produce some saliva because my mouth has become as dry as the Great Basin. "I guess."

He moves closer again, and the smell of his aftershave wafts around me—something fresh and outdoorsy. "It was great to hear you laugh ..."—his eyes trace over the contours of my face—"to see you smile and your eyes sparkle." He holds his hand over his heart. "Stunning."

I swallow and draw in a deep breath. "It felt nice. A little strange and I'm definitely rusty, but it felt ... good to let go and have some fun." I'm still on a high.

He nods a little, and one side of his mouth tips up. "You're beautiful when you're happy." He collects a loose curl and tucks it behind my ear, sliding the back of his fingers down the side of my neck while his eyes watch the action, and I watch him.

The air around us shifts and sizzles as we regard each other quietly. My heart hammers wildly against my ribs, and the concentration I have to dedicate to regulate my breathing is ridiculous. I dart my tongue out to wet my lips, and Ben's eyes drop to my mouth with interest as a low rumble vibrates in his chest.

His warm hand slips under the fall of my hair below my ear, and his thumb slowly strokes up and down my throat. With pupils blown wide, his eyes skip between mine and my mouth and he dips his head down a little closer.

My breathing is out of control, and he has to feel how fast the blood is rushing through my body with his hand pressed against my throat like it is. My knees shake, and my stomach twists inside out. I'm not sure if I want him to close the distance or not.

If he closes the distance, he'll kiss me.

I scrunch my eyes closed, hoping I'll be able to go through with it if I can't see his face. Maybe if I imagine Wyatt's kissing me instead.

My heart fractures.

Sending blood and tissue exploding all over my chest cavity.

I can't do it.

I can't kiss another man while I think of my husband.

When I open my eyes to beg him to stop, he's moved back a little. Smiling gently, he rubs his thumb over my lips and removes his hand from my throat. My breaths stall at his expression.

Compassion and understanding fill my vision, making the backs of my eyes sting and my nose burn.

Needing to apologize, I open my mouth, but Ben shakes his head, and presses his finger against my lips. "Don't apologize to me, Hope." He gently presses a kiss to my forehead for several seconds, then pulls away, sending a riot of butterflies through my stomach. "Thanks for coming out tonight. I had a great time." He takes a step back and another and another until it feels like there's an ocean between us. "C'mon, Rex." He pats his thigh and Rex obediently moves to his side and they both head to his truck.

I watch them climb in and Ben start the engine. There's no way I can let him go like that, so I leap down the porch steps. "Ben!"

He winds down his window, confusion creasing his forehead. My mind and emotions are such a jumble. I don't know what to say, so I lean in the window to kiss his cheek. He turns his face at the same time, and our mouths connect for a moment, like it's happening in slow motion.

The most surprising thing isn't that my lips are pressed to his —or how soft they are—it's that I haven't pulled away.

Instead, I open my mouth slightly and press my lips against his bottom one, then repeat the action with the top pillow. The short bristles around his mouth are rough, but his lips are so very soft, inviting me to kiss them some more.

Ben doesn't move, allowing me to explore his mouth without pressure. When I deepen the kiss, a groan vibrates against my mouth, and his hand slides into my hair, holding me to him gently. I know I can move away if I want to, but I don't.

Emotion clogs my throat, and my heart stutters at the feel of a man's lips against mine.

Of *Ben's* lips against mine.

Stinging burns the backs of my eyes, my heart flips, and my bottom lip quivers, but I keep tasting. I push through the ache that's almost breaking me in two—that threatens to tear me apart from the inside out.

Ben draws back a fraction. "It's okay, Hope," he murmurs, his lips touching mine with each word as he reaches up to stroke my cheek. Wetness spreads at his touch and I didn't realize my emotions had overflowed.

I drop my forehead to his, exchanging my breath for his, trying to combat the grief overwhelming me.

Grief for what I've lost.

Grief for what I've denied myself for too long.

Grief for the deprivation of male affection for too many years to count.

The pain is almost too much to bear.

His hands cup either side of my face, and he softly kisses each damp cheek as I take in a shuddering breath. "Baby steps. Okay?" He looks at me with reassurance. "I'll wait as long as it takes, Cookie." He completes his promise with a kiss on my forehead, and I nod against him.

"I'm sorry I'm such a mess," I murmur on a shaky exhale.

He chuckles quietly, his warm breath coasting across my face. "You're the most beautiful mess I've ever seen."

I grin, and shake my head a little. "You're too good to me."

"Nah. I haven't started being good to you yet." He turns off his engine, nudges me back a little and climbs out of his car. "Let me hold you for a minute."

I eagerly step into his open arms, and he wraps them around me, engulfing me and cocooning me in his warmth, his strength, his compassion. Melding my body to his, I draw his scent deep into my lungs and relax into him.

A kiss is pressed against the top of my head, and I sigh at this overwhelming feeling of contentment filling me. It's not like I haven't received hugs since losing Wyatt, but this one ... it's different ... and so very welcome.

I've missed this contact ... desperately.

Ben's hand strokes my hair, while his other arm snugly holds me to him. His heart beats sure and strong beneath my cheek, and I curl my fingers into the woolen fabric beneath my hands, securing him to me. Closing my eyes, I soak in his vitality and appreciate this moment where my thoughts are finally quiet—and the guilt for being wrapped up in another man's arms isn't quite as loud as it was before.

31

BEN

CARS FILL HOPE'S DRIVEWAY AND MORE ARE PARKED down the street, so I turn around and park in the empty spot behind Sebastian's truck on the opposite side.

He climbs out and meets me, carrying a gift bag.

"Hey, man. Thanks for coming today." We grasp hands and pull each other into a chest bump, careful not to crush our gifts.

"No problem. I was surprised to be invited."

I chuckle as we cross the street. "Ev thinks you're really cool."

"He'd be right about that." Sebastian laughs. He looks around at all the cars. "Looks like we might be the last to arrive."

We pass the spot where I was parked last time I was here. The image of Hope running down the steps and across the grass to my truck replays clearly. And when I remember the soft touch of her mouth against mine, I draw in an essential breath. I'll never, for as long as I live, forget how brave she was that night. Nor will I forget how it felt to have her lips on mine as I fought to allow her the space she needed to kiss me. And I will *never* forget how my heart crumbled to dust when I felt her tears as her mouth explored mine.

I glance back at the street once I reach the porch. "Yeah. I'm not sure what to expect in terms of turn out."

"So, I'm guessing things are progressing?" he asks as we climb the steps.

I tip my head to the side. "Just taking it one day at a time."

He nods. "I can see why you're prepared to wait until she's ready. She's a great person. Beautiful, too. And Evan's a pretty cool kid."

"I think they'll be worth the wait." I knock on the door, worried I won't be heard over the ruckus inside. A few moments later, a silhouette appears, and, as the person walks closer, I recognize Hope's mom. I watch her smile grow as she reaches the door.

"Ben. I'm so happy you came." She pushes the screen door open and throws her arms around my body, much the same way she did when we met the first time in the school gym, and I stiffen slightly, much the same way I did then. I'm not used to such open affection from parental figures.

"Hey, June." I return her embrace. When I finally pull away, her eyes slide to Seb. "This is my friend, Sebastian."

"Hi, June," Sebastian says as he holds out his hand, but she pushes past it, hugging him the same way she did me, and I chuckle at his surprise.

"Nice to meet you, Sebastian. Evan's told me all about you and how you won the mini golf game. And while I have you both here" —she clasps her hands over her heart and rushes to add—"I wanted to thank you for giving my grandson and daughter such a fun evening. It's all Evan can talk about." She leans in and cups the side of her mouth. "He told me Hope laughed and smiled and danced," she whispers as her eyes grow glassy.

I can't fathom how hard it's been for her to watch her daughter and grandson lose so much and struggle in the wake of such a tragedy.

"We had a great time, too. And it was fantastic to help them have fun," I tell her.

Imagine how she'd feel if she knew her daughter kissed me. I think she'd establish a cheer squad. In the short amount of time

I've spent with her, she's made it abundantly clear she'd be happy for me to date her daughter.

The three of us step inside and make our way into the open living, dining, and kitchen area. "Look who's here!" June calls out, and all eyes snap to us, making us the focus of the party.

Raising my eyebrows, I swallow past my nerves, dig deep for my confidence, and wave. "Hi, everyone. I'm Ben and this is my friend—"

"Sebastian!" a woman calls as she walks straight to him with a smirk.

Sebastian chuckles as his eyes widen. "Lucy. What are the chances?" He turns to me. "This is Lucy. Remember we were supposed to meet for drinks a while back? We stayed until closing, but she never showed." He widens his eyes at her in accusation.

She screws up her nose. "Yeah, sorry about that." Jabbing her thumb over her shoulder toward the kitchen, she adds, "I had to look after my girl here. Sisters before misters, you know?"

"Ben!" Evan calls as he races up to us with Donnelly following close behind. I'm thrilled the boys have bonded. It'll be good for both of them. "You came!"

"Of course. You invited me. Where else would I be?" I muss his hair and hand him my gift. "Happy birthday."

His head snaps up. "You even brought me a present?"

Sebastian hands his gift over as well. "Happy birthday, Ev."

"Thanks. I didn't think you'd bring me presents." He doesn't even look at them before he walks away from us toward a table covered in gifts. "Mom! Ben and Seb are here. They got me presents," he shouts. Everyone chuckles at his excitement.

Donnelly nudges me with an exaggerated wink. "I see you took my advice and went after that hot single mom." He nudges me again. "Good for you, man."

I scowl at Don. "How about we have another chat about being respectful toward women next time we catch up? I think you need it."

He has the courtesy of looking chastised. "I didn't mean anything by it. Promise." He holds up his hands in surrender and backs away from me.

I look at all the people jammed into the room, and notice all eyes are still trained on me. I tip my lips up in what I hope looks like a genuine smile and not an uncomfortable grimace. I guess I should have expected this, seeing as we're new. And by the sounds of things, Evan's spoken about Seb and me—a lot. I spot a huge guy with crutches and nod in his direction—that's gotta be Shane. He's a freaking unit. He tips his head in my direction, but his attention snaps toward the kitchen.

"Did you say thank you?" Hope's smooth voice makes its way to me before my eyes land on her. She's wearing wide-leg jeans and a loose sweater that exposes one slender shoulder that I'd love to press a kiss to. Her curls are piled on top of her head with several loosely framing her face. I swallow down my instant desire for her, which heats through my body like a nuclear blast.

She guides Evan back to us. "Hey, thanks for coming." She nudges Evan. "Ev, what do you say?"

"Thanks for my presents."

"You're welcome," Seb and I say at the same time.

Hope glances around. "Let me introduce you guys to everyone."

"I already know Seb," Lucy blurts as she hooks her arm through Seb's.

Hope's eyebrows shoot up as she looks between the two. "How?"

Lucy tips her head toward Seb. "He's the firefighter we were supposed to meet at *Brady's* that night."

Hope's eyes widen, and something like shame slides over her features. "Oh." Then she glances at me. "Were you going to be there, too?"

I raise my eyebrows and nod with a grin, rocking back on my heels. "Yep."

We both chuckle, and the pretty pink blush I love rises up her neck. "I guess we were meant to meet, huh?"

I nod slowly. "It seems that way."

Lucy looks between me and Hope. "Hang on. *You're* Ben. The cop who brought Evan home?"

My gaze slides to Lucy. "That's me."

She looks at her friend with raised brows and mouths, "Wow."

Hope shrugs with a grin, and I desperately want to reach forward and cup her face, so I can bring her mouth to mine, but that's impossible right now. Instead, I settle for tracing her features with my eyes. She has a little makeup on today, so the smattering of freckles across her nose and cheeks isn't as obvious, but whatever she's done to her eyes makes them really pop. "You look beautiful."

She blinks several times, and her friend, Lucy, smirks. Hope tucks her chin to her chest with a shy smile. "Thanks." She looks back up at us and shifts on her feet. "Let me introduce you guys." She leads us to a middle-aged couple. "Ben and Sebastian. These are Wyatt's parents, Tracey and Graeme."

Wow, introducing me to the in-laws right out of the gate. I swallow my nerves, wipe my hand on my jeans, and hold it out to shake theirs, dipping my chin out of respect. "Nice to meet you both."

"You too, Ben. We've heard a lot about you from Evan." Tracey smiles kindly.

I can't imagine what they've been through to lose their son and watch their grandson grow up without his father. After watching Bev lose Tahlia, I know how difficult it is for a parent to lose their child. As Bev used to say, "It's supposed to be the other way around. I'm supposed to go first, not mourn my only child."

I laugh nervously. "Only good things, I hope." I hadn't realized —until this moment—how important it is to me that Wyatt's family approves of me. After all, I want to take care of their son's family. I want to make them mine.

Graeme grips my bicep and squeezes. "Only the best things,

son." He turns to Sebastian. "I hear you're a hose jockey. How long have you been in the job?"

Wyatt's dad called me son, and his mom was warm toward me. Right? I didn't imagine all that. That has to be a positive start to what I hope will be a long-standing relationship.

I blow out a relieved breath, but before we can talk anymore, Hope moves me along, leaving Sebastian and Graeme to talk shop. "This is Wyatt's sister, Clara, my best friend since middle school, and her husband, Ryan."

I hold out my hand. "Hey Clara. Ryan," I greet, dipping my chin.

Clara gives Hope what she must consider a sneaky wink. "So nice to meet you, Ben. Evan's quite smitten with you."

I laugh softly. "That goes both ways. He's an awesome kid."

Her eyes go soft, and her smile widens as she tilts her head to the side a little. "Aww, so sweet. We all love him to pieces." She studies me for a moment and nods. "So, how long have you been a cop?"

I tuck one hand in the pocket of my jeans. "Graduated from the Academy when I was twenty-one, so six years, give or take."

Her eyebrows rise. "What made you want to become a cop?"

Hope sighs beside me and shuffles on her feet. "Clara," she scolds. "This isn't the time for an inquisition."

I'd love to tug her into my side and tuck her under my arm, but it feels disrespectful to do anything like that in front of Wyatt's family. I chuckle and get my head back into the conversation. "I don't mind." I lift and drop one shoulder. "I enjoy helping people. I like that every day, I get to work within the community and build relationships. I like having a positive impact on the people I come into contact with and I enjoy the unpredictability of my job. No two days are ever the same, and it keeps life interesting."

Clara listens intently, then a slow grin tips up her lips. "Not so you can arrest all the people you don't like and throw them in a cell?" She chuckles. "Because that's what I'd do."

"Oh, my god, Clara." Hope rolls her eyes at her friend, then tugs me away. "I'm so sorry about my best friend."

"Hey, I've thought about doing that."

She knocks her shoulder into my arm. "You have not. You're a good man, Ben Taylor." I can't explain the feeling that grows and spreads through my body with her words. Something like pride—pride that she thinks I'm a good man—wraps around me, and it makes me hopeful she'll consider me as more than a friend someday.

I lean down and lower my voice. "I can be bad in the right situation." Pulling away, I wink at her and watch the pink blush rise up her pale throat.

Without a word, she leads me over to the man I assume is Shane and clears her throat. "I want you to meet Wyatt's best friend." He's standing with an attractive woman who's holding the hand of a cute little girl, and a guy who must be in his mid-to-late forties. "Ben, these are Wyatt's friends from the Army, Shane and Nix. And this is Shane's fiancée, Violet, and her little girl, Jasmine." The sweet little girl smiles up at me shyly, then shuffles behind her mother. So cute.

I dip my chin and hold out my hand, shaking Shane's hand, then Nix's. "Thank you for your sacrifice. Good to meet you both."

The sacrifices these men have made for us blows my mind. Service men and women come home with no support and little public regard for what they've experienced, and the government expects them to return to their lives as though nothing's changed for them. It's unreal. And I know for a fact that these two men have survived something truly horrific.

Nix and Shane tilt their chins up, acknowledging my appreciation. "Thank you for yours," Nix says. As if anything I do is remotely similar to what they've experienced.

"Nice to meet you, Violet."

"You, too." She dips her head with a smile, her eyes flicking to Hope.

I crouch, so I'm at eye level with Jasmine. "Hey, Jasmine."

She burrows behind her mom's leg, hiding her face, but not before I see her smile. Then she pops back out. "Hello."

I glance up at her mom. "You have a cutie pie here."

Violet chuckles. "Thank you." She rests her hand on her daughter's head and strokes her silky-looking hair.

Shane readjusts his grip on his crutches. "Thanks for helping with soccer practice, man."

I stand to my full height. "No problem. Happy to help for as long as you need"—I nod to his crutches—"but I might ask for some tips from you, if you don't mind." I rub the back of my neck. "I'd never even watched a full game until Evan asked me to help." I laugh softly. "Then I binged everything I could find on YouTube in an afternoon."

Shane chuckles. "Yeah, sure. No problem. I was the same. It took me a while to find my feet," he says, then takes a drink of his beer. "But Evan tells me you did a great job."

Hope gently rests her hand between my shoulder blades, and it feels so good to have her touching me; I close my eyes briefly to soak up the sensation. "I'll grab you a beer. Back in a minute."

When I open my eyes, Shane's watching me closely, and a slow smile tips up one side of his mouth. "Evan tells me you're part of the K9 unit."

I shake my mind clear and focus back on the conversation. "Uh, yeah. I've worked with Rex for about four years now. He was trained under another handler, but when he retired, I took over. We do a lot of searches for lost people or locating perpetrators on the run. It's rewarding work."

"I bet." He pauses, watching me closely. "Hope was telling me Evan is quite taken with your dog, Rex."

I laugh softly. "The feeling's mutual. When Evan's around, he and Rex are inseparable."

Hope returns with an open beer, which I accept gratefully, and then she rushes off, mentioning something about getting the food out of the oven. Violet steps away to help, leaving me with Nix and Shane. My nerves ratchet up, so I take a drink of the cold beer for something to do. This feeling is completely foreign to me. I don't usually worry what people think of me, but today, it's all I've done.

We talk about my work for a while. "If you're ever thinking about leaving the police force, I could use someone like you on my team," Nix offers. "Rex, too." He glances at Shane. "I need to cut back and spend more time with my family."

I'm unsure what he's talking about, so I tilt my head to the side a little. "He owns a security firm. *Steele Security*. You may have heard of it," Shane tells me, filling in the blanks.

I nod. "I've heard of it. You have a fantastic reputation."

Pride lights Nix's eyes. "Good to know."

Shane glances over my shoulder, and I turn to follow what he's looking at. Hope and Violet are chatting in the kitchen as they plate the hot food. I turn back toward the guys to find both of their eyes locked on me. The need to escape pumps through me, but I lock my feet to the ground.

"So, you and Hope ..." Shane prods, but leaves the sentence hanging.

I'm not sure what he's getting at, so I'm unsure how to respond.

Nix slaps Shane's abs with the back of his hand. "What he's asking is this: what are your intentions with Hope and Evan?" My eyebrows shoot up, and he holds his hands out in a placating move. "We promised Wyatt we'd always keep an eye on his family. This is us watching over them."

I glance around us, satisfied that nobody is listening to our conversation. Picking at the label on my beer, I consider my response. I respect the hell out of Shane and Nix, so it's important to me that they understand how I feel about Hope and Evan—and what I'd like to happen.

"Hope and Evan have quickly become the most important people in my life, and I'd like to keep them in it if I can. Evan and I have already discussed how he would feel if I asked his mom on a date."

Both of their eyebrows shoot up, and grins tug at their lips.

"And after ensuring I was aware his mom still loves his dad, I have his support. Especially after explaining she never has to stop loving him."

They both nod their approval.

"I've also explained to Hope I'd like to take her on a date some time ..." I glance away, then back to the two men in front of me. "I've told her I'm prepared to wait until she's ready." I lock my gazes with both of them. "I'm not going anywhere—unless Hope sends me away."

They're both quiet for a long time, but I sense they approve of what I said.

Nix takes a drink while Shane studies me. "A few months ago, I would have said you're wasting your time. That she'll never be ready to open her heart to someone new." He pauses and I hold my breath, waiting for him to finish. "But after hearing Evan talk about you and Rex ... and watching Hope's reactions when it was just the three of us, and then again today..." His eyes flick over my shoulder, then return to me. "She's changed." He turns to Nix. "Have you noticed?"

Nix nods. "Yeah. It's hard to miss. She seems happier."

Shane hums his agreement, and warmth spreads throughout my chest as it swells with a sense of pride. "I agree." His brown, assessing eyes find mine. "I don't think you'll have to wait all that long."

A long breath escapes my mouth and my entire body sags. Man, I had no idea how tense I was. "You think?"

"Absolutely." He adjusts his crutches and looks at Nix. "I think Wyatt would approve?" Even though he makes the statement, it sounds more like a question aimed at his friend.

Nix turns his stern gaze my way. "I agree. I think he'd want Hope to move on, and I believe you'd be the man he'd want taking care of his family."

Shane casts his gaze to me. "But don't think we won't kick your ass if you hurt either of them."

I hold up my hands in surrender. "You won't have to; I'll kick my own ass. Hurting either of them is the last thing I'd ever do."

Hope calls out, gaining everyone's attention as she tells us the food is ready.

I spend the afternoon talking with Hope's friends and family, who all make Seb and me feel welcome. Some conversations and side glances have me believing I'm under the microscope, which, I guess, is to be expected. My earlier discussion with Nix and Shane has me feeling hopeful, and their observation that Wyatt would approve of me for his family bolsters my belief that I'm where I'm supposed to be.

Cake is served, gifts are opened, and guests slowly trickle out. Sebastian left with Lucy about an hour ago, but I wasn't ready to leave. I don't want to overstay my welcome, but I want some time with Evan and Hope. Just the three of us. I want to know if Evan liked the journals I bought him. Hope wanders back inside alone after saying goodbye to her parents—the last guests to leave.

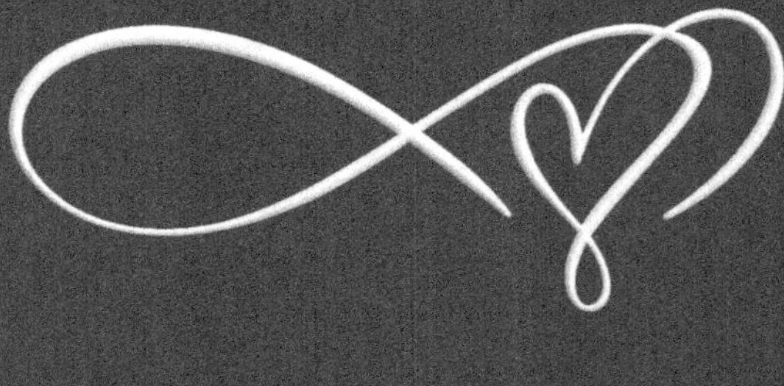

32

BEN

"Where's Ev?"

"He practically begged to have a sleepover at Mom and Dad's." She titters. "She can never say no to him." Walking further into the kitchen, she blows her hair out of her eyes as I'm washing the last tray. She still looks beautiful, even though she didn't stop once all afternoon, but she also looks exhausted. Her eyes widen when they land on me. "You don't have to do that. You've already done so much." She looks around the kitchen and steps closer as if to take over the task.

"I've got this. Why don't you put your feet up?" I suggest, tipping my chin toward the living room I've already put back together.

Her eyes trace over my face, and drop to my hands buried deep beneath bubbles in the sink. A slow grin takes over her face. "Okay."

I finish in the kitchen, wiping down the counters and taking out the trash. With nothing left to do, I pour Hope a glass of wine, grab a beer, and wander into the living room. She's curled up on one end of the couch, and soft music plays as she stares out the front window. I put our drinks on the coffee table, sit next to her —keeping a polite amount of space between us—then collect her sock-covered feet and place them in my lap. Without thinking too deeply, I dig my thumbs into the arch of her foot and massage.

She drops her head back on her shoulders with a soft moan, and my dick twitches in response. The sound of her pleasure vibrates through every cell in my body, heating my blood and waking that primal urge to claim her. "That feels so good," she murmurs.

I adjust my position, making a little more room in my jeans. "Good to know." I continue my ministrations, noting how small her feet are. I trace my eyes up her slender legs, to her narrow hips and even narrower waist. She has such a tiny frame, but from the photographs of her on the wall and mantel, I know she was never as slim as she is now, and I wonder if it's because of the grief she's living with.

"Thanks for coming today," Hope murmurs, and when I lift my eyes from her feet, I find hers locked on me.

I raise and drop a shoulder. "If you or Evan want me here, there's nowhere else I'd be." I hope she understands what I'm saying. But just in case she doesn't, I add. "I hope you know how important the two of you have become to me."

She reaches out and grabs her wine, then sinks further into the couch, and it's like her entire body sighs. "I know," she whispers.

I watch her watching me as she takes a sip of her sweet wine. My eyes trace over her features, cataloging them. Neither of us speaks because there's no need to fill the quiet. It's perfect. This time, this space—it's perfect as is.

"You don't have the TV on."

She snickers. "Yeah. I needed a little quiet after the noisiness of the day. Normally, I can't stand the house being this quiet."

"Why's that?" She's mentioned that the house is too quiet before, but is that all it is?

She adjusts her position, and the heel of her foot inadvertently presses against my dick.

My *hard* dick.

I freeze—unsure what she'll do next. Her eyes widen, but she doesn't pull her foot away. I watch her swallow. When I look more closely, I notice the fast fluttering of her pulse at the base of her neck and her pupils eclipsing the aquamarine I love so much. My body heats, and my blood thrums through my veins as I watch her chest rise and fall quickly.

Neither of us moves or looks away, and the air grows heavy with tension. I wonder if she even realizes she's aroused? Or has she closed herself off for so long that she's forgotten she's a woman who has needs and is allowed to have them fulfilled?

After a long silence, she moistens her lips, and I fight to hold in my groan. "I guess I like the noise, so I don't feel so lonely. It was a strategy I developed whenever Wyatt was deployed before Evan was born. You'd think, with Evan in the house, I wouldn't feel so lonely, but he's often doing his own thing, especially now that he's getting older. He doesn't really like to hang out with me so much." She shrugs and her fingers move to play with some invisible thread on her sweater and I sense her disappointment. "My fault, really. I've been so disengaged, so I can't really blame him."

I hate how hard she is on herself. "You were grieving."

She shakes her head with vigor and places her wine back onto the table. "That's no excuse. He needed me, and I wasn't emotionally available to him. I'll never forgive myself for abandoning my son like that, especially through his formative years. It wasn't good enough to be going through the motions. He needed more. I'm surprised he hasn't gotten himself into more trouble than he did." Her shoulders rise and fall dramatically, and her chest expands and deflates with a loud sigh. "Everyone's given me a pass because *I'm grieving,* but I failed at parenting 101, and I'll work my ass off to make it up to him. He was grieving too, and I left him to flounder." Her eyes glisten, and she presses her lips together, but not before I see them quiver.

Gripping her ankles, I pull her closer, then position her across my lap so I can wrap my arms around her. She presses her body into mine as a sharp sob breaks free, and she may as well have plunged a dagger into my heart and ripped it in two. Needing her closer, I cup the back of her head as she buries her face in my shoulder and cries.

Her pain.

Her guilt.

Her trauma bleeds into me, and I take it all, absorbing it and hoping that, by some miracle, this helps her let go of some of it. Her body shudders, and her tears soak through my sweater, but I don't care. I'll soak up her tears for eternity if she'll let me—and I'll consider it a honor.

All I can do is soothe her with gentle kisses to her hair and stroke her back softly as she purges her guilt and regrets. There are no words I can say to her. Deep down, she knows she's not a terrible parent. If she digs beneath all the self-blaming and shaming, she'll discover she hasn't left Evan to flounder as much as she thinks she has. I've seen some shitty parents, and she's definitely not one of them.

Slowly, her sobs subside, and her breathing evens out. Her body feels heavier against mine, and relief fills every cell in body that she's calm again. I continue to stroke her slowly, but my eyes grow heavy, almost like I was the one to purge my heart.

When Hope doesn't move, I drag the blanket from the back of the couch and gently drape it over her. She snuggles down into me further, burying herself inside my heart as she does.

One day, I'm going to marry this woman.

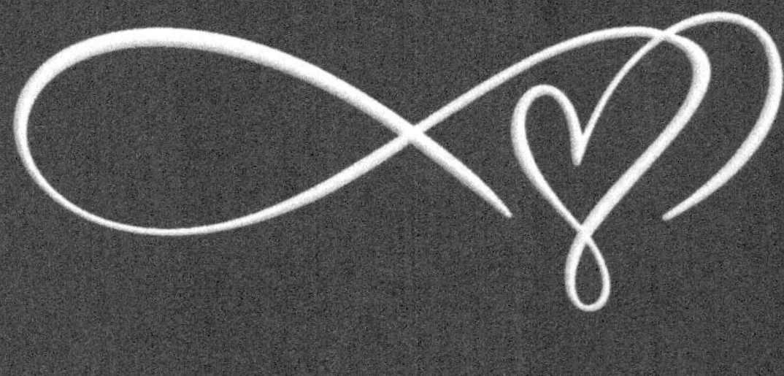

33
HOPE

I FORGOT TO DRAW MY CURTAINS LAST NIGHT, IS MY first thought as the bright morning sunlight sends sharp pins through my eyes.

My second is … where on earth am I?

I curl my fingers into hard muscle, and when I finally open my gritty eyes properly and follow the slab of chest upward, I'm greeted by one of the most handsome faces I've ever seen.

Relaxed in sleep but still cradling me like I'm the most precious thing on earth, he looks so beautiful. Thick, dark lashes rest on the apples of his cheeks, and his short beard has thickened overnight. His lips look as soft as I know them to be, and the urge to push up a little and press my mouth to his is overwhelming.

This man gave me a safe haven to fall apart last night. He didn't judge. He didn't give me false platitudes or promises. He listened and held my broken pieces together. And by doing that, he's slowly putting each piece back into place. This morning, I'm strangely calm. My brain's quiet, and my heart doesn't ache quite as much as it did the night before.

I sink back into his warmth with a sigh, wishing I could stay here all day. It's been a long time since I've felt a man's arms around me—experienced contentment like this. Somehow I feel everything's changed, but when I glance around the room, nothing's changed at all. My muscles draw tight when my eyes land on my wedding photo.

Guilt is swift, slicing through my contentment with the sharpest blade, spilling my shame like blood on a battlefield.

What am I doing, snuggling into another man's arms?

With urgency, I push against Ben's chest, so I can climb to my feet, but his fingers tighten on my hip, and the arm holding me to him tenses, not allowing me to gain my freedom.

A soft rumble vibrates against me, and when I look up, sleepy gray eyes are watching me closely. Creases form between his dark brows as his eyes flick between mine, and I *should* feel trapped as he silently holds me in place. Instead, relief cascades through my body and my mind. I have no other option than to stay where I am. With quiet authority, he's removing my guilt for finding solace in his arms by holding me steady.

I know, down to my core, if I wanted to move away, he would let me go, but somehow he knows I need this connection. He knows I need his embrace. I need the security he's quietly giving me. I relax back into him and soak up this moment of peace.

His fingers loosen on my hip, and his other hand comes up to cup my face reverently. His soft lips press against the top of my head, and I sigh with a long exhale, releasing the tightness across my chest.

I draw in a long breath, taking Ben's outdoorsy scent deep into my lungs. With my next exhale, I release a little of the guilt I feel for waking in another man's arms. With each breath out, I release everything that's been buried deep inside for too long, and with each breath in, I fill the empty spaces with Ben and the peace he's giving me.

Tilting my head back, I gaze into his stormy gaze and see the questions written there. *Are you okay? How can I help?*

Yes, I'm okay. You already have. I answer without words.

A soft smile touches his lips, and his eyes sparkle in the

morning light. His fingers trace my cheek, and his warm breath coats my mouth. It would be so easy to lean upward and show him my gratitude with a kiss ... the problem is ... I don't want to kiss him out of gratitude.

I want to kiss him because I want to feel his mouth against mine again. I want to taste his lips ... to feel his tongue stroke against mine. He's awakened me in ways I never dreamed possible after losing Wyatt.

It should feel wrong to have these thoughts and feelings swirling through me for another man.

A man who isn't my husband.

It should feel wrong to have Ben's arms wrapped around me ... to want his lips against mine.

But none of it does.

It feels right.

After all this time ...

After all the pain and tears and agony.

It feels too good to ignore.

Wyatt wouldn't want me to be alone. He'd want me to find love and happiness again. I know he would. And even though I've fought the idea until now, maybe it was because I was waiting for Ben. Before leaving the party yesterday, everyone made sure to tell me how much they liked him and how they thought Wyatt would like him, too.

I can't ignore the way he makes me feel. His patience and understanding make him incredibly attractive, and it doesn't hurt that the package he comes in is easy on the eyes. He's not playing games and has been honest with me about what he'd like.

With the same patience he's always shown, he watches me silently as I work through my thoughts and come to a decision. His gaze studies me like he can see every thought and doubt I have.

As I give myself permission to be in the moment—to do what my body aches to do—I tilt my head back and straighten in his arms, pushing upward. He must realize what I'm about to do because he sucks in a sharp breath, and when I glance back up at his eyes, the heat I see there gives me the courage to follow through.

I lick my lips, tasting Ben's breath on my tongue. His eyes trace the movement and his pupils blow wide. Dipping his head slightly, he meets me halfway, and I swear, when we finally make contact, flames lick down my spine and heat my blood.

His fingers tighten on my hip once again, but for a completely different reason, as our mouths connect, touch, and taste.

A soft rumble vibrates beneath my hand, and my heart slams against my ribs. I need to be closer to him, so I press against his firm chest and slide my hand into the short strands of his hair to hold him to me—silently demanding more.

His arm tightens around my body, eliminating any space between us. Our kiss is unhurried as he sucks my bottom lip into his mouth, then does the same with my top lip before dipping his tongue inside.

It's been such a long time.

My blood fizzes as our kiss goes on. Slow, sweet strokes of tongue against tongue. Lips sucking and moving against one another in a seductive dance. Giddiness erupts in my stomach and spreads outward through my limbs to my fingers and toes.

I twist in Ben's embrace until I'm straddling his thighs. He wraps his arms around me, pulling me tight against his body, leaving not a single breath of space between us. My breasts are squashed tight against his pecs, and I tilt my head to take the kiss deeper.

A soft moan makes its way up my throat, which he swallows down and answers with a groan of his own. His length is hard between us, and I shuffle my hips forward until my center meets his. We both suck in a sharp breath, and his hands move to the small dip at my waist where he grips firmly to hold me in place. He wrenches his mouth away, his heavy breaths matching mine. Our gazes meet and lock.

"Cookie?" One single word full of so many questions that I can't answer ... *only feel.*

I lick his taste from my lips as I gather my thoughts so I can work out what he's asking me, but my mind is filled with lust.

"What do you need?" he asks, his voice rough with his own restrained desire.

I work against his grip on my waist and grind my center along his hard length. The only thing on my mind is relieving this heavy ache in my core. A whimper escapes at the contact, and I drop my forehead to his chest, breaking eye contact. My heart thunders as lightning skates down my spine at the feel of him against me.

He feels so good.

It won't take much to make me see stars.

I rock again and his hands leave my waist, one sliding across my stomach and up between my breasts until it stops at my throat. With a light grip, he tilts my head back with his thumb until our eyes meet.

"Talk to me."

My breath gushes out of me as the heat of his stare touches mine, and I lick my lips, not even a little embarrassed by my behavior. I feel like I've gone from zero to one hundred in mere seconds, and if I don't quench this ache, I might die. "I need ... this ache ... it almost hurts," I murmur, brokenly.

He presses his hips up from beneath me, and a moan caresses my lips. I couldn't hold it back if I tried.

"Take what you need. I'm yours. Have been since the first moment I laid eyes on you," he whispers roughly, and my heart stutters to a stop.

I close my eyes, blocking his vulnerability. His honesty. His words.

He presses up beneath me, using one hand on my hip to guide me along his length. The friction feels so damn good, and I'm already so close. Sparks sizzle through my blood, and stars appear behind my lids. With the perfect rhythm and pressure,

Ben pushes me closer to the release I'm seeking, but I need something more.

His hand tightens around my throat, and his mouth crashes down on mine in the next moment. He pushes his tongue between my lips without ceremony and kisses me like I'm his everything, showing me with his actions exactly what he meant by his words.

He kisses me like I'm his, and it's enough to shove me over the edge of the cliff I was balancing on. Free-falling into an orgasm that steals my breath and empties my mind of everything except pure pleasure. He swallows my moan as my body shatters into a million tiny shards of light. I grip the longer strands of his hair tight to ground me as I explode.

For beautiful moments, I lose myself in the sensation—the buzz, the thrum of an orgasm so powerful I'm still shaking.

Ben kisses me roughly, still guiding my hips back and forth until a rumble of a groan explodes against my lips. My blood sizzles beneath my burning flesh, his touch branding me in a way that's so powerful it's frightening.

His body tightens and shakes beneath me, much the way mine just did. He rips his mouth away and drops his head to the back of the couch, pushing his hips up into me. "Fuuuck!" he grits as his jaw tightens beneath his stubble.

My eyes widen. *I* came, then *he* came.

Realization dawns as I watch his chest rise and fall with sharp breaths, the veins along his neck protruding with his exertion, and when his satisfied gaze drops to mine, I burst into tears.

Horrible loud sobbing tears.

I bury my face in my hands and try to scramble off his lap, but his arms wrap around me like a tourniquet. Like he can somehow hold all of my broken pieces together.

He can't.

Nobody can.

I'm too broken and there are too many jagged shards.

"L-l-let m-m-e g-g-o," I stutter and, keeping my face averted, drop my hands to his chest to push away.

His hands tighten. Then, a moment later, he releases me. I shuffle back and, with shaky legs, climb to my feet. Spinning away from him, I race upstairs to my bedroom and close myself inside. Drowning in guilt and disgust with myself, I slide down the door until my butt lands on the carpet.

What did I just do?

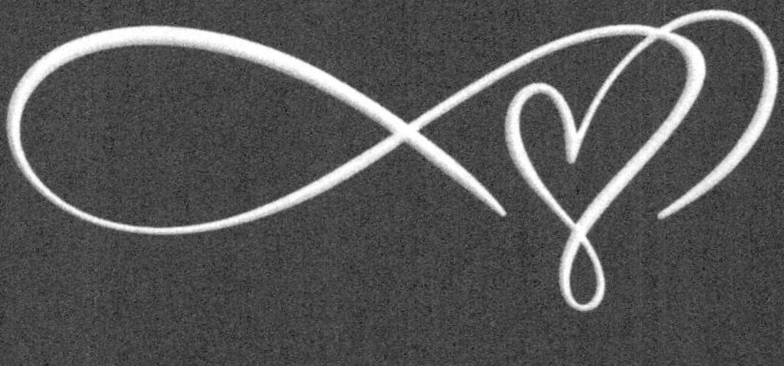

34

HOPE

DRAGGING MY FEET CLOSE TO MY BUTT, I WRAP MY ARMS around my legs and drop my head to my knees and fall apart. Tears fall in thick streams, and I'm certain they'll never stop.

A light knock sounds against my door, and I jolt. "Hope?" Using the back of my hand, I wipe away the mess from beneath my nose. "Can we talk? I need to go home to get ready for work, but I can't leave you like this."

Like a coward, I answer through the door. "I'm sorry, Ben. I sh-shouldn't have gotten so carried away. I ... I'm a mess and I-I-I'm not ready."

A heavy thunk vibrates through the wood and I imagine him dropping his head against the door in frustration. "I think you're more ready than you realize, but I won't push you. We can go at your pace. I just need to check on you before I go. I won't be able to concentrate today if I don't see you before I leave. I'll feel like an asshole if I leave now."

He could never be an asshole, and I don't want him to leave here feeling guilty because of what *I* did ... because of how *I* fell apart.

I draw in a breath for fortification and climb to my feet, shakily crossing the short distance to my dresser for some tissues. I wipe my face the best I can, hopefully cleaning up the worst of the mess, then I open the door a little.

My breath stalls in my lungs at the understanding and concern I see written all over his handsome face and when my eyes finally meet his, I drown in the guilt I see there. I feel like a psychotic bitch—one minute I'm hot, the next I'm cold. I'm surprised the poor guy doesn't have whiplash.

Opening the door wider, I dart forward and wrap my arms around him, pressing my cheek to his chest—feeling his heart thudding heavily. So vital. So alive. So *here*. "I'll be okay."

His arms wrap around me, and I feel him press a kiss to the top of my head. "I hate leaving you like this, but I can't be late for work." He looks down at me. "I'm so sorry, Cookie. I should have stopped before things got out of hand."

"It wasn't your fault." I pull away so I can look up at him. I'm certain I look a mess, and my eyes are red and puffy, but he looks at me like I'm the most beautiful woman he's ever seen. "That was all me and I'm sorry you have to deal with my Dr. Jekyll and Mr. Hyde routine."

He smiles sadly as he strokes the hair away from my face, then rests his thumb on my lips. "You're much sexier than Jekyll or Hyde." Leaning forward, he presses a kiss to my forehead, and my eyes drop closed at his gentleness. "I'm sorry I have to go."

I shake my head. "Don't be sorry. You have to get ready for work, so do I, and I'm sure Evan will be home any minute with Mom to get ready for school."

His eyes widen slightly. "Shit. I should get outta here before he comes home. I don't want to confuse him."

The front door bangs open and sneakers squeak on the timber floor, followed by the sound of Mom's boots. Our eyes widen at the same time.

"Why is Ben's truck still parked in the street?" Evan's voice bounces up the stairs and my panic rises.

Mom makes a scoffing sound. "I don't think that's Ben's truck."

"But it is. I'm sure of it," my son insists. He's familiar with Ben's truck, so I have no doubt he saw it parked across the road in the same place it was last night.

"If it is, I'm sure there's an explanation." She tilts her head up and her eyes land on me and Ben. Her smile is instant and obnoxious as she urges Evan toward the kitchen. "Now, go and make your breakfast."

"I wanna say hi to Mom first."

"She's probably in the shower. You can say hello when she comes downstairs." She gives him a little push. "Now scoot."

As soon as Evan's out of sight, Ben leans forward and presses a delicate kiss to my cheek. "I'm sorry about all of this, Cookie." His eyes lock onto mine, begging me to understand, but there's nothing to understand. "I feel like an asshole."

With my heart pounding in my chest like I've been caught breaking curfew, I push him toward the stairs with urgency. "You're not an asshole. You wouldn't know how to be. None of it was your fault." I widen my eyes. "But you have to go before Evan sees you," I whisper.

He kisses me one more time, and my cheeks flush, then he lightly races down the stairs, and passes Mom, saying hello and goodbye in a single murmured breath. He shoots out the front door, as silent as a ninja, and Mom's eyes snap back to me, her eyebrows resting halfway up her forehead.

She walks to the bottom of the steps and points at me. "I'm going to let this go for now because there are little ears around, but you *will* have lunch with me today. No excuses."

My shoulders slump as my heart rate slows. "Okay." I point over my shoulder with my thumb. "I need to shower. I'm running late."

"I'll get your things ready for you. Go!" She flicks her fingers at me in a shooing motion.

When I come downstairs after my shower, I hurry into the kitchen, heading straight for my boy. "Good morning. How'd you sleep?" I lean down, press a kiss to the top of his head, and breathe him in.

"Okay. How come Ben's truck is still across the street?"

I knew this question was coming, so I concocted a story while I was in the shower. "Sebastian came back and picked him up because his truck wouldn't start."

He scoops more cereal into his mouth. "Oh, okay."

Phew. I hate lying to him, but I don't want him to know Ben spent the night here. It feels disrespectful to Wyatt to have another man stay in his home. The one he paid for and continues to pay for. The guilt I was feeling earlier rears its ugly head once again.

"Hi, sweetie." Mom grins and places my favorite cup on the counter.

I kiss her cheek. "Hi, Mom. Sorry, I can't stop. I'm running late."

"That's okay. We'll chat later," she says with a knowing look. "I've made you a breakfast sandwich you can eat on the way, and here's your coffee."

I grab the cup and take a sip, noting my wine glass from last night draining on the sink. "Thanks, Mom. You're the best." Collecting the sandwich, I scoot past Evan. "Have a good day at school, and I'll see you in the pick-up line."

"Okay." He collects his empty bowl, takes it to the sink, and I head out the front door to my car.

Once I'm secure inside, I finally take a breath.

Shit, that was close!

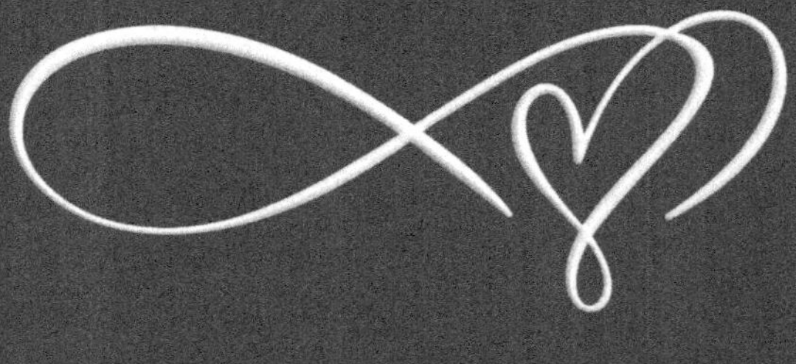

I PULL INTO THE PARKING LOT BEHIND THE SALON, AND Sophie, Lucy, and Savannah are already waiting for me. Lucy's grin is almost as obnoxious as Mom's this morning, and I think I know why. She left with Sebastian yesterday, and I swear I could smell their pheromones in the air.

The minute I climb out of my car, Savannah calls out, "Any particular reason you're late this morning? Wouldn't have anything to do with a certain hottie named Ben?" She wiggles her eyebrows up and down.

I guess I should have expected an inquisition this morning after the girls met him yesterday. There's no way they would let something so juicy go. I decide it's best to deflect. "How's Sebastian?" I ask Lucy with a raised brow, then shove the key into the lock of the back door into the salon.

Her face flushes pink, but not from embarrassment. She fans herself. "So hot!" We all giggle. "I can barely walk this morning, but you will not hear me make one single complaint. What they say about firefighters and their hoses ... completely true!"

The four of us break into peals of laughter as we separate to set up for the day. Phew! My plan worked. Once everything is set up, I lean against my work area and sip of my coffee while I take a moment to breathe. Everything was such a rush from the minute Mom and Evan came home; I haven't had a moment to recalibrate.

A man, other than my husband, gave me a powerful orgasm this morning.

And I know once the euphoria wore off, I fell apart, but while it was happening, it felt fantastic. I'd forgotten what it was like to be kissed like that. Like I was the beginning and end of everything. It was heady, and as upset as I was once reality snuck in, I know, without a doubt, that I want a repeat.

Hopefully next time, I won't break into a million pieces and ruin the moment. I also don't want anything between us. I want to feel him moving inside me. Feel his hands and mouth all over my skin. Trace my mouth and fingers all over his. I dip my head to look at my boots as my cheeks heat.

I shake my head and blow out a long breath.

I'm all over the place.

One minute, I feel as though I'm cheating on my husband. The next, I want to do it all over again. I can't keep up. *What the hell is wrong with me?* I'm not this girl. I've never been so confused. Surely this isn't normal.

Logically, I know it's not cheating. Wyatt's gone and he's never coming back, and after my last conversation with the girls, I realize he wouldn't want me to be alone for the rest of my life—I thought as much this morning before things went as far as they did. He'd want me to find happiness. To find love again. *But can I?*

Ben said he's prepared to wait for me. He's been patient, understanding, compassionate, and he's never pushed me. Both times anything's happened between us have been because I've initiated it. And even then, he's let me take what I've wanted from him without any pressure.

At what point will he think it's all too hard and walk away? Or does he really mean what he says?

A hand lands on my shoulder, and I look up. Lucy's worried gaze pierces straight through me. "Are you okay?"

I swallow past the heavy lump in my throat and force a smile to my lips. "Yeah, of course."

Her brows dip. "Don't lie to me."

I shake my head with a mild laugh. "I wouldn't dare."

The door opens, and our first client walks in, saving me from her inquisition.

I'M NOT sure where the morning went, but the next time I look up, Mom's waiting at the front of the salon for me. My shoulders sag in defeat. I had hoped she'd forget about what she walked in on this morning, but I should know better. The glee written all over her face is unmistakable, so there's no way she would have forfeited catching up for lunch.

I hold up my finger. "I'll just grab my purse. Won't be long."

She nods and I disappear to the back to grab my purse. "I'll be back in thirty minutes!" I call as I head out the door to meet Mom on the sidewalk.

She holds up a paper bag. "I brought lunch for us."

"Thanks, Mom." We wander toward the park and sit at the empty table, and Mom pulls out our sandwiches and a thermos with two plastic cups she had tucked in her purse. I chuckle. "You came prepared."

She looks at me with a grin, her eyes full of mischief. "I didn't want anything to get in the way of our chat. Now spill."

I grab my sandwich and peel the paper away. "Geez, can't a girl eat first?"

"Nope. You can eat and talk. I know how limited your time is." She unwraps her sandwich and takes a bite.

I shrug with an air of nonchalance. "There's not much to tell.

Ben and I were talking last night. I got upset, and we ended up falling asleep on the couch."

She nods slowly as she listens, finishing with, "Mhmm."

"What's with the mhmm, Mom?"

"Nothing. What did you get upset about?" She takes another bite of her sandwich like she's not waiting with bated breath for my answer.

I look down at my boots, noticing a scuff I'll need to polish out when I get home. "I was talking to Ben about how much I've let Evan down since Wyatt died." I swallow past the boulder-sized lump in my throat that seems to show up every time I think about the mistakes I've made. "I got overwhelmed with the amount of guilt I'm carrying about it." Picking at the paper wrapped around my sandwich, I focus on tearing it into strips. "I burst into tears, and he comforted me and then ... I don't know what happened, I-I must have fallen asleep on him. He sat with me all night," I murmur the last part.

Mom's hand shoots across the table to grip mine, stopping my assault on the wrapping paper. "Oh, sweetie." She squeezes my hand and scoots closer, wrapping her arm around my shoulders. "You. Have. Been. Grieving the loss of your husband. The only man you've ever loved. The man you planned to grow old with. The father of your son. Your best friend." She dips down to catch my eyes. "You have done your very best, and when you couldn't, you've had people around you to fill in the gaps. Evan hasn't been forgotten."

"But I've been so selfish in my loss. I haven't supported him the way I should have." I beg her with my eyes to understand. "I failed him and I'll never forgive myself."

She sighs. "I'm going to let you in on a secret. Every single parent on this planet thinks they've failed their child or children for one reason or another. They focus on the mistakes they've made and forget to acknowledge all the things they get right every single day. It's been like this since the dawn of time, and it will continue forever and a day."

"But—"

She shakes her head adamantly. "No buts, Hope. You are no different from any other parent. Yes, you were deep in your grief for a long time, but you still got up every single day and cared for your son. You fed, clothed, and loved him. You made sure he spent time with friends and family. You ensure he plays sports, and you insist he spends time outside. You encourage and support him." She rubs her hand up and down my back. "So stop this. You can't change what's been done. You need to start looking forward and focusing on building a future ... whatever that may look like for you and Evan."

"I'm worried I've screwed him up. Like he'll have mommy issues and won't pursue relationships because I wasn't there for him emotionally during his formative years." The thought that I've caused irreparable damage to my son crushes me under a weight I'm not sure I can carry.

Mom's shoulders shake with a chuckle and pats my hand. "That's every parent's nightmare, Hope. He'll be fine, but if you're worried, why don't you have a chat with him about all of this, and if you still think there's an issue, you can always take him to counseling." She sighs dramatically. "Keep in mind that losing his father *will* have a long-term impact on him. Of course it will. Nobody can deny that. But be logical and reasonable about how much blame you take for that impact."

I understand what she's saying. She's more experienced with parenting than I am. She raised two kids and has helped raise my son too. But none of us grew up experiencing the same loss that Evan has, and I worry myself sick that the damage will be too much. But she's right, I should talk with him about it and get him help if he needs it.

She studies me closely. "I've seen a drastic change in him since Ben came on the scene. I think he's been good for Evan." She pauses and clears her throat. "And maybe he'll be good for you too ... if you let him."

If I let him.

To let him be good for me, I have to let go of my grief—and the promise I made to love Wyatt forever.

36

HOPE

As I watch Evan play soccer with his friends, I blow out a long breath, relax my shoulders, and thank my lucky stars that it's not Ben's week to coach the kids. I need some space to think about things.

Evan passes the ball, and the boy who receives it kicks a goal. The kids run around like goofballs, and I leap to my feet to cheer for the boys. Evan's gaze comes straight to me, and a bright smile lights up his face. I raise my hands higher, clapping so he can see how proud I am.

Maybe Mom's right. I *have* shown up for Evan in all the ways that count. I may have been sad while doing it, but I was still always there for him.

The kids head for the center of the field, and I sit back on the hood of my car, a grin still stuck on my lips. My thoughts return to Ben and what happened this morning, and my neck and cheeks heat instantly as an ache builds between my thighs at the memory. I still can't believe it happened, and while I got upset after the act, I can't deny I enjoyed what we did—and would have done a lot more if my sensibilities hadn't returned when they had.

Loud cheers erupt, and I focus back on the game. It looks like the other team scored a goal this time. Relieved that I missed nothing important, I return to my thoughts.

Ben's made it clear he's interested in a relationship with Evan and me ... whenever I'm ready.

Can I let go of Wyatt to pursue something with Ben? That's the million-dollar question.

I promised Wyatt I'd love him forever.

And I always intended to keep that promise.

But then Ben came along with his easy smiles and compassionate understanding. He's woken a part of me I thought had died with my husband, and he makes me want to live again. He's shown Evan and me nothing but patience and kindness. He's brought fun back into our lives.

I glance across the field to Evan, and my lips tip up. He already loves Ben, but would he feel the same about him if we were dating? That's very different from the arrangement in place now. I don't want Evan to think I'm forgetting his father and leaving him behind, or that I've broken my promise.

I raise my hands and slide them through my hair, gripping the roots. *Why does it have to be so hard? Why do I have to feel so torn?*

My phone vibrates on the hood of my car, and my best friend's face lights up the screen. Shame floods through my system like dirty oil. *What would she think if she knew what happened between Ben and me when I'm supposed to be mourning her brother? If she knew I cheated on her brother when I promised him forever?*

I swallow down my shame and answer. "Hey, Clara," I say, as if it's just like any other day.

"Hey. How are you?" she asks in a way that makes it difficult to gauge her mood.

"I'm good. Just watching Evan at soccer. How about you?" I lift my eyes and watch the boys run and kick the ball around.

I hear her blow out a long breath. "Great. That means you can talk, because I have *so* many questions."

Shit. It's never a good thing when she has questions. I tuck my hair behind my ear, and dread forms like a lead ball in my stomach. I've never kept anything from her in the past, but I'm not sure I can share this. "What about?" I know exactly what she has questions about, but if I act ignorant, maybe I can avoid this discussion.

She chuckles. "I think you know, but I'll spell it out for you. B. E. N." Her sigh is so dramatic, I can't miss it over the cheering from the other team as they score another goal. I watch Evan's shoulders slump and roll forward. "His eyes were glued to you the entire time he was at the party, and don't even get me started on the fact that he was still there when your mom and dad left. Yes. I talked to your mom last night." She sounds so excited, almost like how she was when I finally fessed up to crushing on her big brother.

"Evan invited him to his party, and he stayed behind to help clean up because he likes to be helpful." I keep my voice steady, hopeful she doesn't detect the lie. Thankful she hasn't spoken to Mom today.

"Sure. Yeah. That's totally ... you know what, I'm not playing your game, girly. He's totally into you. Whether he's Evan's friend or not is irrelevant. He could not keep his eyes off of you. And when you were within three feet of him, I watched him clench his hands, as if he were holding himself back. You can lie to yourself all you like, but I know what I saw. Now, I want to know what you're doing about it?"

I narrow my eyes as I look across the field. "Well, I'm not going to stop Evan from being friends with Ben. He's been a wonderful influence, and Evan loves him and his dog, Rex."

She tsks rather loudly. "You know that's not what I'm asking. Stop being so obtuse. The way you're deflecting tells me you're hiding something." Her voice softens. "We've been friends for too long for you to be able to hide stuff from me. Talk to me, Hope," she cajoles softly.

The backs of my eyes sting, and I blink quickly to stem the tears that want to fall when I hear the softness in her voice.

"I cheated." The words gush out of me, and I'm washed under a wave of guilt and shame. I claw for the surface, but I can't make headway. It feels as though the pressure is squeezing all the oxygen out of my lungs, and I'm struggling to breathe.

"On Ben?" Confusion is thick in her voice, and I can imagine her tilting her head to the side and chewing on her nail as she tries to make sense of what I said.

I shake my head and grip my locks, sucking in a sharp breath. "No. Wyatt. I cheated on Wyatt *with* Ben."

I'm not gonna lie, as wrong as it is, it also feels good to get it off my chest. It's been eating away at me since the first time I pressed my mouth to his. Even before that ... when I had that dream. But telling Wyatt's sister that I cheated on her brother is all kinds of messed up. I press the heel of my hand against my forehead, trying to stem the pressure building there.

"Aww. Honey. You didn't cheat on Wyatt," she whispers.

The half-time whistle blows and I watch the boys walk off the field to grab a drink. My eyes burn and my nose fizzes with the telltale sign I won't be able to hold back the tears this time. They well in my eyes and drop over my bottom lashes. I furiously swipe them away, tired of them.

Tired of the buildup of emotions.

Tired of feeling too much ... too little.

Tired of the overwhelming hole in my chest where my heart used to beat for Wyatt.

Tired of feeling so damn broken.

"Hope," Clara says my name, bringing my focus back to our call. "None of us expect you to be alone for the rest of your life. Wyatt wouldn't expect you to be alone. Mom and Dad don't. *I* don't. You're the only one who thinks that way and you're too young to think that way," she says in a tone that can't be misconstrued as anything other than the truth. "You can't possibly think anyone would begrudge you finding happiness after everything. After all these years. You were the best thing to ever happen to my brother. You were a fantastic wife, and you gave him the greatest gift ... a son. You made my brother so happy."

A sob bursts past my lips, and I look around me, embarrassed. Slipping off the hood of my car, I climb inside, where I can have some semblance of privacy.

"He would hate that you're not allowing yourself the opportunity to find happiness with someone else," she murmurs.

"I-it just feels so wrong, Clara. On so many levels." I look out of the windshield, not really seeing anything.

Fabric rustles and a chair scrapes across the floor over the phone. "Tell me about the levels that feel wrong."

Waving my hand around the interior of my car like a crazy person, I snap. "Well, talking to you about a man other than Wyatt, for starters. Inviting a man who isn't Evan's father into our home to spend time with our son. A man who's made it clear he'll wait as long as it takes for me to be ready to date. Kissing that man in the house that Wyatt paid for—and continues to pay for."

Clara sucks in a sharp breath.

"Having sexual dreams and thoughts about a man other than my husband in the bed that I shared with my husband. Appreciating the way another man looks. Wanting him to touch me ... to kiss me. It's wrong. All of it. It's just wrong," I sob, then gasp in a harsh breath. "Breaking my promise to the man I married," I whisper. Broken. There's no stopping the cascade of tears that flood my cheeks. "It's all so wrong. He was supposed to be my first and my only," I say brokenly.

Silence fills the space between me and Clara as I cry. Dropping my head back on the seat, I look up at the roof of my car, hoping the change in angle will stop the tears from falling. All it does is change their direction so they fall down the side of my face and into my hair.

"None of it's wrong, honey," she whispers. "I promise." She

blows out a long breath over the phone. "If Wyatt were still here, he *would* be your one and only, but he's gone, and he's not coming home." Her words stab me painfully. "He wouldn't want you to hold true to your promise to him."

"That's what everyone says, so why does it feel that way for me?" I sigh. "Why am I having so much trouble reconciling what everyone else tells me and what my heart feels?"

She blows out a long breath. "I think it's easier for us to say these things because we haven't experienced the same loss you have but we want you to be happy. I lost my brother, and I feel it every day. It's like there's this missing piece of me. But I didn't lose my life partner or the father of my child, and neither has anyone else in our circle. I can't imagine the depth of your devastation. It's not like you guys fought or the relationship turned sour. You guys loved each other deeply; you were happy. It's not like you got to choose to end your relationship. That has to leave deep scars on your heart. You have to learn to exist without him, Hope. You have to learn to love again with those scars on your heart."

"I'm tr-trying my best."

"We know you are. But you need to stop getting in your own way. You're allowed to live again, Hope. It's what we all want for you. Wyatt would want you to. And whether that be with Ben or someone else, we all want you to be happy." She pauses for a long while, and I think that's the end of it. "If you need our permission to move on, you have it."

It feels like the world falls out from beneath me, and I gasp in a breath, but there's not enough oxygen inside the car. I rush to open my door to get more air into the car to help regulate my breathing. Cool air rushes over me, and it's exactly what I need. I gulp in oxygen like I'm about to do a deep dive, filling my lungs with cool, fresh air. My eyes water, and I swallow past the thickness in my throat.

Is that what I've needed?

To know Wyatt's family will accept me moving on with another relationship?

The thought hadn't even crossed my mind, but the pressure that's lifted from my chest makes me believe maybe it's been lurking in the back of my mind. I know I want to keep my promise ... my vow to my first love, but maybe my struggle has been compounded by my worry about their reaction to me moving on.

"Hope?" Clara sounds uncertain as she calls my name. "You gonna be okay? I can come over."

I gather my composure. "I'm okay."

"Are you sure?"

"Yeah. Promise."

"I didn't mean to upset you."

"I know."

"For what it's worth, we all like Ben, and I think Wyatt would like him for you and Evan."

I tip my head back again and press my lips together, nodding in agreement even though she can't see me. "Thanks, Clara."

I think Wyatt would, too. Ben's so good with Evan and so patient with me. He brings fun back into our lives, which was something Wyatt always tried to do whenever he was home. And most importantly, Ben doesn't look at us like we're broken.

"Any time, my friend. I gotta go, but I can come over later if you want."

"Thanks, but I'm okay."

We say goodbye, and when I look back out at the field, the game has ended and the kids are shaking hands.

37
HOPE

Dragging my rubber gloves up my arms, I turn toward Evan, still sitting at the table as he looks at something on his phone. "Hey, Ev. How about you come and help dry the dishes for me?" I pose it like a question, but he knows I expect him to help.

I learned long ago that, if I want to chat with him, he has to be busy … slightly distracted.

Once the sink is full, I toss him the dish towel and get started. As he's drying the first glass, I watch him out of the corner of my eye. "How are you, Ev?"

"Okay. You?" he asks as he stuffs the dish towel inside the glass, concentrating hard to get the water at the very bottom.

I look at him, so he can see the sincerity of my answer. "I think I'm doing better these days, but I'd like to know if *you* agree?"

He places the glass in the cupboard and turns to me. Leaning against the counter, he takes my breath away. He looks so much like his father. He crosses his arms and studies me closely, making me shift under his scrutiny. "I think you're not so sad. I've even seen you smile and heard you laugh. And I like the way we've been talking about Dad more."

I turn back to the sink. The way he's looking at me, like he can see inside my head, gives me goosebumps. He's twelve, for goodness' sake. He shouldn't be so perceptive. "I'm sorry."

He collects another glass and wipes the outside. "What for?"

"It upsets me you haven't seen me happy for such a long time." I rinse the plate and place it on the dish rack.

His eyebrows scrunch together. "But you've been sad because of Dad."

I smile sadly at my son. "But I still had you here, and it's like I forgot how important you are to me. I should have put my focus on you. On the person I love most in the world rather than the person I lost. It wasn't fair to you, Ev."

He wraps his arm around my waist and rests his head against my shoulder. "You didn't forget me." He squeezes me, and I wrap my arm around him. "You made sure I had everything I needed. You always picked me up from school on time and always took me to soccer practice. Every night you told me how much you love me, and you always helped me with my homework." He looks up at me with a guilty expression. "You even put up with my bad moods and terrible decisions."

I grin down at him and stroke his hair with my glove-covered hand. "I love you all the way to *Knowhere* and back again. You know that, right?"

"I know."

My grin falls, and I study him carefully, noting the changes in the shape of his face. He's growing up so fast. "Would you like to talk to a counselor or psych? Someone who you can talk to about your feelings in a safe place? I know you haven't always been able to talk to me about stuff because I always got too upset."

He shakes his head. "Nah. I could always talk to Shane or Nanna and Grandad, as well as Grandma and Pop, or Aunty Clara." He looks down and back up at me. "Shane even let me take some of my bad mood out on him that time when I was feeling angry and upset."

My relief is overwhelming, and I grip the counter to keep

myself upright. Mom said they'd all picked up where I fell down, but hearing it from Evan settles that deep pit of worry deep in my gut. Knowing he wasn't left floundering and that our friends and family watched out for him when I was unable releases tension deep inside my muscles and it's almost like I can take a full breath for the first time in over six years.

"Do you think we'll be okay?" I ask.

He nods with a grin. "Yeah. I'm pretty sure we're okay." His grin widens. "And we have Ben now."

My heart takes off at a gallop at the joy on my son's face when he says Ben's name. "Well, yeah. He's been a great friend to you."

"And you, too," Evan fires back.

I chuckle, nodding. "Yeah. Me too."

"You know, he told me our heart is elastic. We can love as many people as we want to, and our heart will fit them all in." He looks at me. "He said we didn't have to stop loving Dad to love him. He said we could love both of them."

I swear my heart crashes to a halt and the air in my lungs thins. "Wh-what?"

"Our hearts. He said we can love him *and* Dad. He doesn't expect you or me to stop loving Dad because he knows we have enough room in our hearts to love both of them," he tells me with wide eyes.

"When was this?"

"At the giant bake sale." He pulls away from me and looks down at the floor between us. "I-I got a bit jealous when I thought he liked you more than he liked me. He was my friend first, you know?" My head is spinning with this new information, but I nod for him to continue. "But he told me he liked us both for different reasons—that if I didn't mind, he'd like to ask you on a date some-day." He shakes his head. "I told him how you still love Dad, and that's when he told me it was okay for you to still love Dad. He said he didn't mind because our hearts are elastic. He said he would never expect you to stop loving Dad."

I'm rendered speechless as blood rushes through my ears, and my head becomes filled with cotton. I had no idea such a conversation had taken place, and I'm not sure how I feel about it. Ben's made his intention clear to me, but I'm uncertain how I feel about Evan knowing Ben's intentions before I did.

"He sorta asked me if I thought it'd be okay if he asked you out some day," he tells me quietly.

I finally find my composure and look at Evan. "And ... what did you say?"

"I told him it would be okay with me." His eyes widen and he swallows. "You're not mad, are you?"

How can I be mad? My son just gave me the okay to move forward and date. My in-laws have given me the go-ahead. At this point, I'm the only one holding myself back. I force a smile. "I'm not mad. You're quite something, Evan. You know that, right?"

His body sags as he blows out a long breath. "Phew." He looks down at the dishes, then back to me with a hopeful grin. "Do you think you'll date Ben?"

I shrug and dip my hands back into the soapy water, washing a plate. "Maybe."

Out of the corner of my eye, I watch Evan smile. "Cool."

38

BEN

I PALM MY COCK AS IT THICKENS. MY MIND HAS constantly wandered back to the events of this morning all day, and it's been a constant struggle to keep my focus on my job—something I never had a problem doing before.

Hope was so damn stunning as she fell apart in my lap. The flush to her cheeks and the way her pulse hammered. The way she took what she wanted.

So damn sexy.

It took everything in me not to fall into oblivion until she got what she needed. It took a hell of a lot of control on my part as my orgasm burned and clawed to be released. Once she came, I couldn't hold it back—even if a gun was being held to my head. It rammed through me like a bullet. And nothing had ever felt better because she showed me a level of trust I wasn't sure she'd ever give me.

My heart soared as we shared something so intimate, and then within moments, it shattered into a million bloody pieces when her distress and pain filled the room like a swirling storm. I just wanted to hold her ... to reassure her that everything would be okay.

That we did nothing wrong.

Then it was time to get ready for work ... and Evan came home ... and I hated leaving Hope when she was so vulnerable and raw. I'm gutted something so natural, so beautiful, ended in such sorrow.

What I wouldn't give to make her pain mine and give her the freedom to feel peace. If I could swap places with Wyatt, I would in a heartbeat—if it took away her pain and gave her the happiness she deserves.

I glance across at my phone sitting on the bedside table. Rex raises his head from his prone position on his dog bed and whines at me.

"I know. I should just message her to check she's okay." His golden eyebrows rise and fall as he watches me. "I'm trying to give her some space. I don't want to lose her by pushing too hard."

He adjusts his position, tilts his head to the side as though he understands what I'm saying, and barks at me as my phone lights up with a message.

Snatching the phone like a teenage girl, my eyes greedily scan the screen. A long, relieved breath peels out of my lungs at the name that's lit up like a beacon.

> COOKIE
>
> Hey
>
> I hope it's not too late
>
> Are you free?
>
> Can I call you?

I fumble with the device, cursing myself, and call her. After one ring, her chuckle reaches my ears and the air in my lungs gushes past my lips. It's the best sound I've heard all day, and I soak it up like it's essential for my wellbeing. I should feel scared at how quickly Hope and Evan have gotten under my skin and become an integral part of my life, but I'm not. It's surprising how ready I am to make them mine.

"That was fast," she says with a chuckle.

"Hey," I murmur on a breath.

"Hey." She must still be smiling because I can hear it in that simple greeting.

I lean back against my headboard and get comfortable, resting my free hand behind my head. "How was your day?" I wonder if she can hear the deeper questions—the ones I really want to ask.

Are you okay? Did I break you? Did I break us before we began?

She chuckles softly, and I can imagine her sliding her fingers through her hair and holding it back from her face the way she does. The sound of a long breath fans out across the line, then there's a pause. "Where do I start?"

"Wherever you want, Cookie."

Rex sighs from his bed, still watching me.

"Cookie," she whispers. "Wyatt never gave me a nickname, but I like that you've given me one. The way your voice softens when you say it. It ... uh ... makes me feel really special."

"Good, because you are."

The rustling of fabric and the creak of bed springs fill the silence. "I'm a broken mess, that's what I am."

I shake my head. "You're beautiful ... inside and out."

"You make me feel beautiful for the first time in a really long time," she confesses softly.

"I'm glad." My chest fills with warmth which radiates out through my body. If I can help her see her beauty and bring her back into the light, I'll consider it one of my greatest achievements.

"You make me feel like maybe some of my broken pieces aren't so broken anymore."

"There's beauty in being broken, Hope. You just don't see it."

"Ben," she murmurs in the softest voice.

"Have you ever heard of *kintsugi*?"

"No. I don't think so."

"It's a Japanese method for repairing broken pottery. Using a special Japanese lacquer, artisans glue the pieces back together and then paint the joins with a gold, silver, or platinum powder. Some believe the repaired pottery is even more stunning than it was before it was broken." Her breaths fill the line. "When I look at you, all I see is the most stunning woman I've ever laid eyes on, and the more time I spend with you, the more stunning you become. Your broken pieces make you beautifully unique."

Silence fills the line, and the temptation to fill it with words to lighten the mood is strong, but maybe the silence will give her time to come to terms with what I've said. She clears her throat. "That ... that's beautiful, Ben. I don't know what to say."

"You don't need to say anything. You just need to believe what I'm telling you."

"I can't believe you see me like that," she whispers. The line goes quiet again, except for her breathing. "I wanted to apologize for this morning."

My stomach drops and twists on itself. I know she regrets what happened, but I can't bear to hear her say the words. As much as I know she does, I can't find it in myself to regret it. The only part of what happened this morning I regret is when she broke down. "You don't—"

"Yes, I do. You don't deserve to be dealing with my emotional breakdowns. This morning was all my fault. The other night when I kissed you ... that was my fault, too. You've been so patient, allowing me the space to do things when I'm ready and then when I do ... I fall apart. I'm embarrassed by my behavior."

I can't sit here and listen to her anymore, so I climb from the bed and pace across the cool hardwood floor. "Hope," I rumble. "You have nothing to be embarrassed about."

"Well, thank you, but I think I do. You didn't ask for any of this, but you've continued to be there for me through my tears. You're such a good man." She goes quiet, and I absorb her words, soaking up her compliment. I've always worked hard to be a good person. To be the opposite of everything I grew up with. "I've had an emotional day, and to be honest, I'm beyond exhausted."

"Do you wanna talk about it, or would you rather get some sleep?" I don't want her to hang up, but if she needs sleep …

She sighs. "I'd like to talk with you about it. I mean, if you have time."

"I have nothing but time for you … and for Evan." I drop back onto my bed and get comfortable again, shoving my pillows behind my back.

She blows out a long breath, and I hear the rustle of fabric. "I've had an emotional day all around. First, this morning with you, then Mom insisted on having lunch together. She was adamant I haven't screwed up Evan and that all parents question their ability to parent. And while I'd love to believe that's true, I feel as though she's only saying that to relieve some of the burden from my heart."

I nod even though she can't see me, and when she pauses, I jump in. "I'm not a parent, so I don't know how it works from personal experience, but in my line of work, I see a lot of kids who have definitely been emotionally abandoned or physically forgotten by their parents. The signs of their neglect are as obvious as a neon sign to me, and I want to tell you that Evan doesn't bear any. Sure, he made an error in judgment with his new friends, but he was genuinely remorseful. He's a great kid, Hope. He has a strong moral compass, and he's well cared for and loved. The minute I laid eyes on him in the gas station, I knew he was a good kid who'd made a mistake."

"As much as I wish he'd never gotten caught up with those boys, I'm thankful you're the one who brought him home. I'm not sure if the positive change in Evan would have happened if it weren't for you." I draw in a silent breath, caught off guard by her declaration. Something deep inside me warms with her acknowledgment. "I'm so appreciative of the time and compassion you've given Evan. The change in him has been ... remarkable ... and so good for my soul."

I rub my hand over the top of my head, sending flashes of Hope cutting my hair through my mind. "As I said, he's a good kid."

"He is." She pauses for a long time, and I wonder if that's the end of the conversation. "Then, this afternoon, Clara called while Evan was playing soccer." The tone of her voice has changed, grown heavier, more weighed down. "She wanted the lowdown about you." She chuckles mischievously. *I wonder what she had to say about me?* "I told her I cheated on Wyatt," she murmurs so softly, and I'm unsure if I heard her correctly.

Cheated?

But how?

Then, as if lightning strikes, realization hits me. She still considers herself a married woman. She still wears her wedding ring and still holds herself to the same promises she made when she made her vows to Wyatt. Guilt crawls its way up my throat and tears out of my mouth. "I'm so sorry, Hope. I should have stopped things before they went that far." I can't believe I put her in that position. I'm such a selfish ass.

"You don't need to apologize for anything. That was all on me, and I realized this afternoon that if ... if I had the chance ... if you were even remotely interested ... after my breakdown and all ... I ... uh ... I'd like to do it again some time," she whispers the last part, as if she's worried I'll deny her. *Does she not realize I'd never deny her anything?*

My heart takes off at a gallop. I thought this conversation was her way of telling me nothing could happen between us again. Instead, she's surprised the hell out of me. "Hope." Her name escapes my lips on a breath, mixed with compassion and need. "Don't ever doubt my interest in you," I almost growl—disappointed. Frustrated she hasn't been paying attention.

Her breaths echo across the line. "Oh-kay." Her nervous

chuckle follows after a few seconds. "So … uhm … maybe we could go on a da—"

"Yes!" I almost shout and she chuckles more freely. "I'd love to take you on a date," I rush to add. Feeling like an asshole that she had to ask. "When can we make this happen?"

"Hmm. I'm not sure. When are you free?" Her tone has grown playful.

"I'm on days this Friday, Saturday, and Sunday, so we can do something one of those evenings." I can't believe a date with Hope is within my grasp. Now, to make it memorable for her.

"Leave it to me, and I'll see when I can organize a babysitter for Evan. I'm sure it won't be a problem," she tells me, and I can practically hear the smile in her voice. "I'll let you know tomorrow."

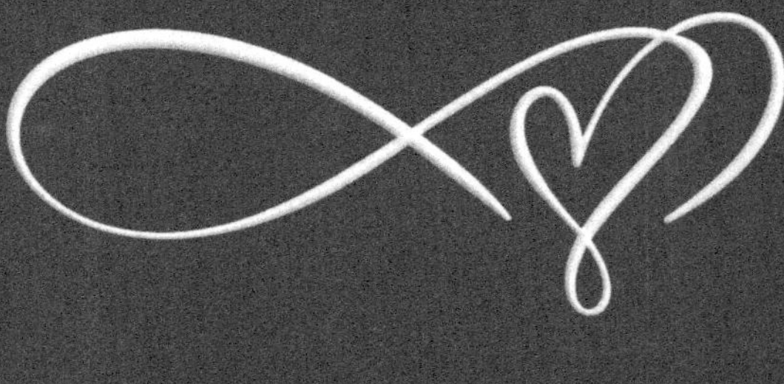

39

BEN

I gave our date a lot of consideration. Wondering if I should reserve a table at a nice restaurant so we can enjoy a meal together, or if I should organize something fun and lighthearted? But when I remembered how much fun Hope had at mini golf, it was an easy decision—indoor archery at *The Golden Circle*.

I figure it'll be a relaxed evening without too much pressure, and hopefully we'll have a few laughs along the way. Then we can grab a couple of pizzas and enjoy a picnic beneath the stars in the back of my truck. You can take the boy out of the country, but you can't take the country out of the boy.

As I pull up to a stop in front of the neat gray-and-white trim home, my heart races like I'm about to perform a search and rescue. Blowing out a nervous breath, I run my hand through my hair and climb out of my truck, then lean in to grab the flowers and gift bag from the passenger seat. I didn't want to be cliché, but I was at a loss as to what to bring, and I wanted to bring something.

Striding up the walkway, I'm unsure what to expect, which sends my mind racing in a hundred different directions—along with contingency plans for each one. There's no way of knowing if she's had second thoughts, or if she's feeling guilty about going on a date with me. I'm hopeful she's as ready as she says she is, but I'm prepared to cut our time short if that's what she needs. I certainly don't want to pressure her; she puts enough pressure on herself.

The door opens suddenly as I breach the top step, and all the air leaves my lungs in a whoosh. My heart beats frantically for a completely different reason as my eyes eat her up. She's wearing tight, dark denim jeans, tan boots up to her knees, and a simple pink knitted top, but she's so damn beautiful. When my gaze finally makes it up to her face, her clear, aquamarine gaze is studying me with uncertainty, and my heart sinks.

She's having second thoughts.

Closing the distance between us, I trace her face carefully, looking for an answer. "You're so beautiful, Hope," I whisper on a breath, unable to contain the words and unwilling to let the disappointment of her change of heart stop me from sharing my thoughts with her.

Her shoulders drop as a puff of air leaves her lips. A smile lights her face, and the uncertainty I saw vanishes. "Thank you," she murmurs, dropping her eyes away from mine.

Realization strikes that she was waiting for my approval, which she absolutely doesn't need. She could wear a paper bag, and she'd still be the most beautiful woman to me. I lean in and press a kiss to her cheek, soaking in the smooth softness of her skin and her addictive vanilla scent. Moving my mouth closer to her ear, I murmur with a heated breath, "You're perfect in every way, Cookie."

A shiver races through her, and my mouth stretches into a smile. Good to know I affect her as much as she affects me. Stepping back a little, I hold out the flowers to her—light pink roses, mixed with baby's breath, wrapped in white tissue paper. The gray-eyed woman at *Blooms and Balloons* said they'd be perfect for a first date, and if the smile on Hope's face is any indication, the florist knew her stuff.

Hope brings them to her nose and dips her head closer to the arrangement, drawing in a deep breath. When she looks back up at me, gratitude fills her gaze. "Thank you. They're beautiful." She chuckles softly. "I'm not gonna say you shouldn't have, because I'm so glad you did. I've never been given flowers before." Her tone relays the disappointment she's felt at not receiving such a simple gift, and I vow then and there that I'll make sure she has fresh flowers regularly for the rest of her days. I hold up the gift bag, and her eyes widen. "Now, I'm gonna say you shouldn't have."

I shrug as she takes it from the tips of my fingers with a gentle brush. "If I'm honest, this is more for me than for you."

She chuckles and looks inside the bag at the army-green cable-knit socks. Her eyes narrow in question, and her gaze lifts to mine in question. "I'm not sure how these are more for you than for me, but I love them. Thank you." She passes the flowers back to me so she can dip her hand inside to pull them out. She rubs them against her cheek with a sigh. "They're so soft. They'll be my coziest pair yet." She pushes up onto her toes and presses a soft kiss to my bristly cheek. "Thanks, Ben. You've spoiled me. Be careful, or I'll expect it all the time." She giggles. I'll buy her gifts every day, if it makes her happy.

I twist the watch on my wrist, so I don't pull her into me. I'm determined not to maul her before our date. All bets are off after, but taking her out and showing her a fun time is my priority tonight. "I thought the green would match Wyatt's sweatshirt." It's my way of letting her know I'm okay with her holding onto him.

Her eyes snap up to mine, and her questions bombard me without her opening her mouth. "Ben?" My name is barely a breath on her trembling lips. She wraps her arms around me and lays her cheek against my chest and I return her embrace.

"I want you to know you don't have to let him go, Hope," I whisper against the top of her soft hair. She squeezes me tighter, burying her face against me, melding her body to mine, and I have to remind myself that I want to take her out—that I want her to let go and have some fun. Shuffling my feet, I settle in and return her hug, doing my utmost to keep it innocent.

WE ARRIVE at the archery center, and Hope's head snaps toward me when she realizes where we are. "What's this?"

I release my seatbelt and hers and raise an eyebrow. "Archery. I thought it might be fun."

She swivels in her seat and narrows her eyes. "You didn't pick up on my total lack of coordination when we played mini golf?" She waves her arm out toward the building. "I'm likely to kill someone in there."

I chuckle and take her hand, kissing the center of her palm. Her shoulders drop, and she seems to relax at my touch. "I won't let you. I promise it's completely safe, and it'll be fun." I open my door and climb out. "Wait there, I'll come around."

I grasp her hand in mine, and we walk inside to check in. We each sign a waiver, then we're given our equipment. Hope studies our bows. "How come yours is so much bigger than mine?" she asks, looking truly offended.

"The size of the bow depends on the size of the archer," the attendant explains.

Hope's mouth forms an O in understanding, but because my mind is permanently in the gutter when I'm around this woman, I instantly imagine pushing my dick into her mouth and watching her eyes water as she swallows me down.

Damn.

I adjust my position and drop my gaze from hers, fearing she'll be able to read my thoughts. It's like the second her lips met mine the first time—my mind goes straight to filthy thoughts whenever I'm with her.

I help her strap the leather arm-guard onto her slender arm, and place the quiver around her slim waist and thigh, subtly breathing in the sweet fragrance that always surrounds her.

The attendant leads us over to an area and demonstrates how to aim and shoot the arrow, ensuring he hits the golden bullseye every single time.

I manage to hit the red and blue circles, but I wouldn't say I was consistent with my technique. Two of Hope's arrows miss the target entirely, landing in the net behind. She looks at me with raised brows and wide eyes over her shoulder as if to say, *I told you so.*

We finish our lesson and the attendant leaves us alone to work our way through the archery range on our own. "Do you really think this is a good idea?" Hope waves her arm back toward the net, where we just had our lesson. "I can't be trusted to hit the target."

Wrapping my arm around her shoulders with a chuckle, I pull her in tight. "I have faith in you." I kiss her temple, then let her go. "You wanna go first?"

She shrugs. "Sure."

She steps up to the line and raises the bow, then pulls back on the string, but her stance is all wrong. "Hold on." Moving in behind her, I place my hands on her hips and twist them slightly, wishing I could keep touching her indefinitely. "Remember, the side of your body should face the boss and your toes need to be in line with the target." I nudge her feet. "These need to be shoulder-width apart."

She adjusts the position of her feet and looks up at me over her shoulder. "Like this?"

My eyes drop to her mouth, the temptation to lean down and kiss her almost too overwhelming for me to control.

When her body connects with my groin, I step back like I'm on fire; there's no need for her to feel what she does to me. Not here, not now. Maybe later.

"Uh, yeah. Yeah. That should do it." I push my lips up into a reassuring smile, hoping like hell I can maintain my equilibrium throughout our date.

With her long fingers wrapped around the string, she pulls it back until it's in line with her cheek. I move back in and reposition her fingers, so there is one above and two below the shaft of the arrow.

"Thanks, Ben."

I step back, and she focuses on the target, then releases the arrow. It flies, landing wide and hitting the net strung up behind the stand.

"Damn it!" The arch of her eyebrows dips, and she mumbles something under her breath, before drawing another arrow from her quiver and nocking it to the string.

I watch her shoulders rise as she draws in a breath, and then she drops them into a relaxed position.

She adjusts her feet and raises her bow, keeping her shoulders square with the target, like I showed her. Raising the bow into position, she draws back the string and, after a moment, releases it. This time, the arrow flies and hits the boss. Granted, it misses the target, but she's closer to making the shot within the circle. Her shoulders drop, and disappointment fills the surrounding air.

"Hey, look at that. You almost hit the paper. Next time, you'll get on the scoreboard."

She whines. "I doubt it. I'm terrible at this stuff."

I frown. "Have you done archery before?" She shakes her head. "Then how can you expect to be good at it from the get-go? It takes practice ... like most things in life."

She toes the fake grass beneath her feet. "I guess so." The action reminds me so much of Evan when we all played mini golf together. Even though she doesn't come across as competitive, maybe she is a little.

"C'mon. You have one more shot this round. Make it count." I wink at her and step backward to watch her take the shot. My eyes drop to her denim-clad ass, and I remember how it felt in my hands the other morning. How sexy she was when she took what she needed from me.

Hope jumps up and down, squealing with delight, like a child in a bouncy castle, pulling me from my salacious thoughts. When I gather my bearings, I notice what has her so excited. Her arrow is proudly sticking out of the outermost white circle of the target. "Did you see that? I actually hit the target!"

I bend down and wrap my arms around her hips, easily lifting her from the ground. Her free hand drops to my shoulder, and she looks down at me with a beaming smile and a face filled with pride for her achievement. "I knew you'd do it!"

She leans down and kisses me chastely, but before I have time to react, she pulls away to look at her arrow. "I can't believe it!"

And I can't believe she kissed me in her excitement.

I take my turn, hitting the target each time I fire an arrow, but I'm nowhere near to getting a bullseye, and the arrows don't even land anywhere near each other. I definitely need to improve my technique.

By the last target of the night, Hope's aim has improved to the point where she hits the rings of the target with all three arrows. Watching her confidence grow—and the excitement in her eyes build whenever she hits the target—has been better than I could have predicted.

Her enjoyment was my number one goal tonight. Seeing her eyes sparkle and her wide smile has made my night—no, my *week*. Her happiness, her joy, her sparkle ... it's better than breathing. I'm so glad I went with a fun night out instead of sitting in a stuffy restaurant.

40

BEN

With her small hand tucked securely in mine, we head out into the cool night to my truck. The extra blankets I packed for the next part of our date will be essential.

Hope squeezes my hand and pulls me to a stop beside my truck. She tugs me around, tips her head back, and her genuine grin rocks my world. "I had the best time tonight. Thank you." She rises onto her toes and presses her lips to mine. Soft and warm. Tender and gentle. Every atom in my body wants to slide my fingers into the fall of her hair and tilt her head back to deepen the kiss, but I want to let her take the lead. She pulls away too soon, her eyes sparkling with mischief. "Next time, I'm gonna beat you." She twists away from me playfully, and I tap her tight ass with a chuckle.

I raise my eyebrows. "That's some smack talk right there. We'll see," I tell her as I open her door—thrilled she's thinking about future dates.

She slides into the seat, and I drag the seatbelt across her body, breathing in her warm vanilla scent that sends my libido into overdrive. As I move back to stand, I turn my head and my eyes automatically drop to Hope's lips. Her breath coasts across mine, and as if I have zero self-control, I lean forward and press my mouth to hers.

She sighs and I slip my tongue inside to taste her, something I've been dying to do all night. Her hand slides up over my shoulder and wraps around the back of my neck, holding me in place. I breathe her in as we kiss, exploring and tasting each other. Her breath becomes mine, and mine becomes hers—as if it were always meant to be this way. We take and we give, as if we've been kissing like this for years.

After too short a time, she pulls back slightly, and I'm relieved when I find her cheeks dry and a lazy, sexy grin on her lips. That look, right there, is all I'll ever need until the end of time. I peck her lips and close her door, then make my way around to my side, adjusting myself discreetly as I slide behind the wheel.

"I thought we could pick up a couple of pizzas and head up the hill to enjoy them above the city lights."

Hope smiles at me and my breath catches. She's so beautiful when she's like this. I mean, she's always beautiful, but there's something mesmerizing about her when she smiles. Especially when it's aimed at me. "Sounds perfect."

WITH THE PIZZAS BETWEEN US, I reverse park so we can enjoy the view over the city from the back of my truck. "Wait here, okay?"

Hope nods, confusion causing crinkles between her eyebrows. "Okay."

I climb out and set up the back with the mattress, cushions, and a ton of blankets that I packed for our date—essential tonight with the brisk temperature. Once it's set up to my liking, I turn on the twinkle lights, set up our picnic, grab the pizzas, then I open Hope's door and hold my hand out to her.

She gasps and her free hand flies up to cover her mouth as we reach the back of my truck and she sees the set up. Her eyes slide up to mine, and the shock and surprise on her face is almost comical. "Ben," she whispers on a breath. "This ... it's gorgeous." She tears her gaze from mine and studies the bed of my truck. "You've thought of everything."

"I hope so," I tell her as I tug her forward and help her up.

She shimmies back, propping herself against the cushions and covers herself with a thick blanket, and I add another for good measure. I don't want her to feel cold, so I place a woolen hat I bought for her on her head and a scarf around her neck. "These are gorgeous. You really have thought of everything."

I grin, then get comfortable, dragging the blankets over myself, cocooning us together. Opening the pizza boxes, I lift the pizza closer to Hope so she can grab a slice. Her eyes drop closed on a moan when she takes her first bite, and suddenly my jeans are too tight. I imagine her responding in much the same way as I swipe my tongue through her lips and circle her clit with gentle strokes. *Damn.*

As much as I love hanging out with Evan, I've been looking forward to spending time alone with Hope. I want to discover if we have enough of a connection to be a couple without Evan as a buffer. I know I'm attracted to her. I also know she's been struggling with her attraction to me out of guilt for her promise to her late husband. I need to know if our attraction goes deeper than the physical and beyond my sense of wanting to make life better for her. *Are we compatible enough to have a friendship ... a deeper bond based on commonalities and understanding, loyalty, and communication?*

We're both quiet as we eat, neither of us feeling the need to fill the silence. The soft hoot of an owl in the distance rings out in the darkness, and a gentle, cool breeze sends strands of Hope's hair across her cheek. She chuckles, trying to push it away with the back of her wrist. I reach across, slide the wayward strands behind her ear, then trace my finger down the side of her soft cheek, eliciting a soft smile and sending my heart skittering across my ribs.

"Mmmm. I don't think I could eat another bite," Hope tells me as she closes the lid on the box, then rests her hand over her stomach.

I stack her box on top of mine and shove them out of the way. Once the space between us is clear, Hope shuffles closer to me. Her body heat seeps through her clothes and mine, and my soul sighs at having her initiate physical contact so freely. Wrapping my arm around her shoulders, I tug her as close as possible and tighten the blankets over us, making the space cozy under a carpet of stars. "Tell me about Evan as a baby."

She glances up at me with a soft smile and pink cheeks from the cool night air. "Gosh, where do I even start? I could talk about him all day."

A soft smile touches my lips because she doesn't even realize how that makes her a great mom.

"He was a terrible sleeper. Up all hours of the night. I don't know how many hours I spent walking around the house in the dark, trying to coax him to sleep. I tried everything the nurses recommended, from making sure he had plenty of access to sunlight during the day, to tiring him out ... nothing worked. Wyatt was overseas, so I was doing it all by myself. Our parents helped me as much as they could, but nighttime was the hardest. I was like a walking zombie for months, and then one day, he got the idea that nighttime was for sleeping. And while I should have been relieved, I panicked the first few nights because I was worried he'd stopped breathing." She chuckles darkly. "Nothing like catastrophizing a situation in the middle of the night when you're sleep deprived."

I press her head against my shoulder and lean down to lay a kiss there. "That had to be a tough time." Stroking my fingers along her temple and down her cheek, I kiss her again. I can't seem to stop. "You're incredible. You know that, right?" She doesn't even realize that she's been doing the single mom thing far longer than she's had the support of a partner.

Her shoulder moves against my side. "I just did what I had to do. It wasn't so bad." She sighs. "I never knew how much a parent loves their child. I worried my heart would burst with how much love I had for Evan. It was almost shocking to realize that I loved him more than I loved Wyatt ... and I loved him a lot."

With my free hand, I drag the cooler over and grab the peach schnapps, pouring each of us a drink. I hand a glass to Hope and then tap my glass against hers in a silent toast. "To being an incredible mom with so much love to give."

Hope scoffs. "Far from it, Ben. You know I've let my son down."

"We all have times when we're not at our best, Hope. That's what it is to be human. It's how you move forward from there that counts. I've seen a huge change in you guys since I first met you. You need to acknowledge those changes rather than always scolding yourself for where you fell down." I watch her throat move as she takes in my words and teases them apart.

She hums her agreement while she smiles ever so slightly, then she takes a sip of the fruity drink. "Mmm, this is delicious." She glances down at the glass, licking her lips, then back up to me, her eyebrows scrunched together. "This isn't the type of drink I would have thought you'd like."

I chuckle. "Funny story." I hold my glass up, studying the contents with a smile. "Tahlia, Sebastian, and I used to sneak Tahlia's mom's peach schnapps. Then we'd top it off with water, so she wouldn't notice. By the time we'd had a few drinks, we were drinking more water than schnapps." I chuckle, then sip my drink. "I'm sure she noticed and didn't say anything. But I got hooked on it and still have it occasionally."

Hope bursts out laughing. "How old were you?"

I tip my head back and gaze at the stars as I think back. "Maybe fifteen or sixteen."

"I can't imagine the law-abiding man next to me drinking stolen alcohol. Underage, no less." She laughs, and it goes straight to my heart. Her laugh has got to be one of the best sounds I've ever heard. I reach into the cooler and grab the dark chocolate I brought to pair with the schnapps. Hope snaps off a square and takes a delicate bite. "Oh, these go great together."

I share more stories about Tahlia, Sebastian, and me, and Hope tells me more about Evan and her friendship with Clara. Time passes as we learn more about each other and it feels natural to share these parts of ourselves. I love the way her face lights up when she speaks of Evan, and I even get a couple of wistful smiles when she shares about her crush on Wyatt as a teen. I feel as though Hope's letting me in behind her broken walls, and it's exactly where I want to be.

She looks up at me with a sleepy smile, and I can't resist sliding my fingers through her gorgeous curls and tracing down along her jaw until I reach her chin. Tipping her head back further, I erase the space between us and gently press my lips to hers. I'll never get enough of kissing Hope. She opens her mouth, inviting me inside, and I don't hesitate to deepen our connection. She tastes of rich dark chocolate, sweet peach schnapps, and *everlasting promises.*

She tastes of everything I've ever wanted ... everything I need.

And as I kiss her beneath the stars, I know she's the last woman I'll ever kiss.

41

HOPE

I may as well be floating for how light I feel after my date with Ben last week. When I pull up in front of *The Paw Palace*, Evan is waiting out front with Ben and Rex, his face beaming. Seeing him happy soothes something deep in my soul. For so long, I felt as though I was failing him, but he seems to have come out the other side reasonably unscathed, which is a miracle.

He opens the door before I come to a complete stop. "Some dogs need a bath today. Can we stay and help Ben, please?" I glance up at Ben and smile to myself at his hopeful expression. "Please, Mom. Say yes."

I chuckle. "Su—"

"Yes!" He pumps his fist in the air.

Widening my eyes, I grin. "Sure. Let me park, and I'll meet you guys inside."

Butterflies erupt in my stomach at the idea of spending unexpected time with Ben. He suggested we keep our budding relationship between us for now until we know where we're heading, and it made me fall for him even more that he has Evan's best interest at heart. Not a surprise, really. Ben constantly puts others before himself. He doesn't know another way to be.

It's such an attractive trait, because as much as I love Wyatt, at the end of the day, he was a selfish man whenever he was home.

Which I completely understood.

Whenever he was deployed, he had to give up so much and live in a constant state of stress. His time at home was always limited, so who was I to stop him from going surfing every day or catching up with old friends? He needed that time to destress and be normal. Even if it meant spending less time with us. As much as I missed him when he was deployed and wanted to spend every moment with him while he was home, he never seemed to feel the same. He always needed his space.

The three of us—Ben, Evan, and I—work like a well-oiled machine and finish bathing the dogs in a short amount of time. And surprisingly, we all manage to stay dry. *Winning!*

Tori steps into the washroom, blowing out a relieved breath as we're cleaning up the mess. "Thanks, guys. I'm so busy today. You really saved my butt." Her gratitude drips with relief, and the tightness around her mouth softens.

Ben wraps his arm around her shoulder. "You okay? Can we help with anything else?"

"Thanks. No, I'm okay. You guys have done more than enough. I appreciate it." She makes a shooing motion with her hands. "You guys go have fun and enjoy what's left of your Saturday afternoon."

We say goodbye to Tori, but I'm really not ready to say goodbye to Ben, and from the way Evan is fidgeting, I'd say he's not ready to say goodbye either.

"So, I was thinking we could go bowling this afternoon," I suggest, hoping Evan takes the bait and invites Ben along.

Evan snaps his head up to me. "That'll be fun. Can Ben come too?"

My heart rejoices, but I temper my external response. "Well, Ben may be busy." I peer at the man who has slowly, but surely broken down my walls, hoping to spend a little more time with him.

Evan snaps his head up to Ben. "Do you wanna come bowling with us?"

Ben musses up Evan's hair with a soft laugh. "Sure. I'll need to drop Rex home first." He looks up at me with a sexy grin, his gray eyes twinkling. "I can meet you guys there."

I shrug. "We can follow you home and then go in my car." That way, we can spend more time together.

I CAN'T WIPE the grin from my face. Bowling is more fun than I ever remember it being, but Ben always seems to make everything light and fun.

Evan and I laugh at Ben's antics as he dances his way back to us after knocking over seven of the ten pins. Anyone would think he'd knocked over all ten with his celebration, but he decided that, each time we knock over at least four pins, we should dance our way back to our little group.

Evan's soaked up every minute, making each of his dances more humorous than the last. It's like they're trying to out-dance each other at this point. Other teams around us cheer and clap each performance, encouraging their outrageous antics—not that they need any encouragement.

Clara, Wyatt, and I used to bowl regularly. They were always so competitive with each other, where I only ever wanted to have fun —primarily because I sucked at bowling, and nothing's changed. I'm last on the leaderboard, even though this is Evan's first time.

Ben took the time to teach Evan the proper techniques—the man seems to be gifted at everything he does—while I took the time to admire Ben's ass every time he rolled the ball. The way the denim of his jeans highlighted his firm thighs and butt had me imagining what he looks like naked. By the end of our first frame, I swear I was ready to combust, and by the end of our game, my underwear was toast.

As much as I try to muster up a feeling of guilt for admiring another man, I can't. I'm sure that makes me a horrible person, but for the first time in a long time, it's nice to *not* feel guilty. It's time to release myself from the self-imposed prison I'd trapped myself in—and it feels incredible to be free.

"I'm hungry. Can we get dinner?" Evan asks as he walks in front of Ben and me out of the bowling alley.

We follow behind, our arms brushing as we walk, sending tingles racing through my body. "Sure. What do you feel like eating?"

"Can we get burgers? Ben, you'll come too, won't you?" he asks as he stops at the car.

I'm unsure if Ben has figured out that Evan is trying to create the opportunity for us to spend even more time together. When I stop to think about it, maybe Evan's been doing it all along and I just didn't realize. He's always been so keen to extend our time with Ben.

Ben looks at me with raised brows. "Burgers sounds great, as long as your mom is happy for me to tag along."

I knock my shoulder into Ben's arm. "You're always welcome."

We drive the short distance to our favorite burger place, *Declan's Diner*. When we arrive, Evan heads straight to our usual table while Ben and I order at the counter. He leans down, sending shivers skittering across my body as his warm breath coasts across the side of my face. "I hope you know it's been torture spending this time with you and not being able to touch you. To kiss you the way I want to."

Heat rises up my neck, and I glance across at Evan playing on his phone while he waits for us. "Trust me, the feeling's mutual." I quickly press up on my toes and kiss him chastely.

He groans when I pull away quickly. "We need to have another date. Just the two of us."

My pulse races. "I agree. Evan stays with Wyatt's parents for the weekend in two weeks."

"Damn, that feels like forever from now, but if that's what I can have, I'll take it."

I grin at the torturous expression on his face, and I know the next two weeks will drag. "We can text," I offer, hopefully.

He nods stiffly, like he doesn't trust what will come out of his mouth.

Our number's called, and we grab our food and head to our table. Conversation flows easily between the three of us, and before I know it, our evening is over and my stomach sinks with disappointment. I never thought I'd feel this way about someone else. Never thought I'd *want* to spend all of my time with someone other than Wyatt.

Not that long ago, I was devoted to the idea of being alone for the rest of my days. It's shocking how my thoughts have shifted so drastically, and yet, once I gave myself permission to move forward, it's been easy.

I love spending time with Ben. I love seeing him with Evan. I'm not sure exactly how things shifted for me, but I'll be damned if I'll willingly give up this feeling of rightness.

We drop Ben at home, and as I pull into the driveway of our house, something feels off. "Did you leave the light on upstairs?"

Evan leans forward and looks up at the house. "Nope." And why would he? We left home this morning.

"Hmmm." I turn off the engine and twist in my seat. "Wait here, okay?"

"No. I'll come with you. What if there's someone inside?" It's sweet that he's being protective.

I widen my eyes at him. "Exactly. Wait here, please."

He reluctantly nods, and I climb out of the car, engaging the locks in case there is someone around and they try to steal our car. Nothing looks amiss, but I trek around the side of the house.

That's when I notice the side door ajar. My hands shake and my legs feel like Jell-O.

Quietly, I make my way back to our car and tug Evan out of the back seat, holding my finger up to my lips, showing we should be silent. I know we wouldn't stand a chance against whoever might be inside our house, so I lock the car again and lead Evan away from our home, even though everything inside me wants to confront the intruder.

With shaky hands, I dial the one person I know can help us.

42

BEN

My phone rings, and when I glance at the screen, my heart takes flight and I beam into the night sky. After weeks of her keeping a careful distance between us, she's already calling me straight after one of the best days of my life.

My smile drops as my thoughts take a darker turn. *What if something's wrong?*

I quickly accept the call. "Hey. Is everything all right?"

"Ben! Oh, thank goodness." Her whispered voice drips with panic.

My senses go on high alert, and I grab my keys, heading straight for my truck after locking the door—Rex close on my heels. "What's wrong?"

"We just got home and found the side door open and a light on upstairs. I know I locked the house this morning when I left to pick up Evan. Y-You were the first person I thought to call," she tells me, her voice shaky and uneven.

"I'm on my way. Wait out front for me. I don't want you in the house in case someone's still inside." I start the engine and floor it out of my driveway and onto the road. I'll be there in less than ten minutes if traffic is on my side. "Stay on the phone with me. Okay?"

I hear rustling and know she's following my instructions. "Okay."

Focusing on the road, I hear their footsteps on the sidewalk, which I know is on the opposite side of the street to their house. I bang on the steering wheel when I get stopped at the third set of traffic signals. "Damn it!"

"Everything okay?"

"Yeah. I keep getting all the red lights. I'm not too far now. Sit tight, okay?" The light turns green, and I floor the gas. I know I should follow the law and travel at the correct speed, but my body won't allow me to go slow.

"We're safe, Ben. Don't rush—" She disconnects the call as soon as we spot each other, my truck barreling down the street toward her and Evan, and I'm happy to see they're as far away from their house as they can be while still keeping watch on their property.

I shut off the engine the second I pull in behind their car and jump out. As I take long strides toward the two most important people in my life, I scan Hope and Evan from top to toe, ensuring they're okay. Gripping Hope's slender shoulders, I pull her into me and wrap my arms around her, pressing us together until I can feel every single inch. Rex barks, and I pull Evan into the embrace.

Hope presses her cheek against me, and she must feel my heart hammering heavily against my ribs. After a few moments, she tilts her head up, and I cup her cheek, pushing her hair away from her face. Looking between her and Evan, I ask, "Are you guys okay?"

She exhales, sending her warm breath ghosting across my chin. "We're fine."

Evan pulls away. "Geez, man, give a guy some breathing room."

"I'm glad neither of you were home." Ignoring my promise to keep things platonic between us in front of Evan, I kiss the top of her head because I need to taste her to reassure every one of my senses she's okay. Evan watches me with interest, and I'm sure he'll have a million questions when things are quiet later.

"Yeah, but it probably wouldn't have happened if we were home."

I shake my head. "Not necessarily. Burglars don't always care if people are home. I'll call it in, then I'm going to go in with Rex to check things out."

She steps away and nods as she wraps her arm around Evan, tugging him to her side. "Okay. We'll wait here." She reaches out to squeeze my arm. "Be careful." It's impossible to miss the worry in her tone.

I nod. "This is what I do. I don't take unnecessary risks. Promise." Before I take her back into my arms and kiss her like I really want to, I tap the side of my leg and head inside with Rex. I detour to my truck, grab my phone, and call it in, then we make our way through each room, finding parts of the house in disarray but thankfully empty. When I study the side door carefully, I note the gouges in the wood where the perp obviously broke the lock.

I step outside to update Hope and Evan. "The house is empty, and I can see where they jimmied the lock to get in. They've left a mess behind where they've gone through your things in some of the rooms. Do you have any security? Cameras ... sensors ... anything?"

Her face grows pale as she shakes her head, bringing her trembling hand up to cover her mouth. "No, just regular locks."

"All right. I've already called it in, but I'm also gonna call Nix and get him out here to fix that back lock. Then we'll see what he can do about a security system for you." He gave me his number at the birthday party, in case I ever decide to leave the force.

Hope's brows scrunch together. "Oh, I don't think that's necessary. I don't want to bother Nix and I can't afford a security system."

While I'm on the phone to Nix, a cruiser pulls up and two officers climb out of the car. Hope explains what she found when she came home, and then I introduce myself and fill the officers in on what I found when Rex and I checked inside. They head inside to gather evidence while we wait out front. After a while, they return to us on the front grass.

"Do you know if anything was stolen?"

Hope shakes her head. "I haven't been inside yet."

"Okay, well, we'll check the neighbors to see if anyone has CCTV footage we can use." The officer shrugs. "No guarantees on that, though. When you go through your things, make notes on anything that's missing."

"Will do. Thank you, officers."

They nod. "We'll be in touch if we discover any new information." He hands her his card. "Here's my card."

As they step away, Nix and Shane pull up in front of the house at the same time. They climb out of their cars and Shane's expression is like thunder as he storms toward us with a slight limp. "Why didn't you call?" he snaps at Hope.

Nix grabs a toolbox from his van and wanders over at a slower pace. "Hey, Hope. Ev."

"Hey, Nix. Thanks for coming," Hope says, then turns to Shane, raising her brows at him. "Hey, Shane. Nice to see you, too."

"Don't *Hey, Shane* me. You're supposed to call me when stuff like this happens." He pushes his huge hand roughly across the top of his cropped hair. The guy is intimidating without even trying. Seeing him like this makes *me* want to put distance between us.

Hope waves toward me. "I called Ben, and he came."

Shane looks at me as if it's the first time he's noticed I'm here and raises his chin. The tension in his jaw and across his shoulders disappears, and he blows out a long breath. "Thanks, Ben."

"No problem. The house needs to be secured, and I'd like Nix to install security cameras and an alarm system."

Shane nods in agreement. "We should've done it years ago."

Hope sighs loudly, but reaches out, placing her hand on my

forearm. "I don't think any of that's necessary. It's expensive, and we've been okay without it until now."

"How about we get the house secure, and we can take a look at some simple measures Hope will be comfortable with?" Nix looks at Hope with raised brows. "No cost."

She shakes her head, sending her curls swaying from side to side. "No. I won't accept a handout. If I can't pay you, then you're not installing anything," she tells him with a firm tone. I've never seen her so adamant before—with her jaw set tight and her arms crossed stubbornly across her chest—but I recognize a woman who's not prepared to budge.

They negotiate an arrangement Hope is happy with, and Nix sets about securing the house, while the rest of us tidy the mess, collecting any items that need repairs.

An hour later, Hope and Evan's home is secure and Nix and Shane have left, promising to return tomorrow to install a couple of motion sensor cameras and an alarm system on the downstairs windows and doors.

Evan slides his zipper up and down his hoodie repeatedly as he chews on his bottom lip. "Mom, do you think whoever broke in will come back tonight?"

"I wouldn't think so," Hope tells him, brushing her hand over the top of his head. Her body sags with exhaustion—it's been a long night—and I can't begin to understand the worry she's feeling about everything that happened here tonight.

Unconvinced, Evan looks up at me. "What do you think, Ben?"

I rest my hand on his shoulder. I don't want to frighten them, but I need to be honest. "Sometimes they do. It depends why they broke in and what they were looking for."

Hope's shoulders stiffen, and a soft gasp punches from her lips.

"It depends on how determined they are to get whatever they were after in the first place—if they didn't get it." I shrug. "I think it would be a good idea if you guys stayed with me tonight. Just to be safe until we can get the security system installed tomorrow."

Hope pulls Evan in close and nods her agreement before I finish speaking. "Okay." She drops her eyes to her son. "That makes sense, if you don't mind us invading your space."

"You guys are always welcome."

"Thanks, Ben. I'll pack us an overnight bag. Won't be long." She disappears upstairs, leaving me and Evan alone.

Evan yawns. "Do you have enough beds at your house?"

I chuckle. "Yeah, buddy. You won't have to sleep on the floor. Maybe Rex can sleep with you tonight?"

43

BEN

I almost swallow my tongue when Hope pads into the kitchen wearing her sexy over-the-knee socks, my Foo Fighters T-shirt, and a long sweater draped over her slim shoulders.

Fuck!

As she climbs onto a stool at the island counter, I avert my gaze and clear my throat. "Feel better?"

"Much. Thank you." From the corner of my eye, I see her lean forward on the counter. "I hope you don't mind. I forgot to pack pajamas, so I borrowed one of your T-shirts."

I glance at her, careful not to stare, but it's damn hard not to when she's wearing my favorite T-shirt. As she tugs her sweater around her body, it pulls down off one shoulder and I have to look away before I lose my self-control and kiss the naked expanse of skin. I clear my throat. "No problem. Anything I have is yours," I tell her as I grab two glasses, then turn back for the bottle of wine.

Keeping my distance, I fill the glasses from the opposite side of the counter. Maybe if I keep a slab of granite and a bank of cupboards between us, I'll be able to keep my hands and mouth to myself.

She lifts the glass to her lips and takes a sip, closing her eyes when the fruity liquid hits her tongue. Slowly, she opens her eyes and tips her glass toward me. "This is just what I needed after tonight. Thank you."

"No problem. We'll have everything sorted tomorrow, and you guys will be back to normal." Her expression shutters, so I rush to add, "But you guys are welcome to stay as long as you need until you feel safe going home."

Her gorgeous sea-colored eyes lift back up to mine. "You're already helping so much, and you don't need us taking up your space more than necessary."

"Don't worry about it. I like having you guys here." I'd have them move in with me if I thought she'd agree. She doesn't look convinced, but there's no way I'll allow her to deal with this on her own. I know she's fully capable, but she's been doing it for too long already and it's time she has someone she can lean on for support. And I plan on being that someone. "You wanna relax in the living room?"

"Sure." She climbs from the stool, collects her glass, and leads the way to the living room. My eyes drop to the small sliver of exposed thigh, and I readjust my sweats, hoping she doesn't notice what's happening below the elastic band.

I grab the bottle of wine and follow behind. When I walk into the living room, she's standing near the shelf looking at the photos of my friends and family. She picks one up and spins to face me, her perfectly shaped eyebrows halfway up her forehead.

I know exactly which photo she has as I place the bottle and my glass on the coffee table, then make my way toward her. She holds it up. Our gazes lock and hold and all the questions that want to tumble past her lips are plain to see.

"You're married?" Her voice carries a little hurt.

I step closer, ensuring I hold her gaze. "Yes and no. Technically widowed."

Her mouth drops open, and sadness fills her eyes. "This is Tahlia? You never said anything."

"It's a different situation from yours." Looking at the photo, I trace my eyes over the young woman, dressed in white, standing by my side. "Tahlia had one dream in life. She wanted to be a bride. Even though she was a tomboy at heart, she wanted to wear white and walk down an aisle covered in pink rose petals. She wanted to carry a bouquet of pink roses and wear a veil."

Hope's hand flies up to her mouth and her eyes grow glassy.

"When she received the diagnosis that she didn't have long to live, I talked to her mom about Tahlia's dream. I loved her enough as a friend that I wanted to make it come true for her. One last wish before she left this earth."

"Oh, Ben." Hope's voice drips with pain—two syllables, but so much feeling.

I draw in a breath, remembering how happy Tahlia was when I asked her to marry me. "She was so excited. She and her mom organized the entire wedding in two weeks. We exchanged vows by the largest lake in Piney Lakes, beneath an arbor of pink roses on the first day of September." I lift my eyes to Hope's. "We didn't live together or anything like that, because it was never like that between us, but I was more than happy to make her dream a reality. Two weeks later, she was gone."

I swallow around the thickness that always forms in my throat whenever I think of Tahlia. Taken from us too soon. Her shining light extinguished before we were ready. It wasn't fair to her or her mom—or us. Hope places the photo on the shelf and wraps her arms around me, pressing herself against the length of my body.

"You're such a good man, Benjamin Taylor." She looks up at me. "Tahlia was lucky to have a best friend like you."

I smile down at her. "I was the lucky one. She taught me how to have fun and make the most of each day. It's almost like she knew she wouldn't be here for a long time." I kiss her forehead, soaking in her softness and the scent of vanilla in her hair. "Your hair always smells so damn delicious," I groan.

She chuckles, her body shaking against mine. "Thanks."

"This house belonged to Tahlia's family. They'd come here

every summer vacation. Sebastian and I even came along a few times. When Tahlia's mom passed away five years ago, she left it to me, which was completely unexpected. That's when I decided to leave Piney Lakes and follow my dream of working as a K9 handler here."

"Oh, Ben. So much loss in one family." The entire Gilbert family is gone.

I nod my agreement and she squeezes me tight, then I kiss her temple and reluctantly pull away from her embrace, grabbing the bottle of wine to top off our glasses.

After the way things quickly escalated when I fell asleep on the couch with her, I need to be mindful about keeping space between us—especially with Evan in the house. I don't want her to think I've offered them a place to stay to get her into my bed. She needs to take the lead and guide the pace between us. I'll never forgive myself if we were to move faster than she's ready for. I'd rather wait a thousand years to touch her than push things too quickly and break her. I'm gonna end up with the bluest balls of all time, but it's a small price to pay.

When it's time for bed, we say goodnight in the hallway and go to our separate rooms. I tell myself it won't be like this forever.

Lying in bed with my hands behind my head, I stare at the ceiling as the shadows from the tree outside move across the ceiling in the wind. I picture her in the bed next door, my T-shirt pushed up over her breasts, leaving them exposed to my tongue as I tease her nipples into hard points. I'd spread her legs wide so her glistening pussy was on display for my perusal. Her lower half bare except for those sexy ass socks she wears. I'd slide my hands up her toned thighs, appreciating their silkiness beneath my rough hands.

My cock hardens, and the temptation to take it in hand and stroke it is almost too much, but I don't want to disrespect Hope like that. She deserves more than lust. She deserves to be cherished and adored. She deserves to be treated like a queen. But I can't switch my mind off that easily. I imagine the heat in her eyes as I lightly swipe my tongue along her pussy, teasing her clit with small, tight circles.

An unfamiliar sound breaks the silence, and I strain to listen. Everything's quiet until a few moments later, it happens again. This time it sounds distinctly like a low moan followed by what sounds like a sob coming from Hope's room. I sit up, straining to listen. It happens again, and before I know it, my feet hit the floor and I'm walking toward my bedroom door. Ripping it open, I stride to her door, then press my forehead against the wood.

Dammit, she's upset. I'm not surprised after the way her day ended. *What should I do?* I want to go in and hold her. Tell her everything will be okay. But I don't want to invade her privacy either.

I fall forward slightly before I realize the door's no longer there. I don't recall touching the doorknob, but maybe my subconscious took over since I couldn't decide.

"Oh." Hope's startled expression and flushed cheeks has me straightening in place.

"Sorry, I heard you moan and sob, and I was worried. I was coming to ask if you were okay," I explain quickly so she doesn't think I'm some kind of creeper hanging outside her bedroom door. Though I wouldn't blame her if that's the impression she has.

I watch her throat move as she swallows, her eyes blown wide and cheeks flushed a gorgeous hue of pink. "Y-you heard that?"

"Uh, yeah." I toss my thumb over my shoulder. "Our beds butt up against the same wall."

She covers her face with both hands. "Oh, my god. I'm so embarrassed."

I drag her hands away from her face and bring them to my mouth to kiss each one. I can't miss the feminine scent lingering on her fingers, and my eyes snap back up to Hope's. If I thought she looked flushed before, she's even more so now. She tries to tug them out of my hold, but I grip onto them, not letting go. I bring them to my nose and draw in a deep breath. "Beautiful." I kiss each finger, never taking my eyes from hers. Her pupils grow, almost overtaking the aquamarine I love so much.

"Ben," she whispers on a shaky breath.

"Yeah, Cookie?"

"What's happening?" Her question is barely a murmur.

"I'm kissing you." I promised myself I wouldn't push her, but she makes it damn hard to keep myself in check. Clearly, I have no self-control where she's concerned. Her shoulders drop, the tension falls away, and I watch her soften as I flip her hand over and kiss her palm. I take my time, slowly stroking my tongue along each finger, tasting the remnants of her self-induced orgasm. "Tell me what you were doing," I murmur, my voice a pained whisper. My dick as hard as a rock.

"Uhm ..." Her wide eyes are almost comical—it's a guilty expression I'm used to seeing in my job. Her chest rises and falls quickly, giving away how turned on she is.

A hard nudge at my thigh breaks my focus and when I look down, Rex is looking up at me. He whines and wags his tail, then takes off for the stairs. I know what that means, and disappointment swiftly floods my body.

Cock blocked by my best friend.

I sigh. "Sorry, I need to take him out," I say to Hope, regret dripping from every single word.

Her smile is timid. "That's okay. It's probably for the best. I'll see you in the morning." She takes a step backward into her room.

"Sleep well, Hope," I whisper, pressing a soft kiss against the top of her head and drawing her delicious scent deep into my lungs to tide me over.

I take the steps two at a time and push the folding patio doors open. Rex bolts outside, and I follow. The cool air is a sharp contrast to the heat boiling beneath my skin—it's just what I need.

Rex comes back and sniffs at me, barking sharply, and I rub his scruff.

"Yeah, thanks, buddy." Waves crash in the distance, and I glance out at my dark backyard, then back to Rex. "It was probably for the best. She's only been here a few hours, and I'm already breaking my promise to myself." I rub between his ears. "Good save, buddy."

He licks my face and races back out into the darkness.

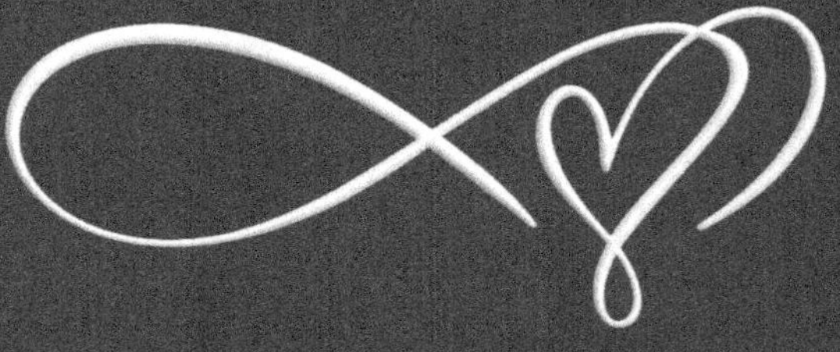

44

I'M ANTSY.

It's the only way to describe the energy thrumming through my body. Knowing Hope and I will be alone tonight is making it hard to focus on anything. After having her and Evan in my space two weeks ago ... looking after them is all I've thought about.

She's been doing the single parent thing for pretty much Evan's entire life. Even though she was married, Wyatt was often away serving our country, leaving Hope to raise their son alone. Then the unthinkable happened, leaving her the sole parent. She works so hard to provide for them both, and even though she'll say she's done a terrible job of raising Evan, she's still given him everything she has.

Tonight, I want to pamper her, care for her, and help her relax. I want to give her the break she deserves.

Wyatt's parents picked up Evan from *The Paw Palace*, and I came straight home to clean up the house and prepare dinner before Hope comes over straight from work. Soft music plays over the speakers, and the steaks are marinating for a special dinner. I have the bathroom upstairs ready and waiting and her favorite shows lined up. I want to make tonight special. She deserves to be treated like a queen, and that's what I intend to do.

Rex races to the front door as a car pulls into the driveway. *She's here.*

I walk to the front door with a glass of wine in hand and push it open. When she reaches the porch, her eyes land on me and sparkle beneath the afternoon sun. "Hey." I kiss her cheek and pass the glass of wine to her in exchange for her purse and overnight bag, then hold the screen door open.

"Hey." She holds up the glass with a sassy smirk. "This is nice," she says as she walks beneath my arm, ducking inside with a familiarity I'm thrilled about.

"It's only the beginning." I close the door behind us, and she bends over to greet Rex. It's hard to believe she was ever concerned about him with the way she loves on him. "How was work?"

She blows out a long breath. "Busy. Saturdays are always crazy busy. I'm glad I only work one Saturday a month." *Something I bet she does so she's not home alone all weekend when Evan is with his grandparents.* She sips her drink as she walks down the hallway toward the back of the house. I've noticed she likes to sit on the back deck and watch the ocean. "I only work because Evan spends the weekend with Wyatt's parents, and I couldn't bear to be home alone all weekend."

"Makes sense." I hook the straps of her purse over the banister and take her hand, tugging her back toward the stairs. "Follow me."

She tilts her head to the side, but follows without question. I lead her through my bedroom and into the ensuite. Her gasp echoes against the tiled walls and floor, and her wide eyes find mine. I smile at her, pleased with her reaction.

"This is gorgeous." She places her glass on the bathroom counter beside a group of lit candles, then slides her fingers across the wall tiles. "I love these tiles." Her eyes scan over the room, taking everything in.

I lean over and start filling the tub, checking the water temperature to make sure it's perfect for her. "I'm happy with how everything turned out. I still need to renovate the main bathroom and downstairs powder room, but with only me here, I didn't see the need to rush." *Maybe I should move it higher up my list of things to do. Just in case.* "Do you think I should use the same combination of tiles and counters in the other bathrooms?"

"I guess so. It would help keep the feel of your home consistent."

Hopefully, one day, it'll be our *home, but I'm getting ahead of myself.*

I stand and turn in time to see Hope snap her eyes away from me, then swallow. That pink blush I love so much makes its way up the side of her neck. I've caught her gaze lingering on me more often since the first time we kissed. It gives me hope that maybe she's getting closer to moving our relationship forward.

She waves her hand around the room. "What's with all the candles and the bath?"

"Well." I step closer to her and lay my hands on her shoulders. My thumbs stroke her delicate collarbones with no direction from me, and I watch as a shiver makes its way through her body. "You work too hard and I want to pamper you ... starting with a quiet glass of wine and a long soak in the tub."

"Oh, yeah?" she asks with a sexy lilt to her voice. It's playful and I love how she's relaxed enough with me that she's letting her flirty side out a little more. "What else do you have planned?"

I tap the end of her cute nose, loving the freckles there. "You'll have to wait and see." I kiss the spot I just tapped and back away before I drop my mouth to hers. Walking backward, I grip the door handle and take one step over the threshold.

"Enjoy your soak, Cookie. If you need anything, just shout." I wink and close the door, dropping my forehead to the wood. It's going to be murder knowing she's sitting in that giant tub for two —completely naked.

Naked *and* wet.

I blow out a long breath and adjust my sweats. I'm doing this for her. She needs this. She deserves this time to herself.

I get busy slicing the potatoes for the bake and rinse the broccoli. Rex watches me from his bed, his eyebrows shifting as his eyes follow my every move. "Yeah, buddy. I know. I've got it bad."

"Ben!"

I drop the knife and race upstairs, taking the stairs three at a time. Gripping the doorknob to the bathroom, I almost jerk it open. Then I remember she's naked and I shouldn't barge in—as much as I want to. "Yeah? You okay?" I call through the door.

"Yeah. Can I please have some more wine?" I hear the tap turn on and water pouring into the tub.

"Uh, sure. Back in a sec." I probably should have thought to bring the bottle up with me before. I race back downstairs, grab the bottle, race upstairs, and freeze at the door. "I'm back with the wine."

"Great," comes her reply.

How in the hell am I going to do this? She's in the tub. *Naked.* I pace back and forth, running my free hand through my hair like a crazy person.

"Are you coming in?" she calls, like it's no big deal she's in the tub.

Naked.

Naked *and* wet.

Fuck.

"Ah, sure." I try to think of as many un-sexy thoughts as I can and steel myself to keep my eyes averted from the tub, picturing where everything is in the bathroom so I don't mistakenly look at her. "Are you covered?" Hopefully, the bubbles I poured in earlier are still intact and will keep her hidden in case I accidentally slip and drop my eyes.

"I'm in the tub. What am I supposed to use to cover myself?" she asks, laughter evident in her voice.

Shit. I roughly push my fingers through my hair, then adjust my sweats. "The bubbles?" *Is that too much to ask? I'm hanging on by a thread here.*

"I hate to tell you the bad news, but they're gone. I can cover the important bits with my hands if it's such a problem," she shares her solution like I haven't been at war with myself to be a gentleman when all I've wanted to do was barge in and wash her back ... and front ... and everywhere in between.

I swallow and grip the door handle like my life depends on it, twisting it until the catch releases, almost crushing the metal in my fist. The *snick* sounds like a gunshot, and my heart ricochets inside my chest. Dropping my eyes to the floor, I take the few steps over to the side of the tub. Picking up her empty glass, I turn my back to Hope and fill it, then place it back on the side of the tub, aware that her exposed shoulder is right there and it would be so damn easy to lean down and place a kiss on her warm, wet flesh.

She chuckles behind me, and I'm glad she finds my predicament amusing. "Ben?"

Sweat trickles down my spine, and my dick grows thick at the rasp in her voice. "Yeah?"

"Turn around, please?"

Does she even understand what she's asking?

She's fucking naked.

Naked and *wet.*

As much as I try to be a decent human being, I'm just a man. A mere mortal who's itching to turn around and lay my eyes on what I've only ever imagined. I clench my empty hand into a fist at my side. "I'm trying to be a gentleman here, Hope. Help a guy out."

The sound of the water sloshing around in the tub breaks the silence in the room, and her wet hand wraps around my fist, teasing it open. Her fingers slide between mine and she tugs. "Ben," she murmurs. Her tone on the brink of begging.

I clear my throat and clench my eyes closed, turning toward the tub. I deserve some kind of award for this torture. "Yeah, Cookie?"

Can she see my hard on? Her face has to be at eye level with my dick, for fuck's sake.

"Open your eyes," she whispers, and I can't miss the desperation in her voice.

I peel my eyes open. My greedy gaze sails over the tub, and within seconds, I have her shape seared into my brain. Her curves are slight, and her breasts are smaller than I'm used to, but she's perfection to me.

Utter perfection.

Stunning porcelain skin, turned pink from the warm water, and neat curls sit at the apex of her thighs. Out of politeness, I drag my gaze away from her body to her face. Her long curls are piled haphazardly on top of her head in that sexy way I've grown used to seeing, leaving her neck and shoulders exposed. Her clear eyes gaze up at me, and I swallow roughly.

She's watching me with a mixture of uncertainty and false bravado. I squeeze her fingers, then flip her hand over and lean down to press a kiss to her palm. Goosebumps race across her body, and her pretty pink nipples pebble into tight points. I place her open palm against the bulge in my sweats. "Do you feel what you've done to me, Hope?"

She swallows and nods slowly as she presses harder against my cock—some of her uncertainty fading. This is a gigantic step for her. It's been a long time since she's been naked in front of a man. On top of that, I'm a man who isn't her husband. I need to remember to slow down and let her take the lead.

Pressing her hand against my dick isn't taking it slow or allowing her to take the lead, but she doesn't pull away. In fact, she rubs her palm along the hard ridge. "I feel it," she murmurs.

I move, dislodging her hand to place the bottle of wine on the shelf behind the tub. "What do you need, Cookie?"

She turns around and leans forward, peering over her shoulder, then back up to me. "I was hoping you'd wash my back for me. And maybe sit and talk for a while."

I nod sharply. "I can do that." My voice comes out gruff, so I clear my throat.

It may kill me, but I can do it for her.

Dragging the wooden stool over, I sit and push up my sleeves. She watches with rapt attention as each inch of my forearms becomes exposed. Grabbing the sponge and the liquid soap, I add a generous amount and encourage her to lean forward further.

Once I'm satisfied, I glide the sponge across her smooth shoulders, watching as I cover every inch, ensuring I don't miss a single spot.

"What do you want to talk about?" I ask, tracing the smattering of freckles scattered across her delicate shoulders.

"Anything." Her back rises and falls with a deep breath. "How was Evan this morning?"

I chuckle. "He was in heaven. Tori had puppies today."

"Oh, god. I bet he asks me for a dog again when I pick him up from his grandparents tomorrow." The water around her ripples with her quiet laugh.

I squeeze the sponge, sending suds streaming over each vertebra down her spine, then dip the sponge into the bath, brushing the side of her body with my knuckles. "Probably."

She looks at me over her shoulder. "I was sorta hoping the time he spends with you and Rex would satisfy his need to have a dog of his own."

"Stay strong." I rub the sponge down her arm, then back up to her shoulder, sweeping it across the slight curve to her neck. She tips her head to the side with a sigh, exposing her throat to me like an offering I can't resist.

I tried.

I lean forward and kiss the pulse point there, relishing the contact for a moment before kissing my way higher until I can press a kiss to the tender spot behind her ear. Her body rises and falls as she sighs softly. I repeat the process on the other side, my erection growing by the second.

The water in the tub sloshes in waves as she turns her body to face me. My eyes follow the line of her throat, to her clavicles and lower still until they land on her pert breasts ... the perfect size to suck and lick.

"Kiss me," she murmurs. Her pupils are blown so wide they almost eclipse the aquamarine I love so much. She's so damn irresistible, but does she have any idea what she's asking of me?

I shift on the stool, making more room for my throbbing dick. "If I kiss you, I'm not sure I'll be able to stop, and I promised myself I'd go at your pace. Let you take the lead." I keep my eyes locked on hers, so she understands what I'm saying. "But if I kiss you, I don't think I'll be able to do that. I won't be able to stop."

"Then don't."

Disappointment shatters every cell in my body, and I pull away, putting much-needed space between us. I push to stand, to give her the privacy she deserves, but she rises to her knees, looking like a wet dream, and shoots her hand out to hold me in place before I can climb to my feet. When she licks her lips and swallows, I watch her throat move with a fascination I've never felt before.

"I meant, don't stop kissing me, Ben." There's a strength to her tone that gives me the assurance I need that this *is* what she truly wants.

I drop my hand to her shoulder, sliding it across the smooth expanse of warm flesh, up the curve to her throat, and grip her gently, reverently ... respectfully. She melts beneath my touch, and I slowly lower my face to hers. Our breaths coat each other's lips, and I savor the seconds leading up to having my mouth on hers again. I stroke my thumb back and forth across her pulse, watching it flutter wildly, then trace my eyes over her soft lips to her stunning eyes.

"Are you sure?" I murmur, studying her closely.

She nods. "So sure."

I don't need anything more. I crush my mouth to hers in a bruising kiss. It's the way I've wanted to kiss her since the moment

I first laid eyes on her. With my hand wrapped around the front of her throat, I tilt her head back so I can kiss her deeply. Her small moan vibrates against my lips, and I swipe my tongue across the seam, pushing my way inside. She opens, teasing her tongue against mine greedily, and it's a relief to know she's as desperate as I am. The sweet, fruity wine tastes delicious on her tongue, and I stay a while.

I'm in no rush.

I want to savor this moment with her.

Savor the intentionality of her request.

Her request for *me* to kiss her.

I take from her, then give double in return. She responds beautifully, participating in our kiss like her life depends on it. We stroke our tongues, tasting and licking. Connecting.

It's sexy and addictive.

I love kissing. It's the most sensual way to connect with someone on a deeper level.

But more than anything, I love kissing Hope.

I love the trust she's giving me.

I love that she's opening herself up to me after years of celibacy and devotion to the promise she made to her husband.

It feels spiritual in a way.

She pushes up higher, changing the angle of our kiss. Our mouths press together firmly, our desire increasing like an inferno. I cup her breast and moan at the feel of her flesh in my hand. The way her beaded nipple presses into my palm and the softness beneath my fingers. I slide my thumb back and forth across the hard point, eager for the moment I can take it in my mouth.

I slow our kiss with gentle pecks, pulling away so I can kiss my way down her body, but Hope's fingers slip into my hair, gripping the longer strands on top, tugging my mouth back to hers. I smile against her lips, feeling the heavy beats of her heart beneath my palm. So vital. So here in the moment with me.

With me.

Pressing her wet body against mine, she deepens the kiss like she's starving. And I guess, in a way, she is. It's been too long since she's been intimate with a man.

I can't imagine the loneliness.

The bone-deep ache.

The emptiness.

I want to fill her up.

I want to soothe the ache and defeat her loneliness.

I never want her to feel that level of intimate isolation again.

I wrap both arms around her, keeping her close, but it's not enough for her.

She climbs out of the tub and straddles my lap, soaking my sweats and my T-shirt, but I couldn't care less. If this is where she wants to be, then this is where she'll be. Wrapping her arms around my neck, she tangles her fingers in my hair, and grinds down over my dick, creating the most torturous friction known to man. A groan vibrates through my body, which Hope matches with a feminine moan.

The diamond points of her nipples rub against my T-shirt, and I wish I were as naked as she is. She rubs her pussy against me through my sweats, her lips still locked with mine. Her long fingers find the back of my T-shirt, and then she drags it up my back, tugging and pulling until I have no choice but to release her so I can tear it over my head. Once I have it off, I toss it to the floor and pull her back against me. A sigh escapes at the beauty of finally having her skin against mine.

Much the same way as the morning we woke together on the couch, I slide my hands down each side of her slender body, my thumbs teasing the sides of her breasts, until I grip her hips and guide her up and down my rock-hard length, still covered by soaking cotton. At this point, the shield between us is essential, or I'll slide into her pussy, and I'm not sure she's ready to go that far.

Delicate moans and whimpers escape Hope's mouth as she works herself toward her release. Her body is flushed pink from the warm bath and her exertion, and I've never seen her look more beautiful as she takes what she wants from me.

"Ben," she whimpers.

"What do you need, Cookie?" I rumble against her lips.

"I-I-I feel so empty," she breathes. "I need you."

"You've got me. Heart, body, and soul." I take her mouth again and slide my hands over the curve of her ass, squeezing the cheeks and following the seam down to her pussy. The heat and slickness are unreal, and a groan rumbles from deep in my gut. I find her opening and slide one finger inside.

So fucking tight and silky.

Hot and perfect.

Hope rewards me with a whimper, pushing herself back onto my digit.

"You're so fucking hot and tight," I whisper against her lips. My dick grows excited at the thought of being inside her slick heat, but I ignore it. "You're so perfect."

Tonight is for her.

All for her.

I push my finger deep and then add another, building a rhythm that she matches easily. "How's that feel for you? Because it feels fucking amazing for me."

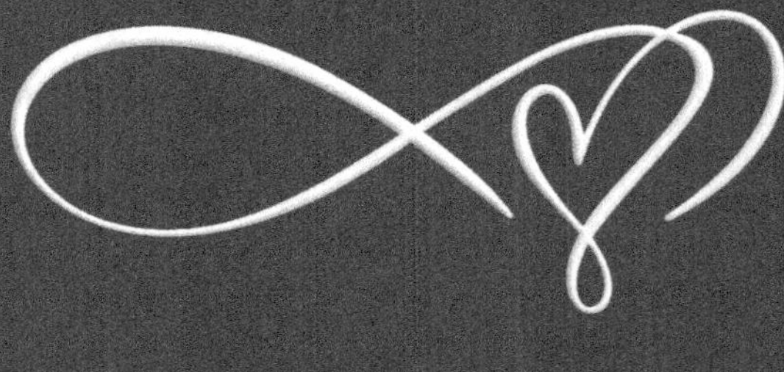

45

HOPE

OH, MY GOD. I SWEAR I'M SEEING STARS AS MY BODY trembles. "So good." I should be embarrassed by my brazenness, but Ben's made me feel safe enough to ask for what I want, and I want him.

I want him inside me.

I want him all around me.

On top of me.

Touching me.

Kissing me.

Filling me up.

I *need* him.

Desperately.

It's ironic I've gone so long without feeling desire, but Ben's brought it blazing to life, and I don't want to extinguish it. I want to fan the flames, catch fire, and burn hot.

With him.

Only with him.

While sitting in the tub Ben prepared for me—surrounded by candles—I allowed my mind to wander over recent discussions with my friends and family. I considered what everyone's been saying and their words *finally* sank in. After years of holding onto

Wyatt and the promises I made to him, my heart loosened its grip. It wasn't as painful as I expected it to be and I feel a little lost without the anchor holding me down, but it's time to let him go and move forward. Pushing past my misconceptions and putting aside old promises isn't easy, but everyone's right. Wyatt wouldn't want me to stay alone forever—so I decided to see how far I could tempt Ben.

I'm so glad I did.

I'm going to enjoy this experience without feeling guilt or shame. I'm not cheating. I'm a single woman in her prime, and I've denied myself for too long. I'm going to live in and enjoy the moment.

I hope.

With everything I am, I hope I don't ruin this moment with tears.

His fingers fill me, stretch me, push me closer to the edge, and drag me out of my head. It's delicious and decadent. It reminds me of my dream, but I want more.

I push up a little and tug his sweats and boxer briefs away from his firm stomach, then dip my hand inside to grip his steely dick.

Oh, my. He's so thick ... and hot. His skin is so smooth and tight.

I swipe my thumb across the crown to collect his essence, and his dick jumps beneath my touch.

"Hope?" he groans as he pushes himself further into my palm.

I watch him fuck my hand while his fingers fuck me. He buries his face in my neck, sucking and biting my pulse point, and I don't think I'll last too much longer.

"Fuck, you feel incredible. Your pussy's sucking my fingers in so deep, like you never want me to leave." He pushes in deep and hard. My walls tighten further, and a whimper escapes my lips.

"I don't," I pant as I trip ever closer to the edge.

"I'll stay here all day," he rumbles.

My muscles spasm and contract around his fingers, and

when I rub his dick against my clit, I fall into oblivion. Free falling into space where everything feels fantastic and nothing can hurt me. I drop my head back as I cry out through my release. Warmth cascades over my hand, the sticky substance sliding through my fingers, and I grin with satisfaction as my body shudders.

"Jesus, fuck!" he groans. "That was embarrassingly fast." He slows his fingers until my aftershocks disappear, then slides them out of me.

I drag my head forward and lock my gaze with his while he brings his fingers to his mouth and pushes them in deep, closing his eyes as if he's savoring the most decadent chocolate cake of all time.

So hot!

When he opens his eyes, I decide to return the favor, bringing my sticky hand to my mouth so I can lick his salty essence. His eyes darken as he watches me lick my fingers clean. The muscle at his jaw tenses, and before I can move, he growls and dips forward, replacing my fingers with his tongue.

"You act innocent, but really, you hide a dirty girl beneath your sweetness," he mumbles before sealing my mouth with his again.

His kisses are drugging. Addictive.

His tongue twists around mine, and our combined tastes linger. It's dirty and oh, so sexy. His hand slides up my body, tweaking my nipples and then continuing until he has it wrapped around my throat. His thumb rests on my chin as he tilts my head to his liking, and he devours me.

Everything around us falls away as I'm consumed by his mouth on mine. This man knows how to kiss. Not that I'm an expert. I've only kissed two men now, but his kiss transcends this world and takes me to places I've never experienced.

All thought processes cease.

My only need ... desire ... is to be kissed by Ben.

The feel of his soft, but firm lips and the rasp of his beard are so completely masculine, calling to my femininity and my arousal skyrockets.

With one hand beneath my ass and the other still holding me by my throat, he stands easily, carrying my slight weight. I'm a little shy about him seeing my body so thin. I've always been slim because of dancing, but since losing Wyatt, I've lost weight, which never returned. I don't really have womanly curves, but judging by the heat in Ben's eyes when he saw me naked, he liked what he saw, and it seems like I turn him on.

"I need to taste you properly," he says, his voice gravelly with need.

Climbing onto his enormous bed, he maneuvers so his head is on the pillow, and I'm balancing on my knees above him. He grips my hips and pulls me down to his mouth, and I almost topple over with surprise. My heart pounds with excitement at what I know is about to happen. Never in my wildest dreams, when I first met this man, did I think we'd be in this position.

Without ceremony, he swipes his tongue aggressively through my swollen lips, and I'm instantly ready to chase another orgasm. He feasts on me, holding me tight to his mouth, not giving me any chance to escape. Not that I'd want to. His fingers dig into my hips, and I know I'll be wearing bruises there for the next week. I smile to myself as I grip the headboard and move my hips in time with his ministrations, my heart pounding like a drum line, and mind focused solely on chasing my pleasure.

"Oh, god. I'm gonna come again." A whimper stumbles past my lips as he pulses his tongue in and out of my opening, his nose rubbing my clit, and his short beard scraping against my lips and thighs, making the muscles in my body tighten.

His hungry groans vibrate against my sensitive lips, adding to the sensations and ensuring I'm pushed to the point of no return. I throw my head back on a long guttural moan as my stomach tightens and white light steals my vision. Every muscle in my body locks tight, and for a moment, I can't breathe. If it weren't for Ben holding me, I'd collapse on his face and suffocate the poor guy as I fall apart for the second time this afternoon.

I sigh as my muscles relax again, leaving me as limp as a noodle. I could curl up into a ball and go to sleep right now and not wake until tomorrow. Satisfaction weaves through every cell of my body and when I lazily open my eyes and look down at Ben, his darkened gaze is locked on me. My arousal coats his mouth and cheeks, and it's possibly the hottest thing I've seen.

"You're so sexy when you fall apart. It's my new favorite thing to watch."

I should feel embarrassed, but I don't.

He releases my hips and guides me down, so I'm lying on top of him like he's my personal mattress. His hard body stretches out beneath me, his warm embrace surrounds me, and his legs cradle mine. I'm wrapped in him, and it feels better than anything has in a long time.

I hum with contentment against his chest, feeling his strong heartbeat against my cheek. I close my eyes for a moment, absorbing his warmth as his fingers lazily glide up and down the middle of my spine and his hardness presses against my thigh. Feeling him hot and hard makes me greedy. I want him inside me. It's as if I haven't just had two incredible orgasms already.

I shift so I'm straddling his hips and push up with my hands on his chest. His eyes widen as his nipples pebble. I lean down and kiss each one, licking around them and nipping them with my teeth. Then I move down his torso, licking and kissing the smooth expanse of tanned skin, tracing the valleys of his abs with my tongue.

He has a gorgeous trail of dark hair leading down from his navel and disappearing beneath his sweatpants. Hooking my fingers under the elastic waistband, I tug his sweatpants along with his boxers. Ben's gaze is wary, but he raises his ass so I can pull them down and remove them, leaving him equally as naked as I am.

"Hope?"

I ignore his question as I trail my eyes up his muscular legs dusted in dark hair and admire their obvious strength. When my eyes land on his dick—long and thick—proudly reaching up his stomach, I suck in a sharp breath. Oh, my gosh. *Could he be any more perfect? He's so defined. So strong.*

So here.

Ben sits up, reaching for me, but I shake my head and gently push him so he lies back. "I want to taste you. I want to make you feel good."

He chuckles darkly. "You've already made me feel fucking fantastic, Cookie. You don't need to do anything else."

I grin seductively. "Imagine how fantastic you'll feel with my mouth on you." I wink, then wrap my hand around his length and dip to lick the precum from his darkened head.

He grunts as his hips bounce up. "Fuck." His fingers slip through my hair, and he tugs until the twist comes loose. "Today was supposed to be all for you."

I pull my mouth away from him. "Who says this isn't for me?"

He groans and dramatically drops his head back on the pillow. "By all means, go ahead then." I chuckle as I take the head of his beautiful penis into my mouth. "Ah, fuck. You're so damn perfect." He cups the side of my face. "Your mouth feels so damn good."

I'm so out of practice as I lick and stroke the length of Ben's dick, but anyone would think I'm a pro from the way his hips shift and writhe. Guttural groans rumble from his throat. The man is sex personified when he's aroused; the way his body tenses and flexes beneath my touch is such a turn on. His muscles ripple beneath his tanned, taut skin like he's holding himself back.

His physical response to me and my touch makes me feel incredibly sexy and spurs me on to give him the best blow job. I double down my efforts, cupping his heavy balls and tightening my grip on his thick length. The corners of my mouth feel like they're going to split apart, but I take him as deep as I can. My gag reflex is pretty much non-existent, always has been, so I take him all the way to the back of my throat and swallow around his thick length.

My eyes water as his fingers tighten their grip on my hair.

His hips thrust up.

I swallow.

He groans.

I squeeze my thighs together to stem the ache growing there.

He grips my arms, drags me off his dick, and flips me to my back, eliciting a surprised squeal.

I'm almost folded in half, with my ankles hooked over his shoulders and his cock pressed to my opening, before I know what's happening. One hand wraps around the front of my throat, securing me to the bed, like his powerful body pinning me like a pretzel isn't enough.

"Tell me I can fuck you," he grumbles like he's pissed off at the world.

This is a side of Ben I haven't seen before. It's a little intimidating and a *lot* hot. He's always so easygoing and gentlemanly.

He's anything but right now.

There's a demand buried in his request, but I feel completely safe with him, knowing if I were to say no, he'd honor my denial. Not that I'm going to say no. He has my blood pumping and my body running so hot I may combust.

Drowning in lust, I nod and raise my hips in invitation. "Please."

His eyes grow darker, more intense, and the veins decorating his neck bulge with power. His hold on my throat tightens a little as he bites his bottom lip as though he's barely holding onto his control.

He notches the tip of his dick against me and pushes slightly.

My mouth drops open at the stretch, and he nudges forward a little more. A string of obscenities burst forth on a panted breath.

He stops moving, the muscles in his back straining beneath my fingers. "You okay?" he murmurs against my lips.

I nod, then lift my head to press my lips to his. He gives me exactly what I want, delving his tongue into my mouth and kissing me deeply. So deeply that I forget to breathe. His taste, mixed with my orgasm heightens my desire. His thumb strokes my throat as he pushes in a little deeper, and I adjust my position so I can open my thighs wider to accommodate him. "God, you feel so big like this."

Male pride overtakes his features, and he smirks down at me. "Keep saying stuff like that to stroke my ego, and I won't be able to go slow like you need."

A chuckle bursts out of me, and I push my hips into him, taking him in a little further. He drops his head and licks my lips in a slow, seductive dance that has me desperate for more. I dig my fingernails into his shoulders for purchase, and I wouldn't be surprised if I leave scratch marks all over him. I should be concerned I'm hurting him, but the hiss that passes from his mouth to mine suggests he likes it.

Finally, his pelvis meets mine, and I breathe through the stretch and burn of having him deep inside me. *It's been so long*. He moves back a little and slides his concerned gaze over every inch of my face.

"How are you doing?"

"It's a little uncomfortable because it's been a while," I pant.

His eyes soften, and he leans down, kissing me gently. "Take a breath and relax. We have time." I nod and suck in a breath, then blow it out slowly, feeling each muscle relax. "I'll happily stay like this all afternoon and night, buried in your hot, tight pussy. I don't even need to move. This is already perfect."

As his gaze drops to where we're joined, I repeat the process again and he slides in a little more, which I didn't think was possible.

I wiggle my hips. "Please move."

Without taking his eyes from mine, he slips out a little, dragging along every sensitive spot inside me, then pushes back in. His eyes roll to the back of his head, and pure satisfaction makes me smile.

"Jesus. I don't think I'll last long, even though I just came in your hand less than thirty minutes ago," he grunts as he buries himself to the hilt. "Your pussy's like a silky fist, sucking me in so fucking deep."

Leaning down, he kisses me again and begins leisurely thrusting his hips, stretching me open and lighting up every single nerve ending I'd forgotten I had. My muscles tremble under his onslaught, and it's a struggle to keep my eyes open and on him. But watching him move, tilting his head at such an angle that makes the muscles in his neck and shoulders stand out in bold relief, is adding to the heat he's building so effortlessly in my body. The connection between us is powerful and heartbreakingly beautiful.

Once my body becomes used to his sexy intrusion, I meet his hips thrust for thrust, push for push. He pushes back onto his heels, dragging my body onto his thighs, and holds my legs wide open with a firm grip around each of my upper thighs.

The way he pulls me around and positions me where he wants, like I'm as light as a feather, ratchets up my desire and makes me feel so damn sexy. He's not treating me like breakable glass. He's treating me like a woman he wants to fuck and it's so damn hot.

My blood fizzes, racing through my body like lava, and my muscles tighten as all my focus narrows to one singular point. Ben's heated gaze drops to where we're joined, and his thumb presses against my clit.

A sheen of sweat coats his golden torso as his muscles ripple in time with his movements. God, he's so handsome. So masculine. All man.

"Fuck, your pussy's squeezing my cock like a fist. I need you to get there, Hope," he grunts, panting heavily. "You're so damn perfect, I don't know how much longer I can hold on."

I pant as sparks race through my blood, tightening my muscles to the point of no return. "I'm so close."

He moves his hips faster. Deeper. Changing the angle so he hits a different trigger point inside. White light streaks across my vision as my body quakes and shatters into a million beautiful pieces.

"Fuck. I wish you could see how beautiful you look right now. All flushed pink, skin shimmering, tits shaking." He drops forward, his hands landing on either side of my head, causing the pillow to sink. His mouth meets mine in a hungry kiss as he pistons in and out of me almost viciously, sending me skyward on the back of an orgasm that hasn't quite finished. "That's it, Hope. Strangle my cock."

He pushes back up and grips my hips, his fingers digging into my ass as he increases his speed. I can't believe he's still going strong. He tilts his head to the side, watching me beneath hooded eyes, his teeth digging into his bottom lip, his muscles flexing, and the veins up the sides of his neck protruding with his effort.

His mouth falls open, and he drops his head back as a deep rumble fills the bedroom. I watch him fall apart in awe as his cock grows impossibly larger, and I feel the telltale throb of his orgasm. His fingers dig into my ass, and I look forward to checking it out in the mirror to see if he's left bruises.

I hope he has.

Our eyes lock and hold, and one side of his mouth tips up in satisfaction. "Ruined."

He drags me up so my legs wrap around his hips and my ass rests on his thighs. Then, he takes my mouth in a scorching kiss that steals my breath and thoughts. As he softens inside of me, I'm utterly consumed by him and what he just did to my body and my heart. He cradles me in his arms—chest to chest, heart to heart— like I'm the most precious gift he's ever been given.

But let's be honest, he's the true gift here. I pepper light kisses along his jaw and neck. "That." *Kiss.* "Was." *Kiss.* "Incredible."

His body vibrates against me when he chuckles. "You've completely ruined me. There'll never be anyone else but you."

I hope that's true.

He kisses me thoroughly as my heart soars with his admission. I'm not sure if it's all the feel-good hormones racing through my body, but I feel exactly the same.

He pulls back slightly, a serious expression causing tension across his eyes and around his jaw. "I didn't hurt you, did I? I got a little carried away."

I shake my head. "I'm definitely tender, but only in a good way."

His shoulders relax, as does his jaw, as he smiles with pride. He kisses the tip of my nose, then scoops one leg up and falls to his side, arranging us so I'm cradled against him. He wraps his muscular arms around me, and I snuggle down until my face nestles against his chest. His heart beats a heavy staccato against my cheek, and I grin.

I swipe my cheeks, relieved and happy to find them dry. This was a huge step for us—one I'm thrilled to have finally taken with the man beneath me. I couldn't have asked for a better person. He's been so patient and understanding.

46

HOPE

MY PUSSY STINGS AS HE SLIDES OUT OF ME, LEAVING wetness between my thighs. Every muscle in my body tenses when I realize what we've done, and I feel Ben tense in response. I specifically bought condoms just in case and then completely forgot to use them. To be fair, Wyatt and I hadn't used condoms since we were teenagers, and it's been a long dry spell for me. His arms tighten around me when I try to put some space between us so I can break the news that I'm not on birth control. There was no need.

Dark, concerned eyes greet me when I look up. "What's wrong?"

I lick my dry lips as panic works its way through my body. *Is he going to be mad?*

"Uhm, I'm ... uh. I'm not on birth control, and we forgot to use condoms."

The tension he was holding in his body releases, and he slides his fingers through my hair, tucking it over my shoulder. His eyes are all soft, and a devastating smile stretches his kiss-swollen lips.

"I'm pretty sure we'll be okay, because I'm due to get my period in a few days."

He kisses my shoulder and shrugs. "That was completely my

fault, and I take full responsibility." He slides his fingers down the side of my cheek, tucking them beneath my chin and tilting my face up to his. He places a tender kiss on my nose. "But, Hope, I'm not opposed to the idea of having a baby with you."

My breath stutters, and I'm certain my eyeballs are about to pop out of my head right now. I shake my head awkwardly.

"It takes two. I was equally irresponsible. I can't believe you're being so cool about it." I slide my eyes over his handsome face. "I was so caught up in the moment. I ... I just didn't think."

Ben chuckles. "That's the point. You should be so caught up that you can't think straight or I'm not doing my job properly." He kisses me lightly. "We'll use condoms from now on, if it'll make you more comfortable." He drops his gaze from mine, and I watch his Adam's apple bob. The mood in the room has shifted as he nudges my nose with his. "Does it make me a terrible person to want to have something between us that ties us together forever?" he murmurs against my cheek.

"Oh, believe me. You did your job *very* thoroughly." I wink playfully, trying to ignore the heaviness of his confession, then run my hand over his shoulder to tease the cropped hair at his nape with my fingers, sending a wave of goosebumps fanning across his skin.

He kisses me again, sliding his tongue between my lips, and nudges his pelvis into mine. I can't miss the fact that he's growing hard again, but I gently push him away.

"Uh, there's no way I can go again this soon." I wave my hand around my hip area. "Need I remind you, it's been a long time. This girl needs a little recovery time."

He chuckles and rolls out of bed, pulling me up with him. "Let's get cleaned up so I can feed you." Picking me up, he carries me bridal style into his bathroom, turns on the faucets until steam bellows out of the glass cubicle, then he attempts to carry me inside.

"Uh, I need to pee." It's been a long time for me, but I do remember post-sex protocol. "I don't want to end up with a UTI."

He nods and places me on my feet. "Sure," he says. "I'll give you a minute."

Once I'm done, I call him back into the bathroom and he drags me into the hot shower. I go willingly, and sigh loudly when the hot water flows over my well-used muscles, eliciting a chuckle from the Adonis next to me.

With no chance to tie up my hair, the steam wreaks havoc on my curls, so I dip them beneath the spray. Ben's about to get a lesson in the life of a girl with curly hair.

He grabs the soap and a sponge and works a lather over every inch of my skin, which is rapidly turning pink from the hot water. I hum dreamily at the attention he's giving me, soaking up his tender touch.

It's been such a long time since I've had a man's hands on me. Emotion builds in my throat, and I swallow quickly to stem it before it overflows and ruins our moment. He lovingly kisses each area once it's rinsed clean of soap and pays special attention to the area between my legs, my boobs, and my ass.

When he turns me around to face him, his beautiful smile falls when his eyes land on mine. He cups the back of my head with one hand and wraps his other arm around me, holding me close against his hard body.

"Cookie," he murmurs against my hair as he rocks me from side to side.

His compassion unleashes the emotion I was trying so hard to keep inside. I didn't want to do this. We've shared such a beautiful experience, and I don't want to drag us down. I don't want to taint this moment. It's not that I'm upset about what we did; it's more about how long I've lived without the affection of a man.

The warm water cascades over us, and Ben continues to hold me in this space, giving me the time I need to collect myself. His patience astounds me and makes me feel safe enough to sit with my feelings for a short while.

I pull my face away from his chest and look up at him. "Thank you."

"Talk to me," he coaxes.

I suck in a deep breath. "As you were washing me and kissing me, it just really hit home how long it's been since I've been intimate with a man—had a man's hands and mouth on my body. You know?" I shake my head and shrug. "It caught me a little off guard. I'm sorry. I didn't mean to ruin our afternoon."

He's shaking his head before I can finish. "You haven't ruined anything. You're allowed to feel how you feel and express it however you wish. I'm here for all of it."

I push up onto my toes and kiss his jaw, covered in bristles. "You're a good man, Ben Taylor."

"I wouldn't say that. I should feed you, not feel you up in the shower."

I giggle as he turns off the water, then leads me out of the cubicle to dry me off with an enormous gray, fluffy towel. Once he dries me, he taps my butt.

"Go get dressed and meet me downstairs."

"So bossy," I chuckle as I step past him.

He wraps his hand around my throat, freezing me in place. "You ain't seen nothing yet, Hope," he tells me, then kisses me roughly and urges me out of his bathroom.

Giddiness is my companion as I dress in one of Ben's T-shirts and sort out my hair the best I can so it doesn't turn into a bird's nest. When I'm satisfied, I follow the delicious smell of dinner downstairs to find Ben crouched next to Rex, giving him plenty of love.

"I know, buddy. I've fallen hard, but I promise I won't forget about you." My heart swoons while he places a bowl of food on the floor. "Here. Your favorite—steak and vegetables." He rubs Rex's scruff, then stands, and that's when he notices me leaning in the doorway. A pink hue paints his cheeks, and he rubs the back of his neck as he walks over to me.

His eyes dance to my hair, and his cheeks rise as his fingers tease the curls. "I love these curls of yours."

I chuckle. "They're freaking hard work."

"I think they're beautiful and definitely worth the time and effort you devote to them." He leans forward and lightly kisses me. "Come. Let me feed you."

"You're completely spoiling me. I might get used to this, and then you'll be stuck having to look after me." I slam my mouth shut. Shit. We had sex once, and I'm acting like a stage-five clinger. Completely his fault. He's been so terrific to me and Evan. And he even hinted that he'd like to have a baby with me. *A baby!*

He tugs me into his hard body and presses his forehead to mine with our eyes locked—my aquamarine to his gray. "I'll happily spoil you until we're wrinkly and gray."

I wrap my arms around his neck, and my heart swells for what feels like the first time in forever. I press up on my toes and kiss him. I kiss him with everything I am and a heart full of *hope*. Hope for a future that is free from the deep sadness I've been drowning in.

He returns it tenfold, picking me up and carrying me to the granite counter in the middle of his kitchen. Our kiss escalates quickly, and dry humping ensues. We tear at each other's clothes with desperate fingers like we didn't have sex less than an hour ago, and when he finally pushes inside me, I know I'll struggle with soreness, but I really don't care.

I just want this connection with him as often as possible. I want this feeling he gives me so freely. The feeling I thought I'd lost forever.

47

BEN

"So, how are things going with you and Hope?" Sebastian asks as he jams a fry in his mouth.

My body heats at the mention of the woman who's always at the forefront of my mind. "Pretty great." Images of her curled up on my chest the morning after we finally crossed the line and all the times we've stolen moments to be together as a couple—and as a *family*—over the last week run across my mind like a movie reel.

I've never felt so content.

So at peace.

Like I've finally found the place I belong.

And I get the impression Hope feels the same. I *hope* she feels the same. It's natural between the three of us, even though we haven't had a *sleepover* with Evan in the house yet.

Seb points at my face. "If that look is anything to go by, I'd have to agree things must be pretty great between you." He lifts his beer to his lips. "I'm happy for you, man. If anyone deserves to find happiness, it's you." He punctuates his sentence by gulping the rest of his drink.

Warmth unfurls in my chest with his words. "You deserve it, too."

He responds with a shrug. "One day." He brushes off any talk about a relationship for himself, but I know he aches to have someone to call his own. "So tell me, what changed?"

I blow out a long breath. "Everything." I can't stop the grin from overtaking my face, then I sober. "I know the road ahead won't always be smooth. I know she'll always mourn everything her and Evan have lost, but hopefully being with me will make it hurt a little less. I've watched her laugh and smile more than she ever did when I first met her. Even her family have noticed the change in her and Evan. She has a sparkle to her eyes and a lightness that was missing. I'm trying to show both of them life is worth living. The way Tahlia taught us."

"That's great. I'm glad things are working out." He pauses for a moment, a thoughtful expression pinching his features. "How does she feel about you being a cop?"

I tip my head to the side, unsure what he means, and he reads my unspoken question.

"Being a cop is dangerous, especially in the city. She could lose you, too." He raises his brows like I'm an idiot for not thinking about it myself.

Maybe I *am* an idiot.

I shift uncomfortably in my seat and glance at the people around us while I gather my thoughts. "She hasn't said anything, and I never gave it any consideration. She knew I was a cop from the start. That's how we met. Do you think it could be an issue?"

He nods solemnly. "For someone like Hope. Yeah, I do. She already lost the love of her life. Her son lost his father because of his job, and while you're not likely to get blown up by an IED, your job has inherent risks. As you spend more time together, she's bound to start thinking about all the things that could go wrong."

I let his words settle for a moment, teasing them apart. "Do you think that's why Nix offered me a job with him? He said it was because he needs to step away and spend more time with his family, but maybe it was his way of watching over Hope?"

Sebastian licks his lips. "Yeah, maybe." He grins and points his empty bottle at me. "That's some dedication to his promise to watch over his friend's family."

"Nix doesn't strike me as a man who half-asses shit."

"Nope, he doesn't." My long-time friend studies me. "Do you think you'd give up your dream for her? For them?"

My stomach sinks at the thought. "You know how much I wanted this job, and it's not so easy to walk away with Rex as my partner. He represents a significant investment, so I'd have to work to transition him to a new handler. I'd have to give him up." My stomach plummets at the thought. Rex and I have a tight working relationship, but above that, we have a close personal bond.

"I do. I know exactly how hard you worked to get here and how important Rex is to you." He shifts, throwing his arm around the back of his chair, giving me the space I need to consider the possibility.

I drop my eyes to the tabletop, tracing the patterns in the wood grain. It takes me less than a minute to make a decision, and I straighten up to deliver it to my friend, who knows me better than anyone. "If Hope needs me to walk away for her peace of mind, I'll do it in a heartbeat." His eyebrows shoot up. "Her and Evan are more important to me than any job. I'd miss Rex more than the job, to be honest." My stomach clenches, and my ribs feel like they're strangling my lungs. Giving up Rex would be the worst. He's my loyal friend and the best partner a cop could ever have. I know I've been fortunate to have him in my life.

A smile stretches his cheeks. "I knew you'd say something like that. That's pretty serious, man. I know how much Rex means to you." He playfully shakes his head. "I guess I've lost my wingman."

I chuckle, but it's hollow. "A married man makes a perfect wingman."

His eyebrows shoot high above his wide eyes. "Married?"

"Yeah. I'm all in, in case you haven't noticed. But I need to wait until she's ready. I don't want to spook her. I need to go slow." I take a drink and smirk at my best friend. "If I'm off the market,

I'm no competition." Not that we were ever competitive when it comes to women. Our tastes are distinctly different. He likes easy. I like connection.

He slaps the table. "Perfect! Why didn't I think of that?"

BUNDLED IN WARM COATS, Hope and I follow Evan and Rex along the sidewalk to my house. Rex stops again to sniff around a streetlight, something he's done several times since we left home for our walk.

Evan tugs on his lead. "C'mon, boy. You don't need to sniff *every* post."

I chuckle. "You're fighting a losing battle, Ev. He can't help himself."

He rolls his eyes. "Yeah, well, it's kinda gross."

Hope chuckles at her son, and I glance up my street. A familiar metallic-gray BMW SUV is parked in my driveway, and dread coils like a snake in the pit of my stomach.

I wish they'd have the courtesy to call before they turn up unannounced, but that would be too much to ask. It would mean they'd have to show consideration for someone else. They've always been too self-centered to think of others.

I'm not ready for them to burst my perfect bubble with Hope and Evan. I don't want my mother's fake pleasantries and private snide comments tainting what I'm building here, nor my father's tendency to ignore anyone he deems beneath him.

"Looks like you have visitors," Hope mentions when she spots the car in my driveway.

I slow down, blow out a breath, and try to release the tension that has drawn every muscle in my body tight at the sight of their car. "Yeah. My parents."

Hope grins and my stomach sinks. Excitement lights her eyes. She would never consider parents could be less than anything but loving and supportive—look at the examples she has in her life. Unfortunately, mine are the polar opposite to what she's used to.

"Really? I can't wait to meet the people who raised such a wonderful man."

I grab her hand and pull her to a stop. "Wonderful, huh?" I say playfully, trying to take my mind off the imminent disaster.

She glances to see Evan and Rex stopped behind my parents' car. "Definitely wonderful. They must be pretty incredible to raise you." Her eyes sparkle with excitement.

I wouldn't say that. Pretty sure I turned out the way I did *despite* their parental influence. I want to warn her, even suggest she escape while she can, but I've always believed people should make their own judgment about others. As much as it pains me to expose two of the most important people in my world to my parents, I should let them draw their own conclusions without input from me.

Maybe my parents have changed in the six months since I saw them last. It's something I've hoped for since I was old enough to realize I'm the son of narcissists.

As I watch my parents climb from their vehicle and Hope's smile light up her face, I vow to run interference wherever I can.

Mom's eyes dart between me, Evan, and Hope. Then she forces her lips to tip up, like she's happy to see everyone. Stepping forward, she holds out her arms like a loving mother. "Benjamin."

She and Dad are the only people who call me by my full name, and it makes me cringe.

I lean in for a hug, like the dutiful son I am so as not to shame Mom. As Dad makes his way around their SUV, Mom air kisses both of my cheeks, then pulls away to straighten her sweater, dusting imaginary dirt from the fabric as if touching me has soiled her somehow.

Out of my periphery, I notice Hope watching us with interest. She told me that, because she works with people all the time, she can read them pretty well.

Dad thrusts his hand out at me. "Benjamin." I slide mine into his, and he gives my arm a quick jerk before letting go. Then, he glances at his hand and wipes it down the length of his trousers. His eyes skate over Hope and Evan, and I see the moment he decides they aren't worth his attention and dismisses them.

He draws his mouth into a tight grimace when he looks down at Rex, sitting beside me. "I see you still have *the dog*." He says *the dog* as though he's tasted something foul. It doesn't matter that Rex is a decorated officer of the law. In his eyes, Rex isn't worth his time.

I don't bother responding. "I didn't know you were back from your vacation, or that you'd be stopping by." I wonder how long they would have waited in my driveway for me to come home instead of calling ahead, like normal people do.

Mom's eyes float over to Hope and Evan, and a plastic smile pushes up her cheeks. "We got back last week and have been recovering from the arduous journey at *The Four Seasons*. We popped in as soon as we could. We haven't seen you for months, and we missed our only son," she says to me, her voice dripping like syrup. She directs her attention to Hope. "And who do we have here?"

They've been here a week and couldn't pick up the phone. I would say I'm disappointed and hurt, but I'm not. Everything is always about them. *Every single time.* I turn my head to Hope, trying to make my apology clear. "This is Hope and her son, Evan. This is Elaine and Robert. They've recently returned from six months in Europe."

It's not like I can introduce her as my girlfriend when Evan is standing right there. He doesn't know we're dating yet. Now I wish we'd already spoken to him about it, but I'm nothing if not determined to take things at Hope's pace.

Hope's attention snaps toward my mother. "Oh, my. What a wonderful experience! Gosh, it must have been incredible." Her eyes literally sparkle with delight on their behalf.

Mom shrugs as if she isn't fortunate to indulge in such experiences. "It was okay, I guess. Sometimes it was a struggle to find someone who spoke English. You'd think they'd learn the language rather than be so ignorant." Dad grunts his agreement, and Mom leans in like she's about to share some big secret. She screws up her nose. "And some places were downright filthy." She pinches her nose and shudders. "Very third-world," she says as she rolls her eyes. "Not at all what we expected."

Europe ... *third world*? Unbelievable.

I can never understand why they travel so much. They've never returned from a vacation and been one hundred percent happy with the experience. They always find something to complain about. Whether it be the food, the water, climate, or the language and culture.

Hope's eyebrows rise slightly, and I watch her swallow. It's obvious she didn't expect Mom's response and is at a loss for how to carry on the conversation, which has already taken a negative turn—as I expected it would. That's gotta be some kind of record, even for Mom.

"Are you in the city for much longer before you head home?" I ask, trying to provide somewhat of a buffer.

Evan tosses the ball to Rex and he leaps across the yard.

"We're driving home in the morning. We thought we should share a nice meal with our only son on our last night in town, but I see you're busy." She raises her eyebrows at me as if to chastise me for having plans and a life of my own. I wonder if Hope noticed Mom say they *should* share a meal with me. Because that's what normal, loving parents who hadn't seen their *only* son for six months *would* do.

Hope places her hand on my forearm, and Mom zones in on the action like a heat-seeking missile. "That's okay. Evan and I were just leaving." *They weren't.* She looks at me. "You should enjoy dinner with your family. It's been such a long time since you've seen them."

I know she thinks she's helping, but I'd rather have a tooth extraction than spend the evening with my parents. I tug her away so we can have a conversation without three pairs of ears listening. "*We* had plans. Plans that are important to me. And I was kinda hoping Evan would fall asleep, so we could ... catch up and you'd have an excuse to stay over." I wiggle my eyebrows up and down.

She chuckles and glances over at my parents and Evan, who they've completely ignored. Luckily, he's too focused on playing ball with Rex to notice their lack of interest. Her fingers squeeze mine and empathy overtakes her features. "We can catch up tomorrow. You haven't seen them for months, and they want to have dinner with you before they go home."

Obviously, she didn't pick up on the wording Mom used, and it's not my place to point it out. If she hasn't picked up any clues as to the type of people they are, then I won't bring it to her attention. I'd rather she not know than feel sorry for me.

I know I'm clutching at straws, but I don't want to miss out on spending this evening with her and Evan. Our time together already feels too limited. "How about you guys come too?"

Her eyes widen, and a hint of worry slides over her face. She shakes her head adamantly. "Oh, no. No way." She leans in close and drops her voice low. "I got the distinct impression that your dad doesn't like us, and, well ... I don't think we're the kind of people your mom would want to share dinner with. It sounds like they want to go somewhere fancy." Her nose crinkles a little as she speaks. So she *did* pick up on the unwelcoming vibes.

I reach out and take her hand, squeezing it. "Please come." I'll beg if I have to. "I'd really like to have you guys there with me." She shifts on her feet and chews on the corner of her plump bottom lip. "For support." I bend my knees to get down to her level and give her my best puppy dog eyes, hoping she can't resist.

She glances around and blows out a long breath. "Okay."

I could kiss her right now, but I won't. I need to honor our plan to keep things platonic in front of Evan. Until we're sure.

Though, I don't know what we're waiting for, because I'm already certain I want them both ... forever.

I squeeze Hope's hand. "Thank you. I'll make it up to you later," I say, then turn back toward my parents. "Hope and Evan are coming to dinner, too."

Mom smiles like she just stepped in Rex's shit and glances between the three of us. "We're dining at *The Four Seasons* tonight." She eyeballs Hope and Evan up and down, then glances at Dad. "I'm not sure we can change the reservation from three to five with such little notice."

"Oh, that's o—" Hope starts, but I squeeze her hand to stop her from bailing on me.

"No problem. You've probably eaten there every night this week. We can order takeout and eat here."

Mom scrunches up her nose, much like Hope did, but it was so much more adorable on Hope. "I don't think so. If you can't give up one evening to have dinner with your parents, then I don't even know why we bothered stopping by." She pouts as she eyes Hope and Evan like they've personally affronted her. "I wouldn't have thought it would be asking too much to spend one evening with our *only* son. It's not like we can see each other often with you *choosing* to live in the city." She points her nose to the darkening sky. "I see I was mistaken, and we're not important enough for you."

I'm reasonably certain she took lessons in how to guilt trip her *only* son. She often made me feel like I was in the way or that I took up too much of her valuable time. There was a time when I would play into her guilt. I would change my plans without question. But I'm older and wiser now, and there's no way I'm prepared to adjust tonight's plans to fit in with them. They could have phoned ahead to make arrangements with me like normal people do, but they chose not to. I'm tired of them assuming I'll drop everything for them.

Not anymore.

I'm no longer that kid who devotes everything I am and pushes aside my wants and needs to make his parents happy when they never returned the sentiment.

I shrug carelessly. "Then I guess we'll have to catch up the next time you and Dad are in town."

Hope's eyes have been following our conversation, progressively growing more concerned. Squeezing my hand, she pulls me back slightly. "I don't understand what's happening here, but I think you should have dinner with your parents. Your mom seems upset. Why are you being so stubborn about this?" she whispers, concern tightening her features. "They're your parents."

Mom folds her arms across her chest and narrows her eyes with a noisy exhale. "I suppose we could stay for a short while."

I smile at Hope and raise my eyebrows. "Sounds good." I hold my arm out toward my front door. "Come on in."

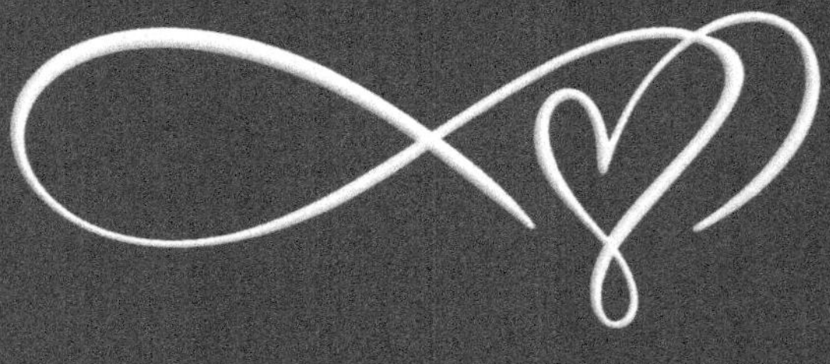

48

HOPE

T HIS IS NOT THE MAN I'VE GROWN TO KNOW. HE'S always so easygoing and amenable, but I think I understand why he's not adjusting his plans to suit his parents. They're certainly not what I expected. Ben's so warm. Considerate. Compassionate. Thoughtful.

And they're ... none of those things, from what I can tell.

"That dog's not coming inside while we're here," Robert states bluntly, pointing at Rex, as if it's his home and his decision.

Evan—who they've failed to acknowledge—looks at me with raised brows, and Ben's shoulders stiffen as he blows out a long breath. "He sure is. This is his home, and I'm not leaving him outside in the cold."

His dad mumbles something under his breath as he crosses the threshold of the front door.

"You'll at least lock him in the laundry," his mom states. She's telling, not asking, and I get the impression that she never asks— she *expects*. I'm truly baffled by how Ben's turned out the way he has, even after this brief interaction with his parents. Maybe they weren't always like this.

Ben ignores her and locks the front door behind us as we remove our coats.

I nudge Evan's arm to get his attention. "Can you please give Rex fresh water while I wash up?"

He nods and says, "Sure, Mom," as we separate to head in different directions.

"I see nothing's changed and you're still collecting strays," Elaine says snidely as soon as I'm out of sight, obviously talking about Evan and me.

My steps stall along with my heart as I wait to hear Ben's response while hoping Evan didn't hear her.

"Enough! I've tried to be a respectful son, but you need to stop," he snaps in a harsh whisper. "Hope and Evan are important to me. If I have my way, they're going to be part of my life for a long time. So, if you can't be a decent human being and be respectful, then you should leave."

I hear her gasp, and a smile grows with no guidance from me. I can't believe what he just said, though I shouldn't be surprised. He's always been honest and open about his feelings and intentions. It boggles my mind that I've met a man like him. So emotionally available. A man who doesn't play games.

The girls often talk about the men they meet and their lack of emotional maturity. It's something I experienced with Wyatt, but I put it down to us being young. I figured he'd mature as we grew older. Ben has it in spades, and it's such an attractive quality. If anything gives me the confidence to move forward with him, it's that.

Stepping into the kitchen, Evan's texting on his phone, Ben's feeding Rex, and his parents are sitting at the dining table with pinched faces, like they're surrounded by filth. Which they're not. Ben's meticulous about keeping his home clean and tidy, something that surprised me the first time we visited. I expected a bachelor pad, but his home was the complete opposite.

I paste on a smile. Ben needs my support; that's why he begged us to stay. For the first time, I can do something for him, and I intend to show him I'm here for him, just as he's been for me and

Evan. "Can I get you both a drink? Ben has beer, wine, juice, and soda."

"You're not … " Elaine squeezes her mouth into a tight line and flicks her eyes to Ben, then pastes on a fake smile. "Thank you. Does Benjamin have any decent wine? Not that cheap store-bought stuff." She wrinkles her nose.

I smile sweetly. "Of course. He always keeps my favorite wine on hand." I won't tell her it's only eight bucks a bottle. Then I turn to Ben's dad. "And you?"

"I'll have the same as Elaine." Sheesh, it must cost extra for him to use his manners.

"Sure." I spin on my heel, grab four wine glasses and fill them, then grab a juice for Evan.

Evan comes over, holding up his phone. "Elliott wants to know if I can stay the night." It wouldn't surprise me if *he* texted Elliott, looking for an escape.

I glance around the kitchen. It's probably best if he's not here, and it's not like our plans for the evening haven't already changed. But it would be rude if I left, and I don't want to abandon Ben when he's obviously on edge with his parents. I've heard of families who aren't close and I guess I've witnessed it, but not this close up. It feels so foreign.

"Do you think they'd come and pick you up from here?" I lean closer and lower my voice. "I don't want to leave Ben alone with his parents."

Evan glances around the room. "I'll ask. I don't think you should leave him alone, either. His parents seem mean."

I nod sadly while he texts Elliott.

"It's bothersome that your son has a phone at such a young age and prefers to bury his face in it rather than converse with the adults in the room," Robert remarks coldly.

Ben's head snaps up, and his eyes narrow. "What conversation, Dad? I'm feeding Rex. You and Mom are sitting at my table looking fearful that you're going to catch a disease at any moment.

You've completely ignored Evan and Hope's waiting on you like she's the help," he points out snappily.

Evan drops his gaze to his shoes. "I'm sorry."

Ben moves closer and grips Evan's shoulder. "You don't need to apologize. You weren't doing anything wrong."

Once I have the drinks and some snacks on the table, we all sit. Evan tucks his phone away, knowing Elliott's mom is on her way. He has an escape from Ben's parents, and I can almost feel relief washing over him. I almost wish I had an escape plan, too, and I'd bet anything Ben would rather spend time with anyone but them, which makes me sad.

I wonder what his childhood was like—and how he turned out to be so wonderful.

Elaine's eyes shift between Ben, Evan, and me. "So, how did you meet?"

Evan looks at me like he's been caught with his hand in the cookie jar, but Ben just chuckles. "I met Evan first. His friends had abandoned him at a gas station, and he needed a ride home. He and Rex became fast friends, and we all started spending time together."

I discreetly blow out a relieved breath, grateful he didn't mention Evan was caught shoplifting. I already feel as though his parents have judged us harshly for some unknown reason. I'd hate to think about what they'd say if they knew he'd broken the law.

Elaine purses her lips and raises a single eyebrow. "You have a phone. Why didn't you call your mother?" she questions Evan.

"He didn't have it with him," I butt in, running my fingers through his hair to offer my support before Evan has to defend himself. A knock at the door interrupts at the perfect moment. "That must be Elliott. Say goodbye, Ev."

We both stand and Evan says his goodbyes to everyone, then drops to bury his face in Rex's neck to say goodbye to him. Ben's dad watches on in sheer horror.

Once Evan's gone, I draw in a deep breath and head back to the kitchen, pasting a smile on my face. "Anyone need a top-up?"

Elaine pushes her glass toward me. "Please." The way she says *please*, like she won't be able to survive another moment without wine, grates on my nerves. This is her son. Her *only* son. The son she hasn't seen for six months. I can't believe they've been here for a week and only decided, on their last night in the city, to contact him.

"I'm gonna order take—"

I place my hand on Ben's forearm to stop him. "I can cook dinner." I force a smile. "Your parents have probably missed home-cooked meals since they've been traveling for so long." I push to my feet, ready to prepare the dinner we'd already planned. We always make too much, so I'm not worried we won't have enough food.

Elaine waves her hand in the air. "Don't bother. The food is better at *The Four Seasons*." She pushes to her feet and checks her watch. "Robert, if we hurry, we can make our reservation. I'm sure they can add another setting to the table now the boy's gone."

Red tinges the edges of my vision. How dare she?

Ben pushes to his feet and leans his closed fists on the edge of the table. "Feel free to have your dinner at *The Four Seasons*. We won't be joining you. You've been nothing but rude and disrespectful, and I already warned you once."

His mother waves her hand around dismissively and collects her purse. "Don't be ridiculous. Let's go."

Robert pushes to his feet and silently follows his wife. I can't move, my feet locked in place with shock at how this afternoon has gone.

Ben kisses my forehead. "Would you mind waiting here for a minute? I'm just going to walk them out. I need to have a word with them."

"But, Ben. You can go to dinner. Don't stay here for me. I can go home. They're your parents," I implore him. Goodness only knows when he'll see them next.

He shakes his head, a look of dejection painting his features. "Only biologically. I can't say they've ever truly been parents. Not in any way that counts." He kisses me again and my already mangled heart cracks for the man who seems to have missed out on so much. "I won't be long."

49

HOPE

My thoughts are erratic as I clear the table and drag on the rubber gloves Ben keeps here for me to wash the dishes. I never imagined his parents would be so cold and rude when he's so warm. When the kitchen is clean, I wander toward the front window and watch him with them.

They're obviously unhappy he's not doing what they want, and I wonder if he normally complies but is choosing not to because of Evan and me. I'd hate for our presence to put a wedge between him and his parents. I know how important it is to have family around. Without the support of my family—and Wyatt's— Evan and I wouldn't have survived the last six years. Hell, even before that, they supported us whenever Wyatt was deployed. Which was often.

The slamming of car doors breaks me from my thoughts, and I focus back on what's happening outside. With his hands on his hips, Ben stands frozen in place as he watches his parents' SUV disappear down the street. He brings his hands to the back of his head, linking his fingers together as he paces in a circle. His pain and disappointment surround him like an aura, and I can't watch him deal with his obvious hurt alone, so I push open the screen door and make my way toward him.

Sliding my hands up over his tense shoulders, I place a kiss to the space between his shoulder blades and feel his muscles relax a little. Slowly, I slide my hands down his strong back, trace his flanks, then wrap my arms around his waist, pressing my cheek and the front of my body to him.

He entangles our fingers together and blows out a long breath, releasing more tension. "I'm sorry."

I kiss his muscular back again. "Why are you apologizing to me?"

Turning in my embrace, he gently pushes my hair over my shoulders as his eyes trace every inch of my face. "Because you didn't deserve to have to experience my parents' toxicity." He drops his forehead to mine and squeezes his eyes closed. "I'm embarrassed and ashamed."

I hold him tighter, giving him as much of my support as I can. "You have nothing to be embarrassed about or ashamed of. You are not your parents, Ben. In fact, you're the exact opposite, which makes me love you that much more. The work you've had to do to *not* be like them must have been astounding. I can't believe you're related to those people."

He opens his eyes, revealing the gorgeous gray irises that are normally playful, but are now filled with uncertainty. "You love me?"

I stop breathing for a moment and run back over what I said, realizing the words I spoke. I ruminate over them for a moment, then nod my head when I conclude I meant them down to the depths of my soul. Mist forms with my hot breath in the cold air as I release the air trapped in my lungs. "Yeah, I love you," I declare with a grin.

A gorgeous, all-encompassing smile overtakes his face, and he suddenly lifts me from my feet, making me squeal in surprise. He chuckles as he spins me around, then tugs me in tight. I wrap my legs around his waist and he looks up at me. "You know I've loved you and Evan for a couple of months, right?"

The muscle in my chest expands, pumping hard and filling up all the available space. I didn't need him to tell me.

I *knew*.

How could I not?

Nodding, I murmur, "I knew."

I watch his lips move closer to mine. "Good," he whispers, his hot breath hitting my skin before his mouth crashes onto mine.

Tightening my hold around his neck, I open eagerly to welcome his kiss. After all, it's his kisses that brought me back to life. It was his patience and compassion that brought me back into the light after more than six years in the darkness.

I'm glad he wants Evan and me forever, because I never want to leave the sanctuary of his embrace. And I hope, with this kiss, he realizes I love him for the man he is … the man he worked so hard to become.

When the need for oxygen becomes too much, we pull away, but Ben drags his lips down the side of my neck, kissing his way to my pulse, his bristles leaving a raspy trail on my sensitive flesh. I grind down on him, and his groan vibrates deliciously against my throat.

As he turns and takes the first step toward his home, excitement bubbles inside me at the prospect of what will happen once we're inside. We unexpectedly have the evening to ourselves, and I can't wait to get started.

His hands grip my ass while I kiss across his jaw to his ear. "I need you inside me. My panties are so wet."

He groans and hurries his steps, slamming the screen door followed by the front door. "Fuck, Hope. I need to be inside you like I need my next breath. Probably more," he pants against my throat.

Pressing my back against the closed front door, our teeth clash as he kisses me savagely. Our heavy breaths mingle and my breasts ache to be free of constraint so I can feel his warm hands on them.

My thoughts and responses solely narrow to Ben and what he's doing to me … to my body. I scramble to drag his T-shirt up his body, and when he realizes what I'm trying to do, he reaches behind his neck, pulls it clear over his head, and tosses it to the floor.

Immediately, I glide my hands over the smooth expanse of his back, feeling every shift of his firm muscles as he effortlessly holds me in place. The thick ridge behind his zipper feels amazing against my throbbing clit, but I need him inside me as well as all around me.

I need him under me, over me … I need him *everywhere*.

We've rarely had moments alone like this—moments we can be with each other without the worry of being caught, and I want to take advantage of every second.

Our kisses turn frantic, the energy between us blazing like an inferno. Ben presses me further into the door, and then his hands trace over my heated flesh beneath my sweater, sending wildfire blazing over my body.

His touch is everything I need.

His kiss is everything I desire.

His love is everything I want.

Never did I imagine I'd be capable of feeling this after the emotional destruction left behind when I lost Wyatt. I realize I'm truly blessed. Not only have I had the soul-deep love of one good man, but now I'm lucky enough to have it for a second time— something I know some people never experience.

I pour my heart and soul into our kiss as I grind down on Ben's steely length.

He peels me away from the door and walks down the hallway without missing a beat. His lips never leave mine, and his kiss never falters.

My ass connects with the kitchen counter, and Ben's hands drop to my pants to tear them away from my body. With deft fingers he has the button and zipper undone and peels them down my legs, removing them completely, along with my shoes and socks. I raise my hips to help him along, then dig my fingers into the sides of my panties to get rid of them, too.

I return the favor and push his jeans and boxers down his thick thighs, using my feet to push them further down his legs. He dips and removes them completely, standing proudly in front of me, stark naked.

My eyes devour his sculpted body with appreciation for the fine specimen of a man he is. I follow the dark happy trail from his navel to his thick cock—glistening at the tip—pointing directly at me, and I squeeze my bare thighs together, smearing the wetness between them.

Ben's heated gaze drops to watch, and he smirks cockily. "Who's a needy girl?"

Me.

I cross my arms to grip the bottom of my sweater and drag it over my body, sending my hair cascading down my back. Ben's hands instantly slide around my body to release the clasp of my bra, and I breathe a sigh of relief when my breasts drop free. "Me," I whisper.

His mouth crashes onto mine, and my hands find the short strands of his hair to hold him in place. Our tongues perform their now-familiar dance, ratcheting up our desire and my need for more. Edging to the lip of the counter, my heated center connects with Ben's erection and my wetness coats his rigid length. We both groan at the contact.

It feels like forever since we've been together like this. Without breaking our kiss, his hand slides up my body, molding to my breast before wrapping around the front of my throat—something I've noticed he likes to do.

He says he likes to feel my pulse jump beneath his grip.

I like the way his grip grounds me.

It feels a little dangerous … and a lot possessive.

The hair on his thighs brush against the inside of mine, and the crown of his dick nudges my opening, so I widen my legs to give him more room and drop my hands to his tight ass to pull him into me. My mouth drops open at the exquisite slide of his thickness entering me and I hook my legs up higher so he can bury himself deep.

His kisses steal my breath and every thought in my head. He slides in and out slowly several times, and I revel in the feel of him inside of me ... the exquisite feel of connecting on such a primitive level.

"Oh, shit. You feel so damn good, Hope," he tells me, his hot breath ghosting across my cheek.

"Same," I grunt when his hips snap forward again. I love how we fit together so perfectly.

He lifts me from the counter and delicately lowers me to the kitchen floor. Keeping his heated gaze locked with mine, he folds me in half like a pretzel with my legs resting over his shoulders, and relentlessly pounds into me like his life depends on it.

Grunts and whimpers leave my lips on hot gusts of air, and I shift my hips as much as I can to meet him thrust for thrust. My heart thumps like it's going to burst right through my ribs as my blood rushes through my body like a tornado. I dig my fingernails into his shoulders for purchase, somewhat cognizant that I'm probably scratching him to pieces.

Our gazes meet and lock, and the heat burning in Ben's half-lidded eyes sends sparks shooting through every cell in my body. His muscles are tight with exertion, and the vein on the side of his neck pulses in stark contrast. Sweat dots his forehead as his eyes beg me to fall apart.

50

I can't get deep enough. I just can't get enough of Hope, period.

Each time we come together, I'm blown away by how well we fit. Better than any sexual experience I've had before. Her tight little body welcomes me like she was made to be mine and mine alone. I know that makes me sound like an archaic asshole.

My hips snap forward as I fight the lightning shooting down my spine, threatening my ability to wait for her. The muscles in my body draw tight and I do everything I can to hold on to what I know will be the supernova of all orgasms. My thighs burn, so I reach between us and rub light circles around her clit and lean down to take one plump breast into my mouth.

She cries out as her hips buck and her walls tighten around me, sending sparks of shooting stars across my vision. "C'mon, Cookie. Milk my cock."

"Oh, god!" Hope murmurs as her walls pulse and tighten around me, strangling me and drawing out every drop of cum.

I slow my movements, easing us both through our climax, and kiss my way up to her swollen lips. I kiss her with appreciation for the privilege she bestows on me when she shares her body—for allowing me to be the one to experience moments like these with her. I kiss her passionately because she turns me on and heats my blood like no other woman ever has.

I kiss her to show how much I fucking *love her*.

She loves *me*. I couldn't believe it when the words tumbled over her lips. I don't think she even realized what she'd said. I never thought I'd be lucky enough to hear them.

Pulling her in tight, I roll to my back and position her on top of me, cradling her head and her body with reverence. We both chase our breath as we slide back to earth from our high. Hope pushes up and captures my lips, kissing me with affection. Her kisses turn to giggles and her entire body vibrates on top of mine. She pulls away, and my breath catches at the sheer joy radiating on her face.

"I can't believe we just had sex on the kitchen floor," she says through her chuckles.

I glance around as if seeing our surroundings for the first time, and laughter bursts from my lips. I drop my head back to the floor. "I'm sorry. You deserve better. I'm supposed to treat you like a queen." Leaning up, I kiss the tip of her nose and the apples of her cheeks.

She lightheartedly hits my chest. "Stop it. I enjoyed every single minute. And who knows when we'll get the opportunity to do that again."

I tangle my fingers through her hair and drag her mouth back to mine. "We'll make opportunities," I murmur against her mouth with a wink, then I devour her again.

My cock quickly grows, and Hope pushes up and notches the head at her slick opening, sliding down until her pelvis meets mine. The tips of her silky hair brush my thighs as she drops her head back on a sigh.

This has to be what it's like to be in heaven. This time we make slow, passionate love with lazy strokes and unhurried touches, neither of us in a rush for this moment to end.

HOPE SITS on my lap as I feed her a bite of egg roll. She tried to sit on a different chair at the table, but this is where I want her. I want her close. I *need* her close after the shit show with my parents.

I don't want to talk about them, but I owe Hope an explanation. She saw a side of me I hoped she never would. She saw the man who no longer accepts being treated like a second-class citizen by the two people who are supposed to love me the most in the world.

I take a sip of beer and nuzzle into her shoulder. "I'm sorry about this afternoon. Sorry about my parents," I breathe into her skin, then press a tender kiss there.

Her fingers feel incredible gliding through my hair, and it's even better when she presses a kiss to the top of my head. "You wanna talk about it?"

I pull back and look up into her concerned gaze. "No. I mean, yeah." I know I need to explain. I want her and Evan in my life, and there's no way to avoid my parents altogether, as much as I'd like to.

"Have they always been like that?" she asks as she plays with the strands of my hair, grounding me and providing the comfort I need to share what I'm about to tell her. I just hope she doesn't look at me like I'm a failure.

"Yeah. My earliest memories include Mom telling me she wasn't interested in what happened at school when I came home and told her I was awarded a citizenship certificate in first grade." Hope gasps. "It never got any better. As I grew older, I wondered why they had a kid, but then I realized Mom's all about appearances. She got pregnant because it was expected of her after she got married." I draw in a sharp breath. "She hugged me today, and I honestly can't remember the last time she embraced me."

Hope's fingernails graze my scalp, sending goosebumps radiating across my body. "Then why did she do it today? Maybe she missed you?" She sounds hopeful. Like maybe she misread the situation.

A disappointed chuckle huffs past my lips. "Nope. It was because there was an audience."

"No." A single word. Two letters. Dripping with disbelief.

"Yeah. Everything she does is for appearances. And he's not much better. He just goes along with her." I swallow my disappointment. The same disappointment I've felt most of my life. I lost count of the amount of times I wished Tahlia's mom, Bev, was mine.

"Ben," she whispers. "I'm so sorry." She drops her forehead against my temple, and her warm breath skates across my cheek.

"Don't be sorry. I'm used to it, but I wanted to explain." I push her hair over her shoulder. "I used to bend over backward to do whatever she—they—wanted. They were never happy. Whatever I did was never enough. Nothing was ever good enough or warranted their interest. *I* was never enough." I shake my head, thinking back to the boy who would do anything to earn his parents' approval and attention. "I was lucky I had Tahlia's mom and Sebastian's parents ... not that they knew what I dealt with at home. Spending time with their families showed me what it meant to have a family that loved unconditionally. In my teens, I spent more time with them than I did at home."

Hope rubs my shoulders with supportive strokes and shakes her head. "I can't imagine how lonely you must have been."

A grin touches my lips. "I was until Seb and Tahlia came along. They were exactly what I needed, and that's partially why we were so close. When things fell apart after Seb's mom and Tahlia's mom passed, we decided it was time to leave Piney Lakes behind. My parents were too toxic, and Seb's dad didn't cope with losing his wife. That's when I resolved to no longer bend to my parents' demands." I stroke my thumb along Hope's waist to maintain our connection as I purge the dynamic of my family. "Now and then, they show up and try to return the status quo. I always fight my instinct to keep the peace, so I can stay true to the promise I made myself when I left home."

Hope drops her forehead to mine. "You should be proud of the man you are, Ben Taylor. Despite having parents like them, you've grown to be a wonderful, thoughtful, compassionate, and considerate human being. You're truly remarkable. And you have us now." She presses her mouth to mine, and it only takes a moment for the kiss to turn into so much more. My heart swells to new proportions with her words.

Words I never thought I'd hear from her lips.

I have them *now.*

Within moments, I have her laid out on the table like an offering. As if she's my greatest reward for all the shit I've dealt with throughout my life. I push her thighs apart and feast on her until she cries out my name, then I bury my cock in her snug pussy until we both fall apart for the third time tonight.

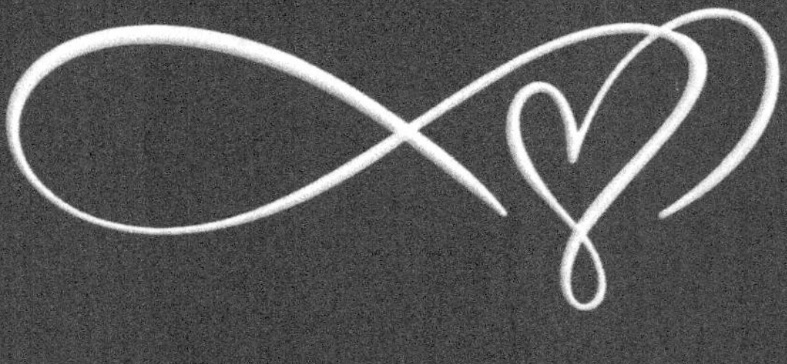

THE SOUND OF HOPE'S CAR PULLING INTO MY DRIVEWAY rips my focus away from attaching the string lights to the gutters. I've never bothered with any of this stuff. There was never a point in doing it when I live alone and work the Christmas holiday, but now I have Hope and Evan, and I want to make the holiday special. She peers up and grins at me through the windshield while Evan climbs out from the back.

Rex leaps from the porch to welcome his buddy home, and Evan gives him plenty of attention, making his entire rump shake from side to side. Evan chuckles. "Yeah, I missed you too, boy."

When I look back at Hope, her genuine smile is breathtaking. Her entire demeanor has changed in the last few weeks, and I'd like to think I'm at least part of the reason for that—I don't think I can take all the credit. *She* made the powerful decision to live her life ... to let go of the pain and the grief. And she looks so much lighter ... freer ... happier. It's been a privilege to witness her wade into the light after drowning in the darkness for so long.

I know she'll still have her moments, but I couldn't feel more proud of her.

I climb down the ladder and meet Evan—who's wearing a cheeky grin—at the bottom. He holds out his fist for a complicated fist-bump-handshake type thing he insists us using, making me chuckle.

When he has my hand in his, he tugs me down so his mouth is at my ear. "So Mom tells me you guys are a thing now." He pulls back and winks at me. "If you hurt her, you have me to deal with. And I don't care if you're a cop, I'll kick your ass." He pats me on the shoulder with a grin and raised eyebrows. "Okay?"

To say I'm surprised she spoke with him so soon would be a gross understatement. I don't want to hide my affection, and I told her as much before she left to collect him from his overnight stay. She was concerned it would be too much too soon, but I explained my discussion with Evan at the bake sale. Surprisingly, she already knew about it, but I still didn't expect her to share the development of our relationship so soon. It's a relief because it means she's not having second thoughts.

She's all in.

Like me.

She's ready to move forward.

And in this moment, I realize the amount of tension I've been holding in my body—worried she'd change her mind and I'd lose them both.

I nod at Evan. "You and your mom are my priority now. If I hurt her *or* you, I'll kick my own ass." I widen my eyes at him. "But don't let your mom hear you saying that you'll kick my ass. I'm pretty sure she'd be mortified."

He chuckles with a shrug. "Yeah, probably. But I *will* kick your ass."

Hope strolls toward us, looking a little unsure, obviously giving us time to talk, but when she sees both of us smiling, her shoulders drop and her face relaxes. Once she's within reach, I wrap my arm around her waist and kiss her temple. "Hey."

"Hey," she murmurs as she leans into me, resting her hand on my stomach and melting into me.

Evan rolls his eyes. "Does this mean I'll have to see you guys kissing and hugging all the time now?" The playful tone of his voice and the tipping up of his lips suggest he won't be bothered at all.

"Maybe," I say.

"Ugh." He rolls his eyes, and Hope chuckles.

"Only because I love your mom." Hope grins up at me, her blue-green eyes glittering beneath the sunlight, and I can't resist kissing the tip of her nose. "I was hoping you guys could help me decorate this afternoon. What do you think?" I want to make our first Christmas together special and start some family traditions.

Hope and Evan snap their heads toward each other with excitement. "Heck yeah!"

"Great. I'll be about another hour with these lights, then we can start inside."

"I think this calls for cookies. I'll check if you have the ingredients, and if not, I'll go to the store."

My stomach rumbles at the thought of Hope's fresh-baked treats. "I won't say no to your cookies." I lean down and kiss her ... *why shouldn't I?*

"Can I help Ben, Mom?"

"Of course."

Evan spins on his heel to head inside, but not before I see his grin. He pats the side of his thigh. "C'mon, Rex. I'm just gonna get a drink first. I'm thirsty."

The screen door slams behind boy and dog, and Hope wraps both arms around me, tilting her head back. "Can I get a proper kiss now?"

I dip my head closer to hers. "Absolutely. I was trying to be respectful in front of Evan." I lower my mouth to hers and kiss her the way she deserves to be kissed.

Every. Single. Time.

She's only been gone a few hours, but I missed her. The house suddenly felt too empty. Too quiet. And I understood Hope's need to always have the television on in the background. It's the reason I went out and purchased more than what I need for Christmas decorating this afternoon. The screen door bangs again, and I know we have a witness, so I slow our kiss with small pecks to her lips, finishing with a satisfied grin.

"Ahhh, here we go! It's started already," Evan sighs as he walks toward us, and I can almost hear his eyes rolling in his voice.

"Sorry. Not sorry." I smile against Hope's lips, and we both chuckle.

Hope heads inside to check the pantry, and Evan and I get to work finishing the lights. An hour later, we stand on the grass to study the lights with a critical eye.

"I don't think we can really get the full effect until it's dark, but they all look evenly spaced to me," Evan says.

I stand with my hands resting on my hips. "I agree." The scent of freshly baked cookies drifts out of the house, and a grin creeps across my lips. "Smells like the cookies are ready. Let's put this stuff away."

We spend the afternoon assembling the Christmas tree, adding the lights after much debate about whether they go on the tree first or last—first, obviously—and eating Hope's delicious ginger shortbread cookies.

Christmas music—including Mariah fucking Carey—fills the room as we hang decoration after decoration on the ten-foot pine tree, complete with fake snow flocked onto the ends of the almost natural-looking pine needles.

Hope stands back as Evan climbs the ladder to place the star at the top of the tree. He plonks it on top and takes one step down. "Ev, you need to tilt it a little to the left. It's wonky." He climbs back up and twists it to the left. "That's too far now."

He looks down at me and rolls his eyes with a grin, but repositions the star, looking over his shoulder for approval from his mom. "How's that, Mom?"

Her smile lights up the room. "Perfect." I watch as she scans the tree with a critical eye. As Evan climbs down the ladder, she steps to the tree and repositions a few decorations. Tilting her head this way and that to ensure everything is precisely where she wants it. This is exactly what I want every Christmas to be like from here on out.

I plug in the lights and move the ladder out of the way to give a clear view of the Christmas tree. We all step back to admire our handiwork, and I press the heel of my hand against my sternum, rubbing it. It actually feels a little like Christmas, something I haven't experienced since moving to the city.

Hope stands next to me and hooks her arm through mine, resting her head against my bicep. I tug my arm out and pull her in front of me, wrapping my arms around her, resting my hands on her flat stomach. She sighs and melts into me. "It's so beautiful."

I nod and kiss the top of her head, drawing her vanilla shampoo deep into my lungs. "I don't usually bother with a tree."

Her body stiffens, and she turns within my embrace. Adorable creases decorate her forehead as she looks up at me. "Why not?"

I shrug like it's unimportant, but I've realized this afternoon that I've missed this, so it kinda is a big deal. "It's just me, and I usually work over the holiday."

Her body sags, and her eyes drop to my chest. "I've never really thought about the work-life balance of a police officer."

Pushing a lock of curly hair behind her ear with my fingers, I chuckle darkly. "Not many people do. It's the worst time of the year for domestic violence and criminal activity. Drunk drivers and intoxicated patrons cause all sorts of problems over the holiday." The mood in the room has darkened considerably, and I don't want Hope dwelling on anything negative—especially regarding my job. I kiss the tip of her nose and grin. "C'mon, let's go outside and see how the tree looks through the window. Evan, can you turn on the Christmas lights across the front of the house, please?"

"Sure." He puts on his coat and pushes out of the front door with Rex close behind, and I drop my hand to grip Hope's so I can tug her outside.

"C'mon."

She chuckles at my enthusiasm as I pull her behind me, grabbing our coats on the way out the door. It's not quite dark, but it's dark enough to get the idea.

Hope pushes her arms through the sleeves of her coat and gasps when she sees all the lights. "It looks gorgeous," she whispers as she soaks everything in. Her eyes scan across the front of the house, pausing on the living room window and the tree inside.

"We did a pretty good job," Evan states, his shoulders pushed back and chest puffed out.

Hope turns toward him and drags him in for a group hug. "You guys did a fantastic job."

Evan shows Hope how we can choose different settings for the lights, and we settle on one that blinks slowly across the string. The cool evening air turns our breath to mist, and I rub Hope's arms when she shivers. "Come on. Let's get you back inside before you freeze."

After dinner, we finish adding the decorations to other areas of the house and watch *The Polar Express* with Hope snuggled into my side.

The house looks and feels festive, and a deep level of peace settles over me. It's ironic how I was happily single until Hope and Evan came into my life. It wasn't until then I realized how lonely and empty my life truly was. I watch them enjoying the movie and count my blessings they're here with me.

52

HOPE

Savannah breezes in as I'm dropping my purse into my locker. "Morning!" she sings, then spins toward me, her eyebrows dancing up and down. "How's lover boy? Have I missed anything this week? Any plans tonight?" When her eyes land on me, all humor vanishes. "You okay, hon?"

Geez, I must look as bad as I feel. I press my hands to my cheeks. "I feel awful. I've been sick every day this week, and I'm exhausted from it." I rub my hand across my stomach, which feels sunken in because I couldn't face the idea of food this morning.

Her eyebrows draw together in worry. "Have you been to see the doctor? I don't think the stomach flu usually lasts that long. Should you even be here?"

I raise my hands and drop them again. "Lucy's away for the weekend, so it's just you, me, and Sophie today. We're too busy, we can't afford for me to take the day off. Hopefully, I'll feel better in an hour or two, then I'll eat something." I hold up the granola bars I brought with me, along with an apple and a bottle of juice. "This'll help when I can stomach the idea of food."

She juts her hip out and rests her hand there. "So you wake up feeling sick, then you're okay by mid-morning?"

I nod. "Yeah, it seems that way."

"And you're feeling exhausted?"

"Yeah." I grab the fresh towels and take my first step toward the front of the salon to set up.

"Any other symptoms?" Savannah asks as she follows me out, turning on the lights.

I rub my hand across my stomach. "I ... uh ... feel bloated all the time. My zippers on my jeans are harder to pull up." Even though I've barely eaten. It's so weird.

She nods. "Uh huh."

I stop in my tracks and spin to face her at the tone of her voice. "What? You sound like you don't believe me."

"Oh, I believe you, but I'm wondering why you haven't thought of the obvious reason you're feeling this way, because it's as obvious as a neon sign to me," she says as she turns on the computer.

I chuckle in confusion as my forehead dampens in response to my stomach rolling again. Before I can ask her what the hell she's talking about, I make a beeline for the bathroom and get there just in time to be sick.

Savannah's voice echoes down the hallway as I brush my teeth. "Yeah, can you stop at the drugstore and grab a pregnancy test kit for me?" *A pregnancy test?* Silence. "Nah, not for me. For Hope. I think she's pregnant."

My eyes almost bulge out of my head. *Whaaaat?*

Savannah giggles. "Yeah, she just told me she's been sick and exhausted all week. I take a week off work, and this is what I come back to. Why didn't you guys pick up on the signs? You've been pregnant. How did you not put two and two together?"

Another pause as my breathing escalates and my heart trips into my ribs.

"Anyway, can you grab a test? I'll cover the reception until you get here."

Music begins to play softly through the speakers, and I wipe my mouth, ensuring there's no toothpaste left behind, then touch up my makeup with shaky hands. We've been using condoms since the first time when we forgot. I couldn't have possibly gotten pregnant the first time we had sex. Surely not. Oh, shit! I palm my forehead. There was also that night after his parents stopped by. Maybe we haven't been as careful as we should have.

"Thanks. See you soon."

I step out of the bathroom on shaky legs to the sound of the bell over the door and Savannah greeting our clients. There's no time to question her about the phone call—or to organize my thoughts. My mind spins in different directions, but I paste on a smile for my first client of the day.

When Sophie arrives twenty minutes later, she gives me a sheepish smile before disappearing through to the back. The phone rings the second she steps back into the salon, and she answers it efficiently as always, however, I can't help but wonder if she bought the test and how soon I can pee on the damn stick to find out if what Savannah thinks is true.

She hangs up and comes over to me. "Morning!" she says brightly.

"Morning." I want to ask her if she bought the test, but I'm doing my best to remain professional when all I want to do is run to the bathroom.

"I put that thing you needed with your stuff," she whispers with a knowing grin and wide eyes.

I swallow past the sand in my mouth. "Thanks, Soph."

Holding a mirror up so my client can see the back of his hair, I count down the moments until I can head to the bathroom. The anticipation of learning if I'm pregnant or not is making my skin itch.

"That looks great. Thanks, Hope." Donovan grins at me in the mirror.

I give him a genuine smile. "You're welcome." I brush off some stray hair from his neck. "I'll see you in six weeks."

"Yep. I'll be back," he says in his best Arnold Schwarzenegger voice as he climbs to his feet, and I chuckle. He has such a great demeanor. I bet all of his elementary students love him.

Glancing at the wall clock, I realize I have five minutes before my next client, so I scurry to the back, grab the test, and close myself in the bathroom. I skim the instructions and get to work. Once I've done my business, I wash my hands and wait.

Pacing the bathroom, I press my hand to my stomach as questions stream through my head. *He said he wouldn't mind if I got pregnant. I wonder if he meant that? Or did he say it in the heat of the post-sex high? What would we do? Where would we live? How would Evan feel if I were pregnant? He's been an only child for so long. How would he adjust? Is this all happening too fast? What if I'm not pregnant?*

I glance down at my wedding rings and twist them around my finger. *How can I wear these if I'm pregnant with Ben's baby?*

I jump as two sharp raps on the door snap me from my thoughts. I wrench it open to find Sophie and Savannah at the door with expectant looks. "So?"

"I don't know. I'm too afraid to look." I realize that, in the time since I overheard Savannah on the phone, hope has grown within me. For as many questions as I have rushing through my mind, there's joy and excitement too. *Hope.*

Their eyes soften, and their lips curl into supportive smiles. "I'd have no idea what I'm looking at," Savannah announces, then nudges Sophie's arm. "You look."

Sophie's startled eyes lock with mine. "I can look, if you want me to."

I bite my bottom lip, my eyes flicking between the two women. Appreciation grows for their unwavering support. "I'll look, but will you guys stay while I do?"

They both nod. "Of course. Why in the hell do you think

we're here? I've got about a minute and a half before I need to get back out there, so hurry up!" Savannah cries.

I flap my hands and draw in a deep breath. "Okay, okay." I grab the stick from the counter and glance at the window, spotting two solid dark pink lines. "Oh, my god," I whisper, shock dripping from the three syllables.

Sophie and Savannah crowd me as they look at the test. "Holy shit. You're preggers!" Savannah blurts.

I finally peel my eyes away from the test to look at the girls. "We haven't been as careful as we should. This might be a result of the first time we had sex ..." I count in my head. "Five weeks ago. It's not like we've had a lot of opportunities to do the deed."

Sophie smiles. "I got pregnant the first time I *ever* had sex."

Savannah playfully punches her arm. "No way! That's some bullshit, right there."

With a nod, Sophie agrees and says, "I know, but I ended up with James, so I'm not complaining. He's the best thing that's ever happened to me." I think she says something else, but all I hear is the buzzing in my head and my blood thrumming through my veins.

I'm pregnant.

Something I never thought I'd experience again. I lay my hand across my stomach in awe, knowing there's a little piece of me and a little piece of Ben in there.

Ben and I are having a baby.

"Shit. I gotta go," Savannah curses, then wraps her arm around me, hugging me awkwardly in the tight space. "Congrats, momma!" She kisses my cheek and rushes out.

When it's just Sophie and me, she looks at me cautiously. "What are you gonna do?"

A grin touches my lips. Something that's been happening a lot lately. "I'm gonna tell Ben tonight after he finishes work."

"Do you think he'll be happy?"

I ponder the question, and there's no doubt in my mind when

I finally answer. "Yeah." My grin is broad and my heart expands as I answer.

She beams and leans in to embrace me. "I'm so happy for you, Hope."

I suck in a deep breath, feeling the oxygen fill my lungs. "Me too." And I really am. For the first time in a long time, I'm genuinely happy and looking forward to the future.

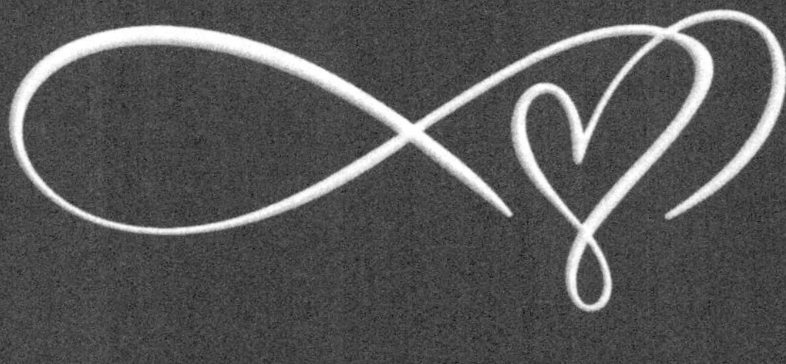

53

HOPE

Happiness fills every cell in my body, and I feel like I've been floating on clouds ever since seeing the two pink lines on the white stick this morning. I've been smiling so much my cheeks hurt. Deep down, I know Ben will be as thrilled as I am about having a baby, but there's a minuscule niggle in the back of my mind that maybe it isn't such a good idea.

We haven't been together all that long. Is this too soon? His job is dangerous, and what if something happens to him? What would I do? I don't think I could bring another child into the world and have them lose their father like Evan has. I understand the devastation that would cause and know it wouldn't be fair to put another child through it.

I twist my rings around my finger, something I've been doing more often. I slide them along my finger to the tip, then push them back down. Rubbing the small diamond of my engagement ring, I sink to my butt on the edge of my bed. I drag both rings off my finger and study them. My heart stutters for a moment, then beats like a drum.

I never thought I'd take them off.

Tears well and slip over my lashes, and I let them fall. I held onto my promise to love only one man for the rest of my life, but it's time to put the past where it belongs. Behind me. "You'll always be my first love," I murmur as I close my fist around the precious jewelry. "But Ben will be my last."

Climbing to my feet, I dig around in my drawer for the box where I keep Wyatt's dog tags and place the rings inside. Then I snap the lid closed and tuck it safely away, wiping away my tears. I blow out a long breath and push back my shoulders, feeling a weight lifted. A small smile touches my lips as I walk out of my bedroom.

MY PHONE BUZZES on the coffee table, and Evan's smiling face lights up the screen. Placing my book down, I grab my phone to answer.

"Hey, Mom. Ben and Rex are on the news. Turn to A2Z News. That's what Pop has on the TV."

"Uh, okay." I grab the remote and turn on the television, navigating to Wyatt's dad's favorite news station.

The news anchor wears a serious expression, instantly telling me it's not a feel-good news story. "Can you tell us what's happening on the ground, Paul?" she asks the reporter, taking up the other half of the screen.

My blood pounds in my ears as the reporter's image fills the entire screen. Police cars, cruisers, and SUVs are haphazardly parked everywhere in the background, and police officers are crouched low behind their vehicles. As the camera pans the area, I spot Ben and Rex off to the side and my heart hammers like a maniac in my chest. My breaths grow shallow and my vision narrows to him.

Only him.

God. I instinctively place my hand over my stomach.

"A woman called authorities this afternoon, telling the operator her husband had been beating her and she was bleeding from several wounds. She said he'd gone out, so an ambulance was dispatched to the property. When paramedics arrived at the scene, it's alleged the husband returned and fired shots, killing—"

Gunshots ring out, and the reporter ducks with a wince, trying to remain professional in a terrifying situation. A scream—*my* scream—shatters the air, and my phone clatters to the floor. My knees give out, and I drop to the couch.

No. No. No. This can't be happening.

"Mom!" Evan's voice sounds far away, but I gather my wits, reaching down to search for the device on the floor without taking my eyes from the television screen.

"Evan," I almost screech, then quickly calm myself. "Can you go ask Grandma what time I should come over tomorrow, please, and pass your phone to Pop? I need to talk to him for a sec."

What is Graeme thinking, letting Evan watch this? What if something happens?

"Uh, sure. But it's probably the usual time."

I force a smile into my voice as I watch officers storm toward the dilapidated house and use a heavy-looking cylinder thing to bash the door. "Thanks, big guy."

"Hey, are you watching the news?" Graeme asks, excitement in his voice.

"Yeah. But why would you let Evan watch that? What if something happens? We both know they'll show anything on the news for shock value, and I don't want him to see stuff like that," I rush to say.

"Ah," he growls. "Sorry. I wasn't thinking." More shots ring out, and I snap my hand up to cover my mouth, trapping another scream. Oh, my god! Tears moisten my hand, and I jump to my feet to pace. "I-I'll turn it off."

Silence rings loud on the other end of the phone, and a relieved sigh puffs over my lips while my eyes stay glued to the screen in front of me.

"Shots are being fired as the police break through the front door of the house, Alison," the reporter announces.

The image on the television changes to aerial footage of the property, and I scan it, frantically looking for Ben and Rex.

"A man has escaped out the rear of the property," the reporter announces with excitement.

More gunshots are fired, and the drone zooms in on the man as he runs through his backyard and jumps the fence into the park next door.

I press my hand to my stomach and hope there aren't any kids playing there.

"Our drone is capturing the alleged gunman as he escapes, Alison," Paul announces, like we can't see what's happening for ourselves, even though the footage is fuzzy. "The police are hot on his heels."

From the bottom right-hand corner, a dark blur races at speed toward the man. "Rex!"

"What's happening?" Graeme calls out as Ben also comes into view, reminding me I'm still on the phone.

"Rex and Ben are chasing the guy, and he still has his gun! He's still shooting!" I scream, horrified at what I'm seeing. It's one thing watching them chase down a young guy who stole a backpack at the beach. It's an entirely different experience watching them chase down a madman with a gun. I know he wouldn't have thought twice about chasing after the gunman.

I can't get enough oxygen in my lungs, and my vision darkens around the edges. I can't watch. But it's like driving past a car wreck—I can't turn away. My legs shake uncontrollably, and I'm certain my heart is going to pound its way right out of my chest and fall into a bloody blob on the floor.

"Hope. Calm down. Everything will be all right," Graeme calmly says.

The man disappears beneath a copse of trees, shielding him from the drone, but gunshots ring out again, followed by the unmistakable yelp of a dog echoing through the speakers and into my living room.

"Oh, my god! Graeme. I think Rex has been shot!" Hysteria builds inside me and I struggle to suck oxygen into my lungs.

Another gunshot rings out, and I scream.

"Hope. Stay calm. You don't know that for sure. We're coming over. We'll stay on the phone with you until we get there."

No. No. No. No. This can't possibly be happening. I slide my fingers through my hair, gripping the strands tightly as I curl my body over.

The world can't possibly be so cruel as send Ben to us, only to steal him away.

The reporter presses his finger against his ear. "We've just received news that an officer has been shot. Alison, we have ..." He presses his ear again. "We have reports of at least one officer down. I repeat. There is an officer down. Shot in the line of duty."

"Have they caught the perpetrator, Paul?" Alison asks. Her voice drips with sheer joy that they're the team breaking this horrifying story. Reporters really are the scum of the earth. They don't care about the lives of the people in the story, how this could change the lives of the people involved ... only about the story.

He presses his ear again. "No word, Alison."

The image changes to the newsroom. "Thanks, Paul. We'll check back in with you for an update soon. In other news, a tire factory has exploded, sending plumes of black smoke billowing into the sky. Surrounding businesses and homes have been evacuated, and fire and emergency services are fighting the blaze."

No!

I need to see what's happening *now*! I press the heel of my hand against my sternum in an attempt to keep my heart in place. *Thump. Thump. Thump.* The sound is deafening to my ears.

I stand to pace, walking a shaky circuit through my empty house as my heart threatens to cease beating one minute and escape my chest the next. Each time I loop through the living room, I study the screen like a crazy person looking for my next hit. My eyes fixate on the banner across the bottom of the frame, searching for some sort of update, but there's nothing.

"Hope, we're not far away. What's happening?" Tracey's voice breaches the buzzing in my ears.

I swallow the nausea that's threatening to rise and press my hand tight to my stomach. "I-I don't know. They're not ... they're not showing anything. Don't they know I need to know what's happening? God, what if something's happened to him? I don't think I'd survive," I sob brokenly, my knees finally giving out, leaving me in a puddle on the floor in front of the useless television.

"Hope. Everything will be fine. They'll be home before you know it, and this will all be a terrible memory," she cajoles.

I already have enough terrible memories. I don't need to add another to the list. I don't *want* to add another to the list. I won't survive it. I *know* I won't. My lunch threatens to make a reappearance as more tears track down my face.

I press my hand to my stomach, like I can somehow protect our baby from the loss of its father.

"Mom! Hold it together, we're just around the corner," Evan's stern voice breaks through the haze of my despair, and I jolt upright. I can't let him see me fall apart. He's had enough of that and I promised to do better.

I clear my throat and try to push confidence instead of fear into my voice. "I'm okay, Ev," I choke. "I'm just worried about Ben and Rex."

The sound of a car pulling into my driveway and doors opening and closing has me wiping beneath my eyes and sniffing as I climb to my feet on unsteady legs. Footsteps sound on the porch, and the door swings open. Before I can brace, Evan barrels into me, wrapping his arms around me, holding me up.

"They'll be okay, Mom. Rex is a badass, and so is Ben. You've seen how fast he runs. He doesn't mess around. Stop crying.

They'll be okay." He squeezes me tight. "They'll be okay," he murmurs the last part, as if he's trying to convince himself as well as me.

Cupping the back of his head, I lean down and press a kiss to his short hair, soaking his scent into my lungs. "You're r-right. They're both badass, and they'll be f-fine. Ben's been doing this a long time, and he knows what he's doing. He wouldn't take unnecessary r-risks. He told us he doesn't."

Tracey and Graeme come to a stop in the doorway to the living room. Another car pulls up outside, and a car door slams. Clara barrels inside, bypassing her parents and coming straight for me and Evan. She wraps both of us in her embrace. "I saw the news and came straight here. Have you heard anything?"

I shake my head. "No, and I dou-doubt we will. If so-some-something ha-happens, no-nobody would know to call m-me," I sob as my body quakes in Evan and Clara's arms. Her hand comes up to my cheek, and the sympathy in her eyes undoes me. She knows. She knows if something happens to Ben, it would break me beyond repair.

There'd be no coming back this time.

Another engine sounds, and more doors open and slam shut. Footsteps thud on the porch, and Mom and Dad charge inside, worry etched into their faces when their eyes land on Evan and me. Mom's eyes are red and wet with tears, while Dad holds himself stiffly. Tracey walks straight to her, offering comfort while I'm unable, and Graeme shakes Dad's hand.

Clara guides Evan and me into the living room and onto the sofa. The men stand behind us, murmuring, while Mom and Tracey move about in the kitchen. My eyes land back on the TV, and I search for information.

They show the woman at the news desk again. "We have an update on the situation in Almond Creek. Paul, what do you have for us?"

The screen cuts back to the reporter standing in front of the house that looks more like a war zone. The camera zooms in on paramedics wheeling a woman on a gurney from the house. "Yes, Alison. The police have apprehended the perpetrator and currently have him in custody. Crime scene investigators have also arrived to collect evidence from the scene, as well as the medical examiner to collect the deceased paramedics who were shot in the line of duty when they arrived on scene." God, those poor families. My heart breaks for them.

The screen splits, showing Alison nodding seriously—as if she's truly concerned. "And, any news on the officer who's been shot, Paul?"

He shakes his head. "I'm afraid we've been told we have to wait for an update on that, Alison."

My stomach drops, and my body shakes violently.

"That sounds serious, Paul."

I lose all sense of what's happening around me as I fall apart. Sickness rises up my throat, and I sprint into the bathroom, collapsing to my knees as I slam into the cold tile and vomit. They have to wait for an update. If the police aren't forthcoming with the information, that must mean ... that must mean someone ... someone died.

Rex's yelp replays in my ears, and I press my hands over them to quiet the awful sound. It's a sound I'll never forget for as long as I live. Wherever Rex went, Ben went. They were inseparable. A package deal.

A sob falls from my lips, and my body shudders.

Strong hands on my shoulders pull me back, and I look up through bleary eyes to find Shane looking at me with sympathy ... compassion. "Hey. C'mon, let's get you up off the floor," he says softly as he lifts me into his arms and carries me like a child back into the living room, placing me like I'm a piece of delicate porcelain on the sofa. Wrapping his arm around me, he tugs me in close. "Nix is on the phone with his contact in the police department to find out what's going on."

I nod hopelessly, aware of noises and that my living room seems full of people, but it's like I'm falling through golden syrup. Everything feels slow. Colors and sounds, muted. Yet, inside me, everything feels like it's moving too fast, and my blood rushing through my veins fills my ears. My limbs are heavy and sluggish, and I just want to sleep. Sleep through this nightmare and wake up to find it didn't really happen. *Is that too much to ask?*

A weight lands on my thighs, and when I look up, Nix's worried gaze traps mine. "Hope."

I trace my eyes over his face, cataloging his stern features. They look softer today, not as harsh and intimidating. He reaches up and slides my hair behind my ear, tracing the back of his hand down my cheek and over my tears.

"Hope. I've spoken to a friend on the force. Ben's okay. He's shaken up, but he's okay." He squeezes my thigh, and my eyes drop to watch his rough hands. "Hope. Did you hear me?" He pauses and I lift my eyes back to his. He raises a single brow. "Ben's okay." He nods. "He's okay, Hope."

Hope sparks deep in my stomach, and Evan sits beside me, shaking my shoulders. "Ben's okay, Mom. Did you hear Uncle Nix?" As if in slow motion, I turn toward him. He grins at me with pure happiness. "Ben wasn't hurt!"

My breath gushes out on a whoosh, and a fresh stream of tears falls from my eyes. This time, they're full of relief, releasing my premature devastation.

I snap my head up and look at everyone around me as we collectively sigh with relief. Shoulders drop and stress lines disappear from everyone's faces. Ben hasn't been part of our lives all that long, but as I look around my living room, all I see are people who have accepted him into our family with love. Something he desperately needed after being raised by two people who never showed him the love and support he deserves.

Nix squeezes my thighs again, and I focus on him. Even though he's just delivered fantastic news, he still looks grim. His eyes skate between me and Evan, and I watch him swallow, suddenly looking uncomfortable. "Ben's okay, but Rex is the officer that was shot by the perpetrator."

Evan shoots to his feet. "No!" he shouts. "He, he, can't …"

Nix stands and Shane grabs Evan before I can, pulling him close and tucking him in tight to his body. He looks so small, wrapped in Shane's thick arms, with his big hand cradling his head.

"Wh-What?" I stutter. Not Rex. No. No. No. His yelp replays in my mind on repeat. My relief that Ben's okay is short-lived as renewed pain surges through my body. Poor Ben. "Is he going to be okay?"

Nix swallows. Shaking his head, he holds up his hands. "I don't know Rex's condition. My friend didn't know any more than that."

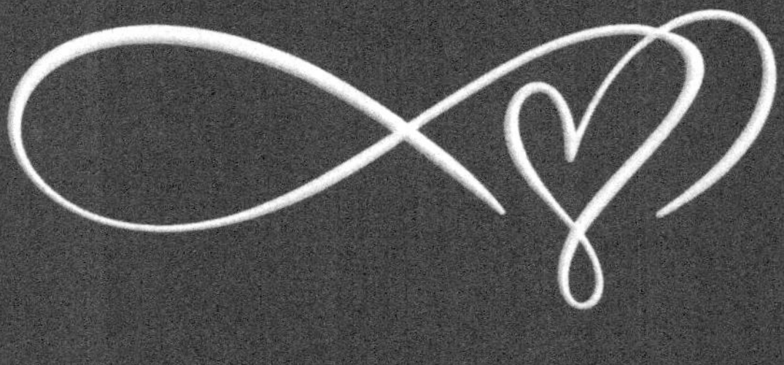

54

BEN

I slide down the icy wall until my ass hits the hard concrete floor. Covered head to toe in my partner's blood, I drop my head into my hands. Everything replays like a slow-motion movie reel in my mind, forcing me to relive one of the top three worst moments of my life.

There was nothing I could do. I was too far away and too inept to protect him. He was so fearless, so mighty, as he went after the perpetrator like the hero he is.

Shoving my fingers roughly through my hair, I tug hard on the strands, causing pain, hoping it will distract me from the devastation ripping me apart, but it barely scratches the surface.

The graze from the bullet on the side of my neck burns and aches, but it's nothing compared to the ache that's shattered my soul. The paramedics wanted to check me over, but it was more important to get Rex the help he needed. I didn't care about myself; getting him to the vet was my only priority.

The fluorescent lights buzz overhead, the smell of antiseptic fills my nose, and I shift on my numb ass. Exhaustion tries to drag me into its depths, but I can't give in. I need to fight ... to be here. For Rex. I refuse to let him down a second time today.

I shake my head and squeeze my eyes closed, dropping my head between my shoulders. I try to draw in a deep breath and shut everything out so I can focus on my best friend. He's been privy to my deepest confessions, some of my darkest nights, and my heartbreak. He's been my salvation. My best friend. The best work partner a guy could ask for.

Soft, familiar fingers slide into my hair, and I look up into the most gorgeous sea-colored eyes I've ever seen. Without words, she drops to her knees and pushes her way between my legs, draping herself around me despite the blood covering my uniform and flesh.

My heart stutters and stops before taking off at a gallop, and I swallow the earthquake of emotions that want to break free. I wrap my weary arms around her, soaking up her warmth and silent comfort.

A sob drags my attention to the left, and I lift my gaze to find Evan with bloodshot eyes and tears pouring down his cheeks. I grip his slender wrist and tug him down to join me and Hope on the floor. Then, I wrap my arm around him and pull him in tight. His body shudders against mine, and it takes everything inside of me not to fall apart with him.

With the three of us huddled on the cold floor of the vet clinic, my loneliness dissipates. A surge of energy, a second wind of sorts, slides through my body. "How did you guys know where we were?" I murmur into Hope's soft hair.

"Nix made some calls, and Shane dropped us off because I was in no state to drive." She sucks in a sharp breath, her bottom lip wobbling, tearing the remnants of my heart to pieces. "A-at first"— she swallows, tears shimmering in her gorgeous eyes, adding an ethereal quality to the pools of blue/green, her lips quivering with broken pain—"w-we thought it was you. We thought you'd been shot, but Nix ... he made some calls ... he has a friend on the force, and he found out you were okay, but Rex ... wasn't."

Heartbreak is etched into every movement of her lips, every word ... every shuddering breath she takes. I can't fathom the pain she suffered—the utter heartbreak, and yet she's here. Beside me. Offering her love and comfort.

She's so fucking strong.

She thought she lost me today, but here she is, beside me, supporting me.

Fissures form across my heart, splintering outward. I've hurt her in the worst possible way—something I never wanted to do. My career causes her pain and distress, which means I need to leave it behind, just like Seb and I discussed.

He was right. If I want to build a life with Hope and Evan, it's unfair for me to work in a job that will cause them distress every time I leave for work.

Especially after today.

They'll always worry and I don't want to put either of them through that. They've experienced enough tragedy and only deserve peace and calm. They deserve to know they come first and that I love them enough to remove any unnecessary risk from our lives.

"I'm never leaving you. Either of you." I declare, then drop a kiss to the top of her head, then I do the same with Evan. "I promise you with everything I am. My promise is *everlasting*."

Evan drags his tear-stained face from my shoulder, anguish painting his boyish features. He shouldn't have to feel this kind of pain. Not after everything he's already lost. "I-I don't wanna say goodbye to Rex. I l-love him so much." A sob explodes over his lips, and his body shudders.

I tug him back in and kiss the top of his head. "He's in expert hands here." I swallow past the sawdust on my tongue, hoping I'm not lying to him. "We won't have to say goodbye."

Both he and Hope jolt back. "You mean ..." Hope murmurs.

"He's not dead?" Evan shouts.

I shake my head, my heart thundering in my chest, my blood rushing through my veins. "No. He's in a bad way. The perpetrator shot his shoulder, and he lost a lot of blood because he got straight back up and continued his pursuit until he took the gunman down. He's done a lot of damage. The vet is going to do her best, but it's a long, complicated surgery, and she can't promise anything." I run my hand through my hair in agitation. "We need to stay positive."

Evan and Hope both breathe a relieved sigh, the tension in their shoulders falling away. "That's better news than I thought we'd hear." Hope looks at Evan. "We can stay positive, right, Ev?"

He nods like a bobble doll, his eyes wide like saucers and filled with hope. If the situation wasn't so dire, I'd laugh. "Definitely!" He looks around us, then back at me. "Why are we sitting on the floor?"

I chuckle darkly, scrub my hands tiredly down my face, then look at the boy who's become a son to me. "I was feeling pretty low, and this felt like an appropriate place to be."

He climbs to his feet and yanks on my arm. "We're here now. We've got you."

Warmth moves through my chest and radiates out through my body like sunlight, and gratitude for my small family fills my soul. Hope pulls away, grabbing my other arm, and together they tug me to my feet, then guide me to a chair. Bone-weary exhaustion floods my body like a tsunami as the adrenaline drains from my system, and I collapse into the plastic chair. Everything aches and I feel eighty-seven, not twenty-seven.

Evan and Hope sit on either side of me, taking my hand in each of theirs. Hope drops her head to my shoulder, and Evan's eyes take in our surroundings. "How come you didn't take him to see Tori?"

"I wish I could. Whenever he's injured or sick, I have to bring him here because this is the clinic approved by the police force."

Evan nods and we fall into silence as shadows lengthen across the floor of the waiting room. I've lost track of the hours, but I'm also grateful for the time it's taking—it means they're working on Rex. It means I still have hope that he'll be okay. Maybe not the same as he was before, but as long as he's here, I don't care. He'll still be my Rex.

The doors that lead through to the surgery swing open like a gunshot in the silence, and with energy I didn't think I had, I jump to my feet and stalk forward, aware of Hope and Evan following close behind. "How is he?"

The doctor gives me a smile full of pity and my guts drop to the floor. My knees threaten to give out, so I lock them in place, preparing for the worst.

"We've had to give Rex several infusions, and we've removed the bullet which shattered his scapula. An inch to the right and it would have hit his heart. As it was, the bullet scraped his lung. He has pins and rods holding the bone together. He's under heavy sedation and will need to remain here for at least forty-eight hours once he wakes properly. He'll need physiotherapy once the bone knits together."

My breath gushes out of me, and my weary muscles relax. The doctor's eyebrows knit together, and sadness washes over her features.

"I'm not sure how to tell you, but my previous experience with injuries like these leaves me with little doubt that the extensive damage caused will be career-ending for Rex. I'm so sorry." She lays her hand on my forearm and squeezes.

How many times can a heart break? Can it really shatter and put itself back together, only to get broken again with different news? In the grand scheme of things, I'm just glad he's still alive. The rest doesn't matter. "Thank you, doctor. Can we see him?"

She nods. "Sure. Just give us a few minutes to clean him up and settle him in his crate."

She heads back through the doors, and I drop my head, breathing deeply for the first time since Rex was shot. Cupping my face in my hands, the tears that have been threatening to fall escape in sheer relief.

Hope gently strokes along my spine, and Evan wraps his arms

around my waist, reminding me I'm not dealing with this alone. They love Rex as much as I do. I wrap my arms around them, holding them close, drawing strength from them and giving it in return.

"YOU GUYS really should go home. There's nothing you can do here. Get some sleep and something to eat and come back tomorrow," the night nurse murmurs.

If it were only me, I'd stay, but as I look at Hope's exhausted face and Evan sleeping on the hard plastic chair, I realize I need to take them home. I nod at the nurse and climb to my feet, stretching my arms above my head. "We'll be back in a few hours."

Hope's questioning gaze locks with mine. "Are you sure? We can stay."

I tuck a loose curly lock behind her ear and trace the line of her delicate jaw with the back of my hand. "We all need to rest. I need to feed you guys, and I desperately need to shower."

Her eyes drop to my body, tracing over every inch of my blood-stained uniform—not that the blood is overly visible on the dark navy material—and widen when they land on the dried blood on my neck and arms. I can't imagine what I must look like. She nods, then leans over Evan, rubbing his back and whispering in his ear until he rouses.

He jolts upright, looking around in confusion. "Is Rex okay?"

She smiles gently. "He's fine. The nurses are looking after him, so we're going home to eat and sleep. We'll come back tomorrow." She glances at the clock on the wall and winces. "Actually, later today. Okay?"

He nods. "Yeah, okay. I could eat, and I'm pretty tired."

I drag out my phone. "I'll call an Uber."

"No need. My car's here. Nix followed Shane, so we wouldn't be stranded," she tells me as she drags her keys out of her purse.

Gratitude fills every cell of my body for the support of Hope's friends. The nurse unlocks the glass doors, and we step out into the chilly night, my arms wrapped around my two most favorite people.

When we breach the doorway and I look up, the sight that greets me steals every molecule of oxygen from my lungs. At least one hundred people, wrapped in blankets and warm clothes, holding candles in the darkness of the earliest hours of the morning.

"Oh, wow," Hope murmurs, her fingers gripping tightly to the back of my shirt.

"Are they here for Rex?" Evan asks, his voice full of wonder.

"I guess so." I nod as the three of us move toward the large group.

As we grow closer to the crowd, familiar faces catch my attention. Donnelly, Eva, Samuel, and Peter huddled together with Brett, Francine, Connor, Michael, and Scott. Tori's standing with them, and Evan breaks away from us to jog over to his friends. They greet him like they've been friends forever, not a few months, pulling him into their huddle.

I watch the tension fall away from the group when Evan tells them Rex is going to be okay. Tori's eyes snap up to mine, and I know she'll want all the medical details later.

Looking around at the gathered crowd, out here in the middle of a freezing night, holding a vigil for Rex, my chest expands with thankfulness.

Keeping Hope close, I clear my throat. "Thank you so much for coming out to support Rex. He's undergone extensive surgery to repair the damage he sustained today. He's still heavily sedated, but the doctors and nurses believe he'll pull through. We don't yet know how his injury will impact his future as a K9 officer, but at this time, I'm just grateful he's alive."

Cheers, applause, and loud whoops of joy fill the night air, bringing a smile to my lips. I lean down and kiss the top of Hope's head, needing her to ground me after my shitty day. I stop to talk to the kids and Tori, as well as other members of the community holding vigil.

Eventually, everyone disperses, and we head home, grabbing burgers from a twenty-four-hour drive-thru. When Hope pulls up in front of my place, my stomach drops and dread consumes me.

I don't want to be alone tonight.

Hope answers my unspoken plea when she turns off the engine and climbs out of the car, Evan following close behind after pulling a small carry bag from the back seat. I drag my weary bones out of her car and follow them to my front door.

We're quiet as we make it inside and eat, each of us emotionally and physically exhausted.

"It feels weird not having Rex here," Evan murmurs.

I rub the top of his head. "Sure does. Hopefully, he'll be home where he belongs soon."

After we clean up, Evan puts himself to bed in the bedroom he's claimed. Hope locks the house, turns out the lights, and leads me upstairs to my ensuite without saying a single word.

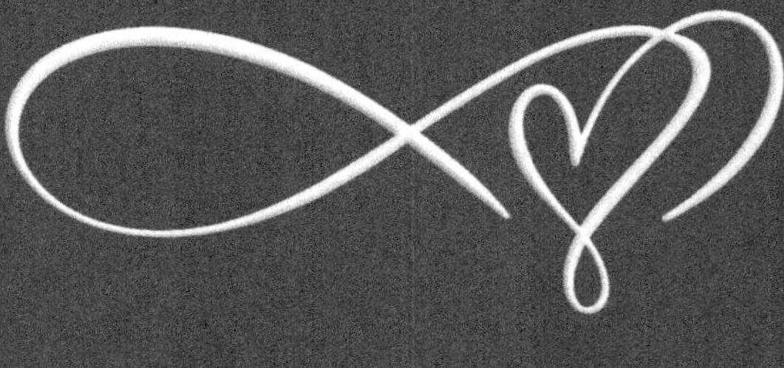

55

BEN

Steam fills the bathroom shortly after Hope turns on the hot water. She turns to me, like the angel she is, and methodically removes every last stitch of cotton from my body—and hers—then tenderly leads me into the shower. The hot water scalds my tired muscles, easing the tension and loosening the knots a little. The wound on my neck stings when the water hits it, and I wince at the burn of pain.

The clear water turns light pink as the blood on my skin washes down my body in rivulets. With a weird fixation, I watch it disappearing down the drain and out of sight, taking my premature grief with it.

Soapy hands slide over my back and across my shoulders, rubbing soothing circles on my skin and easing my aches. Pressing my hands against the tile and dropping my head between my shoulders, I relish in having Hope's soft hands on me, massaging my flesh, soothing me, caressing me. And even though there's nothing sexual about her actions, my cock doesn't know the difference and grows hard, just as it always does whenever I'm with her.

She makes her way around to the front of my body, her gaze full of concern. The moment her gaze lands on my neck, her eyes widen and her mouth drops open. Her body trembles as she presses up on her toes to look more closely, gently stroking her fingers alongside the graze.

"What's this?" she murmurs.

I shrug carelessly. "Just a graze." Using my fingers to tip her chin up so I can drown in her gorgeous eyes, I add, "It's nothing."

Her sculpted eyebrows dip low. "What's it from?" she asks as her worried eyes flick between mine.

Should I be honest or gloss over the fact a bullet almost pierced my jugular?

Should I protect her or deliver news that could mean she walks away from me forever to protect her and her son?

Long moments pass, steam builds in the bathroom, and my mind slips back to the moment when everything changed for me. In a split second, things I considered important no longer were. My job, the one I worked so hard for, no longer held the appeal it once did. All because of Hope and Evan. Because I value keeping their hearts safe and sharing a long life with them more than I value following my dream.

I cup Hope's face in my hands and prepare to deliver the devastation I know my words will cause the woman I love. I swallow past the anxiety that I may lose her for good. "A bullet grazed me," I whisper, the four words laced with guilt. Guilt that I've put her through something she should never have to experience.

Tears spring forth instantly, and she drops her forehead to my chest with a shuddery breath. Her legs collapse beneath her and I capture her before she falls. I can do nothing but stand with her wrapped in my arms, holding her as she falls apart. Her soft body presses harder against mine, not a breath of space between us, and I cradle the back of her head, pressing kisses to the top of it.

She mumbles something against my chest, but I can't understand a single word. Dread and exhaustion has me almost deciding to ignore it, but my rational side knows we need to deal with what happened today.

I guide her head back a little so I can look at her face and hear what she has to say. Red, swollen eyes are my punishment for putting her through hell today. I cradle her tear-stained cheeks reverently. "What did you say, Cookie?" I murmur.

Her eyes lock with mine, and my heart shreds to pieces at the pain I see haunting the aqua pools. "I thought I'd lost you. It was the worst pain thinking I'd never see you again. And then to see how close I really came to losing you ..." She sucks in a shuddering breath, her lips trembling. "I-I can't go through that again, Ben. I-I know I have no right to feel that way. I've always known—"

I stoop and bring her trembling lips to mine, stroking my thumbs along her delicate cheekbones. She returns my kiss with desperation, and the heat between us flames into an inferno. She climbs my body, wraps her arms around my neck and her toned legs around my hips, lining our bodies up and sinking down on my cock, which never got the memo that now isn't the time. We both groan into each other's mouths as her hot, tight heat wraps around me and steals all thoughts about our discussion.

But this is important.

I need to tell her she won't have to worry. Not ever.

I tear my mouth from hers, panting. "I'll never leave you, Hope. I promise."

She shakes her head, sending damp curls swaying. Her eyes look so damn sad. "You can't promise me that. Not with the important work you do. You don't know what each day will bring."

"I can." I study her eyes carefully. "I decided to resign from the police force today. I'm handing in my notice in the morning." Her hot breath fans across my lips, and she sags in my arms. "As I carried Rex's unconscious body, I realized it could have easily been me." I kiss the tip of her nose. "I don't want to hurt you like that. I love you and Evan so much ..." I glance away, then back to the woman who made me realize exactly what's important. "My job used to be my world. It used to be the most important part of my life ... but it's not anymore. You and Evan—you're my world. Our family is all that matters."

She crushes her mouth to mine and kisses me fiercely. "I'd never ask you to give it up for us."

"You didn't ask. I talked to Seb about it weeks ago and said I'd give it away for you. The thought of leaving you and Evan behind turns my bones to ash and my heart to a useless organ taking up space in my chest. I can't do it." I shake my head. "Not anymore."

Her eyes go all soft and dreamy as she melts into my embrace, my cock still nestled in her tight heat. "It wouldn't just be Evan and me you left behind."

I nod once. "I know. Seb would feel lost, and I guess, on some level, my parents would miss me too."

She shakes her head as her mouth slowly morphs into a smile, sending her freckled cheeks up higher. "Of course they'd miss you, but there's someone else, too." Her eyes sparkle beneath the bathroom light, and I'm so damn relieved to see the sorrow and pain that was haunting her gone. I narrow my eyes, trying to think about who I've missed. She bites her bottom lip and tightens her hold around my neck, then nudges my nose with hers. "We're having a baby," she murmurs.

It takes me longer than it should for her words to sink in. I look at her for confirmation that I heard her correctly. My mouth won't form the questions rushing through my head. *How? When? We haven't been all that careful, but can it happen that quickly? Is she sure?*

"I guess it was meant to be ..." Her words trail off as she shrugs her slender shoulder.

I crush her mouth with mine, tightening my grip on her as the warm water from the shower rains down on us. She squeals against my lips, but it doesn't take long for her to catch up and return my kiss with heat of her own.

My heart thunders against my ribs, trying to crack through them to physically join with Hope's as we kiss like we need this to breathe. Joy replaces the ache in every muscle, and happiness lights up every part of my body.

Cupping the back of her head, I pull away enough to speak. "You've turned one of the shittiest days into one of the happiest." I squeeze her tighter, probably crushing her ribs, and kiss her. "I can't tell you how happy I am." I press my lips to hers again, kissing her in a way I hope shows how much I love her and how ecstatic I am to become a dad.

And then it hits me.

The pain and terror she would have experienced today when she thought she'd lost me.

The wave of memories that would have washed over her.

The heartbreak of losing Wyatt and having to raise Evan alone.

For a moment in time, she would have thought history was repeating itself.

Guilt ties itself around me like a noose for the grief she experienced today because of *me*.

Never again.

Never again will she experience that soul-shattering devastating pain.

"I love you. I'm so sorry I put you through what I did today. I'll spend the rest of my life making it up to you and Evan. And I'll be the best dad and husband I can be." Her eyes widen. "That's not a proposal. I'll do a proper one. One you deserve."

She uses her thighs to push up and then slides back down my cock. "That was perfect. I don't need a fancy proposal. I just need you."

The connection forged between us is stronger than anything I've felt before, and I can't believe I'm the lucky son of a bitch who gets to call this woman mine. I grip her perfect ass and spread my feet, then pump my hips, sliding in deep with the help of gravity. Soft grunts and whimpers bounce off the tiles each time I bottom out in heaven, and I drown in the desire I see in Hope's heavy-lidded gaze.

Sliding my hand up her smooth back, I guide her mouth to mine. I tease her with small bites and licks as my labored breaths puff across her lips. My heart hammers with love, and my skin flames with lust as we climb closer to our release. I have no idea how I was lucky enough to capture this woman's heart, but there's no way I'll ever do anything to break it and I'm never letting her go.

Hope's peaked nipples slide against my pecs, and I angle our bodies so her clit rubs against my pelvis. Her hot, velvet sheath grips my cock. "So good. You fist me so good," I mumble against her lips, panting. "I love you so much," I grunt.

"I love you, too," she sighs into my mouth.

I take a step forward, pressing her back against the tile, and she gasps. I take advantage, darting my tongue inside to dance with hers, mimicking the action of my hips, driving us both closer to the edge.

Fire shoots down my spine, sending flames licking over every part of my body as I work to hold back my release. I increase my pace, pumping harder as I pull Hope onto my dick over and over again. "Come on, Hope. Come for me," I grunt.

She moans against my mouth and grinds her hips. Her panting breaths paint my cheek as I kiss my way to her ear and the spot just behind it. Swiping my tongue along the sensitive zone, I count in my head to hold off my orgasm.

Gripping her butt cheek hard, I slip my thumb to her puckered hole and breach the tight ring of muscle. Hope's legs tighten around my hips as she uses me for leverage, and her pussy strangles my cock with rhythmic squeezes.

"Oh, god. Ben!" she moans, seeking my mouth and kissing me violently as she falls apart in my arms.

Her orgasm releases mine from its imprisonment, and my cum splashes inside her, filling her up. Satisfaction slices through my body; I'll be the last man to ever see her like this.

Feel her like this.

Be with her like this.

I return her kiss with vigor, pouring every ounce of love and gratitude into it.

When we finish in the shower and dry off, Hope grabs my first aid kit and applies antiseptic ointment along my graze, then covers it with a dressing. I feel like she's fussing too much, but when I look at the pain still shadowing her eyes, I keep my mouth shut. She needs to do this for herself as much as she's taking care of me.

I rub my hands up the back of her thighs while she works, offering her a semblance of comfort. I can't take away her pain—her fears—but I can do my best to limit them.

I'm still floating on a cloud. Hope is *pregnant*. I'm going to be a dad. The news is so unexpected, but so welcome. I capture her hand in mine to press a kiss to her palm when I notice something missing. I glance up at her to find her watching me.

"Are you sure? You don't have to take them off for me." I don't ever want her to feel she has to give him up. He was everything to her.

She tilts her head to the side. "It was time. I never thought I'd take them off, but it felt like the time was right. I'm ready to put the past behind me and concentrate on our future. Wyatt would understand."

I kiss her bare finger, knowing it won't be bare for long. Emotion wells in my throat, and pride for her strength overwhelms me. "I love you. I hope you know how much."

She smiles down at me. "I know and I love you, too," she tells me as she slides her fingers lovingly through my damp hair.

"I can't believe I'm gonna be a dad," I whisper, leaning forward to kiss her still-flat stomach.

She smiles down at me, and some of the pain recedes from her gaze as it fills with warmth and tenderness. She slides her fingers through the longer lengths of my hair. "You're gonna be a great dad."

I hope so.

I didn't have a great role model, but I'll do my best to be the father Evan and this baby deserves. Leaning down, she presses a kiss to my lips, and I quickly bury my fingers in her hair to hold her to me.

"Thank you," I murmur against her lips, which spread in a gentle smile. "This is the greatest gift."

She pulls back a little, her eyes skipping between mine. "Do you mind if we tell Evan when we all get up?"

"Of course not. You didn't tell him already?"

She shakes her head. "Nope. I thought you should be the first to know." She glances away, then back to me, and if I'm not mistaken, her eyes carry a little guilt, and her shoulders are more tense than they were a moment ago. "Well ... not technically first. Savannah figured out that my symptoms pointed to a possible pregnancy, and Sophie bought the test. They were both with me when I found out. Sorry." The words rush out of her, and her shoulders sag when she finally takes a breath.

Shaking my head, I chuckle. "That's okay." I tap her ass lightly. "Let's get some sleep, and we'll tell Evan in the morning."

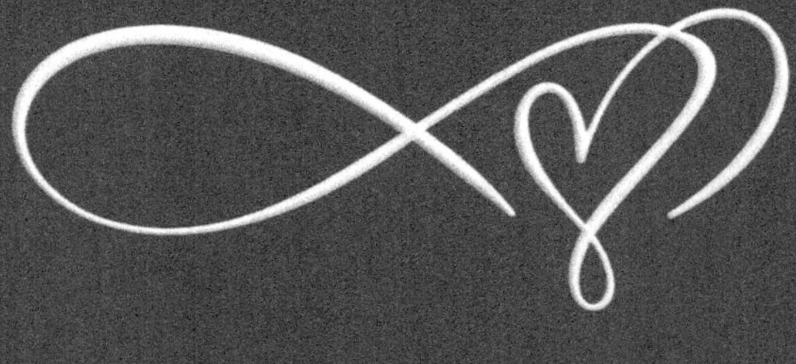

56

HOPE

Queasiness is once again my companion when I wander into the kitchen the next morning and find Ben leaning against the cabinet, eating toast. He holds out his arm, silently inviting me in for a cuddle—which I'll never refuse—then offers me a bite of his breakfast.

I hold up my hand and shake my head. "Not yet. Maybe later." I rub my stomach. "Morning sickness," I murmur in explanation.

His brows drop, and his hand covers mine. "Anything I can do to make it better? Is there anything I can get for you?" He drops to his knees, pressing a kiss to my stomach. "You're not giving your mom a hard time, are you?"

My lips spread at how cute he's being, and I shake my head again, hopefully dismissing his concern. "Give me a couple of hours and I usually feel better. I'll eat then." Creases form between his eyebrows like he doesn't believe me as he climbs to his feet. "Promise."

Wrapping his arms around me, he holds me close, and I drop my head to his chest, enjoying the quiet moment together. Feeling the strong thump of his heart against my cheek and the heat of his body beneath my touch is exactly what I need after yesterday's scare.

Evan shuffles through the kitchen door—hair a mess—and rolls his eyes, but I can't miss him fighting a smile. He didn't make a big deal out of Ben and me being together, and I'm hoping he'll react similarly to this morning's news.

"Hey, big guy. How'd you sleep?" I ask as I pull away from Ben to snuggle with my boy.

He returns my embrace with a tight squeeze. "I'm still worried about Rex."

I pull away slightly and smooth back his hair. "I know, Ev. We all are. We'll see him soon."

Ben swallows a mouthful of coffee and places his cup back on the counter. "I called the vet this morning. Rex is still sleeping, but everything's looking as it should at this stage. She said we could come down whenever we're ready."

Evan's body softens against mine, then he pulls away. "Okay. I'll get dressed, and we should go. I'll be quick."

I chuckle softly at his eagerness. "We will. But I want you to eat breakfast, then Ben and I have something we'd like to tell you." I glance up at Ben.

Nervousness wafts like a cloud around him as he twists the leather band at his wrist—something I've noticed he does when he's anxious.

Evan looks between us with suspicion. "Oh-kay," he drags the word out, then takes a seat at the counter.

I quickly make him some toast and slice an apple, forcing myself to eat a little. Ben pours him some juice, and I grab a small glass for myself.

Once Evan's initial hunger is sated, he looks up at me. "What did you want to tell me?"

I glance at Ben, and he gives me an encouraging smile as he moves next to me, taking my hand in his. I lick my dry lips and draw in a deep breath, thankful smells aren't affecting my delicate stomach. "Well. You know how I've been feeling tired and sick the last week?"

Evan nods. "Yeah."

"Uhm, well, I found out why." He studies me closely, waiting for me to reveal the reason. "Ben and I ..." I glance at Ben, then back to Evan. "We're going to have a baby." His eyes shuttle between me and Ben and down to my stomach, where Ben's hand rests protectively. "You're going to be a big brother."

Evan's eyes widen, and his mouth spreads so wide the edges almost touch his ears. "Really?"

Ben and I nod, our grins equally wide as Evan bolts around to our side of the island counter and barrels into us.

"This is the best news. Is it a boy or a girl? I hope it's a boy."

I laugh, brightness and warmth filling my world. Lightness and love exploding out of me. "It's too early to know, but you'll be there when we find out."

EVAN RACES ahead and pushes open the glass door to the veterinary hospital. Ben holds it open for me, and we make our way to the desk. The nurse takes us back to the ward so we can see Rex. His tail swishes slowly when he sees us, and he uses his uninjured front paw, whimpering with each movement, to edge closer to the barrier between us. When Evan reaches in to rub his snout, he whines and wriggles forward a little more, nuzzling into his hand.

It's unnatural to see him so subdued.

We all lavish him with love. I can't believe we almost lost him yesterday. Tears sting the backs of my eyes at the devastating thought. "I'm so glad you're still with us, Rex," I murmur as I rub the top of his head, bumping the plastic cone he's wearing to stop him from licking or biting his wound.

Rex dozes and wakes periodically, still under the influence of the pain medication being administered through a drip. Every time he wakes, we give him the love and attention he deserves.

Footsteps sound on the polished floor, drawing our focus away from him and Ben stands to greet the uniformed officer walking toward us, holding out his hand. "Sir," he says with a sharp nod as they shake hands.

"Sergeant." The man looks over at Rex for a long moment, and when his eyes return to Ben, he studies him closely, his gaze stopping on the bandage I used to cover his wound. "I wanted to drop by to check on Rex's condition and see how you're doing after yesterday."

Ben blows out a long breath as a different vet from last night approaches the two men. Introductions are made, and the vet explains Rex's surgery and the unlikelihood of Rex returning to service as a K9 officer. All the while, Ben's boss has his eyes locked on Rex, nodding occasionally. The vet wanders away to check on his other patients, leaving the two men to talk.

The captain drops his hand to Ben's shoulder and squeezes. "I'm just glad he's still with us. I'll let the commander know, and we'll work on his release from service. He's been a fantastic asset to our unit, and we'll miss him." He glances at Rex, then back at Ben. "How are you holding up, Sergeant?"

I watch Ben's shoulders rise and fall; his chest expands as he draws in a breath. He looks at me and Evan with a soft smile, then directs his attention back to his boss. "Yesterday was tough, Sir. I'm not gonna lie. It was a wakeup call, and while I was carrying Rex to safety, I decided it's time to resign from the police force."

The captain's eyes widen with shock. I bet he wasn't expecting that. "Don't make any hasty decisions, son. I understand you're shaken. Anyone would be. But you're an exemplary officer. You were born for this job." He squeezes Ben's shoulder again. "Take some time off. Consider this decision carefully."

Ben shakes his head and looks over at me and Evan with another soft smile, then looks back at his boss. "I've already thought about it. This job was great when it was just me, but I have a family now. A family I want to be with for many years to come. My priorities have changed. My job is no longer the most important thing to me." He nods toward us. "They are."

Evan leans in close and whispers, "Does Ben mean that?"

I glance at Evan. "Mean what?"

He widens his eyes at me. "That we're his family?"

I grin at my son. "You know Ben only says things he means."

I watch my son's eyes sparkle with delight. I can't believe we're lucky enough to have Ben claim us as his, and for a moment, I wonder if Wyatt sent Ben our way. And for the first time, I'm thankful we have a guardian angel.

Ben's captain looks at us, taking us in with a soft smile. "I see." He folds his arms across his broad chest. "So I'm losing two of my best officers." Ben dips his head, hiding his smile, and I can see his boss's words mean the world to him.

"I'm sorry, Sir."

The older man chuckles. "No, you're not." He raises his chin in our direction. "Are you going to introduce me to your family?"

Evan and I stand as Ben says, "Yes, Sir." They walk toward us, Ben taking up his position between the two of us, wrapping his arms around our shoulders to hold us close. "This is Hope and her son, Evan. This is Captain Thoms."

I hold out my hand to him and dip my head with respect. "Nice to meet you, Captain."

Evan does the same, and we spend a few minutes chatting before he leaves to have Sunday lunch with his family.

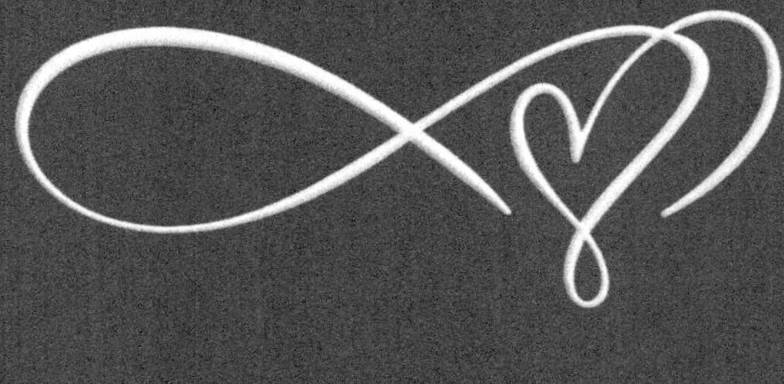

So far, this week's been a blur of bringing Rex home from the vet, caring for him, changing dressings, and visiting my doctor with Ben in tow to confirm my pregnancy. I'm exhausted, and it's only Wednesday, but within the busyness, there's been one thing playing on my mind—and I need to talk with Evan about it.

The back door opens and Evan drops into the back seat. "Hi, Mom."

"Hi, big guy. How was your day?" I ask, peering over my shoulder.

He shrugs. "Okay. I just want to go to Ben's and hang out with Rex, so it felt like it took forever."

"Same. But there's something I want to talk with you about. Do you mind if we stop off for milkshakes first?" I turn toward the front and put my foot on the gas, pulling away from the sidewalk.

I watch him narrow his eyes at me in my rearview mirror. "Can't we just talk on the way? I really want to see Rex."

I scrunch up my nose. "It's important, Ev."

"Okay, I guess." He blows out a frustrated breath.

"Thanks."

I find a parking spot not too far from our favorite diner, and we walk along the pier, enjoying a brief appearance from the sun.

When we arrive, I place our order with butterflies in my stomach that are making me feel a little off-balance. As I carry our food to the table Evan secured, I think about what I want to say and how I should say it.

I slide the tray to the middle of the table and slip into the seat opposite my son, who's eyeing me with suspicion. He grabs a fry and shoves it in his mouth, then sucks on the straw in his milkshake and I watch him, marveling at how fast he's growing up.

"So, what did you want to talk about?" he asks, then pushes another fry into his mouth, like he's in a hurry to finish his food so we can leave.

I fidget with the napkin in front of me, then trace the condensation forming on the outside of my shake. "Uhm ... well. You know it's Ben's birthday tomorrow, and I'd like us to do something special for him."

Evan's eyes light up, and he grins. "Oh yeah. Good idea." He leans forward. "What are we gonna do?"

I drop my eyes to the tabletop, sorting my words in my head so they make sense. I suck in a deep breath and blow it out slowly. "Well. You know how I'm pregnant, right?" He nods. "And you know ... Ben considers us a family now." He nods again. "So, I was thinking ... you know"—I widen my eyes and swallow my nerves—"families live together in one house."

He nods again. "Yeah," he says slowly.

I blink and take another deep breath. "I was thinking we could move in with Ben and Rex. We could tell him as his birthday present." Evan just stares at me, making my stomach twist. "What do you think?"

Without taking his eyes from me, he grabs another fry and jams it in his mouth, then takes another drink of his shake. It feels as though hours tick by, but I know it's only been seconds, maybe a minute or two.

I steal a fry and pop it in my mouth to prevent the verbal diarrhea that's burning its way up my throat. I need to give him time to sit with the idea. I've been thinking about it since I discovered I was pregnant, and if I'm being completely honest, before that, even.

"I like Ben's house. It's close to the beach, and my bedroom's bigger there." He chews on a couple more fries and washes them down. His initial response gives me hope he'll agree with the idea. "Do you think he'll want us to live with him?"

To me, that's a no-brainer. I raise my eyebrows. "What do you think?"

"I think he'd want us with him. He really loves us." I'm so glad Evan can see how much Ben cares for the both of us. "We're more important to him than being a cop."

I nod. "We are."

He's quiet again for several moments, and I'm unsure what he's thinking. Then his eyebrows drop over his eyes, and he steals my breath. He looks just like Wyatt did when he was making an important decision. "But will we be leaving Dad behind if we move out of our house?"

His words wrap around my heart like a fist, squeezing tightly. I never want to leave Wyatt behind, and Ben understands that. Wyatt is incredibly important to both Evan and me. But I've thought about this, and I don't think it's fair to ask Ben to move into our house with Wyatt's ghost. I also want a fresh start with Ben without the shadows of our life from before surrounding us.

I swallow past the tears that desperately want to flow and move to Evan's side of the booth, wrapping my arm around his shoulder. Like this, we're eye to eye. I squeeze his arm and study his face, especially his warm brown eyes, which are so much like his dad's.

When did he grow up?

I suck in a deep breath for courage and place my hand over his heart. "You know, no matter where we are, your dad will always be in here." I move my hand to his head. "And here. I know I wasn't able to talk about him with you for a long time, but I promise I won't let you forget."

He's quiet again, and I can almost see the cogs turning in his head. "But that's where Dad taught me to ride my bike and where he used to measure how much I'd grown on my bedroom doorframe. And Shane built you those bookshelves."

It's my turn to be quiet with my thoughts. *Am I being selfish? Maybe I should put my wish for a fresh start aside and ask Ben to move in with us? Would he want to leave behind the home gifted to him by Tahlia's mom? It's special to him.*

"But then ... Ben's house *is* close to the beach, and I like that. It means I could surf on the weekends like Dad used to, and you wouldn't have to drive me or find parking. And maybe it wouldn't be fair to expect Rex to move house when he loves running along the beach every day." He chews on another fry thoughtfully and narrows his eyes. "Do you think we could take my doorframe with us?" He shrugs. "Cuz that's really special to me." My lungs constrict, making it difficult to take a breath as he sucks his shake through his straw. "And do you think Ben would let us put up photos of Dad?"

This kid is trying to kill me, I'm certain of it.

"I can ask Shane how hard it would be to switch out the timber of the doorframe. I don't think we'd need the entire frame, just the part that has your measurements on it in Dad's writing."

He nods. "Yeah, that'd work."

I grin. "And we have that video on the laptop of you learning to ride your bike with Dad, which you can watch any time you like." I smooth my hand over the top of his hair. "I also think Ben would encourage us to have photos of Dad on display. I really don't think that's something we need to worry about."

His shoulders drop from around his ears and he grins at me. "I have an idea."

My eyebrows shoot up. "Oh, yeah?"

"I think we should pack some of our things and turn up at his house with our bags and a birthday cake. Maybe balloons or something. Oh, and party hats." His voice rises with excitement, and I can't stop my lips from spreading wide.

"I love that idea. I think it's the perfect way to wish Ben happy birthday."

As we leave the diner, Evan bumps his shoulder into me. "You know what this means?" he asks, excitement brightening his face.

I widen my eyes. "What does what mean?"

"When we move in with Ben, it means I'll finally have a dog!" he almost shouts, his eyes alight with pure happiness. My heart expands at his joy.

I chuckle and muss his hair. Wrapping my arm around his neck, I pull him close and kiss the top of his head. "I guess it does."

"Finally!" he sighs.

58

BEN

REX SPRAWLS OUT ON THE LIVING ROOM FLOOR between Seb and me as we enjoy a cold beer to celebrate my birthday. His eyebrows rise and fall as his eyes move between us. The stark white bandage on his shoulder is due to be changed in a couple of hours, and I need to clean his cone. He sighs loudly as Seb taps the neck of his bottle against mine. "Happy birthday, old man," he says with a snicker.

I chuckle with my lips around the opening of my beer. "Oh yeah, a whole nine days older than you."

He shrugs. "Still older."

I take a drink, savoring the slide of the cool liquid down my throat—a sigh escapes unbidden, like a natural reflex, whenever I enjoy a cold brew. It's been a huge week.

Even though I've had time off work, I had to go in on Monday to hand in my resignation. It'll take about a month for it to be finalized, which gives me some time to work out my next steps. Nix has already offered me a job, but I'm considering the idea of learning how to train service dogs. I'm not sure, but maybe I can balance both.

"Any plans tonight? You need me to stay here and watch Rex for you?"

A smile curves my lips, and happiness unfurls in my chest. Life is good. No, life is fucking fantastic. "Hope and Evan are coming over. She suggested we stay in so we could monitor Rex. You can stay if you'd like. I'm gonna grill some chicken breasts, and she's making salad and potato bake." I point my bottle at him. "You need to taste her potato bake, man. So freaking good."

He pats his stomach. "Only if you're sure she won't mind. I don't wanna be a fourth wheel." A knock sounds through the house. "Sounds like she's here."

I glance at the time with narrowed eyes. "It's too early, and she knows they can just walk in. They don't need to knock because I gave them a set of keys." They're my family now.

He raises his eyebrows, looking at me with pride. "Things *are* serious. I mean, I figured they were since you quit the force." He shakes his head with a smile. "Still can't believe it."

I climb to my feet when there's another knock at the door. "Can't get any more serious," I tell him as I drag open the front door. Maybe we can tell him our other news over dinner.

It takes me longer than it should to make sense of what I'm seeing. Hope is holding a fancy homemade birthday cake, while Evan has a bunch of brightly colored helium balloons secured in one hand. Keeping with the party theme, both of them are wearing outrageous party hats, but it's the numerous cases and boxes surrounding them that don't compute.

"Happy birthday!" they both cheer, wearing grins at least a mile wide. Their eyes sparkle with happiness and I want to see that same sparkle every single day.

Pleasure and happiness explode in my chest as I feel Sebastian at my back. *How did I get so damn lucky?* I step out of the house, studying the boxes and luggage. "What's all this?" I wave my hand around.

"Your birthday present," Hope says, as if it's so obvious I should already know. She must read the confusion written all over my face, because she grins at Evan. "We thought we'd give you us for your birthday. We're moving in!"

My heart thuds to a stop. Sebastian's intake of air fills the silence, then my heart takes off at a gallop. My long-time friend slaps me on the back, and I smile so wide, it takes up all the real estate on my face. I rush forward, carefully taking the cake from Hope to hand to Seb, then I scoop her into my arms and spin her around. Hope's giggles ring out and it's a sound I want to hear every day. I carefully place her on her feet and pull Evan in for a hug. "This has to be the best birthday gift I've ever received!" I announce.

Sebastian laughs behind me and collects a box to carry inside.

"I have a few requests," Evan tells me in a serious tone.

I step back with a nod. "Hit me."

"We need to be allowed to put up photos of my dad."

"Done." As if he needs to ask.

"I need to switch out the door frame from my bedroom to this one." He waves his hand toward a piece of timber leaning against the porch railing. "It's where Dad measured me as I grew." My heart splinters and bleeds for everything he's lost.

"Done."

He nods stiffly and his bottom lip trembles. He holds up one finger. "One more thing." I nod for him to continue. "You can't die."

Fuck!

Hope's gasp cracks the air like a whip, Sebastian freezes, and I cup the back of Evan's head to drag him into me. Tucking his face into my chest and kissing the top of his head, I hold him tight. He has to feel my heart thumping heavily as his hands grip each side of my sweater. His body trembles against mine, and I draw in a deep breath.

"I can't make that promise, Ev. Nobody can." I wish I could. I hate that it's even something he felt he needed to say. A promise he's so desperate to have. "But I promise never to put myself at unnecessary risk. You have my word. I'll do everything I can to be here for a long time. I don't want to leave you guys. I love you so much."

He nods against my chest and pulls away. His tear-stained cheeks and red eyes reach into my chest and punch a hole right through my heart. "I know you can't promise, but I don't want to lose you, too." He smiles a shaky smile. "Sorry to ruin your birthday."

I pull him back into me and hold my other arm open to invite Hope to join us. She burrows into my side, wrapping one arm around me and one around her son. I can't imagine how hard it was to make the decision to leave their family home behind and move in with me. They're leaving behind their memories as well as a major connection to Wyatt.

"You haven't ruined anything. This is the best gift you could ever give me. This family is my world. I've wanted us to live together for a while. This works perfectly."

By the time we pull apart, Evan's more composed and Sebastian has most of their things stacked neatly in the living room. I get the grill hot and cook while Hope prepares the rest of the food.

The cold air is biting against my exposed skin, but I barely notice it with the absolute joy I'm feeling. The back door opens and closes, and Sebastian hands me a beer, tapping his bottle against mine with a smirk.

"Life's pretty great right now," I comment.

He nods, his eyes twinkling in the fading light. "I can see that." He lifts the bottle to his lips, then points it at me. "You ready for this?"

Shaking my head, I chuckle. "More than you'll ever know."

Raising an eyebrow, he takes a drink. "I feel like I'm missing something."

I turn over the chicken. "I'll fill you in over dinner."

We're all quiet as we dig into the delicious meal; the only sounds in the room are the utensils as they strike the plates. Seb's watching us closely, and I can read the questions behind his gaze. He's being unusually patient, waiting for us to spill the beans. His gaze flicks between Hope and me as he finishes chewing, clears his throat, and picks up his beer.

It's sorta fun keeping up the suspense, but I should put him out of his misery.

I nudge Evan's foot with mine to get his attention. I tip my chin toward Sebastian. "Do you wanna tell Seb our news?"

"Please, someone tell me already. I'm dying over here."

Hope chuckles. "Quick, Ev. You'd better tell him. We don't want Seb's death on our hands."

Seb turns as white as the counter behind him. "Shit! Sorry, I didn't mean anything ..."

Wearing a grin, Hope waves off his concern. "We know." She turns to Evan and raises her eyebrows.

Evan's smile is magnificent as he puffs up his chest. "I'm gonna be a big brother."

Sebastian blinks several times, frozen in place, as if the words don't compute. Slowly, a grin grows, and he jumps up from his seat, rounding the table to pull Hope out of her chair. Wrapping his arms around her, he lifts her from her feet in a bear hug, placing a kiss on her cheek. Her laughter is free, and her smile is broad, making my heart skip a beat. She's so damn beautiful. "Congratulations!"

"Thanks," she says between chuckles.

He gently places her back on her feet, then moves to Evan. They perform the complicated handshake they were working on while Hope and I made dinner. Then, Seb drags me from my chair and engulfs me in a bear hug—one I'm surprised doesn't leave me with cracked ribs. "Congrats, man. I'm thrilled for you and the future you have spread out in front of you." He pulls away and looks at the three of us. "In front of all of you."

"Thanks, man."

He jabs his thumb into his chest. "I'm gonna be the best damn uncle." He looks at Evan. "I mean, I'm already pretty great, right?"

Evan grins and nods his agreement, realizing Sebastian already considers him to be family.

We finish our meal and clean up, then Hope sets her home-made birthday cake on the table. I can't even remember the last time I had a cake for my birthday. Probably before we lost Tahlia; she used to bake them for me. My heart constricts a little at the thought of her. I think she would have loved Hope and Evan, and I know she'd be thrilled we're having a baby together. That I'm creating a family of my own.

Sebastian nudges me. "This beats a couple of beers at the pub to celebrate your birthday."

"It certainly does." Satisfaction and a sense of peace roll through my body. It's a feeling that's been happening more often lately. At first, it was unfamiliar, and I couldn't place it, but I've come to realize the feeling is contentment. I thought my life was satisfying. I thought it was everything I wanted ... until Hope and Evan. They showed me how empty my life was.

They all sing to me, I blow out the candles, and then Hope cuts pieces of birthday cake for each of us. I watch Sebastian with my family, how seamlessly they fit together, and I'm grateful I was the one to answer the call when Evan was caught shoplifting.

That call changed my life.

It saved me from loneliness. It's given me a family to call my own. Sebastian's always been the brother I never had, but now I have more. So much more. And I hope, one day, he has this, too.

I raise my drink. "To spending birthdays with family."

Sebastian tips his chin to me as he raises his beer. "To family."

Hope and Evan follow suit, and then we all enjoy the delicious cake Hope lovingly baked and decorated for me.

Leaning into Hope, I whisper. "I need to take Rex out. Back in a minute." She nods, never taking her eyes from the television. I kiss her temple, then head through to the back door with Rex.

The cool night air hits me square in the face as Rex hobbles out into the backyard. I take the steps down to the grass and dig my hands deep into my pockets to keep them warm, then look up at the stars. I organize my thoughts and clear my throat. "You can rest easy, Wyatt. I've got them now, and I won't let anything destroy their happiness." I blow out a long breath. "I'm sorry for what happened to you and for everything you've lost, but I promise to love and cherish your family the way they deserve." An arc of light shoots across the sky as if Wyatt's giving his approval. "Thanks, man."

Rex wanders up to me and barks, nudging his muzzle into my thigh. When I turn to go back inside, I freeze at the sight of Hope standing at the base of the steps. Shit, I wonder how long she's been out here.

She smiles softly and swipes at her cheek. I guess she was out here long enough. I walk straight to her and wrap her slight frame in my embrace. She buries her face against my pecs and slides her hands beneath my sweater until her chilly hands rest flat against my shoulder blades. "Thank you," she mumbles against me.

I kiss the top of her head. "I love you."

She looks up at me, a smile touching her lips. "I love you, too."

I take her hand in mine to lead her inside, rubbing her bare finger. I still can't believe she took her wedding rings off. "Are you sure?" She knows what I'm asking.

She shrugs. "Absolutely certain. It was time."

"I love you, Cookie. I hope you know how much." I lean down to kiss her soft lips.

"I'm pretty sure I do." She presses up on her toes to return my kiss. "I hope you know how special you are to me, Ben Taylor. I love you."

EPILOGUE

I MONTH LATER ...

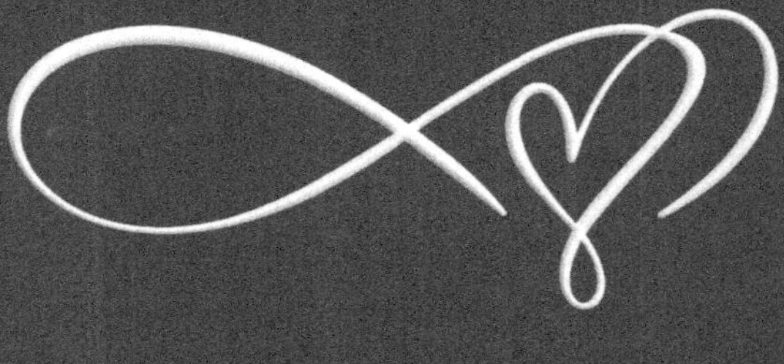

59

BEN

"Come on, Rex." I pat my thigh as I hold the back door to the cruiser open. He's mostly moving freely again, but he still can't put his full weight on the leg that was injured, which means he can't run yet. I've been told he'll be able to run again, but not as fast as before, so we've settled for short, slow walks around the block for now.

Evan gives him a small boost, and once he's securely inside the cruiser for his very last ride into the precinct, I close the door. Nervous energy rockets through my system. It's our last day on the job—not that Rex will be working. Hope will take him home while I go on patrol for the last time.

She leans in and kisses me. "See you there," she murmurs.

I return her kiss, keeping it chaste in front of Evan. "Thanks for coming."

"We wouldn't be anywhere else. This is an important day for both of you."

Evan and Hope follow in her car, and when I arrive at the precinct, I find an empty parking spot out back. I open the gate that separates me from Rex and he surges forward. We need to be together for this special moment. Then, I put the planned call into dispatch. "Car three-Adam-twenty-five."

A static buzz sounds. "Car three-Adam-twenty-five." Katie's voice sounds over the radio, and Rex tilts his head to the side, his ears twitching. Normally, when he hears her voice over the radio, it's to call us out to work. Not today, though.

I get choked up with the next words I'm about to speak. "Will you show K9 Rex 10-42?"

"Copy break," Katie announces. "All units prepare to copy a special transmission. This transmission is for decorated K9 Officer Rex." I look at the best partner an officer could ever hope for. "Rex is coming in for his final goodbye. Due to a career-ending injury, he's heading into retirement after serving our city for the past six and a half years. We want to thank him for his service and his dedication to keeping our city and its citizens safe." Katie pauses, and I hear her take a deep breath.

"With more than three hundred deployments, Rex has made a significant impact in our community. We thank him for bringing fifty-five children home safely to their parents, eleven missing adults home to their families, and aiding in the apprehension of 186 offenders over the course of his career. He's been instrumental in seizing over $120,000 in illegal drug money and twenty-five pounds of methamphetamine, as well as locating and seizing other illegal substances. He has participated in forty-two demonstrations at public elementary and high schools, as well as at community events, showcasing his skills and tenacity in taking down criminals."

My eyes sting, and my nose tingles as I listen to Katie list his achievements. I press my lips together to stem the emotions threatening to spill over as I rub Rex's jaw. He nuzzles into me, almost as if he knows this is his goodbye.

"Rex has earned the respect and admiration of his peers, and deserves a much-needed rest."

A tear falls over my lashes and trails down my cheek as Rex and I watch each other, his eyebrows moving up and down as his eyes trace over my face.

"We thank him for keeping his handler safe over the course of his career and for bringing him home after every shift. We wish him the best in his retirement and hope he enjoys his time being a dog with long days resting in the sunshine, belly rubs, and indulging in his favorite treats. You will be missed, Rex. K9 Rex, you are 10-42 for the final time at 1809." Emotion drips from Katie's words. Everyone at the precinct loves Rex, and I know they're all going to miss him.

"We all copy. Thank you," announces Captain Thoms.

"Everybody copies."

"Good job, boy," I tell him through sniffles. "What do you say?"

I hold the radio close to his face so Rex can sign off with a bark, and I follow him with a simple acknowledgement of appreciation.

I blow out a long breath. That was tough. Tougher than I expected. I climb out of the cruiser and adjust my belt, then help Rex down, protecting his injured leg.

Once I have his lead, I head toward the back entrance of the building. When we step inside the door, my breath catches. Unexpectedly, a guard of honor lines the hallway with what looks like every available police and dispatch officer, as well as admin staff.

I grin proudly, and Rex wags his tail excitedly, making his rump shake from side to side. His claws clip—unevenly because of his limp—on the polished linoleum as I lead him down the passage amid pats and words of congratulations.

At the end of the line are Captain Thoms and Commander Stiles, as well as Hope and Evan. Once Rex notices them, he tugs on the lead, his feet slipping on the polished floor while his tail goes ballistic. Everyone laughs at his excitement, and when Evan drops to his knees, I release the lead so boy and dog can be reunited. He's so excited that Rex is his now.

I shake hands with my captain and commander, then pull Hope in for a hug, chastely kissing her cheek in front of my colleagues. She squeezes me tight as she looks up at me, checking that I'm okay because she knows this is a tough day for me, but I wouldn't have it any other way. Hope, Evan, and the jellybean are my priorities now, and I'm thankful I'm allowed to keep Rex in his retirement.

Everyone gathers around to listen to our commander's retirement speech, reiterating most of what Katie announced in Rex's special announcement. Snacks and drinks are set up on a table, and officers grab something to eat on their way out after saying goodbye to Rex. Katie presents Rex with his own small cake, which he demolishes in around fourteen seconds flat.

"Well, I'm glad he liked it," she says with a chuckle as she rubs his scruff. She leans down, nuzzles him between his ears, and lays a kiss there. When she pulls away, her blue eyes are shiny with tears. "I'm gonna miss you, buddy."

"You're welcome to come and visit him any time, Katie."

She pushes to her feet and wraps her arms around me. "Thank you. I just might do that." When she pulls away, she jabs her thumb over her shoulder. "I'd better get back. Good luck with your last shift, Ben."

"Thanks."

I glance at the time and share a smile with Hope. "I need to get out on patrol." I rub Rex's head. "I'll see you guys tomorrow."

"You sure you don't want us to pick you up?"

I shake my head. "Nah. Seb's coming off the night shift too, so he's happy to pick me up and bring me home. I need to make a stop on the way, so I'll be a little late." As much as I miss them, I'm hoping they'll already be at work and school by the time I get home, which will be ideal for my plan to work.

Hope presses up on her toes to place a soft kiss on my cheek. "Be careful, please." I can't miss the worry in her eyes.

"I will. Promise." I squeeze her in reassurance.

I say my goodbyes, then sign in for my last shift. I never thought I'd leave the police force before I turned thirty. I imagined I'd be retiring in my sixties after a very long career. I imagined climbing the ranks and possibly becoming the commander, but it wasn't meant to be. As much as I've always wanted to be a cop, I want to be here for my family more.

I CLIMB into Seb's truck, dump my bag on the floor, and pull the seatbelt across my body. "Thanks, man."

"No problem. How was your last shift?" he asks as he checks over his shoulder and presses the gas.

"Uneventful," I tell him as he pulls away from the curb and I mentally say farewell to the precinct.

"That's good. Better than having to deal with a ton of crap." I nod. "Still want to make that stop?"

"Yes, please, if you don't mind. Did you bring the beers?"

He tips his head toward the backseat. "Yep."

I glance into the back and see three bottles of beer, a black velvet ring box I had asked him to hold for me so Hope wouldn't discover it before I was ready, and the box set of *Theodore Boone* by John Grisham. I'm hoping Evan will love these—especially since I sourced a signed edition.

Sebastian pulls into the parking lot closest to the main gate, and we climb out, collecting the beer and Hope's engagement ring. We make our way through the large iron gate and follow the path to Wyatt's final resting place. The area around his headstone is well maintained, and I crouch in front of it to trace the chiseled letters with my finger.

I shake my head and look up at my long-time friend. "He was so fucking young, and he left so much behind."

He heaves a loud sigh. "Life's so fucking cruel." Something we both fully understand.

We both drop our asses onto the grass, and I crack open my beer and Wyatt's, even though it's only 7:30 in the morning. Seb and I catch up like we normally do as we drink our beer. For every drink I take, I pour Wyatt's into the grass as if we're sharing a drink.

I tell Seb all about the special broadcast and the fuss everyone made for Rex's retirement yesterday evening, and he tells me all about a guy who overcorrected while speeding and drove over a sidewalk, collecting a stop sign before coming to a stop in someone's front yard.

I take my last swig of beer. "Hey, do you mind giving us a minute?"

He nods and climbs to his feet, collecting the empty bottles. "Meet you at my truck."

I dig the box out of my pocket and fidget with it as I gather my thoughts. "So ... ah ... you probably already know I love Hope and Evan more than I've ever loved anyone before. I gave up my dream job as a cop so they wouldn't experience the daily trauma of worrying about my safety." I swallow the lump in my throat that feels like sawdust. "They've already lost enough, and I'd do anything to keep their hearts safe."

I repeatedly snap the lid of the small velvet box open and closed and shift on my butt. "Uh, you probably also know we're expecting a baby." I glance around, then back to the headstone, paying close attention to Wyatt's name. "I'd like to call him or her Sullivan, if that's okay with you. I figure it works whether we have a boy or girl. And I'd like to honor you in some small way."

I open the box and look at the engagement ring that's nestled in the black velvet cushion inside. A simple princess-cut diamond centered on a channel-set platinum band. It's classically beautiful, and it reminds me of Hope.

"I also wanted to ask if it would be okay with you if I proposed to your wife. I know she'll always love you, and I'm okay with that. You were her first love, and you're the father of her son. I would never expect her to stop, but I hope I've shown her that she can love both of us. I've already asked Evan, as well as your parents and hers. I even asked Shane and Nix, because I know they were important to you." I snap the lid closed. "I promise to always make Hope and Evan my top priority and to keep them safe. To make sure they're loved every day; the way they deserve."

I climb to my feet and touch the headstone. "They'll always be your everything, but now they're mine too."

60

I push my way inside, balancing two bags of groceries for dinner in my arms. "We're home!" I call. It's been almost twenty-two hours since I've seen Ben, and I miss him. His overnight shifts are the worst, and I'm glad last night was his last one. Evan steps in behind me with his backpack hanging off one shoulder. "Close the door, please."

Rex barks from out the back, so they must be out there. I carry the groceries down the hallway, past our family photos—which also include photos from our old home, as well as Ben with Tahlia and Sebastian—into the kitchen. I place the groceries on the counter, and Evan drops his backpack onto the kitchen floor and heads for the back door. I get busy storing the cold items in the fridge so they don't spoil.

"Uh, Mom. You might wanna come here," Evan says. His tone is strained, causing worry to take root in my gut.

I close the fridge door and spin around as my heart takes off at a gallop. "What is it? What's wrong?"

He glances at me with wide eyes and, if I'm not mistaken, a mischievous grin. "Nothing. But you need to see this."

"Can I at least finish putting the groceries away?"

"No. You'll want to see this now."

I shrug. "Okay."

He slips outside, closing the door behind him before I make it there. When I open it again and step onto the porch, my eyes blow wide. It takes a moment for the scene to register, and when it does, I can't believe what I'm seeing.

Three-foot tall letters light up the middle of the backyard. Seven simple letters that each mean nothing on their own, but together, make up two words that mean everything.

Ben's on bended knee with Rex sitting beside him, his rump shaking from side to side and his tongue hanging out of his mouth. On his other side is a canvas tent decorated in fairy lights. Inside sits a low table with a picnic basket and a gift wrapped in a bow that matches the one around Rex's neck.

I drift across the porch and down the steps, aware of Evan holding his phone up. I hope he's recording this, because I'm not sure I'll be able to remember everything with my heart pounding the way it is.

Ben's lips spread in a beautiful smile, and butterflies erupt in my stomach. When I stop in front of him, he reaches out and takes one of my hands in his. "Welcome home, Cookie."

I study him, my mouth forming a grin to match his, then glance around us. "What's all this?" I ask with raised brows.

"I have something important I want to ask you," he says, looking up at me from his lowered position. Rex fidgets on his feet, but he maintains his spot next to his dad like the well-trained animal he is.

I lower myself to my knees, because I don't think they're going to hold me up with all the blood rushing to my head. "What do you want to know?" I murmur as if the two words lit up behind him and this entire setting doesn't give me a clue.

He grins, but when I look more carefully, it's strained. There's a tightness around his eyes that's not usually there, so I entwine our fingers together and squeeze his hand. His shoulders rise as his chest expands with a deep breath. He blows it out, and I watch some of the tension ease from his features.

"I've never told you this, but I was attracted to you the second you opened your front door that very first day when I brought Evan home."

What?

Gosh, I was so focused on Evan arriving home with a police officer in tow, Ben could have been fat and balding, and I would never have noticed.

"It wasn't long after that I discovered I liked the person you are. And then it took no time at all for like to turn into love. There are so many reasons I fell in love with you and Evan that we'd be here all night, and, well, I just want to get to the point."

Evan chuckles from beside us, and Rex's tail sweeps back and forth across the grass. My heart thumps against my sternum, and my breath is becoming more and more difficult to control.

"It has been a privilege to get to know you and Evan over these last months and an honor to have you both in my life. You say I brought you into the light, but you saved me from loneliness. For the first time I have a family to belong to, but I'd like to make it official."

He swallows and nudges Rex, who steps forward to nuzzle me. I chuckle and reach around his neck to cuddle him when my fingers glide over something unexpected. Dropping my eyes, I see a gorgeous ring. I barely register it before snapping my head back up to Ben.

"I've asked Evan, and I've asked your family and Wyatt's. I also checked with Shane and Nix ... and this morning, I stopped by the cemetery to share a beer with Wyatt. They've all given me their blessing. So, Hope, you're really the last one I need to ask."

I swallow thickly as my eyes well with tears. My heart feels like it's going to beat out of my chest with happiness. I glance at Evan to find him beaming at me, then return my gaze to the man I love beyond reason.

I can't believe he included Wyatt and his family and friends in this moment. But I shouldn't be surprised at all, because this is Ben. He's kind and thoughtful. Considerate and patient. He's everything to me. I can't imagine loving a better man.

"I love you and Evan so much." He pauses. "Will you marry me?"

I lean forward, pressing my mouth gently to his as tears track down my cheeks. "Yes," I whisper against his soft lips. "Yes, I'll marry you," I tell him with a smile. "I love you so much."

His arms wrap around me, and everything disappears as we get lost in a kiss to seal a promise of forever ... an *everlasting promise*.

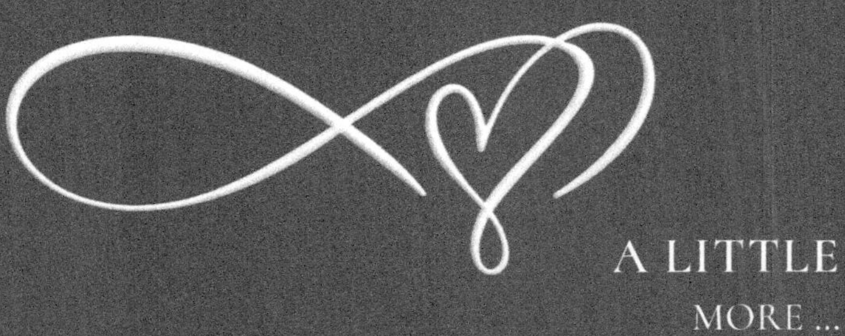

A LITTLE

MORE ...

61

EVAN

It's weird every time I see them kissing. Like nobody wants to see their mom kissing all the time. But it makes her happy. I've never seen her smile as much as she does now, and I think it's Ben's kisses that make it happen, so I'm not gonna complain too much. Though, I'd prefer they didn't do it in front of me.

I stopped recording once they started kissing because ... well, I don't think I need to record *that*. Instead, I untie the ring from Rex's ribbon so Mom can wear it. I think they've forgotten all about it. I clear my throat, because a guy can only put up with so much of the romantic baloney. When they finally pull apart, I shove the ring in front of Ben's face. "I think you're supposed to put this on Mom's finger," I remind him with wide eyes.

Like, come on. *Do I need to do everything around here?*

Ben chuckles. "Thanks, Ev."

He slides it on Mom's finger, and she starts crying all over again. At least they're happy tears now. I've had enough of her sad ones to last me a lifetime. Ben tugs her back into him and rubs his hands up and down her back, whispering something in her ear.

I just want to get to the food. Whatever's in the picnic basket smells really good.

What's a guy gotta do to get fed?

"Hey, Ev. I got something for you, too," Ben calls, waving me over to the tent. *Something for me?* He grabs the gift bag from the table. Huh. I figured that was for Mom. "I wanted to give you something special to remember this day."

I'll always remember this day. It's the day I finally feel like I'm part of a family again. Like I won't be the only kid at school without a dad. I don't need anything special, but if he wants to give me a present, I won't say no.

I take the bag from his fingers and dip my hand inside as he and Mom watch on. My eyes almost bug out of my head when I pull out the box set of John Grisham's *Theodore Boone*. I've borrowed these from the school library because they're awesome stories … and Mom loves reading his books, so I figured he must be a pretty good author. Turns out, he *is* an awesome writer. If I can be half as good as him one day, I'd be proud. I flick my eyes back up to Ben and lunge at him. "Thank you. This is one of my favorite series."

Ben blows out a long breath. "I'm glad. I was worried, but I asked around at work, and several people recommended this series." He points at the box. "Open it."

I move closer to the light so I can see better and pull out the first book, peeling open the cover. It takes me a second to work out what I'm seeing. "You got me signed editions?" I ask softly as I drag my finger over the signature.

I can't believe it. I've never had a signed book before, and to have this from one of my favorite authors is incredible.

"You like it?"

I look up at him. "Like it? I love it!" I wrap my arms around him. "I love you, Ben."

He ruffles my hair and returns my hug. "I love you, too, Ev."

Would you like to check in with Ben, Hope, Evan, and Sullivan nine years into the future?
If you have the time, the inclination, and a few more tears to shed, sign up for my newsletter to find out what they've been up to here:
https://tinyurl.com/everlastingpromises-bonus

Have you met Shane in **Everlasting Love?**
A scarred cinnamon roll Hero/single mom romance
An emotional, steam-filled contemporary romance about a damaged cinnamon roll veteran who believes he's undeserving of the sexy single mom with a sweet daughter even though they may be exactly what he needs.
https://books2read.com/dsj-everlastinglove

PINTEREST

I put together a Pinterest board for Hope and Ben's story. If you're interested, you can check it out here:

https://tinyurl.com/everlastingpromises-pinterest

DEBRA'S BOOKS

The Summer Twins

Loving Summer | *Kate Summer & Oliver Stone*

Second Chance Summer | *Toby Summer & Cassia Phillips*

The Summer Twins | Complete Series

Kisses

Stolen Kisses | *Emma Miller & Theo Drivas*

Moonlit Kisses | *Max Stanfield & Molly Lewis*

Unexpected Kisses | *Sarah Stanfield & AJ*

Kisses | Complete Series

Monday Knights | *novellas*

Enemy Kisses | *Finn Brady & Harriet Dubois*

Wicked Kisses | *Lincoln Kingsley & Sophie Chalmers*

Everlasting

Everlasting Love | *Shane Sutton & Violet Jamison*

Everlasting Promises | *Hope Sullivan & Benjamin Taylor*

Everlasting Vows | *Nixon Steele & Abigail Steele*

Debra has a list of her books available on her website.

You can find them here:

https://debrastjamesbooks.com

CONNECT WITH DEBRA

stalk me

You can stalk me pretty much everywhere!
https://debrastjamesbooks.com/connect/

How about joining my Facebook group?
https://www.facebook.com/groups/DebsBibliomaniacs

newsletter

Join Debra's newsletter to receive important updates before anyone else. Newsletters will be sent twice per month unless something really exciting is happening.

https://debrastjamesbooks.com/newsletter/

Thank you so much for reading Ben, Hope, and Evan's story. I know it's been a long time coming for my dedicated readers and I'd like to thank you for your patience—I only hope I've done their story justice after such a long wait.

Grief has been a long-standing part of my psyche since I lost my fiancé suddenly when I was 22 years old.

One day, he was proposing to me and we were planning our future and literally the next he was killed in a motorcycle accident. That event changed me fundamentally.

At the time, my one wish (apart from him not dying) was that I was pregnant with his baby, so I'd at least have something left of him. It wasn't to be. We were always careful. But it got me thinking how I would have coped if I'd been a mum. You see, I wallowed in my grief for six long years until I met my hubby. It was his patience and understanding that helped me move beyond my grief to see I still had a lot of years to left to live.

Thank goodness for him.

All of that isn't to say that I've ever forgotten my love ... I still think of him often.

I hope that my emotions and experiences bled through her story, and you felt Hope's pain and awakening on the page.

As always, I would like to thank Mr. St James and our two sons for their support and patience with me. Writing and everything associated with getting these stories out to readers takes a lot of my time away from my family, and their understanding and support is always appreciated.

Rachel. My gorgeous alpha reader. If it weren't for you, this book would be riddled with 'Aussie-isms'. Thank you for always digging deep into the story to ensure no plot hole is left unfilled and no question unanswered. You wanted to be punched in the gut from the very beginning of chapter one, and I hope it left you breathless! Thank you for your suggestion. It made the beginning of Hope's story that much more compelling.

To my beta readers, Rachel, Kelly, and W :) Thank you so much for your candid and thoughtful feedback while you read **Everlasting Promises**. You ladies provided me with plenty of points to consider. Your love for this story boosted my confidence.

A special thank you to Nancy for your insight into the world of a hairstylist. Your suggestions helped to make this story more authentic, which is always my aim.

To my online support network and my readers in Deb's Bibliomaniacs, as always, you were there for me on the days when I doubted myself. Ladies, you are so very important to me. I'm grateful we connected and I can call you my friends.

To you, the reader. Thank you for taking a chance on me; for reading my book. I truly do appreciate your time. If you've enjoyed reading about Ben, Hope, and Evan, I'd love to hear from you.

ABOUT THE AUTHOR

Debra St James is an author of spicy, slow-burn contemporary romance that features cinnamon roll heroes who listen to their women's hearts and their words. She takes her time to weave a detailed tapestry of genuine characters, real-life struggles, love, and romance to create engaging stories that will have you so immersed in the story that you'll never want to leave. Her stories are always guaranteed to take you on an emotional journey that ultimately ends with a HEA!

Debra loves to read romance. Her family often finds her with her nose stuck in her iPad, swooning over her latest book boyfriend. She writes part-time from her Perth home, which she shares with Mr St James and their two sons, whose antics often make her roll her eyes and laugh in equal measure.

Writing a novel had never been on her radar. One morning, she was enjoying a coffee by the river and a story sprouted, seemingly from nowhere. At 51, she pulled up the Pages app on her phone and began to type, giving life to her debut, *Loving Summer*.

The rest, as they say, is history!

Debra xo

amazon.com/author/debrastjames

facebook.com/debra.stjames.books

instagram.com/debrastjames_books

bookbub.com/authors/debra-st-james

goodreads.com/debrastjames

pinterest.com/debrastjamesbooks